AS TIME
GOES BY

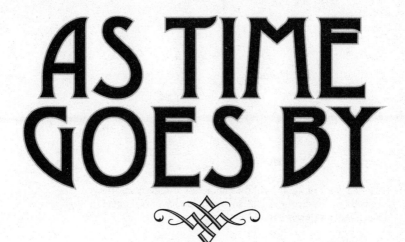

AS TIME GOES BY

EDITED BY

HANK DAVIS

AS TIME GOES BY

This is a work of fiction. All the characters and events portrayed
in this book are fictional, and any resemblance to real people
or incidents is purely coincidental.

A Baen Book

Baen Publishing Enterprises
P.O. Box 1403
Riverdale, NY 10471

ISBN 13: 978-1-4767-8052-8

Cover art by Adam Burn

First Baen printing, February 2015

Distributed by Simon & Schuster
1230 Avenue of the Americas
New York, NY 10020

Library of Congress Cataloging-in-Publication Data

As time goes by / edited by Hank Davis.
    pages cm
  ISBN 978-1-4767-8052-8 (paperback)
  1. Science fiction, American. 2. Time travel--Fiction. I. Davis, Hank, 1944-
  editor.
   PS648.S3A7255 2015
   813'.0876208--dc23
                                    2014043650

Printed in the United States of America

10 9 8 7 6 5 4 3 2 1

Contents

Copyrights of Stories

Dedication

For Robert A. Heinlein, who lifted himself by his bootstraps and pulled science fiction up with him, and showed us where the zombies were, in more stories than one.

Acknowledgements

My thanks to all the contributors, as well as those who helped with advice, permissions, contact information, and other kindnesses, including Lara Allen, David Drake, Moshe Feder, Vaughne Hansen, Jeffrey and Mary Ann Henderson, Mags of Pollinger, Ltd., Barry Malzberg, Bud Webster, Eleanor Wood, and probably other helpful carbon units which my decrepit memory has unforgivably overlooked.

AS TIME GOES BY

A Time Machine Built for Two

by **Hank Davis**

It may still be the fight for love and glory (I always wondered what "glory" meant in the song's context), but it's *not* still the same old story. After all, in this book we're in science fiction territory, and "play it again" can take on a whole new meaning . . .

As has often been observed, we are all involuntary time travelers, stuck on a one-way trip into the future, with no option for getting off or going back to an earlier stop. The urge to go back is universal in human imagination, involving what someone called the saddest words of all: "If" and "might have been . . ." *If* I had (or had not) made that phone call. *If* I hadn't gotten into that poker game. *If* I had studied more for that final exam. *If* I hadn't had that one for the road. *If* I had known then what I know now. And so on. To quote a title of one of John Collier's stories, "If youth knew, if age could."

The irrational (or apparently irrational) urge of the imagination to try to replay the past with a more favorable outcome is particularly true with one's love life. *If* I had met her before that bum that she married. *If* I had kept my temper and apologized. (As Lazarus Long puts it, "Apologize to her immediately—especially if you were right.")

1

If I hadn't made fun of her relatives. *If, if, if* . . . But as Omar Khayyám puts it in Edward Fitzgerald's translation, "The Moving Finger writes: and, having writ/Moves on: nor all thy Piety nor Wit/ Shall lure it back to cancel half a Line/ Nor all thy Tears wash out a Word of it."

Unless, of course, time travel is possible. If dismal fate left one with only a loaf of bread and a jug of wine, one might go back in time and try to do something about the lack of the *thou* part.

I'm not going to linger on the question of whether or not time travel (TT) is possible. Like that other science fiction standby, faster than light (FTL) travel, most physicists think it is impossible. On the other hand, for both TT and FTL, there are far-out and unproven theories (rotating massive cylinders; tachyons; wormholes; etc.) which might make one or both possible. There are critics of SF who complain that since TT and FTL are definitely impossible, all stories involving either concept are fantasy disguised as science fiction. It's an old argument, but not a profitable one. Both TT and FTL, possible or impossible, are far too fascinating to cast aside, have given rise to many enjoyable, even brilliant stories, and doubtless will give rise to many more.

Some consider Charles Dickens' *A Christmas Carol* (1843) one of the earliest time travel stories, though others argue that the three ghosts are only showing Scrooge visions of his past and possible future, and not actually transporting him to other times. Scrooge is only an observer, unseen by the residents of the past, present, or future. The question of changing his past, as with the woman he was once involved with but whom he considered less important than making money, doesn't arise.

A later classic which does definitely involve time travel is Mark Twain's *A Connecticut Yankee in King Arthur's Court* (1889). Hank Morgan, after a serious rap on the noggin somehow puts him back in the Middle Ages, romances and marries Sandy, but the story would have been much the same without the romantic aspect. And while Morgan does industrialize medieval England, circumstances near the end of the novel compel him to blow it all up, which presumably is the reason why the present, to which Morgan returns via a long and magically induced sleep, is unchanged. Twain obviously had no idea how to get his hero back into the past, and probably didn't much care if having a blow to the head cause a temporal dislocation was "scientific" or not. As with Edgar Rice Burroughs' *Under the Moons of Mars/A Princess of Mars* (1912, 1917), in which John Carter practically *wishes* himself to Mars, the mechanism was clunky, but deserved forgiveness for the sake of the absorbing story which followed. I do wonder if there are critics who contend that Morgan dreamed the whole thing after that blow on the head, though it's obvious from the story's frame that the affair was no dream. (If such critics exist, I suspect they're the same ones who contend that the ghosts in *The Turn of the Screw* are products of the narrator's imagination.)

H.G. Wells, in *The Time Machine* (1895), changed time travel stories forever by imagining a machine, instead of ghosts or other supernatural influences, that could carry its operator forward or backward in time. Of course, Wells gives no explanation of how the machine works, distracting the reader with a fascinating discussion by the Time Traveller (for so it was convenient for Wells to name him, with a double-L) of time as a fourth dimension. Some readers may not realize that Wells wrote this years before Einstein also treated time as a fourth dimension. On his journey into the far future, his first and longest stop is 802,701 A.D. where (or when) he encounters the childlike Eloi and acquires a lady friend named Weena, but there is no romance involved. In fact, the Traveller says that he "believes" Weena is a "little woman," indicating that he isn't quite certain about it. Earlier he noted that he has difficulty distinguishing the male Eloi from the females, since they are all of the same short height (about four feet) and have the same delicacy of face and body. When Weena eventually disappears, either carried off by the Morlocks or incinerated (fortunately while unconscious) in a forest fire, the Traveller's regrets are not those of someone in love. His relationship with Weena was more like that of a man with a pet, or a very young child not related to him with whom he has formed an unofficial uncle-niece friendship.

Not surprisingly, the three movie versions saw no reason to repeat the platonic relationship of the novel, beginning with George Pal and

David Duncan's flawed but memorable 1960 movie with Yvette Mimeux as an unmistakably female Weena. Nor did the leisure-suited time traveller (upper case is not deserved in this case) have any doubt about Priscilla Barnes' Weena in the 1978 TV movie version, about which the less said, the better, though it does *almost* make the appalling 2002 movie look acceptable by comparison. And Samantha Mumba, playing "Mara," rather than Weena, again was decidedly female, as the (lower case) time traveller noticed. Incidentally and imho, the best adaptation of the Wells novel into another medium is still the Classics Illustrated comic book version—which is ironic, since the 1978 fiasco was originally broadcast as a Classics Illustrated TV movie.

Again getting away from "scientific" modes of time travel, Henry James began, but did not finish, a novel involving time travel called *The Sense of the Past*, which was adapted by John L. Balderston into a very successful play, *Berkeley Square*. (Balderston's other notable scripts include several of the classic Universal horror movies, beginning with *Dracula* and *Frankenstein*, as well as the best movie version of *the Prisoner of Zenda*, with Ronald Colman.) In the play, a man in the twentieth century either changes places or personalities (there's some ambiguity here) with his eighteenth century ancestor,who looks just like him, and falls in love with his ancestor's intended. Leslie Howard, better known as the Scarlet Pimpernel, played both time-linked relatives on stage, and in a later movie version, which I wish Criterion or Kino or somebody would restore and release on DVD. The only existing DVD, currently out of print, is taken from a very poor print, and looks as if one is watching it though a dirty dishrag and listening to it with ears packed with cotton. My first contact with the story was a TV version in 1959, which I liked a lot, though TV critic Harriet Van Horne complained that a classic story had been reduced to science fiction. (*Excuse* me? Van Horne later went from being a dense TV critic to an even denser political columnist. Some people *deserved* to be on Nixon's Enemies List.)

Later SF writers went for less platonic tales of twisted time, such as, to cite a few examples, Poul Anderson's *The Corridors of Time* and *There Will Be Time*, Richard Matheson's *Bid Time Return* (filmed as

Somewhere in Time, a movie I liked a *lot* better than most critics did), Christopher Priest's *The Space Machine* (an ingenious amalgam of *The Time Machine* and *The War of the Worlds*), A.E. van Vogt's "The Search" and "Recruiting Station," Isaac Asimov's *Pebble in the Sky* and *The End of Eternity*, Keith Laumer's *The Great Time Machine Hoax* and *Dinosaur Beach*, Jack McDevitt's *Time Travelers Never Die*, and others, notably Robert A. Heinlein with *The Door into Summer*, *Time Enough for Love*, and "All You Zombies," the ultimate story of time-traveling star-crossed lovers, with its unforgettable last two lines. I originally hoped to include the story in this book, but the forthcoming movie version (let's hope it's not the disappointment that the cinematic renditions of *The Puppet Masters* and *Starship Troopers* were) made that impossible.

Regrettably, I also was unable to include a story by Jack Finney, best known for his classic novel, *The Body Snatchers*, usually reprinted as *Invasion of the Body Snatchers* to match the title of the equally classic movie. Finney was also known for time travel love stories, as in his novel *Time and Again* and also in such short stories as "Second Chance" and "The Love Letter," two stories which immediately sprang to mind when I started making a little list for this anthology.

I don't wish to shock anyone, but an anthologist cannot always get all the stories which she or he wants to include in a book. Some others which eluded me were Roger Zelazny's "Divine Madness," Ray Bradbury's "Tomorrow and Tomorrow," and Bob Shaw's "Light of Other Days." I list them to call them to the reader's attention. I am completely happy with the stories which I was able to incude in *As Time Goes by*, but I'm mentioning these stories as a recommendation. If you liked this book, I think you'll like these stories, and I suggest that you seek them out.

On a closing note, there is a whole category of fiction which I'm not competent to comment on, not having read widely (well, actually, not read at all) in its examples, and these are the paranormal romance novels, which, from the descriptions of others who *have* read them, usually involve a modern feisty feminist woman who's somehow plopped back in time, and gets involved with a man of the period, usually a bad boy of a nobleman. There's also a more unusual type of story, which has a modern woman hurled *way* back in time who has sex with a dinosaur (T. Rexes not excluded). My understanding is that the stories in the last category are so far only available online as self-published e-books, but romance is not a field I follow, and for all I know, Harlequin has just started up a dino-line.

Getting back to the book in your hands, Theodore Sturgeon once defined a good science fiction story as one like a mainstream story, except that if you take out the science part, there's no story. I think the stories following this pedantic introduction fit that criterion, with the added distinction that if you take out the romance, there's also no story. Happy reading, and may your real-life love affairs go smoothly with no need of any time traveling.

—**Hank Davis**
October 2014

Gibraltar Falls

INTRODUCTION

The job of an agent of the Time Patrol is to keep anyone from changing the past, whether for good motives or ill, and thereby changing the future. But when a patrolman has lost someone in a disaster, someone who means more to him than either the Patrol or the security of the known future, and he might save her by breaking the rules, what will he do?

* * *

Poul Anderson (1926-2001) was one of the most prolific and popular writers in science fiction. He won the Hugo Award seven times and the Nebula Award three times, as well as many other awards, notably including the Grand Master Award of the Science Fiction Writers of America for a lifetime of distinguished achievement. With a degree in physics, and a wide knowledge of other fields of science, he was noted for building stories on a solid foundation of real science, as well as for being one of the most skilled creators of fast-paced adventure stories. He was author of over a hundred science fiction and fantasy novels and story collections, and several hundred short stories, as well as historical novels, mysteries and non-fiction books. He wrote several series, notably the Technic Civilization novels and stories, the Psychotechnic League series, the Harvest of Stars novels, and his Time Patrol series, represented here by "Gibraltar Falls." The basic assumption was that, if time travel is possible, and the past can be changed, thereby changing the present, then necessarily a patrol will have to be established to insure that no one, be they would-be dictator or misguided idealist (if there's a difference), meddles with the past. Starting from this "what if?" notion, Poul Anderson wrote an impressive number of short stories, novelettes, and novellas, which have been collected in a massive volume as *Time Patrol*, (currently available as a Baen e-book), and a novel, *The Shield of Time*. I would say that all are worth seeking out, but then, they were written by Poul Anderson, so that really goes without saying.

Gibraltar Falls

by Poul Anderson

The Time Patrol base would only remain for the hundred-odd years of inflow. During that while, few people other than scientists and maintenance crew would stay there for long at a stretch. Thus it was small, a lodge and a couple of service buildings, nearly lost in the land.

Five and a half million years before he was born, Tom Nomura found that southern end of Iberia still more steep than he remembered it. Hills climbed sharply northward until they became low mountains walling the sky, riven by canyons where shadows lay blue. It was dry country, rained on violently but briefly in winter, its streams shrunken to runnels or nothing as its grass burnt yellow in summer. Trees and shrubs grew far apart, thorn, mimosa, acacia, pine, aloe; around the water holes palm, fern, orchid.

Withal, it was rich in life. Hawks and vultures were always at hover in cloudless heaven. Grazing herds mingled their millions together; among their scores of kinds were zebra-striped ponies, primitive rhinoceros, okapi-like ancestors of the giraffe, sometimes mastodon—thinly red-haired, hugely tusked—or peculiar elephants. Among the predators and scavengers were sabertooths, early forms of the big cats, hyenas, and scuttering ground apes which occasionally

9

walked on their hind legs. Ant heaps lifted six feet into the air. Marmots whistled.

It smelled of hay, scorch, baked dung and warm flesh. When wind awoke, it boomed, pushed, threw dust and heat into the face. Often the earth resounded to hoofbeats, birds clamored or beasts trumpeted. At night a sudden chill struck down, and the stars were so many that one didn't much notice the alienness of their constellations.

Thus had things been until lately. And as yet there was no great change. But now had begun a hundred years of thunder. When that was done, nothing would ever be the same again.

Manse Everard regarded Tom Nomura and Feliz a Rach for a squinting moment before he smiled and said, "No, thanks, I'll just poke around here today. You go have fun."

Did an eyelid of the big, bent-nosed, slightly grizzled man droop a little in Nomura's direction? The latter couldn't be sure. They were from the same milieu, indeed the same country. That Everard had been recruited in New York, A.D. 1954, and Nomura in San Francisco, 1972, ought to make scant difference. The upheavals of that generation were bubble pops against what had happened before and what would happen after. However, Nomura was fresh out of the Academy, a bare twenty-five years of lifespan behind him. Everard hadn't told how much time his own farings through the world's duration added up to; and given the longevity treatment the Patrol offered its people, it was impossible to guess. Nomura suspected the Unattached agent had seen enough existence to have become more foreign to him than Feliz— who was born two millenniums past either of them.

"Very well, let's start," she said. Curt though it was, Nomura thought her voice made music of the Temporal language.

They stepped from the veranda and walked across the yard. A couple of other corpsmen hailed them, with a pleasure directed at her. Nomura agreed. She was young and tall, the curve-nosed strength of her features softened by large green eyes, large mobile mouth, hair that shone auburn in spite of being hacked off at the ears. The usual gray coverall and stout boots could not hide her figure or the suppleness of her stride. Nomura knew he himself wasn't bad-looking—a stocky but limber frame, high-cheeked regular features, tawny skin—but she made him feel drab.

Also inside, he thought. How does a new-minted Patrolman—not even slated for police duty, a mere naturalist—how does he tell an aristocrat of the First Matriarchy that he's fallen in love with her?

The rumbling which always filled the air, these miles from the cataracts, sounded to him like a chorus. Was it imagination, or did he really sense an endless shudder through the ground, up into his bones?

Feliz opened a shed. Several hoppers stood inside, vaguely resembling wheelless two-seater motorcycles, propelled by antigravity and capable of leaping across several thousand years. (They and their present riders had been transported hither in heavy-duty shuttles.) Hers was loaded with recording gear. He had failed to convince her it was overburdened and knew she'd never forgive him if he finked on her. His invitation to Everard—the ranking officer in hand, though here-now simply on vacation—to join them today had been made in a slight hope that the latter would see that load and order her to let her assistant carry part of it.

She sprang to the saddle. "Come on!" she said. "The morning's getting old."

He mounted his vehicle and touched controls. Both glided outside and aloft. At eagle height, they leveled off and bore south, where the River Ocean poured into the Middle of the World.

Banks of upflung mist always edged that horizon, argent smoking off into azure. As one drew near afoot, they loomed topplingly overhead. Farther on, the universe swirled gray, shaken by the roar, bitter on human lips, while water flowed off rock and gouged through mud. So thick was the cold salt fog that it was unsafe to breathe for more than a few minutes.

From well above, the sight was yet more awesome. There one could see the end of a geological epoch. For a million and a half years the Mediterranean basin had lain a desert. Now the Gates of Hercules stood open and the Atlantic was coming through.

The wind of his passage around him, Nomura peered west across unrestful, many-hued and intricately foam-streaked immensity. He could see the currents run, sucked toward the new-made gap between Europe and Africa. There they clashed together and recoiled, a white and green chaos whose violence toned from earth to heaven and back, crumbled cliffs, overwhelmed valleys, blanketed the shore in spume for miles inland. From them came a stream, snow-colored in its fury, with flashes of livid emerald, to stand in an eight-mile wall between the continents and bellow. Spray roiled aloft, dimming the torrent after torrent wherein the sea crashed onward.

Rainbows wheeled through the clouds it made. This far aloft, the noise was no more than a monstrous millstone grinding. Nomura could clearly hear Feliz's voice out of his receiver, as she stopped her vehicle and lifted an arm. "Hold. I want a few more takes before we go on."

"Haven't you enough?" he asked.

Her words softened. "How can we get enough of a miracle?"

His heart jumped. *She's not a she-soldier, born to lord it over a ruck of underlings. In spite of her early life and ways, she isn't. She feels the dread, the beauty, yes, the sense of God at work—*

A wry grin at himself: *She'd better!*

After all, her task was to make a full-sensory record of the whole thing, from its beginning until that day when, a hundred years hence, the basin was full and the sea lapped calm where Odysseus would sail. It would take months of her lifespan. *(And mine, please, mine.)* Everybody in the corps wanted to experience this stupendousness; the hope of adventure was practically required for recruitment. But it wasn't feasible for many to come so far downstairs, crowding into so narrow a time-slot. Most would have to do it vicariously. Their chiefs would not have picked someone who was not a considerable artist, to live it on their behalf and pass it on to them.

Nomura remembered his astonishment when he was assigned to assist her. Short-handed as it was, could the Patrol afford artists?

Well, after he answered a cryptic advertisement and took several puzzling tests and learned about intertemporal traffic, he had wondered if police and rescue work were possible and been told that, usually, they were. He could see the need for administrative and clerical personnel, resident agents, historiographers, anthropologists, and, yes, natural scientists like himself. In the weeks they had been working together, Feliz convinced him that a few artists were at least as vital. Man does not live by bread alone, nor guns, paperwork, theses, naked practicalities.

She restowed her apparatus. "Come," she ordered. As she flashed eastward ahead of him, her hair caught a sunbeam and shone as if molten. He trudged mute in her wake.

The Mediterranean floor lay ten thousand feet below sea level. The inflow took most of that drop within a fifty-mile strait. Its volume amounted to ten thousand cubic miles a year, a hundred Victoria Falls or a thousand Niagaras.

Thus the statistics. The reality was a roar of white water, spray-shrouded, earth-sundering, mountain-shaking. Men could see, hear, feel, smell, taste the thing; they could not imagine it.

When the channel widened, the flow grew smoother, until it ran green and black. Then mists diminished and islands appeared, like ships which cast up huge bow waves; and life could again grow or go clear to the shore. Yet most of those islands would be eroded away before the century was out, and much of that life would perish in weather turned strange. For this event would move the planet from its Miocene to its Pliocene epoch.

And as he flitted onward, Nomura did not hear less noise, but more. Though the stream itself was quieter here, it moved toward a bass clamor which grew and grew till heaven was one brazen bell. He recognized a headland whose worn-down remnant would someday bear the name Gibraltar. Not far beyond, a cataract twenty miles wide made almost half the total plunge.

With terrifying ease, the waters slipped over that brink. They were glass-green against the darkling cliffs and umber grass of the continents. Light flamed off their heights. At their bottom another cloud bank rolled white in never-ending winds. Beyond reached a blue sheet, a lake whence rivers hewed canyons, out and out across the alkaline sparkle, dust devils, and mirage shimmers of the furnace land which they would make into a sea.

It boomed, it brawled, it querned.

Again Feliz poised her flyer. Nomura drew alongside. They were high; the air whittered chilly around them.

"Today," she told him, "I want to try for an impression of the sheer size. I'll move in close to the top, recording as I go, and then down."

"Not too close," he warned.

She bridled. "I'll judge that."

"Uh, I . . . I'm not trying to boss you or anything." *I'd better not. I, a plebe and a male.* "As a favor, please—" Nomura flinched at his own clumsy speech. "—be careful, will you? I mean, you're important to me."

Her smile burst upon him. She leaned hard against her safety harness to catch his hand. "Thank you, Tom." After a moment, turned grave: "Men like you make me understand what is wrong in the age I come from."

She had often spoken kindly to him: most times, in fact. Had she been a strident militant, no amount of comeliness would have kept him awake nights. He wondered if perhaps he had begun loving her when first he noticed how conscientiously she strove to regard him as her equal. It was not easy for her, she being almost as new in the Patrol as he—no easier than it was for men from other areas to believe, down inside where it counted, that she had the same capabilities they did and that it was right she use herself to the full.

She couldn't stay solemn. "Come on!" she shouted. "Hurry! That straight dropoff won't last another twenty years!"

Her machine darted. He slapped down the face screen of his helmet and plunged after, bearing the tapes and power cells and other auxiliary items. *Be careful,* he pleaded, *oh, be careful, my darling.*

She had gotten well ahead. He saw her like a comet, a dragonfly, everything vivid and swift, limned athwart yonder mile-high precipice of sea. The noise grew in him till there was nothing else, his skull was full of its doomsday.

Yards from the waters, she rode her hopper chasmward. Her head was buried in a dial-studded box, her hands at work on its settings; she steered with her knees. Salt spray began to fog Nomura's screen.

He activated the self-cleaner. Turbulence clawed at him; his carrier lurched. His eardrums, guarded against sound but not changing pressure, stabbed with pain.

He had come quite near Feliz when her vehicle went crazy. He saw it spin, saw it strike the green immensity, saw it and her engulfed. He could not hear himself scream through the thunder.

He rammed the speed switch, swooped after her. Was it blind instinct which sent him whirling away again, inches before the torrent grabbed him too? She was gone from sight. There was only the water wall, clouds below and unpitying blue calm above, the noise that took him in its jaws to shake him apart, the cold, the damp, the salt on his mouth that tasted like tears.

He fled for help.

Noonday glowered outside. The land looked bleached, lay moveless and lifeless except for a carrion bird. The distant falls alone had voice.

A knock on the door of his room brought Nomura off the bed, onto his feet. Through an immediately rackety pulse he croaked, "Come in. Do."

Everard entered. In spite of air conditioning, sweat spotted his garments. He gnawed a fireless pipe and his shoulders slumped.

"What's the word?" Nomura begged of him.

"As I feared. Nothing. She never returned home."

Nomura sank into a chair and stared before him. "You're certain?"

Everard sat down on the bed, which creaked beneath his weight. "Yeah. The message capsule just arrived. In answer to my inquiry, et cetera, Agent Feliz a Rach has not reported back to her home milieu base from the Gibraltar assignment, and they have no further record of her."

"Not in *any* era?"

"The way agents move around in time and space, nobody keeps dossiers, except maybe the Danellians."

"Ask them!"

"Do you imagine they'd reply?" Everard snapped—they, the

supermen of the remote future who were the founders and ultimate masters of the Patrol. One big fist clenched on his knee. "And don't tell me we ordinary mortals could keep closer tabs if we wanted to. Have you checked your personal future, son? We don't want to, and that's that."

The roughness left him. He shifted the pipe about in his grip and said most gently, "If we live long enough, we outlive those we've cared for. The common fate of man; nothing unique to our corps. But I'm sorry you had to strike it so young."

"Never mind me!" Nomura exclaimed. "What of her?"

"Yes . . . I've been thinking about your account. My guess is, the airflow patterns are worse than tricky around that fall. What should've been expected, no doubt. Overloaded, her hopper was less controllable than usual. An air pocket, a flaw, whatever it was, something like that grabbed her without warning and tossed her into the stream."

Nomura's fingers writhed against each other. "And I was supposed to look after her."

Everard shook his head. "Don't punish yourself worse. You were simply her assistant. She should have been more careful."

"But—God damn it, we can rescue her still, and you won't allow us to?" Nomura half screamed.

"Stop," Everard warned. "Stop right there."

Never say it: that several Patrolmen could ride backward in time, lay hold on her with tractor beams and haul her free of the abyss. Or that I could tell her and my earlier self to beware. It did not happen, therefore it will not happen.

It must *not happen.*

For the past becomes in fact mutable, as soon as we on our machines have transformed it into our present. And if ever a mortal takes himself that power, where can the changing end? We start by saving a glad girl; we go on to save Lincoln, but somebody else tries to save the Confederate States—No, none less than God can be trusted with time. The Patrol exists to guard what is real. Its men may no more violate that faith than they may violate their own mothers.

"I'm sorry," Nomura mumbled.

"It's okay, Tom."

"No, I . . . I thought . . . when I saw her vanish, my first thought was that we could make up a party, ride back to that very instant and snatch her clear—"

"A natural thought in a new man. Old habits of the mind die hard. The fact is, we did not. It'd scarcely have been authorized anyway. Too dangerous. We can ill afford to lose more. Certainly we can't when the record shows that our rescue attempt would be foredoomed if we made it."

"Is there no way to get around that?"

Everard sighed. "I can't think of any. Make your peace with fate, Tom." He hesitated. "Can I . . . can we do anything for you?"

"No." It came harsh out of Nomura's throat. "Except leave me be for a while."

"Sure." Everard rose. "You weren't the only person who thought a lot of her," he reminded, and left.

When the door had closed behind him, the sound of the falls seemed to wax, grinding, grinding. Nomura stared at emptiness. The sun passed its apex and began to slide very slowly toward night.

I should have gone after her myself, at once.

And risked my life.

Why not follow her into death, then?

No. That's senseless. Two deaths do not make a life. I couldn't have saved her. I didn't have the equipment or—The sane thing was to fetch help.

Only the help was denied—whether by man or by fate hardly matters, does it?—and so she went down. The stream hurled her into the gulf, she had a moment's terror before it smashed the awareness out of her, then at the bottom it crushed her, plucked her apart, strewed the pieces of her bones across the floor of a sea that I, a youngster, will sail upon one holiday, unknowing that there is a Time Patrol or ever was a Feliz. Oh, God, I want my dust down with hers, five and a half million years from this hour!

A remote cannonade went through the air, a tremor through earth and floor. An undercut bank must have crumbled into the torrent. It was the kind of scene she would have loved to capture.

"Would have?" Nomura yelled and surged from the chair. The ground still vibrated beneath him.

"She will!"

He ought to have consulted Everard, but feared—perhaps mistakenly, in his grief and his inexperience—that he would be refused permission and sent upstairs at once.

He ought to have rested for several days, but feared that his manner would betray him. A stimulant pill must serve in place of nature.

He ought to have checked out a tractor unit, not smuggled it into the locker on his vehicle.

When he took the hopper forth, a Patrolman who saw asked where he was bound. "For a ride," Nomura answered. The other nodded sympathetically. He might not suspect that a love had been lost, but the loss of a comrade was bad enough. Nomura was careful to get well over the northern horizon before he swung toward the seafall.

Right and left, it reached farther than he could see. Here, more than halfway down that cliff of green glass, the very curve of the planet hid its ends from him. Then as he entered the spume clouds, whiteness enfolded him, roiling and stinging.

His face shield stayed clear, but vision was ragged, upward along immensity. The helmet warded his hearing but could not stave off the storm which rattled his teeth and heart and skeleton. Winds whirled and smote, the carrier staggered, he must fight for every inch of control.

And to find the exact second—

Back and forth he leaped across time, reset the verniers, reflicked the main switch, glimpsed himself vague in the mists, and peered through them toward heaven; over and over, until abruptly he was *then*.

Twin gleams far above . . . He saw the one strike and go under, go down, while the other darted around until soon it ran away. Its rider had not seen him, where he lurked in the chill salt mists. His presence was not on any damned record.

He darted forward. Yet patience was upon him. He could cruise for a long piece of lifespan if need be, seeking the trice which would be his. The fear of death, even the knowing that she might be dead when he found her, were like half-remembered dreams. The elemental powers had taken him. He was a will that flew.

He hovered within a yard of the water. Gusts tried to cast him into its grip, as they had done to her. He was ready for them, danced free, returned to peer—returned through time as well as space, so that a score of him searched along the fall in that span of seconds when Feliz might be alive.

He paid his other selves no heed. They were merely stages he had gone through or must still go through.

THERE!

The dim dark shape tumbled past him, beneath the flood, on its way to destruction. He spun a control. A tractor beam locked onto the other machine. His reeled and went after it, unable to pull such a mass free of such a might.

The tide nearly had him when help came. Two vehicles, three, four, all straining together, they hauled Feliz's loose. She sagged horribly limp in her saddle harness. He didn't go to her at once. First he went back those few blinks in time, and back, to be her rescuer and his own.

When finally they were alone among fogs and furies, she freed and in his arms, he would have burnt a hole through the sky to get ashore where he could care for her. But she stirred, her eyes blinked open, after a minute she smiled at him. Then he wept.

Beside them, the ocean roared onward.

The sunset to which Nomura had leaped ahead was not on anybody's record either. It turned the land golden. The falls must be afire with it. Their song resounded beneath the evening star.

Feliz propped pillows against headboard, sat straighter in the bed where she was resting, and told Everard: "If you lay charges against him, that he broke regulations or whatever male stupidity you are thinking of, I'll also quit your bloody Patrol."

"Oh, no." The big man lifted a palm as if to fend off attack.

"Please. You misunderstand. I only meant to say, we're in a slightly awkward position."

"How?" Nomura demanded, from the chair in which he sat and held Feliz's hand. "I wasn't under any orders not to attempt this, was I? All right, agents are supposed to safeguard their own lives if possible, as being valuable to the corps. Well, doesn't it follow that the salvaging of a life is worthwhile too?"

"Yes. Sure." Everard paced the floor. It thudded beneath his boots, above the drumbeat of the flood. "Nobody quarrels with success, even in a much tighter organization than ours. In fact, Tom, the initiative you showed today makes your future prospects look good, believe me." A grin went lopsided around his pipestem. "As for an old soldier like myself, it'll be forgiven that I was too ready to give up." A flick of somberness: "I've seen so many lost beyond hope."

He stopped in his treading, confronted them both, and stated: "But we cannot have loose ends. The fact is, her unit does not list Feliz a Rach as returning, ever."

Their clasps tightened on each other.

Everard gave him and her a smile—haunted, nevertheless a smile—before he continued: "Don't get scared, though. Tom, earlier you wondered why we, we ordinary humans at least, don't keep closer track of our people. Now do you see the reason?

"Feliz a Rach never checked back into her original base. She may have visited her former home, of course, but we don't ask officially what agents do on their furloughs." He drew breath. "As for the rest of her career, if she should want to transfer to a different headquarters and adopt a different name, why, any officer of sufficient rank could approve that. Me, for example.

"We operate loose in the Patrol. We dare not do otherwise."

Nomura understood, and shivered.

Feliz recalled him to the ordinary world. "But who might I become?" she wondered.

He pounced on the cue. "Well," he said, half in laughter and half in thunder, "how about Mrs. Thomas Nomura?"

Triceratops Summer

INTRODUCTION

Here's a summer memorable for more than the sudden appearance of a herd of triceratopsies, or whatever the plural is, with a comfortable relationship contrasted with a brand-new, more intense one. If it is better to have loved and lost than not have loved at all, how does having loved and lost *and* not having loved at all stack up?

* * *

Michael Swanwick has received the Hugo (six times), Nebula, Theodore Sturgeon, and World Fantasy Awards for his work. His novel *Stations of the Tide* was honored with the Nebula Award and was also nominated for the Hugo and Arthur C. Clarke Awards. His short work, "The Edge of the World," was awarded the Theodore Sturgeon Memorial Award in 1989. It was also nominated for both the Hugo and World Fantasy Awards. "Radio Waves" received the World Fantasy Award in 1996. "The Very Pulse of the Machine" received the Hugo Award in 1999, as did "Scherzo with Tyrannosaur" in 2000. His stories have appeared in *Omni*, *Penthouse*, *Amazing Stories*, *Asimov's Science Fiction Magazine*, *High Times*, *New Dimensions*, *Starlight*, *Universe*, *Full Spectrum*, *Triquarterly* and elsewhere. Many have been reprinted in best of the year anthologies, and translated for Japanese, Dutch, German, Italian, Portuguese, Spanish, Swedish, French and Croatian publications. His recent novels include *Bones of the Earth*, *The Dragons of Babel*, and *Dancing* *with Bears*. Another novel, *Chasing the Phoenix*, is forthcoming. His short fiction has been collected in *Gravity's Angels*, *A Geography of Unknown Lands*, *Moon Dogs*, *Tales of Old Earth*, *Cigar-Box Faust and Other Miniatures* (a collection of short-shorts), *The Dog Said Bow-Wow* and *The Best of Michael Swanwick*. . He lives in Philadelphia with his wife, Marianne Porter.

Triceratops Summer

by Michael Swanwick

The dinosaurs looked all wobbly in the summer heat shimmering up from the pavement. There were about thirty of them, a small herd of what appeared to be *Triceratops*. They were crossing the road—don't ask me why—so I downshifted and brought the truck to a halt, and waited.

Waited and watched.

They were interesting creatures, and surprisingly graceful for all their bulk. They picked their way delicately across the road, looking neither to the right nor the left. I was pretty sure I'd correctly identified them by now—they had those three horns on their faces. I used to be a kid. I'd owned the plastic models.

My next-door neighbor, Gretta, who was sitting in the cab next to me with her eyes closed, said, "Why aren't we moving?"

"Dinosaurs in the road," I said.

She opened her eyes.

"Son of a bitch," she said.

Then, before I could stop her, she leaned over and honked the horn, three times. Loud.

As one, every *Triceratops* in the herd froze in its tracks, and swung its head around to face the truck.

I practically fell over laughing.

"What's so goddamn funny?" Gretta wanted to know. But I could only point and shake my head helplessly, tears of laughter rolling down my cheeks.

It was the frills. They were beyond garish. They were as bright as any circus poster, with red whorls and yellow slashes and electric orange diamonds—too many shapes and colors to catalog, and each one different. They looked like Chinese kites! Like butterflies with six-foot wingspans! Like Las Vegas on acid! And then, under those carnival-bright displays, the most stupid faces imaginable, blinking and gaping like brain-damaged cows. Oh, they were funny, all right, but if you couldn't see that at a glance, you never were going to.

Gretta was getting fairly steamed. She climbed down out of the cab and slammed the door behind her. At the sound, a couple of the *Triceratops* pissed themselves with excitement, and the lot shied away a step or two. Then they began huddling a little closer, to see what would happen next.

Gretta hastily climbed back into the cab. "What are those bastards up to now?" she demanded irritably. She seemed to blame me for their behavior. Not that she could say so, considering she was in my truck and her BMW was still in the garage in South Burlington.

"They're curious," I said. "Just stand still. Don't move or make any noise, and after a bit they'll lose interest and wander off."

"How do you know? You ever see anything like them before?"

"No," I admitted. "But I worked on a dairy farm when I was a young fella, thirty, forty years ago, and the behavior seems similar."

In fact, the *Triceratops* were already getting bored and starting to wander off again when a battered old Hyundai pulled wildly up beside us, and a skinny young man with the worst-combed hair I'd seen in a long time jumped out. They decided to stay and watch.

The young man came running over to us, arms waving. I leaned out the window. "What's the problem, son?"

He was pretty bad upset. "There's been an accident—an *incident*, I mean. At the Institute." He was talking about the Institute for Advanced Physics, which was not all that far from here. It was government-funded and affiliated in some way I'd never been able to get straight with the University of Vermont. "The verge stabilizers failed and the meson-field inverted and vectorized. The congruence factors went to infinity and . . ." He seized control of himself. "You're not supposed to see *any* of this."

"These things are yours, then?" I said. "So you'd know. They're *Triceratops*, right?"

"*Triceratops horridus,*" he said distractedly. I felt unreasonably pleased with myself. "For the most part. There might be a couple other species of *Triceratops* mixed in there as well. They're like ducks in that regard. They're not fussy about what company they keep."

Gretta shot out her wrist and glanced meaningfully at her watch. Like everything else she owned, it was expensive. She worked for a firm in Essex Junction that did systems analysis for companies that were considering downsizing. Her job was to find out exactly what everybody did and then tell the CEO who could be safely cut. "I'm losing money," she grumbled.

I ignored her.

"Listen," the kid said. "You've got to keep quiet about this. We can't afford to have it get out. It has to be kept a secret."

"A secret?" On the far side of the herd, three cars had drawn up and stopped. Their passengers were standing in the road, gawking. A Ford Taurus pulled up behind us, and its driver rolled down his window for a better look. "You're planning to keep a herd of dinosaurs secret? There must be dozens of these things."

"Hundreds," he said despairingly. "They were migrating. The herd broke up after it came through. This is only a fragment of it."

"Then I don't see how you're going to keep this a secret. I mean, just look at them. They're practically the size of tanks. People are bound to notice."

"My God, my God."

Somebody on the other side had a camera out and was taking pictures. I didn't point this out to the young man.

Gretta had been getting more and more impatient as the conversation proceeded. Now she climbed down out of the truck and said, "I can't afford to waste any more time here. I've got work to do."

"Well, so do I, Gretta."

She snorted derisively. "Ripping out toilets, and nailing up sheet rock! Already, I've lost more money than you earn in a week."

She stuck out her hand at the young man. "Give me your car keys."

Dazed, the kid obeyed. Gretta climbed down, got in the Hyundai, and wheeled it around. "I'll have somebody return this to the Institute later today."

Then she was gone, off to find another route around the herd.

She should have waited, because a minute later the beasts decided to leave, and in no time at all were nowhere to be seen. They'd be easy enough to find, though. They pretty much trampled everything flat in their wake.

The kid shook himself, as if coming out of a trance. "Hey," he said. "She took my *car*."

"Climb into the cab," I said. "There's a bar a ways up the road. I think you need a drink."

He said his name was Everett McCoughlan, and he clutched his glass like he would fall off the face of the Earth if he were to let go. It took a couple of whiskeys to get the full story out of him. Then I sat silent for a long time. I don't mind admitting that what he'd said made me feel a little funny. "How long?" I asked at last.

"Ten weeks, maybe three months, tops. No more."

I took a long swig of my soda water. (I've never been much of a drinker. Also, it was pretty early in the morning.) Then I told Everett that I'd be right back.

I went out to the truck, and dug the cell phone out of the glove compartment.

First I called home. Delia had already left for the bridal shop, and they didn't like her getting personal calls at work, so I left a message saying that I loved her. Then I called Green Mountain Books. It wasn't open yet, but Randy likes to come in early and he picked up the phone when he heard my voice on the machine. I asked him if he had anything on *Triceratops*. He said to hold on a minute, and then said yes, he had one copy of *The Horned Dinosaurs* by Peter Dodson. I told him I'd pick it up next time I was in town.

Then I went back in the bar. Everett had just ordered a third whiskey, but I pried it out of his hand. "You've had enough of that," I said. "Go home, take a nap. Maybe putter around in the garden."

"I don't have my car," he pointed out.

"Where do you live? I'll take you home."

"Anyway, I'm supposed to be at work. I didn't log out. And technically I'm still on probation."

"What difference does that make," I asked, "now?"

Everett had an apartment in Winooski at the Woolen Mill, so I guess the Institute paid him good money. Either that or he wasn't very smart how he spent it. After I dropped him off, I called a couple contractors I knew and arranged for them to take over what jobs I was already committed to. Then I called the *Free Press* to cancel my regular ad, and all my customers to explain I was having scheduling problems and had to subcontract their jobs. Only old Mrs. Bremmer gave me any trouble over that, and even she came around after I said that in any case I wouldn't be able to get around to her Jacuzzi until sometime late July.

Finally, I went to the bank and arranged for a second mortgage on my house.

It took me a while to convince Art Letourneau I was serious. I'd been doing business with him for a long while, and he knew how I felt about debt. Also, I was pretty evasive about what I wanted the money for. He was half-suspicious I was having some kind of late onset mid-life crisis. But the deed was in my name and property values were booming locally, so in the end the deal went through.

On the way home, I stopped at a jewelry store and at the florist's.

Delia's eyes widened when she saw the flowers, and then narrowed at the size of the stone on the ring. She didn't look at all the way I'd thought she would. "This better be good," she said.

So I sat down at the kitchen table and told her the whole story. When I was done, Delia was silent for a long while, just as I'd been. Then she said, "How much time do we have?"

"Three months if we're lucky. Ten weeks in any case," Everett said.

"You believe him?"

"He seemed pretty sure of himself."

If there's one thing I am, it's a good judge of character, and Delia knew it. When Gretta moved into the rehabbed barn next door, I'd said right from the start she was going to be a difficult neighbor. And that was before she'd smothered the grass on her property under three different colors of mulch, and then complained about me keeping my pickup parked in the driveway, out in plain sight.

Delia thought seriously for a few minutes, frowning in that way she has when she's concentrating, and then she smiled. It was a wan little thing, but a smile nonetheless. "Well, I've always wished we could afford a real first-class vacation."

I was glad to hear her say so, because that was exactly the direction my own thought had been trending in. And happier than that when she flung out her arms and whooped, "I'm going to *Disney*world!"

"Hell," I said. "We've got enough money to go to Disney World, Disneyland, *and* Eurodisney, one after the other. I think there's one in Japan too."

We were both laughing at this point, and then she dragged me up out of the chair, and the two of us were dancing around and round the kitchen, still a little spooked under it all, but mostly being as giddy and happy as kids.

We were going to sleep in the next morning, but old habits die hard and anyway, Delia felt she owed it to the bridal shop to give them a week's notice. So, after she'd left, I went out to see if I could find where the *Triceratops* had gone.

Only to discover Everett standing by the side of the road with his thumb out.

I pulled over. "Couldn't get somebody at the Institute to drive your car home?" I asked when we were underway again.

"It never got there," he said gloomily. "That woman who was with you the other day drove it into a ditch. Stripped the clutch and bent the frame out of shape. She said she wouldn't have had the accident if my dinosaurs hadn't gotten her upset. Then she hung up on me. I just started at this job. I don't have the savings to buy a new car."

"Lease one instead," I said. "Put it on your credit card and pay the minimum for the next two or three months."

"I hadn't thought of that."

We drove on for a while and then I asked, "How'd she manage to get in touch with you?" She'd driven off before he mentioned his name.

"She called the Institute and asked for the guy with the bad hair. They gave her my home phone number."

The parking lot for the Institute for Advanced Physics had a card system, so I let Everett off by the side of the road. "Thanks for not telling anybody," he said as he climbed out. "About . . . you know."

"It seemed wisest not to."

He started away and then turned back suddenly and asked, "Is my hair really that bad?"

"Nothing that a barber couldn't fix," I said.

I'd driven to the Institute by the main highway. Returning, I went by back ways, through farmland. When I came to where I'd seen the *Triceratops*, I thought for an instant there'd been an accident, there were so many vehicles by the side of the road. But it turned out they were mostly gawkers and television crews. So apparently the herd hadn't gone far. There were cameras up and down the road and lots of good looking young women standing in front of them with wireless microphones.

I pulled over to take a look. One *Triceratops* had come right up to the fence and was browsing on some tall weeds there. It didn't seem to have any fear of human beings, possibly because in its day mammals never got much bigger than badgers. I walked up and stroked its back, which was hard and pebbly and warm. It was the warmth that got to me. It made the experience real.

A newswoman came over with her cameraman in tow. "You certainly look happy," she said.

"Well, I always wanted to meet a real live dinosaur." I turned to face her, but I kept one hand on the critter's frill. "They're something to see, I'll tell you. Dumb as mud but lots more fun to look at."

She asked me a few questions, and I answered them as best I

could. Then, after she did her wrap, she got out a notebook and took down my name and asked me what I did. I told her I was a contractor but that I used to work on a dairy farm. She seemed to like that.

I watched for a while more, and then drove over to Burlington to pick up my book. The store wasn't open yet, but Randy let me in when I knocked. "You bastard," he said after he'd locked the door behind me. "Do you have any idea how much I could have sold this for? I had a foreigner," by which I understood him to mean somebody from New York State or possibly New Hampshire, "offer me two hundred dollars for it. And I could have got more if I'd had something to dicker with!"

"I'm obliged," I said, and paid him in paper bills. He waved off the tax but kept the nickel. "Have you gone out to see 'em yet?"

"Are you nuts? There's thousands of people coming into the state to look at those things. It's going to be a madhouse out there."

"I thought the roads seemed crowded. But it wasn't as bad as all of that."

"It's early still. You just wait."

Randy was right. By evening the roads were so congested that Delia was an hour late getting home. I had a casserole in the oven and the book open on the kitchen table when she staggered in. "The males have longer, more elevated horns, where the females have shorter, more forward-directed horns," I told her. "Also, the males are bigger than the females, but the females outnumber the males by a ratio of two to one."

I leaned back in my chair with a smile. "Two to one. Imagine that."

Delia hit me. "Let me see that thing."

I handed her the book. It kind of reminded me of when we were new-married, and used to go out bird-watching. Before things got so busy. Then Delia's friend Martha called and said to turn on Channel 3 quick. We did, and there I was saying, "dumb as mud."

"So you're a cattle farmer now?" Delia said, when the spot was over.

"That's not what I told her. She got it mixed up. Hey, look what I got." I'd been to three separate travel agents that afternoon. Now I spread out the brochures: Paris, Dubai, Rome, Australia, Rio de Janeiro, Marrakech. Even Disney World. I'd grabbed everything that looked interesting. "Take your pick, we can be there tomorrow."

Delia looked embarrassed.

"What?" I said.

"You know that June is our busy season. All those young brides. Francesca begged me to stay on through the end of the month."

"But—"

"It's not that long," she said.

For a couple of days it was like Woodstock, the Super Bowl, and the World Series all rolled into one—the Interstates came to a standstill, and it was worth your life to actually have to go somewhere. Then the governor called in the National Guard, and they cordoned off Chittenden County so you had to show your ID to get in or out. The *Triceratops* had scattered into little groups by then. Then a dozen or two were captured and shipped out of state to zoos where they could be more easily seen. So things returned to normal, almost.

I was painting the trim on the house that next Saturday when Everett drove up in a beat-up old clunker. "I like your new haircut," I said. "Looks good. You here to see the trikes?"

"Trikes?"

"That's what they're calling your dinos. *Triceratops* is too long for common use. We got a colony of eight or nine hanging around the neighborhood." There were woods out back of the house and beyond them a little marsh. They liked to browse the margins of the wood and wallow in the mud.

"No, uh . . . I came to find out the name of that woman you were with. The one who took my car."

"Gretta Houck, you mean?"

"I guess. I've been thinking it over, and I think she really ought to pay for the repairs. I mean, right's right."

"I noticed you decided against leasing."

"It felt dishonest. This car's cheap. But it's not very good. One door is wired shut with a coat hanger."

Delia came out of the house with the picnic basket then and I introduced them. "Ev's looking for Gretta," I said.

"Well, your timing couldn't be better," Delia said. "We were just about to go out trike-watching with her. You can join us."

"Oh, I can't—"

"Don't give it a second thought. There's plenty of food." Then, to me, "I'll go fetch Gretta while you clean up."

So that's how we found ourselves following the little trail through the woods and out to the meadow on the bluff above the Tylers' farm. The trikes slept in the field there. They'd torn up the crops pretty bad. But the state was covering damages, so the Tylers didn't seem to mind. It made me wonder if the governor knew what we knew. If he'd been talking with the folks at the Institute.

I spread out the blanket, and Delia got out cold cuts, deviled eggs, lemonade, all the usual stuff. I'd brought along two pairs of binoculars, which I handed out to our guests. Gretta had been pretty surly so far, which made me wonder how Delia'd browbeat her into coming along. But now she said, "Oh, look! They've got babies!"

There were three little ones, only a few feet long. Two of them were mock-fighting, head-butting and tumbling over and over each other. The third just sat in the sun, blinking. They were all as cute as the dickens, with their tiny little nubs of horns and their great big eyes.

The other trikes were wandering around, pulling up bushes and such and eating them. Except for one that stood near the babies, looking big and grumpy and protective. "Is that the mother?" Gretta asked.

"That one's male," Everett said. "You can tell by the horns." He launched into an explanation, which I didn't listen to, having read the book.

On the way back to the house, Gretta grumbled, "I suppose you want the number for my insurance company."

"I guess," Everett said.

They disappeared into her house for maybe twenty minutes and then Everett got into his clunker and drove away. Afterwards, I said to Delia, "I thought the whole point of the picnic was you and I were going to finally work out where we were going on vacation." She hadn't even brought along the travel books I'd bought her.

"I think they like each other."

"Is that what this was about? You know, you've done some damn fool things in your time—"

"Like what?" Delia said indignantly. "When have I ever done anything that was less than wisdom incarnate?"

"Well . . . you married me."

"Oh, that." She put her arms around me. "That was just the exception that proves the rule."

So, what with one thing and the other, the summer drifted by. Delia took to luring the *Triceratops* closer and closer to the house with cabbages and bunches of celery and such. Cabbages were their favorite. It got so that we were feeding the trikes off the back porch in the evenings. They'd come clomping up around sunset, hoping for cabbages but willing to settle for pretty much anything.

It ruined the yard, but so what? Delia was a little upset when they got into her garden, but I spent a day putting up a good strong fence around it, and she replanted. She made manure tea by mixing their dung with water, and its effect on the plants was bracing. The roses blossomed like never before, and in August the tomatoes came up spectacular.

I mentioned this to Dave Jenkins down at the home-and-garden and he looked thoughtful. "I believe there's a market for that," he said. "I'll buy as much of their manure as you can haul over here."

"Sorry," I told him, "I'm on vacation."

Still, I couldn't get Delia to commit to a destination. Not that I quit trying. I was telling her about the Atlantis Hotel on Paradise Island one evening when suddenly she said, "Well, look at this."

I stopped reading about swimming with dolphins and the fake undersea ruined city, and joined her at the door. There was Everett's car—the new one that Gretta's insurance had paid for—parked out front of her house. There was only one light on, in the kitchen. Then that one went out too.

We figured those two had worked through their differences.

An hour later, though, we heard doors slamming, and the screech of Everett's car pulling out too fast. Then somebody was banging on our screen door. It was Gretta. When Delia let her in, she burst out into tears. Which surprised me. I wouldn't have pegged Everett as that kind of guy.

I made some coffee while Delia guided her into a kitchen chair, and got her some tissues, and soothed her down enough that she could tell us why she'd thrown Everett out of her house. It wasn't anything he'd done apparently, but something he'd said.

"Do you know what he *told* me?" she sobbed.

"I think I do," Delia said.

"About timelike—"

"—loops. Yes, dear."

Gretta looked stricken. "You too? Why didn't you tell me? Why didn't you tell everybody?"

"I considered it," I said. "Only then I thought, what would folks do if they knew their actions no longer mattered? Most would behave decently enough. But a few would do some pretty bad things, I'd think. I didn't want to be responsible for that."

She was silent for a while.

"Explain to me again about timelike loops," she said at last. "Ev tried, but by then I was too upset to listen. "

"Well, I'm not so sure myself. But the way he explained it to me, they're going to fix the problem by going back to the moment before the rupture occurred and preventing it from ever happening in the first place. When that happens, everything from the moment of rupture to the moment when they go back to apply the patch separates from the trunk timeline. It just sort of drifts away, and dissolves into nothingness—never was, never will be."

"And what becomes of us?"

"We just go back to whatever we were doing when the accident happened. None the worse for wear."

"But without memories."

"How can you remember something that never happened?"

"So Ev and I—"

"No, dear," Delia said gently.

"How much time do we have?"

"With a little luck, we have the rest of the summer," Delia said. "The question is, how do you want to spend it?"

"What does it matter," Gretta said bitterly. "If it's all going to end?"

"Everything ends eventually. But after all is said and done, it's what we do in the meantime that matters, isn't it?"

The conversation went on for a while more. But that was the gist of it.

Eventually, Gretta got out her cell and called Everett. She had him on speed dial, I noticed. In her most corporate voice, she said, "Get your ass over here," and snapped the phone shut without waiting for a response.

She didn't say another word until Everett's car pulled up in front of her place. Then she went out and confronted him. He put his hands on his hips. She grabbed him and kissed him. Then she took him by the hand and led him back into the house.

They didn't bother to turn on the lights.

I stared at the silent house for a little bit. Then I realized that Delia wasn't with me anymore, so I went looking for her.

She was out on the back porch. "Look," she whispered.

There was a full moon and by its light we could see the *Triceratops* settling down to sleep in our backyard. Delia had managed to lure them all the way in at last. Their skin was all silvery in the moonlight; you couldn't make out the patterns on their frills. The big trikes formed a kind of circle around the little ones. One by one, they closed their eyes and fell asleep.

Believe it or not, the big bull male snored.

It came to me then that we didn't have much time left. One morning soon we'd wake up and it would be the end of spring and everything would be exactly as it was before the dinosaurs came. "We never did get to Paris or London or Rome or Marrakech," I said sadly. "Or even Disney World."

Without taking her eyes off the sleeping trikes, Delia put an arm around my waist. "Why are you so fixated on going places?" she asked. "We had a nice time here, didn't we?"

"I just wanted to make you happy."

"Oh, you idiot. You did that decades ago."

So there we stood, in the late summer of our lives. Out of nowhere, we'd been given a vacation from our ordinary lives, and now it was almost over. A pessimist would have said that we were just waiting for oblivion. But Delia and I didn't see it that way. Life is strange. Sometimes it's hard, and other times it's painful enough to break your heart. But sometimes it's grotesque and beautiful. Sometimes it fills you with wonder, like a *Triceratops* sleeping in the moonlight.

The Chronoclasm

INTRODUCTION

Romeo and Juliet had their problems, being from different feuding families, but suppose that the lovers were from different times, and their love was even more strictly taboo?

* * *

John Wyndham Parkes Lucas Beynon Harris (1903-1969) wrote under a number of permutations of his six names (try fitting *that* on a driver's license!), and even published his novelized story collection, *The Outward Urge*, as a collaboration with one of his pen names. Still, he is best known as "John Wyndham," the name under which he published the now-classic novels *The Day of the Triffids* (also known as *Revolt of the Triffids*), *The Kraken Wakes* (published in the U.S.A. in a cut version with a slightly altered ending as *Out of the Deeps*), *The Chrysalids* (known as *Re-Birth* in the U.S.A.), and *The Midwich Cuckoos*, which became the very good, very scary movie, *Village of the Damned*, unlike the movie version of *Triffids*, which was a profound disappointment. The first two novels involve global catastrophes, while *The Chrysalids* is set long after what obviously was an atomic war, and they established Wyndham as a master of disaster. Wyndham's characters are often common-sensical, unquirky Brits in desperate situations, which led Brian Aldiss to dismiss the author's novels as "cosy catastrophes" (feel free to rewrite "cosy" as "cozy"), an absurd claim which can be sustained only by ignoring how desperate those situations in the novels are. In any case, Wyndham's novels are rarely out of print and still sell, and if he were still alive, he'd probably cry all the way to the bank. (Incidentally, if he were alive, I'd like to ask him why it is that in the *Collier's* magazine serial version of *Triffids*, the killer plants came from Venus, while in the book version, they came from behind the Iron Curtain.) Unlike the novels, Wyndham's short stories are painted on a smaller canvas, and any catastrophe is far more personal.

The Chronoclasm

by John Wyndham

I first heard of Tavia in a sort of semi-detached way. An elderly gentleman, a stranger, approached me in Plyton High Street one morning. He raised his hat, bowed, with perhaps a touch of foreignness, and introduced himself politely:

"My name is Donald Gobie, Dr. Gobie. I should be most grateful, Sir Gerald, if you could spare me just a few minutes of your time. I am so sorry to trouble you, but it is a matter of some urgency, and considerable importance." I looked at him carefully.

"I think there must be some mistake," I told him. "I have no handle to my name—not even a knighthood." He looked taken aback.

"Dear me. I am sorry. Such a likeness—I was quite sure you must be Sir Gerald Lattery."

It was my turn to be taken aback.

"My name *is* Gerald Lattery," I admitted, "but Mister, not Sir."

He grew a little confused.

"Oh, dear. Of course. How very stupid of me. Is there—" he looked about us, "—is there somewhere where we could have a few words in private?" he asked.

I hesitated, but only for a brief moment. He was clearly a

39

gentleman of education and some culture. Might have been a lawyer. Certainly not on the touch, or anything of that kind. We were close to *The Bull,* so I led the way into the lounge there. It was conveniently empty. He declined the offer of a drink, and we sat down.

"Well, what is this trouble, Dr. Gobie?" I asked him.

He hesitated, obviously a little embarrassed. Then he spoke, with an air of plunging:

"It is concerning Tavia, Sir Gerald—er, Mr. Lattery. I think perhaps you don't understand the degree to which the whole situation is fraught with unpredictable consequences. It is not just my own responsibility, you understand, though that troubles me greatly—it is the results that cannot be foreseen. She really must come back before very great harm is done. She *must,* Mr. Lattery."

I watched him. His earnestness was beyond question, his distress perfectly genuine.

"But, Dr. Gobie—" I began.

"I can understand what it may mean to you, sir, nevertheless I do implore you to persuade her. Not just for my sake and her family's, but for everyone's. One has to be so careful; the results of the least action are incalculable. There has to be order, harmony; it must be preserved. Let one single seed fall out of place, and who can say what may come of it? So I beg you to persuade her—"

I broke in, speaking gently because whatever it was all about, he obviously had it very much at heart.

"Just a minute, Dr. Gobie. I'm afraid there *is* some mistake. I haven't the least idea what you are talking about."

He checked himself. A dismayed expression came over his face.

"You—?" he began, and then paused in thought, frowning. "You don't mean you haven't met Tavia yet?" he asked.

"As far as I know, I do. I've never even heard of anyone called Tavia," I assured him.

He looked winded by that, and I was sorry. I renewed my offer of a drink. But he shook his head, and presently he recovered himself.

"I am so sorry," he said. "There has been a mistake indeed. Please accept my apologies, Mr. Lattery. You must think me quite light-headed, I'm afraid. It's so difficult to explain. May I ask you just to forget it, please forget it entirely."

Presently he left, looking forlorn. I remained a little puzzled, but in the course of the next day or two, I carried out his final request—or so I thought.

The first time I did see Tavia was a couple of years later, and, of course, I did not at the time know it was she.

I had just left *The Bull.* There were a number of people about in the High Street, but just as I laid a hand on the car door, I became aware that one of them on the other side of the road had stopped dead, and was watching me. I looked up, and our eyes met. Hers were hazel.

She was tall, and slender, and good-looking—not pretty, something better than that. And I went on looking.

She wore a rather ordinary tweed skirt and dark-green knitted jumper. Her shoes, however, were a little odd: low-heeled, but a bit fancy; they didn't seem to go with the rest. There was something else out of place, too, though I did not fix it at the moment. Only afterwards did I realize that it must have been the way her fair hair was dressed—very becoming to her, but the style was a bit off the beam. You might say that hair is just hair, and hairdressers have infinite variety of touch, but they haven't. There is a kind of period-style overriding current fashion; look at any photograph taken thirty years ago. Her hair, like her shoes, didn't quite suit the rest.

For some seconds she stood there frozen, quite unsmiling. Then, as if she were not quite awake, she took a step forward to cross the road. At that moment the Market Hall clock chimed. She glanced up at it; her expression was suddenly all alarm. She turned, and started running up the pavement, like Cinderella after the last bus.

I got into my car wondering who she had mistaken me for. I was perfectly certain I had never set eyes on her before.

The next day when the barman at The *Bull* set down my pint, he told me:

"Young woman in here asking after you, Mr. Lattery. Did she find you? I told her where your place is."

I shook my head. "Who was she?"

"She didn't say her name, but—" he went on to describe her. Recollection of the girl on the other side of the street came back to me. I nodded.

"I saw her just across the road. I wondered who she was," I told him.

"Well, she seemed to know you all right. 'Was that Mr. Lattery who was in here earlier on?' she says to me. I says yes, you was one of them. She nodded and thought a bit. 'He lives at Bagford House, doesn't he?' she asks. 'Why, no, Miss,' I says, 'that's Major Flacken's place. Mr. Lattery, he lives out at Chatcombe Cottage.' So she asks me where that is, an' I told her. Hope that was all right. Seemed a nice young lady."

I reassured him. "She could have got the address anywhere. Funny she should ask about Bagford House—that's a place I might hanker for, if I ever had any money."

"Better hurry up and make it, sir. The old Major's getting on a bit now," he said.

Nothing came of it. Whatever the girl had wanted my address for, she didn't follow it up, and the matter dropped out of my mind.

It was about a month later that I saw her again. I'd kind of slipped into the habit of going riding once or twice a week with a girl called Marjorie Cranshaw, and running her home from the stables afterwards. The way took us by one of those narrow lanes between high banks where there is barely room for two cars to pass. Round a corner I had to brake and pull right in because an oncoming car was in the middle of the road after overtaking a pedestrian. It pulled over, and squeezed past me. Then I looked at the pedestrian, and saw it was this girl again. She recognized me at the same moment, and gave a slight start. I saw her hesitate, and then make up her mind to come across and speak. She came a few steps nearer with obvious intention. Then she caught sight of Marjorie beside me, changed her mind, with as bad an imitation of not having intended to come our way at all as you could hope to see. I put the gear in.

"Oh," said Marjorie in a voice that penetrated naturally, and a tone that was meant to, "who was that?"

I told her I didn't know.

"She certainly seemed to know you," she said, disbelievingly.

Her tone irritated me. In any case, it was no business of hers. I didn't reply.

She was not willing to let it drop. "I don't think I've seen her about before," she said presently.

"She may be a holiday-maker for all I know," I said. "There are plenty of them about."

"That doesn't sound very convincing, considering the way she looked at you."

"I don't care for being thought, or called, a liar," I said.

"Oh, I thought I asked a perfectly ordinary question. Of course, if I've said anything to embarrass you—"

"Nor do I care for sustained innuendo. Perhaps you'd prefer to walk the rest of the way. It's not far."

"I see. I am sorry to have intruded. It's a pity it's too narrow for you to turn the car here," she said as she got out. "Goodbye, Mr. Lattery."

With the help of a gateway it was not too narrow, but I did not see the girl when I went back. Marjorie had roused my interest in her, so that I rather hoped I would. Besides, though I still had no idea who she might be, I was feeling grateful to her. You will have experienced, perhaps, that feeling of being relieved of a weight that you had not properly realized was there?

Our third meeting was on a different plane altogether.

My cottage stood, as its name suggests, in a coombe—which, in Devonshire, is a small valley that is, or once was, wooded. It was somewhat isolated from the other four or five cottages there, being set in the lower part, at the end of the track. The heathered hills swept steeply up on either side. A few narrow grazing fields bordered both banks of the stream. What was left of the original woods fringed between them and the heather, and survived in small clumps and spinneys here and there.

It was in the closest of these spinneys, on an afternoon when I was surveying my plot and deciding that it was about time the beans came out, that I heard a sound of small branches breaking underfoot. I needed no more than a glance to find the cause of it; her fair hair gave her away. For a moment we looked at one another as we had before.

"Er—hullo," I said.

She did not reply at once. She went on staring. Then:

"Is there anyone in sight?" she asked.

I looked up as much of the track as I could see from where I stood, and then up at the opposite hillside.

"I can't see anyone," I told her.

She pushed the bushes aside, and stepped out cautiously, looking this way and that. She was dressed just as she had been when I first saw her—except that her hair had been a trifle raked about by branches. On the rough ground the shoes looked even more inappropriate. Seeming a little reassured, she took a few steps forward.

"I—" she began.

Then, higher up the coombe, a man's voice called, and another answered it. The girl froze for a moment, looking scared.

"They're coming. Hide me somewhere, quickly, please," she said.

"Er—" I began, inadequately.

"Oh, quick, quick. They're coming," she said urgently.

She certainly looked alarmed.

"Better come inside," I told her, and led the way into the cottage.

She followed swiftly, and when I had shut the door she slid the bolt.

"Don't let them catch me. Don't let them," she begged.

"Look here, what's all this about. Who are 'they'?" I asked.

She did not answer that; her eyes, roving round the room, found the telephone.

"Call the police," she said. "Call the police, quickly." I hesitated. "Don't you have any police?" she added.

"Of course we have police, but—"

"Then call them, please."

"But look here—" I began.

She clenched her hands.

"You must call them, please. Quickly."

She looked very anxious.

"All right, I'll call them. You can do the explaining," I said, and picked up the instrument.

I was used to the rustic leisure of communications in those parts, and waited patiently. The girl did not; she stood twining her fingers together. At last the connection was made:

"Hullo," I said, "is that the Plyton Police?"

"Plyton Police—" an answering voice had begun when there was an interruption of steps on the gravel path, followed by a heavy knocking at the door. I handed the instrument to the girl and went to the door.

"Don't let them in," she said, and then gave her attention to the telephone.

I hesitated. The rather peremptory knocking came again. One can't just stand about, not letting people in; besides, to take a strange young lady hurriedly into one's cottage, and immediately bolt the door against all comers—? At the third knocking I opened up.

The aspect of the man on my doorstep took me aback. Not his face—that was suitable enough in a young man of, say, twenty-five—it was his clothes. One is not prepared to encounter something that looks like a close-fitting skating-suit, worn with a full-cut, hip-length, glass-buttoned jacket; certainly not on Dartmoor, at the end of the summer season. However, I pulled myself together enough to ask what he wanted. He paid no attention to that as he stood looking over my shoulder at the girl.

"Tavia," he said. "Come here!"

She didn't stop talking hurriedly into the telephone. The man stepped forward.

"Steady on!" I said. "First, I'd like to know what all this is about."

He looked at me squarely. "You wouldn't understand," he said, and raised his arm to push me out of the way.

I have always felt that I would strongly dislike people who tell me that I don't understand, and try to push me off my own threshold. I socked him hard in the stomach, and as he doubled up I pushed him outside and closed the door.

"They're coming," said the girl's voice behind me. "The police are coming."

"If you'd just tell me—" I began. But she pointed.

"Look out!—at the window," she said.

I turned. There was another man outside, dressed similarly to the first who was still audibly wheezing on the doorstep. He was hesitating. I reached my twelve-bore off the wall, grabbed some cartridges from the drawer and loaded it. Then I stood back, facing the door.

"Open it, and keep behind it," I told her.

She obeyed, doubtfully.

Outside, the second man was now bending solicitously over the first. A third man was coming up the path. They saw the gun, and we had a brief tableau.

"You, there," I said. "You can either beat it quick, or stay and argue it out with the police. Which is it to be?"

"But you don't understand. It is most important—" began one of them.

"All right. Then you can stay there and tell the police how important it is," I said, and nodded to the girl to close the door again.

We watched through the window as the two of them helped the winded man away.

The police, when they arrived, were not amiable. They took clown my description of the men reluctantly, and departed coolly. Meanwhile, there was the girl.

She had told the police as little as she well could—simply that she had been pursued by three oddly dressed men, and had appealed to me for help. She had refused their offer of a lift to Plyton in the police car, so here she still was.

"Well, now," I suggested, "perhaps you'd like to explain to me just what seems to be going on?"

She sat quite still facing me with a long level look which had a tinge of—sadness?—disappointment?—well, unsatisfactoriness of some kind. For a moment, I wondered if she were going to cry, but in a small voice she said:

"I had your letter—and now I've burned my boats." I sat down opposite to her. After fumbling a bit I found my cigarettes and lit one.

"You—er—had my letter, and now you've—er—burnt your boats?" I repeated.

"Yes," she said. Her eyes left mine and strayed round the room, not seeing much.

"And now you don't even know me," she said.

Whereupon the tears came, fast.

I sat there helplessly for a half-minute. Then I decided to go into the kitchen and put on the kettle while she had it out. All my female relatives have always regarded tea as the prime panacea, so I brought the pot and cups back with me when I returned.

I found her recovered, sitting staring pensively at the unlit fire. I put a match to it. She watched it take light and burn, with the expression of a child who has just received a present.

"Lovely," she said, as though a fire were something completely novel. She looked all round the room again. "Lovely," she repeated.

"Would you like to pour?" I suggested, but she shook her head, and watched me do it.

"Tea," she said. "By a fireside!"

Which was true enough, but scarcely remarkable.

"I think it is about time we introduced ourselves," I suggested. "I am Gerald Lattery."

"Of course," she said, nodding. It was not to my mind an altogether appropriate reply, but she followed it up by: "I am Octavia Lattery—they usually call me Tavia."

Tavia?—Something clinked in my mind, but did not quite chime.

"We are related in some way?" I asked her.

"Yes—very distantly," she said, looking at me oddly. "Oh, dear," she added, "this is difficult," and looked as if she were about to cry again.

"Tavia..?" I repeated, trying to remember. "There's something..."

Then I had a sudden vision of an embarrassed elderly gentleman. "Why, of course; now what was the name? Doctor—Dr. Bogey, or something?"

She suddenly sat quite still.

"Not—not Dr. Gobie?" she suggested.

"Yes, that's it. He asked me about somebody called Tavia. That would be you?"

"He isn't here?" she said, looking round as if he might be hiding in a corner.

I told her it would be about two years ago now. She relaxed.

"Silly old Uncle Donald. How like him! And naturally you'd have no idea what he was talking about?"

"I've very little more now," I pointed out, "though I can understand how even an uncle might be agitated at losing you."

"Yes. I'm afraid he will be—very," she said.

"Was: this was two years ago," I reminded her.

"Oh, of course you don't really understand yet, do you?"

"Look," I told her, "one after another, people keep on telling me that I don't understand. I know that already—it is about the only thing I do understand."

"Yes. I'd better explain. Oh dear, where shall I begin?" I let her ponder that, uninterrupted. Presently she said: "Do you believe in predestination?"

"I don't think so," I told her.

"Oh—no, well perhaps it isn't quite that, after all—more like a sort of affinity. You see, ever since I was quite tiny I remember thinking this was the most thrilling and wonderful age—and then, of course, it was the time in which the only famous person in our family lived. So I thought it was marvelous. Romantic, I suppose you'd call it."

"It depends whether you mean the thought or the age—" I began, but she took no notice.

"I used to picture the great fleets of funny little aircraft during the wars, and think how they were like David going out to hit Goliath, so tiny and brave. And there were the huge clumsy ships, wallowing slowly along, but getting there somehow in the end, and nobody minding how slow they were. And quaint, black and white movies; and horses in the streets; and shaky old internal combustion engines; and coal fires; and exciting bombings; and trains running on rails; and telephones with wires; and, oh, lots of things. And the things one could do! Fancy being at the first night of a new Shaw play, or a new Coward play, in a real theater! Or getting a brand new T.S. Eliot, on publishing day. Or seeing the Queen drive by to open Parliament. A wonderful, thrilling time!"

"Well, it's nice to hear somebody think so," I said. "My own view of the age doesn't quite—"

"Ah, but that's only to be expected. You haven't any perspective on it, so you can't appreciate it. It'd do you good to live in ours for a bit, and see how flat and stale and uniform everything is—so deadly, deadly dull."

I boggled a little: "I don't think I quite—er, live in your what?"

"Century, of course. The twenty-second. Oh, of course, you don't know. How silly of me."

I concentrated on pouring out some more tea.

"Oh dear, I knew this was going to be difficult," she remarked. "Do you find it difficult?"

I said I did, rather. She went on with a dogged air:

"Well, you see, feeling like that about it is why I took up history. I mean, I could really *think* myself into history—some of it. And then getting your letter on my birthday was really what made me take the mid-twentieth century as my Special Period for my Honors Degree, and, of course, it made up my mind for me to go on and do postgraduate work."

"Er—my letter did all this?"

"Well, that was the only way, wasn't it? I mean there simply wasn't any other way I could have got near a history-machine except by working in a history laboratory, was there? And even then I doubt whether I'd have had a chance to use it on my own if it hadn't been Uncle Donald's lab."

"History-machine," I said, grasping a straw out of all this. "What is a history-machine?"

She looked puzzled.

"It's, well—a history-machine. You learn history with it."

"Not lucid," I said. "You might as well tell me you make history with it."

"Oh, no. One's not supposed to do that. It's a very serious offense."

"Oh," I said. I tried again: "About this letter—"

"Well, I had to bring that in to explain about history, but you won't have written it yet, of course, so I expect you find it a bit confusing."

"Confusing," I told her, "is scarcely the word. Can't we get hold of something concrete? This letter I'm supposed to have written, for instance. What was it about?"

She looked at me hard, and then away. A most surprising blush swept up her face, and ran into her hair. She made herself look back at me again. I watched her eyes go shiny, and then pucker at the corners. She dropped her face suddenly into her hands.

"Oh, you don't love me, you *don't*," she wailed. "I wish I'd never come. I wish I was dead!"

"She sort of—sniffed at me," said Tavia.

"Well, she's gone now, and my reputation with her," I said. "An excellent worker, our Mrs. Toombs, but conventional. She'll probably throw up the job."

"Because I'm here? How silly!"

"Perhaps your conventions are different."

"But where else could I go? I've only a few shillings of your kind of money, and nobody to go to."

"Mrs. Toombs could scarcely know that."

"But we weren't, I mean we didn't—"

"Night, and the figure two," I told her, "are plenty for our conventions. In fact, two is enough, anyway. You will recall that the animals simply went in two by two; their emotional relationships didn't interest anyone. Two; and all is assumed."

"Oh, of course, I remember, there was no probative then—now, I mean. You have a sort of rigid, lucky-dip, take-it-or-leave-it system."

"There are other ways of expressing it, but—well, ostensibly at any rate, yes, I suppose."

"Rather crude, these old customs, when one sees them at close range—but fascinating," she remarked. Her eyes rested thoughtfully upon me for a second. "You—" she began.

"You," I reminded her, "promised to give me a more explanatory explanation of all this than you achieved yesterday."

"You didn't believe me."

"The first wallop took my breath," I admitted, "but you've given me enough evidence since. Nobody could keep up an act like that."

She frowned. "I don't think that's very kind of you. I've studied the mid-twentieth very thoroughly. It was my Special Period."

"So you told me, but that doesn't get me far. All historical scholars have Special Periods, but that doesn't mean that they suddenly turn up in them."

She stared at me. "But of course they do—licensed historians. How else would they make close studies?"

"There's too much of this 'of course' business," I told her. "I suggest we just begin at the beginning. Now this letter of mine—no, we'll skip the letter," I added hastily as I caught her expression. "Now, you went to work in your uncle's laboratory with something called a history-machine. What's that—a kind of tape-recorder?"

"Good gracious, no. It's a kind of cupboard thing you get into to go to times and places."

"Oh," I said. "You—you mean you can walk into it in twenty-one-something, and walk out into nineteen-something?"

"Or any other past time," she said, nodding. "But, of course, not anybody can do it. You have to be qualified and licensed and all that kind of thing. There are only six permitted history-machines in England, and only about a hundred in the whole world, and they're very strict about them.

"When the first ones were made they didn't realize what trouble they might cause, but after a time historians began to check the trips made against the written records of the periods, and started to find funny things. There was Hero demonstrating a simple steam-turbine at Alexandria sometime B.C.; and Archimedes using a kind of napalm at the siege of Syracuse; and Leonardo da Vinci drawing parachutes when there wasn't anything to parachute from; and Eric the Red discovering America in a sort of off-the-record way before Columbus got there; and Napoleon wondering about submarines; and lots of other suspicious things. So it was clear that some people had been careless when they used the machine, and had been causing chronoclasms."

"Causing—what?"

"Chronoclasms—that's when a thing goes and happens at the wrong time because somebody was careless, or talked rashly.

"Well, most of those things had happened without causing very much harm—as far as we can tell—though it *is* possible that the natural course of history was altered several times, and people write very clever papers to show how. But everybody saw that the results might be extremely dangerous. Just suppose that somebody had carelessly given Napoleon the idea of the internal combustion engine to add to the idea of the submarine; there's no telling what would have happened. So they decided that tampering must be stopped at once, and all history-machines were forbidden except those licensed by the Historians' Council."

"Just hold it a minute," I said. "Look, if a thing is done, it's done. I mean, well, for example, I am here. I couldn't suddenly cease to be, or to have been, if somebody were to go back and kill my grandfather when he was a boy."

"But you certainly couldn't be here if they did, could you?" she asked. "No, the fallacy that the past is unchangeable didn't matter a bit as long as there was no means of changing it, but once there was, and the fallacy of the idea was shown, we had to be very careful indeed. That's what a historian has to worry about; the other side— just *how* it happens—we leave to the higher mathematicians.

"Now, before you are allowed to use the history-machine you have to have special courses, tests, permits, and give solemn undertakings, and then do several years on probation before you get your license to practice. Only then are you allowed to visit and observe on your own. And that is all you may do, observe. The rule is very, very strict."

I thought that over. "If it isn't an unkind question—aren't you breaking rather a lot of these rules every minute?" I suggested.

"Of course I am. That's why they came after me," she said.

"You'd have had your license revoked, or something, if they'd caught you?"

"Good gracious. I could never qualify for a license. I've just sneaked my trips when the lab has been empty. It being Uncle Donald's lab made things easier because unless I was actually caught at the machine, I could always pretend I was doing something special for him.

"I had to have the right clothes to come in, but I dared not go to the historians' regular costume-makers, so I sketched some things in a museum and got them copied—they're all right, aren't they?"

"Very successful, and becoming, too," I assured her. "—Though there is a little something about the shoes."

She looked down at her feet. "I was afraid so. I couldn't find any of quite the right date," she admitted. "Well, then," she went on, "I was able to make a few short trial trips. They had to be short because duration is constant—that is, an hour here is the same as an hour there—and I couldn't get the machine to myself for long at a time. But yesterday a man came into the lab just as I was getting back. When he saw these clothes he knew at once what I was doing, so the only thing I could do was to jump straight back into the machine— I'd never have had another chance. And they came after me without even bothering to change."

"Do you think they'll come again?" I asked her.

"I expect so. But they'll be wearing proper clothes for the period next time."

"Are they likely to be desperate? I mean, would they shoot, or anything like that?"

She shook her head. "Oh, no. That'd be a pretty bad chronoclasm— particularly if they happened to kill somebody."

"But you being here must be setting up a series of pretty resounding chronoclasms. Which would be worse?"

"Oh, mine are all accounted for. I looked it up," she assured me, obscurely. "They'll be less worried about me when they've thought of looking it up, too."

She paused briefly. Then, with an air of turning to a more interesting subject, she went on:

"When people in your time get married they have to dress up in a special way for it, don't they?"

The topic seemed to have a fascination for her.

"M'm," mumbled Tavia. "I think I rather like twentieth-century marriage."

"It has risen higher in my own estimation, darling," I admitted. And, indeed, I was quite surprised to find how much higher it had risen in the course of the last month or so.

"Do twentieth-century marrieds always have one big bed, darling?" she inquired.

"Invariably, darling," I assured her.

"Funny," she said. "Not very hygienic, of course, but quite nice all the same."

We reflected on that.

"Darling, have you noticed she doesn't sniff at me anymore?" she remarked.

"We always cease to sniff on production of a certificate, darling," I explained.

Conversation pursued its desultory way on topics of personal, but limited, interest for a while. Eventually it reached a point where I was saying:

"It begins to look as if we don't need to worry any more about those men who were chasing you, darling. They'd have been back long before now if they had been as worried as you thought."

She shook her head.

"We'll have to go on being careful, but it is queer. Something to do with Uncle Donald, I expect. He's not really mechanically minded, poor dear. Well, you can tell that by the way he set the machine two years wrong when he came to see you. But there's nothing we can do except wait, and be careful."

I went on reflecting. Presently:

"I shall have to get a job soon. That may make it difficult to keep a watch for them," I told her.

"Job?" she said.

"In spite of what they say, two can't live as cheap as one. And wives hanker after certain standards, and ought to have them—within reason, of course. The little money I have won't run to them."

"You don't need to worry about that, darling," Tavia assured me. "You can just invent something."

"Me? Invent?" I exclaimed.

"Yes. You're already fairly well up on radio, aren't you?"

"They put me on a few radar courses when I was in the R.A.F."

"Ah! The R.A.F.!" she said, ecstatically. "To think that you actually fought in the Second Great War! Did you know Monty and Ike and all those wonderful people?"

"Not personally. Different arm of the Services," I said.

"What a pity, everyone liked Ike. But about the other thing. All you have to do is to get some advanced radio and electronics books, and I'll show you what to invent."

"You'll—? Oh, I see. But do you think that would be quite ethical?" I asked, doubtfully.

"I don't see why not. After all the things have got to be invented by somebody, or I couldn't have learnt about them at school, could I?"

"I—er, I think I'll have to think a bit about that," I told her.

It was, I suppose, coincidence that I should have mentioned the lack of interruption that particular morning—at least, it may have been: I have become increasingly suspicious of coincidences since I first saw Tavia. At any rate, in the middle of that same morning Tavia, looking out of the window, said:

"Darling, there's somebody waving from the trees over there."

I went over to have a look, and sure enough I had a view of a stick with a white handkerchief tied to it, swinging slowly from side to side. Through field glasses, I was able to distinguish the operator, an elderly man almost hidden in the bushes. I handed the glasses to Tavia.

"Oh, dear! Uncle Donald," she exclaimed. "I suppose we had better see him. He seems to be alone."

I went outside, down to the end of my path, and waved him forward. Presently he emerged, carrying the stick and handkerchief bannerwise. His voice reached me faintly: "Don't shoot!"

I spread my hand wide to show that I was unarmed. Tavia came down the path and stood beside me. As he drew close, he transferred the stick to his left hand, lifted his hat with the other, and inclined his head politely.

"Ah, Sir Gerald! A pleasure to meet you again," he said.

"He isn't Sir Gerald, Uncle. He's Mr. Lattery," said Tavia.

"Dear me. Stupid of me. Mr. Lattery," he went on, "I am sure you'll be glad to hear that the wound was more uncomfortable than serious. Just a matter of the poor fellow having to lie on his front for a while."

"Poor fellow—?" I repeated, blankly.

"The one you shot yesterday."

"*I shot?*"

"Probably tomorrow or the next day," Tavia said, briskly. "Uncle, you really are dreadful with those settings, you know."

"I understand the *principles* well enough, my dear. It's just the operation that I sometimes find a little confusing."

"Never mind. Now you are here you'd better come indoors," she told him. "And you can put that handkerchief away in your pocket," she added.

As he entered I saw him give a quick glance round the room, and nod to himself as if satisfied with the authenticity of its contents. We sat down. Tavia said:

"Just before we go any further, Uncle Donald, I think you ought to know that I am married to Gerald—Mr. Lattery."

Dr. Gobie peered closely at her.

"*Married?*" he repeated. "What for?"

"Oh, dear," said Tavia. She explained patiently: "I am in love with him, and he's in love with me, so I am his wife. It's the way things happen here."

"Tch, tch!" said Dr. Gobie, and shook his head. "Of course I am well-aware of your sentimental penchant for the twentieth century and its ways, my dear, but surely it wasn't quite necessary for you to—er—go native?"

"I like it, quite a lot," Tavia told him.

"Young women will be romantic, I know. But have you thought of the trouble you will be causing Sir Ger—er, Mr. Lattery?"

"But I'm *saving* him trouble, Uncle Donald. They *sniff* at you here if you don't get married, and I didn't like him being sniffed at."

"I wasn't thinking so much of while you're here, as of after you have left. They have a great many rules about presuming death, and proving desertion, and so on; most dilatory and complex. Meanwhile, he can't marry anyone else."

"I'm sure he wouldn't want to marry anyone else, would you, darling?" she said to me.

"Certainly not," I protested.

"You're quite sure of that, darling?"

"Darling," I said, taking her hand, "if all the other women in the world—"

Dr. Gobie recalled our attention with an apologetic cough.

"The real purpose of my visit," he explained, "is to persuade my niece that she must come back, and at once. There is the greatest consternation and alarm throughout the faculty over this affair, and I am being held largely to blame. Our chief anxiety is to get her back before any serious damage is done. Any chronoclasm goes ringing unendingly down the ages—and at any moment a really serious one may come of this escapade. It has put all of us into a highly nervous condition."

"I'm sorry about that, Uncle Donald—and about you getting the blame. But I am *not* coming back. I'm very happy here."

"But the possible chronoclasms, my dear. It keeps me awake at night thinking—"

"Uncle dear, they'd be nothing to the chronoclasms that would happen if I *did* come back just now. You must see that I simply can't, and explain it to the others."

"Can't—?" he repeated.

"Now, if you look in the books you'll see that my husband—isn't that a funny, ugly, old-fashioned word? I rather like it, though. It comes from two ancient Icelandic roots—"

"You were speaking about not coming back," Dr. Gobie reminded her.

"Oh, yes. Well, you'll see in the books that first he invented submarine radio communication, and then later on he invented curved-beam transmission, which is what he got knighted for."

"I'm perfectly well-aware of that, Tavia. I do not see—"

"But, Uncle Donald, you must. How on earth can he possibly invent those things if I'm not here to show him how to do it? If you take me away now, they'll just not be invented, and then what will happen?"

Dr. Gobie stared at her steadily for some moments.

"Yes," he said. "Yes, I must admit that that point had not occurred to me," and sank deeply into thought for a while.

"Besides," Tavia added, "Gerald would hate me to go, wouldn't you darling?"

"I—" I began, but Dr. Gobie cut me short by standing up.

"Yes," he said. "I can see there will have to be a postponement for a while. I shall put your point to them, but it will be only for a while."

On his way to the door he paused.

"Meanwhile, my dear, do be careful. These things are so delicate and complicated. I tremble to think of the complexities you might set up if you—well, say, if you were to do something irresponsible like becoming your own progenetrix."

"That is one thing I can't do, Uncle Donald. I'm on the collateral branch."

"Oh, yes. Yes, that's a very lucky thing. Then I'll say *au revoir*, my dear, and to you, too, Sir—er—Mr. Lattery. I trust that we may meet again—it has had its pleasant side to be here as more than a mere observer for once."

"Uncle Donald, you've said a mouthful there," Tavia agreed.

He shook his head reprovingly at her.

"I'm afraid you would never have got to the top of the historical tree, my dear. You aren't thorough enough. That phrase is early-twentieth century, and, if I may say so, inelegant even then."

The expected shooting incident took place about a week later. Three men, dressed in quite convincing imitation of farmhands, made the approach. Tavia recognized one of them through the glasses. When I appeared, gun in hand, at the door, they tried to make for cover. I peppered one at considerable range, and he ran on, limping.

After that we were left unmolested. A little later we began to get down to the business of underwater radio—surprisingly simple, once the principle had been pointed out—and I filed my applications for patents. With that well in-hand, we turned to the curved-beam transmission.

Tavia hurried me along with that. She said:

"You see, I don't know how long we've got, darling. I've been trying to remember ever since I got here what the date was on your letter, and I can't—even though I remember yon underlined it. I know there's a record that your first wife deserted you—'deserted,' isn't that a dreadful word to use? As if I would, my sweet—but it doesn't say when. So I must get you properly briefed on this because there'd be the most frightful chronoclasm if you failed to invent it."

And then, instead of buckling down to it as her words suggested, she became pensive.

"As a matter of fact," she said, "I think there's going to be a pretty bad chronoclasm anyway. You see, I'm going to have a baby."

"No!" I exclaimed delightedly.

"What do you mean, 'no'? I am. And I'm worried. I don't think it has ever happened to a traveling historian before. Uncle Donald would be terribly annoyed if he knew."

"To hell with Uncle Donald," I said. "And to hell with chronoclasms. We're going to celebrate, darling."

The weeks slid quickly by. My patents were granted provisionally. I got a good grip on the theory of curved-beam transmission. Everything was going nicely. We discussed the future: whether he was to be called Donald, or whether she was going to be called Alexandra. How soon the royalties would begin to come in so that we could make an offer for Bagford House. How funny it would feel at first to be addressed as Lady Lattery, and other allied themes . . .

And then came that December afternoon when I got back from discussing a modification with a manufacturer in London and found that she wasn't there anymore . . .

Not a note, not a last word. Just the open front door, and a chair overturned in the sitting room . . .

Oh, Tavia, my dear . . .

I began to write this down because I still have an uneasy feeling about the ethics of not being the inventor of my inventions, and that there should be a straightening out. Now that I have reached the end, I perceive that "straightening out" is scarcely an appropriate description of it. In fact, I can foresee so much trouble attached to putting this forward as a conscientious reason for refusing a knighthood, that I think I shall say nothing, and just accept the knighthood when it comes. After all, when I consider a number of "inspired" inventions that I can call to mind, I begin to wonder whether certain others have not done that before me.

I have never pretended to understand the finer points of action and interaction comprehended in this matter, but I have a pressing sense that one action now on my part is basically necessary: not just to avoid dropping an almighty chronoclasm myself, but for fear that if I neglect it I may find that the whole thing never happened. So I must write a letter.

First, the envelope:

To my great, great grandniece, Miss Octavia Lattery.

(To be opened by her on her 21st birthday 6th June 2136.)

Then the letter. Date it. Underline the date.

My sweet, far-off, lovely Tavia,

Oh, my darling . . .

The Girl Who
Made Time Stop

INTRODUCTION

He was, of course, the luckiest man in the world, engaged to a gorgeous woman . . . and then an adorable ditz showed up and claimed that (a) they were made for each other, (b) and by the way, she was from another planet, and (c) also by the way, he wasn't at all the luckiest man in the world, because his fiancé wasn't what she seemed to be and he was making a *big* mistake. She must have been a nutjob, of course—but she was such a *cute* nutjob. And what if she *was* telling the truth?

* * *

Robert F. Young (1915-1986) was known for writing polished stories with a delicate emotional touch. His first story appeared in *Startling Stories* in 1953, and he frequently sold to the leading SF magazines, such as *Analog*, the Cele Goldsmith Lalli-edited *Amazing Stories*, *If*, and *Galaxy*, but he was a frequent contributor to *The Magazine of Fantasy and Science Fiction*, where his most memorable stories appeared, and also sold to *The Saturday Evening Post*, where "The Girl Who Made Time Stop" first appeared. His work ranged from warmly romantic to slyly satirical. He wrote prolifically for three decades, but most of his output was in the short story length, with few novels, one of which has the distinction of having been published only in French.

His only two short story collections, *The Worlds of Robert F. Young* and *A Glass of Stars* are both long out of print, as are his novels *Starfinder*, *The Vizier's Second Daughter*, *The Last Yggdrasil*, and *Eridahn*—the last being a story which would fit the theme of this anthology. Young is definitely a writer long overdue for rediscovery.

The Girl Who
Made Time Stop

by Robert F. Young

Little did Roger Thompson dream when he sat down on the park bench that Friday morning in June that in a celibate sense his goose was already in the oven and that soon it would be cooked. He may have had an inkling of things to come when he saw the tall brunette in the red sheath walking down the winding walk some several minutes later, but that inkling could not conceivably have apprised him of the vast convolutions of time and space which the bowing out of his bachelorhood would shortly set in motion.

The tall brunette was opposite the bench, and it was beginning to look as though Roger's goose was in no imminent danger of being roasted after all when one of those incidents that so much inspire our boy-meets-girl literature occurred: one of her spike heels sank into a crevice in the walk and brought her to an abrupt halt. Our hero rose to the occasion admirably—especially in view of the fact that he was in the midst of a brown study concerning a particularly abstruse phase of the poetic analysis of science which he was working on and was even less aware of girls than usual. In a millisecond he was at her side; in another he had slipped his arm around her waist. He freed her foot from the shoe, noticing as he did so that there were three narrow golden bands encircling her bare leg just above her ankle, and helped her over to the bench. "I'll have it out of there in a jiffy," he said.

He was as good as his word, and seconds later he slipped the shoe back upon the girl's dainty foot.

"Oh, thank you, Mr. . . . . Mr. . . ." she began.

Her voice was husky, her face was oval; her lips were red and full. Looking into the pearly depths of her gray eyes, he had the feeling that he was falling—as in a sense he was—and he sat dizzily down beside her. "Thompson," he said. "Roger Thompson."

The pearly depths grew deeper still. "I'm glad to meet you, Roger. My name is Becky Fisher."

"I'm glad to meet you, Becky."

So far, so good. Boy has met girl, and girl has met boy. Boy is suitably smitten; girl is amenable. Both are young. The month is June. A romance is virtually bound to blossom, and soon a romance does.

Nevertheless it is a romance that will never be recorded in the annals of time.

Why not? you ask.

You'll see.

They spent the rest of the day together. It was Becky's day off from the Silver Spoon, where she waited on tables. Roger, who was sweating out the sixth application he had tendered since graduating from the Lakeport Institute of Technology, had every day off for the moment.

That evening they dined in a modest cafe, and afterward they played the jukebox and danced. The midnight moment upon the steps of the apartment house where Becky lived was a precious one, and their first kiss was so sweet and lingering on Roger's lips that he did not even wonder, until he reached his hotel room, how a young man such as himself —who saw love as an impediment to a scientific career—could have fallen so deeply into it in so short a span of time.

In his mind's eye the bench in the park had already taken on the aspect of a shrine, and the very next morning saw him walking down the winding walk, eager to view the sacred object once again. Consider his chagrin when he rounded the last curve and saw a girl in a blue dress sitting on the very section of the hallowed object that his goddess had consecrated the most!

He sat down as far away from her as the length of the bench permitted. Perhaps if she had been glamorous he wouldn't have minded so much But she . . . Her face was too thin, and her legs were too long. Compared with the red dress Becky had worn, hers was a lackluster rag, and as for her feather-cut titian hair, it was an insult to cosmetology.

She was writing something in a little red notebook and didn't appear to notice him at first. Presently, however, she glanced at her wrist watch, and then—as though the time of day had somehow apprised her of his presence—she looked in his direction.

It was a rather mild—if startled—look, and did not in the least deserve the dirty one he squelched it with. He had a glimpse, just before she hastily returned her attention to her notebook, of a dusting of golden freckles, a pair of eyes the hue of bluebirds and a small mouth the color of sumac leaves after the first hard frost. He wondered idly if his initial reaction to her might not have been different if he had used a less consummate creature than Becky for a criterion.

Suddenly he became aware that she was looking at him again. "How do you xpell matrimony?" she asked.

He gave a start "Matrimony?"

"Yes. How do you xpell it?'

"M-a-t-r-i-m-o-n-y," Roger said.

"Thankx." She made a correction in her notebook, then she turned toward him again. "I'm a very poor xpeller—expexially when it comex to foreign wordx."

"Oh, you're from another country, then?" That would explain her bizarre accent.

"Yex, from Buzenborg. It'x a xmall provinxe on the xouthernmoxt continent of the xixth plsanet of the xtar you call Altair. I juxt arrived on earth thix morning."

From the matter-of-fact way she said it, you'd have thought that the southernmost continent of Altair VI was no more remote from Lakeport than the southernmost continent of Sol III and that spaceships were as common as automobiles. Small wonder that the scientist in Roger was incensed. Small wonder that he girded himself immediately to do battle.

His best bet, be decided, would be a questions-and-answers campaign designed to lure her into deeper and deeper water until finally she went under. "What's your name?" he began casually.

"Alayne. What'x yourx?"

He told her. Then: "Don't you have a surname?"

"No. In Buzenborg we dixpenxed with xurnamex xenturiex ago."

He let that go by. "All right, then, where's your spaceship?'

"I parked it by a barn on a dexerted farm a few milex outxide the xity. With the forxe field turned on, it lookx xomething like a xilo. People never notixe an obvious object, even if it'x right under their noxex, xo long ax it blendx in with itx xurroundingx."

"A xilo?'

"Yex. A—a silo. I see I've been getting my 'X's' mixed up with my 'S's' again. You see," she went on, pronouncing each word carefully, "in the Buzenborg alphabet the nearest sound to the 'S' sound is the 'X' sound, so if I don't watch myself, whenever I say 'S' it comes out 'X,' unless it is followed or preceded by a letter that softens its sibilance."

Roger looked at her closely. But her blue eyes were disarming, and not so much as a smidgin of a smile disturbed the serene line of her lips. He decided to humor her. "What you need is a good diction teacher," he said.

She nodded solemnly. "But how do I go about getting one?"

"The phone directory is full of them. Just call one up and make an appointment." Probably, he thought cynically, if he had met her before Becky swam into his ken he would have thought her accent charming and have advised her not to go to a diction teacher. "But let's get back to what we were talking about," he went on. "You say you left your ship in plain sight because people never notice an obvious object so long as it doesn't clash with its surroundings, which means that you want to keep your presence on Earth a secret. Right?"

"Yes, that's right."

"Then why," Roger pounced, "are you sitting here in broad daylight practically throwing the secret in my face?"

"Because the law of obviousness works with people too. The surest way to make everybody believe I'm not from Altair VI is to keep saying that I am."

"O.K., we'll let that pass." Eagerly Roger launched Phase Two of his campaign. "Let's consider your trip instead."

Inwardly he gloated. He was sure he had her now. However, as matters turned out, he didn't have her at all, for in drawing up his plans to lure her into deeper and deeper water he had overlooked a very pertinent possibility—the possibility that she might be able to swim. And not only could she swim, she was even more at home in the scientific sea than he was.

For instance, when he pointed out that, owing to the ratio between the mass and the velocity of a moving body, the speed of light cannot be equaled and that therefore her journey from Altair VI to Earth must have required more than the sixteen years needed by light to travel the same distance, she said, "You're not taking the Lorentz transformation into consideration. Moving clocks slow down with reference to stationary clocks, so if I traveled at just under the velocity of light my journey wouldn't have lasted over a few hours."

For instance, when he pointed out that more than sixteen years would still have gone by on Altair VI, and that her family and friends would be that much older, she said, "Yes, but you're only assuming that the speed of light can't be equaled. As a matter of fact, it can be doubled, tripled and quadrupled. True, the mass of a moving body increases in proportion to its velocity, but not when a demassifier—a device invented by our scientists to cancel out mass—is used."

For instance, when he conceded for the sake of argument that the velocity of light could be exceeded and pointed out that if she had traveled a little in excess of twice its velocity she not only would have traveled backward in time but would have finished her journey before she began it, thereby giving birth to a rather awkward paradox, she said, "There wouldn't be a paradox because the minute one became imminent a cosmic time shift would cancel it. Anyway, we don't use faster-than-light drives any more. We used to, and our ships are still equipped with them, but we aren't supposed to resort to them except in cases of emergency because too many time shifts occurring simultaneously could disrupt the space-time continuum."

And for instance, when he demanded how she had made her trip then, she said, "I took the short cut, the same as anyone else on Altair VI does when he wishes to travel vast distances. Space is warped, just as your own scientists have theorized, and with the new warp drive our Altairian VI scientists have developed it's no trick at all, even for an amateur to *travel* to any place he wants to in the galaxy in a matter of just a few days."

It was a classic dodge, but dodge or not, it was still unassailable. Roger stood up. He knew when he was beaten. "Well, don't take any wooden meteorites," he said.

"Where—where are you going, Roger?"

"To a certain tavern I know of for a sandwich and a beer, after which I'm going to watch the New York—Chicago game on TV."

"But—but aren't you going to ask me to come with you?"

"Of course not. Why should I?"

A transformation Lorentz had never dreamed of took place in her eyes, leaving them a misted and an incredulous blue. Abruptly she lowered them to her wrist watch. "I—I can't understand it. My wodget registers ninety, and even eighty is considered a high-compatibility reading."

A tear the size of a large dewdrop rolled down her cheek and fell with a soundless splash upon her blue bodice. The scientist in Roger was unmoved, but the poet in him was touched.

"Oh, all right, come along if you want to," he said.

The tavern was just off Main Street. After phoning a diction teacher at the request of Alayne of Altair and making an appointment for her for four-thirty that afternoon, he chose a booth that afforded an unobstructed view of the TV screen and ordered two roast beefs on kummelweck and two glasses of beer.

Alayne of Altair's sandwich disappeared as fast as his did. "Like another one?" he asked.

"No, thanks. Though the beef was really quite tasty considering the low chlorophyllic content of Earth grass."

"So you've got better grass than we have. I suppose you've got better cars and better TV sets too!"

"No, they're about the same. Except for its phenomenal advance in *space travel*, our technology is practically parallel with yours."

"How about baseball? Do you have that too?'

"What's baseball?" Alayne of Altair wanted to know.

"You'll see," said Roger of Earth gloatingly. Pretending to be from Altair VI was one thing, but pretending to be ignorant of baseball was quite another. She was bound to betray herself by at least one slip of the tongue before the afternoon was very much older.

However, she did nothing of the sort. As a matter of fact, her reactions strengthened rather than weakened her claim to extraterrestrialism. "Why do they keep shouting, 'Go, go, go, Aparicio?'" she asked during the bottom half of the fourth.

"Because Aparicio is famous for his base stealing. Watch him now—he's going to try to steal second."

Aparicio not only tried, he made it too. "See?" Roger said.

It was clear from the befuddled expression on Alayne of Altair's face that she did not see. "It doesn't make any sense," she said. "If he's so good at stealing bases, why didn't he steal first base instead of standing there swinging at that silly sphere?"

Roger gaped at her. "Look, you're not getting this at all. You can't steal first base."

"But suppose somebody did steal it. Would they let him stay there?"

"But you can't steal first base. It's impossible!"

"Nothing is impossible," Alayne of Altair said.

Disgusted, Roger let it go at that, and throughout the rest of the game he ignored her. However, he was a White Sox fan, and when his idols came through with a 5-4 win his disgust dissipated like mist on a summer morning, and so great was his euphoria that he told her he'd walk uptown with her to the diction teacher's studio. On the way he talked about his poetic analysis of science, and he even quoted a few lines from a Petrarchan sonnet he had done on the atom. Her warm enthusiasm sent his euphoria soaring even higher. "I hope you had a pleasant afternoon," he said when they paused in front of the building in which the diction teacher's studio was located.

"Oh, I did!" Excitedly she wrote something down in her notebook, tore out the page and handed it to him. "My Earth address," she explained. "What time are you going to call for me tonight, Rog?"

Abruptly his euphoria vanished. "Whatever gave you the idea we had a date for tonight?"

"I—I took it for granted. According to my wodget—"

"Stop!" Roger said. "I've had all I can take for one day of wodgets and demassifiers and faster-than-light drives. Besides, it just so happens that I've got a date for tonight, and it also just so happens that the girl I've got the date with is the girl I—I've been unconsciously searching for all my life and didn't find till yesterday morning, and . . ."

He paused. Sudden sadness had roiled the blue depths of Alayne of Altair's eyes, and her mouth was quivering like a frost-kissed sumac leaf in a November wind. "I—I understand now," she said. "Wodgets react to compatibility of body chemistry and intellectual proclivities. They aren't sensitive enough to detect superficial emotional attachments. I—I guess I came a day too late."

"You can't prove it by me. Well, give my regards to the Buzenborgians."

"Will—will you be in the park tomorrow morning?"

He opened his mouth to deliver an emphatic no—and saw the second tear. It was even larger than the first one had been and glimmered like a transparent pearl in the corner of her left eye. "I suppose so," he said resignedly.

"I'll be waiting for you on the bench."

He killed three hours in a movie house and picked up Becky at her apartment at seven-thirty. She was wearing a black sheath that made her shape shout, and a pair of pointed shoes with metal tips that matched the three golden bands around her ankle. He took one look into her gray eyes and knew then and there that he was going to propose to her before the evening ended.

They dined in the same cafe. When they were halfway through their meal, Alayne of Altair walked in the door on the arm of a sartorially elegant young man with a lean, hungry face and a long bushy tail.

Roger nearly fell out of his chair.

She spotted him right away and brought her escort over to the table. "Roger, this is Ashley Ames," she said excitedly. "He invited me out to dinner so he could continue my diction lesson. Afterward he's going to take me to his apartment and show me his first edition of *Pygmalion*." She got her eyes on Becky then and gave a start. Abruptly her gaze traveled floorward to where Becky's trim ankles were visible just beneath the tablecloth, and when she raised her eyes again they had transmuted from blue to green. "Three down and one to go," she said. "I should have known it would be one of you!"

Becky's eyes had undergone a metamorphosis too. They were yellow now instead of gray. "I saw him first, and you know the rules as well as I do. So lay off!"

"Come on," Alayne of Altair said haughtily to Ashley Ames, who was hovering predatorily just behind her. "There must be better restaurants on Earth than this!"

Bewildered, Roger watched them leave. All he could think of was Little Red Riding Hood and the wolf. "Do you know her?" he asked Becky.

"She's a real gone crackpot with an outer-space complex who comes in the Silver Spoon sometimes and babbles about life on other planets. Let's change the subject, shall we?"

Roger did so. Dinner over, he took Becky to a show, and afterward he suggested a walk in the park.

She squeezed his arm in an eloquent answer. The sacred bench stood like an island in a tarn of purest moonlight, and they waded through the silvery shallows to its iron-wrought shores and sat down upon its shelving hills. Her second kiss made the first seem sisterly, and when it was over Roger knew he would never be the same again. "Will you marry me, Becky?" he blurted.

She didn't seem particularly surprised. "Do you really want me to?"

"I'll say! Just as soon as I get a job and—"

"Kiss me, Roger."

He didn't get back to the subject till they were standing on her apartment-house steps.

"Why, of course I'll marry you, Roger," she said. "Tomorrow we'll take a drive into the country and make plans."

"Fine! I'll rent a car, and we'll take a lunch and—"

"Never mind a lunch. Just pick me up at two." She kissed him so hard that his toes turned up. "Good night, Roger."

"See you tomorrow at two," he said when his breath came back.

"Maybe I'll ask you in for a cocktail."

His feet never touched the ground once all the way back to the hotel. He came back down to earth with a jar, though, when he read the letter the night clerk handed him. The wording was different from that of the five others he had received in answer to his five other applications, but the essential message was the same: "Don't call us, we'll call you."

He went upstairs sadly and undressed and got into bed. After five failures in a row he should have known better than to tell the sixth interviewer about his poetic analysis of science. Modern industrial corporations wanted men with hard unadorned facts in their heads, not frustrated poets seeking symmetry in the microcosm. But, as usual, his enthusiasm had carried him away.

It was a long time before he fell asleep. When he finally did so he dreamed a long and involved dream about a girl in an Alice-blue gown, a wolf in a Brooks Brothers suit and a siren in a black sheath.

True to her word, Alayne of Altair was sitting on the bench when he came down the walk the next morning. "Hi, Rog," she said brightly.

He sat glumly down beside her. "How was Ashley's first edition?'

"I didn't see it yet. Last night after we had dinner I was so tired I told him to take me straight home. He's going to show it to me tonight. We're going to dine by candlelight in his apartment." She hesitated for a moment—then, with a rush: "She's not the one for you, Rog. Becky, I mean."

He sat up straight on the bench. "What makes you think so?"

"I—I tracked you last night on my fleglinder. It's a little TV receiver that you beam in on whoever you want to see and hear. Last—last night I beamed it in on you and Becky."

"You followed us, you mean! Why, you snooping little—"

"Please don't get mad at me, Roger. I was worried about you. Oh, Rog, you've fallen into the clutches of a witch-woman from Muggenwort!"

It was too much. He stood up to leave, but she grabbed his arm and pulled him back down again.

"Now you listen to me, Rog," she went on. "This is serious. I don't know what she told you about me, but whatever it was, it's a lie. Girls from Muggenwort are mean and cruel and crafty and will do anything to further their evil ends. They come to Earth in spaceships just as we girls from Buzenborg do—only their spaceships are big enough to hold five people instead of only two—then they take an assumed name, get a job where they'll come into contact with lots of men and *start* filling their quota of four husbands—"

"Are you sitting there in broad daylight trying to tell me that the girl I—I'm going to marry is a witch from Muggenwort who came to Earth to collect four husbands?"

"Yes—to collect them and take them back to Muggenwort with her. You see, Muggenwort is a small matriarchal province near the Altair VI equator, and their mating customs are as different from ours as they are from yours. All Muggenwort women have to have four husbands in order to be accepted into Muggenwort society, and as there are no longer enough men in Muggenwort to go around, they have to travel to other planets to get them. But that's not the worst of it. After they capture them and bring them back to Muggenwort, they put them to work twelve hours a day in the kritch fields while they lie around all day in their air-conditioned barkenwood huts chewing rutenstuga nuts and watching TV!"

Roger was more amused than angry now. "And how about the husbands? I suppose they take to all this docilely and don't mind in the least sharing their wife with three other men!"

"But you don't understand!" Alayne of Altair was becoming more agitated by the second. "The husbands have no choice. They're bewitched—the same way Becky is bewitching you. Do you think it was your idea to ask her to marry you? Well, it wasn't! It was her idea, planted in your mind by hypnosis. Didn't you notice those gleaming gray eyes of hers? She's a witch, Roger, and once she gets you completely in her clutches you will be her slave for life, and she must be pretty sure of you already or she wouldn't be taking you out to her spaceship this afternoon!"

"What about her other three husbands-to-be? Are they going to accompany us on our drive into the country?"

"Of course not. They're already in the ship, hopelessly bewitched, waiting for her. Didn't you notice the three anklets on her leg? Well, each of them stands for a man she has conquered. It's an old Muggenwort custom. Probably today she is wearing four. Didn't you ever wonder what happens to all the men who disappear from the face of the Earth each year, Roger?"

"No, I never did," Roger said. "But there is one thing I'm wondering about. Why did you come to Earth?"

Alayne of Altair's bluebird eyes dropped to his chin. "I—I was coming to that," she said. "You see, in Buzenborg, girls chase boys instead of boys chasing girls."

"That seems to be a standard operating procedure on Altair VI."

"That's because the man shortage isn't confined to Muggenwort alone but encompasses the whole planet. When push-button-type spaceships became available, Buzenborg as well as Muggenwort girls began renting them and traveling to other planets in search of husbands, and Buzenborg as well as Muggenwort girls schools started teaching alien languages and customs. The information was easily available because the Altair VI world government has been sending secret anthropological expeditions to Earth, and planets like it, for years, so that we will be ready to make contact with you when you finally lick space travel and qualify for membership in the League of Super Planets."

"What's the Buzenborg husband quota?" Roger asked acidly.

"One. That's why we Buzenborg girls wear wodgets. We're not like those witches from Muggenwort. They don't care whom they get, just so they have strong backs; but we girls from Buzenborg do. Anyway, when my wodget registered ninety, I knew that you and I were ideally suited for each other, and that's why I struck up a conversation with you. I—I didn't know at the time that you were half bewitched."

"Suppose your wodget had been right. What then?"

"Why, I'd have taken you back to Buzenborg with me, of course. Oh, you'd have loved it there, Rog," she rushed on. "Our industrial corporations would be crazy about your poetic analysis of science, and you could have got a swell job, and my folks would have built us a house and we could have settled down and raised—and—raised—" Her voice grew sad. "But I guess I'll have to settle for Ashley instead. He only registers sixty on my wodget, but sixty is better than nothing."

"Are you naive enough to believe that if you go to his apartment tonight he'll marry you and return to Buzenborg with you?"

"I have to take a chance. I only had enough money to rent the ship for a week. What do you think I am—a rich witch from Muggenwort?'

She had raised her eyes to his, and he searched them vainly for the deceit that should have been in them. There must be some way he could trap her. She had eluded his time trap and his baseball trap and—

Wait a minute! Maybe she hadn't eluded his time trap after all. If she was telling the truth and really did want to cut Becky out and really did have a spaceship equipped with faster-than-light drive, she was overlooking a very large ace up her sleeve.

"Did you ever hear the limerick about Miss Bright?" he asked. She shook her head. "It goes something like this:

> *There was a young lady named Bright,*
> *Whose speed was far faster than light;*
> *She set out one day*
> *In a relative way,*
> *And returned home the previous night.* *

"Let me elaborate," Roger went on. "I met Becky a little less than twenty-four hours before I met you, and I met her the same as I did you—on the very bench we're sitting on now. So if you're telling

(*By Arthur H. B. Buller; in *Punch*.)

thetruth you really don't have a problem at all. All you have to do is make a round trip to Altair VI enough in excess of the velocity of light to bring you back to Earth twenty-four hours before your original arrival. Then you simply come walking down the walk to where I'm sitting on the bench, and if your wodget is worth a plugged nickel I'll feel the same way toward you as you feel toward me."

"But that would involve a paradox, and the cosmos would have to create a time shift to compensate for it," Alayne of Altair objected. "The millisecond I attained the necessary velocity and the extent of the paradox became evident, time would go *whoom*! And you, I and everybody else in the cosmos would be catapulted back to the moment when the paradox began, and we'd have no memory of the last few days. It would be as though I'd never met you, as though you'd never met me—"

"And as though I'd never met Becky. What more do you want?"

She was staring at him. "Why—why, it just might work at that. It—it would be sort of like Aparicio stealing first base. Let me see now, if I take a bus out to the farm, Ill get there in less than an hour. Then if I set the grodgel for Lapse Two, and the borque for—"

"Oh, for Pete's sake," Roger said, "come off it, will you!"

"Sh-sh!" Alayne of Altair said. "I'm trying to think."

He stood up. "Well, think then! I'm going back to my room and get ready for my date with Becky!"

Angrily he walked away. In his room, he laid his best suit out on the bed. He shaved and showered leisurely and spent a long time getting dressed. Then he went out, rented a car and drove to Becky's apartment. It was 2:00 P.M. on the nose when he rang her bell. She must have been taking a shower, because when she opened the door all she had on was a terry-cloth towel and three anklets. No, four.

"Hi, Roger," she said warmly. "Come on in."

Eagerly he stepped across the threshold and made—

Whoom! Time went.

Little did Roger Thompson dream when he sat down on the park bench that Friday morning in June that in a celibate sense his goose was already in the oven and that soon it would be cooked. He may have had an inkling of things to come when he saw the cute blonde in the blue dress walking down the winding walk some several seconds later, but that inkling could not conceivably have apprised him of the vast convolutions of time and space which the bowing out of his bachelorhood had already set in motion.

The cute blonde sat down at the other end of the bench, produced a little red notebook and began writing in it. Presently she glanced at her wrist watch. Then she gave a start and looked over at him.

He returned the look cordially. He saw a dusting of golden freckles, a pair of eyes the hue of bluebirds and a small mouth the color of sumac leaves after the first hard frost.

A tall brunette in a red sheath came down the walk. Roger hardly even noticed her. Just as she was opposite the bench one of her spike heels sank into a crevice and brought her to an abrupt halt. She slipped her foot out of the shoe and, kneeling down, jerked the shoe free with her hands. Then she put it back on, gave him a dirty look and continued on her way.

The cute blonde had returned her attention to her note book. Now she faced him again. Roger's heart turned three somersaults and made an entrechat.

"How do you xpell matrimony?" she said.

The Other Now

INTRODUCTION

His wife was dead, killed in an accident that might instead have killed him, or neither of them. He had seen her buried, but their home was somehow haunted by her presence. Suppose there was a parallel world where *he* had died and *she* had survived? Could that gulf between dimensions be crossed?

* * *

William F. Jenkins (1986-1975) was a prolific and successful writer, selling stories to magazines of all sorts, from pulps like *Argosy* to the higher-paying slicks such as *Collier's* and *The Saturday Evening Post*, writing stories ranging from westerns, to mysteries, to science fiction. However, for SF he usually used the pen name of Murray Leinster, and he used it often. Even though SF was a less lucrative field than other categories of fiction, he enjoyed writing it (fortunately for SF readers everywhere) and wrote a great deal of it, including such classics as "Sidewise in Time" (which introduced the concept of parallel time tracks into SF). "First Contact," and "A Logic Named Joe," the last being a story you should keep in mind the next time someone repeats the canard that SF never predicted the home computer or the Internet. Leinster did it (though under his real name, this time) in *Astounding Science-Fiction* in 1946! His first SF story was "The Runaway Skyscraper," published in 1919, and his last was the third of three novelization of the *Land of the Giants* TV show. For the length of his career, his prolificity, and his introduction of original concepts into SF, fans in the 1940s began calling him the Dean of Science Fiction, a title he richly deserved.

The Other Now

by Murray Leinster

This story is self-evident nonsense. If Jimmy Patterson had told anybody but Haynes, nice men in white jackets would have taken him away for psychiatric treatment, which undoubtedly would have been effective. He'd have been restored to sanity and common sense, and he'd probably have died of it. So, to anyone who liked Jimmy and Jane, it is good that things worked out as they did. The facts are patently impossible, but they are satisfying.

Haynes, though, would like very much to know exactly why it happened in the case of Jimmy and Jane and nobody else. There must have been some specific reason, but there's absolutely no clue to it.

It began about three months after Jane was killed in that freak accident. Jimmy had taken her death hard. This night seemed no different from any other. He came home, just as usual, and his throat tightened a little, just as usual, as he went up to the door. It was still intolerable to know that Jane wouldn't be waiting for him. The hurt in his throat was a very familiar sensation, which he was doggedly trying to wear out. But it was extra-strong tonight, and he wondered rather desperately if he'd sleep or, if he did, if he'd dream. Sometimes he had dreams of Jane and was very, very happy until he woke up—and then he wanted to cut his throat. But he wasn't at that point tonight. Not yet.

As he explained it to Haynes later, he simply put his key in the

81

door, opened it and started to walk in. But he bumped into the closed door instead, so he absently put his key in the door and opened it and started to walk in. Yes. That's what happened. He was halfway through before he realized. Then he stared blankly. The door looked perfectly normal. He closed it behind him, feeling queer. He tried to reason out what had happened.

Then he felt a slight draught. The door wasn't shut. It was wide open. He had to close it again.

That was all that happened to mark this night off from any other, and there is no explanation why it happened—began, rather—this night instead of any other. Jimmy went to bed with a rather taut feeling. He had the conviction that he had opened the door twice— the same door. Then he had the conviction that he had had to close it twice. He'd heard of that feeling. Queer, but fairly commonplace.

He slept, blessedly without dreams. He woke next morning and found his muscles tense. That was an acquired habit. Before he opened his eyes every morning, he reminded himself that Jane wasn't beside him. It was necessary. If he forgot and turned contentedly—to emptiness—the ache of being alive when Jane wasn't was unbearable. This morning he lay with his eyes closed to remind himself, and instead he found himself thinking about that business of the door. He'd kicked the door between the two openings, so it wasn't just an illusion of repetition. And he puzzled over closing the door and then finding he had to close it again. So it wasn't a standard mental vagary. It looked like a delusion. But his memory insisted that it had happened that way, whether it was impossible or not.

Frowning, he went out, got his breakfast at a restaurant and went to work. Work was blessed, because he had to think about it. The main trouble was that sometimes something turned up that Jane would have been amused to hear, and he had to remind himself that there was no use making a mental note to tell her. Jane was dead.

Today he thought a good deal about the door, but when he went home he knew that he was going to have a black night. He wouldn't sleep, and oblivion would seem infinitely tempting. Because the ache of being alive when Jane wasn't was horribly tedious, and he couldn't imagine an end to it. Tonight would be a very bad one, indeed.

He opened the door and started in. Then he went crashing *into* the door. He stood still for an instant and then fumbled for the lock. But the door was open. He'd opened it. There hadn't been anything for him to run into. But his forehead hurt where he'd bumped into the door that hadn't been closed at all.

There wasn't anything he could do about it, though. He went in, hung up his coat and sat down wearily. He filled his pipe and grimly faced a night that was going to be one of the worst. He struck a match, lighted the pipe and put the match in an ashtray. And he glanced in the tray. There were cigarette stubs in it. Jane's brand. Freshly smoked.

He touched them with his fingers. They were real. Then a furious anger filled him. Maybe the cleaning woman had had the intolerable insolence to smoke Jane's cigarettes. He got up and stormed through the house, raging as he searched for signs of further impertinence. He found none. He came back, seething, to his chair. The ashtray was empty. And there'd been nobody around to empty it.

It was logical to question his own sanity, and the question gave him a sort of grim cheer. The matter of the recurrent oddities could be used to fight the abysmal depression ahead. He tried to reason them out, and, always, they added up to mere delusions. But he kept his mind resolutely on the problem. Sometimes at work he was able to thrust aside for whole half-hours the fact that Jane was dead. Now he grappled relievedly with the question of his sanity or lunacy. He went to the desk where Jane had kept her household accounts. He'd set the whole thing down on paper and examined it methodically, checking this item against that . . .

Jane's diary lay on the desk-blotter, with a pencil between two of its pages. He picked it up with an inward wrench. Some day he might read it—an absurd chronicle Jane had never offered him—but not now. Not now!

Then he realized that it shouldn't be here. His hands jumped, and the book fell open. He saw Jane's angular writing, and it hurt. He closed it quickly, aching all over. But the printed date at the top of the page registered on his brain even as he snapped the cover shut.

Then he sat still for minutes, every muscle taut.

It was a long time before he opened the book again, and by that time he had a perfectly reasonable explanation. It must be that Jane hadn't restricted herself to assigned spaces. When she had extra much to write, she wrote on past the page allotted for a given date. Of course! So Jimmy fumbled back to the last written page, where the pencil had been, with a tense matter-of-factness. It was—as he'd noticed—today's date. The page was filled. The writing was fresh. It was Jane's handwriting.

> *Went to the cemetery,* said the sprawling letters. *It was very bad. This is three months since the accident, and it doesn't get any easier. I'm developing a personal enmity to chance. It doesn't seem like an abstraction anymore. It was chance that killed Jimmy. It could have been me instead, or neither of us. I wish . . .*

Jimmy went quietly mad for a moment or two. When he came to himself he was staring at an empty desk-blotter. There wasn't any book before him. There wasn't any pencil between his fingers. He remembered picking up the pencil and writing desperately under Jane's entry. *Jane!* he'd written—and he could remember the look of his scrawled script under Jane's—*where are you? I'm not dead! I thought you were! In God's name, where are you?*

But certainly nothing of the sort could possibly have happened. It was delusion.

That night was very, very bad, but, curiously, not as bad as some other nights had been. Jimmy had a normal man's horror of insanity, but this wasn't normal insanity. A lunatic has always an explanation for his delusions. Jimmy had none. He noted the fact.

Next morning he bought a small camera with a flashbulb attachment and carefully memorized the directions for its use. This was the thing that would tell the story. And that night, when he got home— as usual after dark—he had the camera ready. He unlocked the door and opened it. He put his hand out tentatively. The door was still closed. He stepped back and quickly snapped the camera, and there was a blinding flash from the bulb. The glare blinded him. But, when he put out his hand again, the door was open. He stepped into the living room without having to unlock and open the door a second time.

He looked at the desk as he turned the film and put in a new flashbulb. It was as empty as he'd left it in the morning. He hung up his coat and settled down tensely with his pipe. Presently he knocked out the ashes. There were cigarette butts in the tray. He quivered a little. He smoked again, carefully avoiding looking at the desk. It was not until he knocked out the second pipeful of ashes that he let himself look where Jane's diary had been.

It was there again, and it was open. There was a ruler laid across it to keep it open.

Jimmy wasn't frightened, and he wasn't hopeful. There was absolutely no reason why this should happen to him. He was simply desperate and grim when he went across the room. He saw yesterday's entry, and his own hysterical message. And there was more writing beyond that. In Jane's hand.

> *Darling, maybe I'm going crazy. But I think you wrote me as if you were alive. Maybe I'm crazy to answer you. But please, darling, if you are alive somewhere and somehow . . .*

There was a tear-blot here. The rest was frightened, and tender, and as desperate as Jimmy's own sensations.

He wrote, with trembling fingers, before he put the camera into position and pressed the shutter-control for the second time.

When his eyes recovered from the flash, there was nothing on the desk.

He did not sleep at all that night. Nor did he work the next day. He went to a photographer with the film and paid an extravagant fee to have the film developed and enlarged at once. He got back two prints, quite distinct—very distinct, considering everything. One looked like a trick shot, showing a door twice, once open and once closed, in the same photograph. The other was a picture of an open book, and he could read every word on its pages. It was inconceivable that such a picture should have come out.

He walked around almost at random for a couple of hours, looking at the pictures from time to time. Pictures or no pictures, the thing was nonsense. The facts were preposterous. It must be that he only imagined seeing these prints. But there was a way to find out.

He went to Haynes. Haynes was his friend and, reluctantly, a lawyer—reluctantly, because law practice interfered with a large number of unlikely hobbies.

"Haynes," said Jimmy, "I want you to look at a couple of pictures and see if you see what I do. I may have gone out of my head."

He passed over the pictures of the door. It looked to Jimmy like two doors, nearly at right angles—in the same door frame and hung from the same hinges.

Haynes looked at it and said tolerantly, "Didn't know you went in for trick photography." He picked up a reading-glass and examined it in detail. "A futile but highly competent job. You covered half the film and exposed with the door closed, and then exposed for the other half of the film with the door open. A neat job of matching, though. You've a good tripod."

"I held the camera in my hand," said Jimmy, with restraint.

"You couldn't do it that way, Jimmy," said Haynes. "Don't try to kid me!"

"I'm trying not to fool myself," said Jimmy. He was very pale. He handed over the other enlargement. "What do you see in this?"

Haynes looked. Then he jumped. He read through what was so plainly photographed on the pages of a diary that hadn't been before the camera. Then he looked at Jimmy in palpable uneasiness.

"Any explanation?" asked Jimmy. He swallowed. "I—haven't any."

He told what had happened to date, baldly and without any attempt to make it reasonable. Haynes gaped at him. But presently his eyes grew shrewd and compassionate. He had a number of unlikely hobbies, and he loudly insisted on his belief in a fourth dimension and other esoteric ideas, because it was good fun to talk authoritatively about them. But he had common sense, had Haynes, and a good and varied law practice.

Presently he said gently, "If you want it straight, Jimmy . . . I had a client once. She accused a chap of beating her up. It was very pathetic. She was absolutely sincere. She really believed it. But her own family admitted that she'd made the marks on herself—and the doctors agreed that she'd blotted it out of her mind afterward."

"You suggest," said Jimmy composedly, "that I might have forged all that to comfort myself with, as soon as I could forget the forging. I don't think that's the case, Haynes. What's left?"

Haynes hesitated a long time. He looked at the pictures again, scrutinizing especially the one that looked like a trick shot.

"This is an amazingly good job of matching," he said wryly. "I can't pick the place where the two exposures join. Some people might manage to swallow this. And the theoretic explanation is a lot better. The only trouble is that it couldn't happen."

Jimmy waited.

Haynes said awkwardly, "The accident in which Jane was killed. You were in your car. You came up behind a truck carrying structural steel. There was a long slim girder sticking way out behind, with a red rag on it. The truck had air brakes. The driver jammed them on just after he'd passed over a bit of wet pavement. The truck stopped. Your car slid, even with the brakes locked—This is nonsense, Jimmy!"

"I'd rather you went on," said Jimmy, very white.

"You—ran into the truck, your car swinging a little as it slid. The girder came through the windshield. It could have hit you. It could have missed both of you. By pure chance, it happened to hit Jane."

"And killed her," said Jimmy very quietly. "Yes. But it might have been me. That diary entry is written as if it had been me. Did you notice?"

There was a long pause in Haynes' office. The world outside the windows was highly prosaic and commonplace and normal. Haynes wriggled in his chair.

"I think," he said unhappily, "you acted like my girl client—you forged that writing and then forgot it. Have you seen a doctor yet?"

"Presently," said Jimmy. "Systematize my lunacy for me first, Haynes. If it can be done."

"It's not accepted science," said Haynes. "In fact, it's considered eyewash. But there have been speculations. . . ." He grimaced. "But remember that it was pure chance that Jane was hit. It was just as likely to be you instead, or neither of you. If it had been you—"

"Jane," said Jimmy, "would be living in our house alone, and she might very well have written that entry in the diary."

"Yes," agreed Haynes uncomfortably. "I shouldn't suggest this, but—there are a lot of possible futures. We don't know which one will come about, for us. When today was in the future, there were a lot of possible todays. The present moment—now—is only one of a lot nows that might have been. So it's been suggested—mind you, this isn't science, but pure charlatanry—hit's been suggested that there may be more than one actual now. Before the girder actually hit, there were three nows in the possible future. One in which neither of you was hit, one in which you were hit, and one—" He paused, embarrassed. "So some people would say, 'How do we know that the one in which Jane was hit is the only now?' They'd say that the others could have happened and that maybe they did. And—"

Jimmy nodded confirmatorily. "If that were true," he said detachedly, "Jane would be in a present moment, a now, where it was me who was killed. As I'm in a now where she was killed. Is that it?"

Haynes shrugged.

Jimmy thought, then said gravely, "Thanks. Queer, isn't it?"

He picked up the two pictures and went out.

Haynes was worried. But it is not easy to denounce someone as insane, when there is no evidence that he is apt to be dangerous. He did go to the trouble to find out that Jimmy acted in a reasonably normal manner. For two weeks he worked industriously and talked quite sanely in the daytime. Only Haynes suspected that of nights he went home and experienced the impossible. Sometimes, Haynes suspected that the impossible might be the fact—that has been an amazingly good bit of trick photography—but it was too preposterous! Also, there was no reason for such a thing to happen to Jimmy.

Actually, there is still no explanation. But, for a week after Haynes' pseudo-scientific explanation, Jimmy was almost lighthearted. He no longer had to remind himself that Jane was dead. He had evidence that she wasn't. She wrote to him in the diary, which he always found on her desk, and he read her message and wrote in return. For a full week the sheer joy of simply being able to communicate with each other was enough.

But the second week was not so good. To know that Jane was alive was good, but to be separated from her without hope was not. There was no meaning in a cosmos in which one could only write love letters to one's wife or husband in another now that only might have been. But for a while, both Jimmy and Jane tried to hide this new hopelessness from each other—so Jimmy explained carefully to Haynes before it was all over. Their letters were tender and very natural, and presently there was even time for gossip and actual everyday conversation. . . .

Haynes met Jimmy on the street one day, after about two weeks. Jimmy looked better, but he was drawn very fine. He greeted Haynes without constraint, but Haynes felt awkward. After a little he said, "Er—Jimmy. That matter we were talking about the other day—those photographs—"

"Yes. You were right," said Jimmy casually. "Jane agrees. There is more than one now. In the now I'm in, Jane was killed. In the now she's in, I was killed."

Haynes fidgeted.

"Would you let me see that picture of the door again?" he asked. "A trick film like that simply can't be perfect! I'd like to enlarge that picture a little more. May I?"

"You can have the film," said Jimmy. "I don't want it."

Haynes hesitated. Jimmy, quite matter-of-factly, told him most of what had happened to date. But he had no idea what had started it. Haynes almost wrung his hands.

"The thing can't be so!" he said desperately. "You have to be crazy, Jimmy!"

But he would not have said that to a man whose sanity he really suspected. Jimmy nodded.

"Jane told me something, by the way. . . . Did you have a near-accident night before last? Somebody almost ran into you out on the Saw Mill Road?"

Haynes jumped and went pale.

"I went around a curve and a car plunged out of nowhere on the wrong side of the road. We both swung hard. He smashed my fender and almost went off the road himself. But he went racing off without stopping to see if I'd gone in the ditch and killed myself. If I'd been five feet nearer the curve when he came out of it—"

"Where Jane is you were," said Jimmy. "Just about five feet nearer the curve. It was a bad smash. Tony Shields was in the other car. It killed him—where Jane is."

Haynes licked his lips. It was absurd, but he said, "How about me?"

"Where Jane is," Jimmy told him, "you're in the hospital."

Haynes swore in unreasonable irritation. There wasn't any way for Jimmy to know about that near-accident. He hadn't mentioned it because he'd had no idea who had been in the other car.

"I don't believe it!" But then he said pleadingly, "Jimmy—it isn't so, is it? How the hell could you account for it?"

Jimmy shrugged.

"Jane and I—we're rather fond of each other." The understatement was so patent that he smiled faintly. "Chance separated us. The feeling we have for each other draws us together. There's a saying about two people becoming one flesh. If such a thing could happen, it would be Jane and me. After all, maybe only a tiny pebble or a single extra drop of water made my car swerve enough to get her killed—where I am, that is. That's a very little thing. So with such a trifle separating us, and with so much pulling us together, why—sometimes the barrier wears thin. She leaves a door closed in the house where she is. I open that same door where I am. Sometimes I have to open the door she left closed, too. That's all."

Haynes didn't say a word, but the question he wouldn't ask was so self-evident that Jimmy answered it.

"Why, we're hoping," he said. "It's pretty bad being separated, but the—phenomena keep up. So we hope. Her diary is sometimes in the now where she is and sometimes in the now of mine. Cigarette butts, too. Maybe—" And that was the only time he showed any sign of emotion. He spoke as though his mouther was dry. "If ever I'm in her now or she's in mine, even for an instant, all the devils in hell couldn't separate us again! We hope."

Which was insanity. In fact, it was the third week of insanity. He'd told Haynes quite calmly that Jane's diary was on her desk every night, that there was a letter to him in it and that he wrote to one to her. He said, quite calmly, that the barrier between them seemed to be growing thinner and that at least once, when he went to bed, he was sure that there was one more cigarette stub in the ashtray than had been there in the evening. They were very near indeed. They were separated only by the difference between what was and what might have been. In one sense, the difference was a pebble or a drop of water. In another, the difference was that between life and death. But they hoped. They convinced themselves that the barrier was growing thinner. Once it seemed to Jimmy that they touched hands. But he was not sure. And he told all this to Haynes in a matter-of-fact fashion and speculated mildly on what had started it all . . .

Then, one night, Haynes called Jimmy on the telephone. Jimmy answered somewhat impatiently.

"Jimmy!" said Haynes. He was almost hysterical. "I think I'm in insane! You know you said Tony Shields was in the car that hit me?"

"Yes," said Jimmy politely. "What's the matter?"

"It's been driving me crazy," wailed Haynes feverishly. "You said he was killed—there. But I hadn't told a soul about the thing! So—so just now I broke down and phoned him. And it had been Tony Shields! That near-crash scared him to death and I gave him hell and—he's paying for my fender! I didn't tell him he was killed."

Jimmy didn't answer. It didn't seem to matter to him.

"I'm coming over!" said Haynes feverishly. "I've got to talk!"

"No," said Jimmy. "Jane and I—we're pretty close to each other. We've—touched each other once. We're hoping. The barrier's pretty thin. We hope it's going to break."

"But it can't," protested Haynes, shocked at the idea of improbabilities in the preposterous. "It—it can't! What'd happen if you turned up where she is, or—or if she turned up here?"

"I don't know," said Jimmy, "but we'd be together."

"You're crazy! You mustn't—"

"Good-by," said Jimmy, politely. "I'm hoping, Haynes. Something has to happen. It has to!"

His voice stopped. And then there was a noise in the room behind him—Haynes heard it. Only two words—faintly, and over a telephone—but he swore to himself that it was Jane's voice apparently sobbing with happiness. The two words Haynes heard were, *"Jimmy! Darling!"*

Then the telephone crashed and Haynes heard no more. Even though he called back frantically again and again, Jimmy didn't answer.

And that's all. The whole thing is nonsense, of course. Even granting Jimmy's sincerity, any psychiatrist can tell you about patients who write letters to themselves, then apparently blot the fact out of their minds and are elated or depressed by the missives of their own composition. There's no evidence for any other view.

But Haynes sat up all that night, practically gibbering. He tried to call Jimmy again the next morning, then tried his office and at last went to the police. He explained to them that Jimmy had been in a highly nervous state since the death of his wife. So finally, the police broke into the house. They had to break in because every door and window had been carefully fastened from the inside, as though Jimmy has been very careful to make sure nobody could interrupt what he and Jane hoped would occur. But Jimmy wasn't in the house. There was no trace of him. It was exactly as if he'd vanished into thin air. Ultimately, the police even dragged ponds and such things for his body, but they never found any clues. Nobody ever saw Jimmy again.

The thing that really bothers Haynes, though, is the fact that Jimmy told him who'd almost crashed into him on Saw Mill Road— and it was true, and he got a dented fender paid for. Which is hard to take. And there's that double-exposed picture of Jimmy's front door, which is much more convincing than any other trick pictures Haynes had ever seen. But, on the other hand, if it did happen, why did it only happen to Jimmy and Jane? What set it off? What started it? Why, in effect, did those oddities start at that particular time, to those particular people, in that particular fashion? In fact, did anything happen at all?

These are things that Haynes would very much like to know, but he keeps his mouth shut, or the men in white coats would come and take him away for treatment. As they would have taken Jimmy.

The only thing that is really sure is that it's all impossible. But, to someone who liked Jimmy and Jane, it's rather satisfying, too.

A Dry, Quiet War

INTRODUCTION

Soldiers returning home from war often have trouble resuming their civilian lives, and this soldier, back from a time war in the far future, had things even harder. He had a choice of standing by and doing nothing, and losing everything important to him—or fighting back, and *still* losing everything important . . .

* * *

Tony Daniel is the author of seven science fiction books, the latest of which is *Guardian of Night*, as well as an award-winning short story collection, *The Robot's Twilight Companion*. He also collaborated with David Drake on the novel *The Heretic*, and its sequel, *The Savior*, new novels in the popular military science fiction series, The General. His story "Life on the Moon" was a Hugo finalist and also won the *Asimov's* Reader's Choice Award. Daniel's short fiction has been much anthologized and has been collected in multiple year's best anthologies. Daniel has also co-written screen plays for SyFy Channel horror movies, and during the early 2000s was the writer and director of numerous audio dramas for critically-acclaimed SCIFICOM's Seeing Ear theater. Born in Alabama, Daniel has lived in St. Louis, Los Angeles, Seattle, Prague, and New York City. He is now an editor at Baen Books and lives in Wake Forest, North Carolina with his wife and two children.

A Dry, Quiet War

by Tony Daniel

I cannot tell you what it meant to me to see the two suns of Ferro set behind the dry mountain east of my home. I had been away twelve billion years. I passed my cabin to the pump well, and taking a metal cup from where it hung from a set-pin, I worked the handle three times. At first it creaked, and I believed it was rusted tight, but then it loosened, and within fifteen pulls, I had a cup of water.

Someone had kept the pump up. Someone had seen to the house and the land while I was away at the war. For me, it had been fifteen years; I wasn't sure how long it had been for Ferro. The water was tinged red and tasted of iron. Good. I drank it down in a long draft, then put the cup back onto its hanger. When the big sun, Hemingway, set, a slight breeze kicked up. Then Fitzgerald went down and a cold, cloudless night spanked down onto the plateau. I shivered a little, adjusted my internals, and stood motionless, waiting for the last of twilight to pass, and the stars—my stars—to come out. Steiner, the planet that is Ferro's evening star, was the first to emerge, low in the west, methane blue. Then the constellations. Ngal. Gilgamesh. The Big Snake, half-coiled over the southwestern horizon. There was no moon tonight. There was never a moon on Ferro, and that was right.

After a time, I walked to the house, climbed up the porch, and the house recognized me and turned on the lights. I went inside. The place was dusty, the furniture covered with sheets, but there were no signs of rats or jinjas, and all seemed in repair. I sighed, blinked, tried to feel something. Too early, probably. I started to take a covering from a chair, then let it be. I went to the kitchen and checked the cupboard. An old malt-whiskey bottle, some dry cereal, some spices. The spices had been my mother's, and I seldom used them before I left for the end of time. I considered that the whiskey might be perfectly aged by now. But, as the saying goes on Ferro, we like a bit of food with our drink, so I left the house and took the road to town, to Heidel.

It was a five-mile walk, and though I could have enhanced and covered the ground in ten minutes or so, I walked at a regular pace under my homeworld stars. The road was dirt, of course, and my pant legs were dusted red when I stopped under the outside light of Thredmartin's Pub. I took a last breath of cold air, then went inside to the warm.

It was a good night at Thredmartin's. There were men and women gathered around the fire hearth, usas and splices in the cold corners. The regulars were at the bar, a couple of whom I recognized—so old now, wizened like stored apples in a barrel. I looked around for a particular face, but she was not there. A jukebox sputtered some core-cloud deak, and the air was thick with smoke and conversation. Or was, until I walked in. Nobody turned to face me. Most of them couldn't have seen me. But a signal passed and conversation fell to a quiet murmur. Somebody quickly killed the jukebox.

I blinked up an internals menu into my peripheral vision and adjusted to the room's temperature. Then I went to the edge of the bar. The room got even quieter. . . .

The bartender, old Thredmartin himself, reluctantly came over to me.

"What can I do for you, sir?" he asked me.

I looked over him, to the selection of bottles, tubes, and cans on display behind him. "I don't see it," I said.

"Eh?" He glanced back over his shoulder, then quickly returned to peering at me.

"Bone's Barley," I said.

"We don't have any more of that," Thredmartin said, with a suspicious tone.

"Why not?"

"The man who made it died."

"How long ago?"

"Twenty years, more or less. I don't see what business of—"

"What about his son?"

Thredmartin backed up a step. Then another. "Henry," he whispered. "Henry Bone."

"Just give me the best that you do have, Peter Thredmartin." I said. "In fact, I'd like to buy everybody a round on me."

"Henry Bone! Why, you looked to me like a bad 'un indeed when you walked in here. I took you for one of them glims, I did," Thredmartin said. I did not know what he was talking about. Then he smiled an old devil's crooked smile. "Your money's no good here, Henry Bone. I do happen to have a couple of bottles of your old dad's whiskey stowed away in back. Drinks are on the house."

And so I returned to my world, and for most of those I'd left behind it seemed as if I'd never really gone. My neighbors hadn't changed much in the twenty years local that had passed, and of course, they had no conception of what had happened to me. They knew only that I'd been to the war—the Big War at the End of Time— and evidently everything turned out okay, for here I was, back in my own time and my own place. I planted Ferro's desert barley, brought in peat from the mountain bogs, bred the biomass that would extract the minerals from my hard groundwater, and got ready for making whiskey once again. Most of the inhabitants of Ferro were divided between whiskey families and beer families. Bones were distillers, never brewers, since the Settlement, ten generations before.

It wasn't until she called upon me that I heard the first hints of the troubles that had come. Her name was Alinda Bexter, but since we played together under the floorplanks of her father's hotel, I had always called her Bex. When I left for the war, she was twenty, and I twenty-one. I still recognized her at forty, five years older than I was now, as she came walking down the road to my house, a week after I'd returned. She was taller than most women on Ferro, and she might be mistaken for a usa-human splice anywhere else. She was rangy, and she wore a khaki dress that whipped in the dry wind as she came toward me. I stood on the porch, waiting for her, wondering what she would say.

"Well, this is a load off of me," she said. She was wearing a brimmed hat. It had ribbon to tie under her chin, but Bex had not done that. She held her hand on it to keep it from blowing from her head. "This damn ranch has been one big thankless task."

"So it was you who kept it up," I said.

"Just kept it from falling apart as fast as it would have otherwise," she replied. We stood and looked at one another for a moment. Her eyes were green. Now that I had seen an ocean, I could understand the kind of green they were.

"Well then," I finally said. "Come on in."

I offered her some sweetcake I'd fried up, and some beer that my neighbor, Shin, had brought by, both of which she declined. We sat in the living room, on furniture covered with the white sheets I had yet to remove. Bex and I took it slow, getting to know each other again. She ran her father's place now. For years, the only way to get to Heidel was by freighter, but we had finally gotten a node on the Flash, and even though Ferro was still a backwater planet, there were more strangers passing through than there ever had been—usually en route to other places. But they sometimes stayed a night or two in the Bexter Hotel. Its reputation was spreading, Bex claimed, and I believed her. Even when she was young, she had been shrewd but honest, a combination you don't often find in an innkeeper. She was a quiet woman—that is, until she got to know you well—and some most likely thought her conceited. I got the feeling that she hadn't let down her reserve for a long time. When I knew her before, Bex did not have many close friends, but for the ones she had, such as me, she poured out her thoughts, and her heart. I found that she hadn't changed much in that way.

"Did you marry?" I asked her, after hearing about the hotel and her father's bad health.

"No," she said. "No, I very nearly did, but then I did not. Did you?"

"No. Who was it?"

"Rail Kenton."

"Rail Kenton? Rail Kenton whose parents run the hops market?" He was a quarter-splice, a tall man on a world of tall men. Yet, when I knew him, his long shadow had been deceptive. There was no spark or force in him. "I can't see that, Bex."

"Tom Kenton died ten years ago," she said. "Marjorie retired, and Rail owned the business until just last year. Rail did all right; you'd be surprised. Something about his father's passing gave him a backbone. Too much of one, maybe."

"What happened?"

"He died," she said. "He died too, just as I thought you had." Now she told me she would like a beer after all, and I went to get her a bottle of Shin's ale. When I returned, I could tell that she'd been crying a little.

"The glims killed Rail," said Bex, before I could ask her about him. "That's their name for themselves, anyway. Humans, repons, kaliwaks, and I don't know what else. They passed through last year and stayed for a week in Heidel. Very bad. They made my father give over the whole hotel to them, and then they had a . . . trial, they called it. Every house was called and made to pay a tithe. The glims decided how much. Rail refused to pay. He brought along a pistol—Lord knows where he got it—and tried to shoot one of them. They just laughed and took it from him." Now the tears started again.

"And then they hauled him out into the street in front of the hotel." Bex took a moment and got control of herself. "They burnt him up with a p-gun. Burned his legs off first, then his arms, then the rest of him after they'd let him lie there a while. There wasn't a trace of him after that; we couldn't even bury him."

I couldn't take her to me, hold her, not after she'd told me about Rail. Needing something to do, I took some tangled banwood from the tinder box and struggled to get a fire going from the burnt-down coals in my hearth. I blew into the fireplace and only got a nose full of ashes for my trouble. "Didn't anybody fight?" I asked.

"Not after that. We just waited them out. Or they got bored. I don't know. It was bad for everybody, not just Rail." Bex shook her head, sighed, then saw the trouble I was having and bent down to help me. She was much better at it than I, and the fire was soon ablaze. We sat back down and watched it flicker.

"Sounds like war-ghosts," I said.

"The glims?"

"Soldiers who don't go home after the war. The fighting gets into them and they don't want to give it up, or can't. Sometimes they have . . . modifications that won't let them give it up. They wander the timeways—and since they don't belong to the time they show up in, they're hard to kill. In the early times, where people don't know about the war, or have only heard rumors of it, they had lots of names. Vampires. Hagamonsters. Zombies."

"What can you do?"

I put my arm around her. It had been so long. She tensed up, then breathed deeply, serenely.

"Hope they don't come back," I said. "They are bad ones. Not the worst, but bad."

We were quiet for a while, and the wind, blowing over the chimney's top, made the flue moan as if it were a big stone flute.

"Did you love him, Bex?" I asked. "Rail?"

She didn't even hesitate in her answer this time. "Of course not, Henry Bone. How could you ever think such a thing? I was waiting to catch up with you. Now tell me about the future."

And so I drew away from her for a while, and told her—part of it at least. About how there is not enough dark matter to pull the cosmos back together again, not enough mass to undulate in an eternal cycle. Instead, there *is* an end, and all the stars are either dead or dying, and all that there is is nothing but dim night. I told her about the twilight armies gathered there, culled from all times, all places. Creatures, presences, machines, weapons fighting galaxy-to-galaxy, system-to-system, fighting until the critical point is reached, when entropy flows no more, but pools, pools in endless, stagnant pools of nothing. No light. No heat. No effect. And the universe is dead, and so those who remain . . . inherit the dark field. They win.

"And did you win?" she asked me. "If that's the word for it."

The suns were going down. Instead of answering, I went outside to the woodpile and brought in enough banwood to fuel the fire for the night. I thought maybe she would forget what she'd asked me—but not Bex.

"How does the war end, Henry?"

"You must never ask me that." I spoke the words carefully, making sure I was giving away nothing in my reply. "Every time a returning soldier tells that answer, he changes everything. Then he has two choices. He can either go away, leave his own time, and go back to fight again. Or he can stay, and it will all mean nothing, what he did. Not just who won and who lost, but all the things he did in the war spin off into nothing."

Bex thought about this for a while. "What could it matter? What in God's name could be worth fighting *for?*" she finally asked. "Time ends. Nothing matters after that. What could it possibly matter who won . . . who wins?"

"It means you can go back home," I said. "After it's over."

"I don't understand."

I shook my head and was silent. I had said enough. There was no way to tell her more, in any case—not without changing things. And no way to *say* what it was that had brought those forces together at the end of everything. And what the hell do *I* know, even now? All I know is what I was told, and what I was trained to do. If we don't fight at the end, there won't be a beginning. For there to be people, there has to be a war to fight at the end of things. We live in that kind of universe, and not another, they told me. They told me, and then I told myself. And I did what I had to do so that it would be over and I could go home, come back.

"Bex, I never forgot you," I said. She came to sit with me by the fire. We didn't touch at first, but I felt her next to me, breathed the flush of her skin as the fire warmed her. Then she ran her hand along my arm, felt the bumps from the operational enhancements.

"What have they done to you?" she whispered.

Unbidden the old words of the skyfallers' scream, the words that were yet to be, surfaced in my mind.

> They sucked down my heart
> to a little black hole.
> You cannot stab me.

They wrote down my brain
on a hard knot of space.
You cannot turn me.

Icicle spike
from the eye of a star.
I've come to kill you.

I almost spoke them, from sheer habit. But I did not. The war was over. Bex was here, and I knew it was over. I was going to *feel* something, once again, something besides guile, hate, and rage. I didn't yet, that was true, but I *could* feel the possibility.

"I don't really breathe anymore, Bex; I pretend to so I won't put people off," I told her. "It's been so long, I can't even remember what it was like to *have* to."

Bex kissed me then. At first, I didn't remember how to do that either. And then I did. I added wood to the fire, then ran my hand along Bex's neck and shoulder. Her skin had the health of youth still, but years in the sun and wind had made a supple leather of it, tanned and grained fine. We took the sheet from the couch and pulled it near to the warmth, and she drew me down to her on it, to her neck and breasts.

"Did they leave enough of you for me?" she whispered.

I had not known until now. "Yes," I answered, "there's enough." I found my way inside her, and we made love slowly, in a way that might seem sad to any others but us, for there were memories and years of longing that flowed from us, around us, like amber just at the melting point, and we were inside and there was nothing but this present with all of what was, and what would be, already passed. No time. Finally, only Bex and no time between us.

We fell asleep on the old couch, and it was dim half-morning when we awoke, with Fitzgerald yet to rise in the west and the fire a bed of coals as red as the sky.

Two months later, I was in Thredmartin's when Bex came in with an evil look on her face. We had taken getting back together slow and easy up till then, but the more time we spent around each other, the more we understood that nothing basic had changed. Bex kept coming to the ranch and I took to spending a couple of nights a week in a room her father made up for me at the hotel. Furly Bexter was an old-style McKinnonite. Men and women were to live separately and only meet for business and copulation. But he liked me well enough, and when I insisted on paying for my room, he found a loophole somewhere in the Tracts of McKinnon about cohabitation being all right in hotels and hostels.

"The glims are back," Bex said, sitting down at my table. I was in a dark corner of the pub. I left the fire for those who could not adjust their own internals to keep them warm. "They've taken over the top floor of the hotel. What should we do?"

I took a draw of beer—Thredmartin's own thick porter—and looked at her. She was visibly shivering, probably more from agitation than fright.

"How many of them are there?" I asked.

"Six. And something else, some splice I've never seen, however many that makes."

I took another sip of beer. "Let it be," I said. "They'll get tired, and they'll move on."

"What?" Bex's voice was full of astonishment. "What are you saying?"

"You don't want a war here, Bex," I replied. "You have no idea how bad it can get."

"They killed Rail. They took our *money.*"

"Money." My voice sounded many years away, even to me.

"It's muscle and worry and care. You know how hard people work on Ferro. And for those . . . *things* . . . to come in and take it! We cannot let them—"

"—Bex," I said. "I am not going to do anything."

She said nothing; she put a hand on her forehead as if she had a sickening fever, stared at me for a moment, then looked away.

One of the glims chose that moment to come into Thredmartin's. It was a halandana, a splice—human and jan—from up-time and a couple of possible universes over. It was nearly seven feet tall, with a two-foot-long neck, and it stooped to enter Thredmartin's. Without stopping, it went to the bar and demanded morphine.

Thredmartin was at the bar. He pulled out a dusty rubber, little used, and before he could get out an injector, the halandana reached over, took the entire rubber and put it in the pocket of the long gray coat it wore. Thredmartin started to speak, then shook his head, and found a spray shooter. He slapped it on the bar, and started to walk away. The halandana's hand shot out and pushed the old man. Thredmartin stumbled to his knees.

I felt the fingers of my hands clawing, clenching. Let them loosen; let them go.

Thredmartin rose slowly to one knee. Bex was up, around the bar, and over to him, steadying his shoulder. The glim watched this for a moment, then took its drug and shooter to a table, where it got itself ready for an injection.

I looked at it closely now. It was female, but that did not mean much in halandana splices. I could see it phase around the edges with dead, gray flames. I clicked in wideband overspace, and I could see through the halandana to the chair it was sitting in and the unpainted wood of the wall behind it. And I saw more, in the spaces between spaces. The halandana was keyed in to a websquad; it wasn't really an individual anymore. Its fate was tied to that of its unit commander. So the war-ghosts—the glims—were a renegade squad, most likely, with a single leader calling the shots. For a moment, the halandana glanced in my direction, maybe feeling my gaze somewhere outside of local time, and I banded down to human normal. It quickly went back to what it was doing. Bex made sure Thredmartin was all right, then came back over to my table.

"We're not even in its timeline," I said. "It doesn't think of us as really being alive."

"Oh God," Bex said. "This is just like before."

I got up and walked out. It was the only solution. I could not say anything to Bex. She would not understand. I understood—not acting was the rational, the *only*, way, but not *my* way. Not until now.

I enhanced my legs and loped along the road to my house. But when I got there, I kept running, running off into the red sands of

Ferro's outback. The night came down, and as the planet turned, I ran along the length of the Big Snake, bright and hard to the southwest, and then under the blue glow of Steiner, when she arose in the moonless, trackless night. I ran for miles and miles, as fast as a jaguar, but never tiring. How could I tire when parts of me stretched off into dimensions of utter stillness, utter rest? Could Bex see me for what I was, she would not see a man, but a kind of colonial creature, a mash of life pressed into the niches and fault lines of existence like so much grit and lichen. A human is anchored with only his heart and his mind; sever those, and he floats away. Floats away. What was I? A medusa fish in an ocean of time? A tight clump of nothing, disguised as a man? Something else?

Something damned hard to kill, that was certain. And so were the glims. When I returned to my house in the star-bright night, I half-expected to find Bex, but she was not there. And so I rattled about for a while, powered down for an hour at dawn and rested on a living-room chair, dreaming in one part of my mind, completely alert in another. The next day, Bex still did not come, and I began to fear something had happened to her. I walked partway into Heidel, then cut off the road and stole around the outskirts, to a mound of shattered, volcanic rocks—the tailings of some early prospector's pit—not far from the town's edge. There I stepped up my vision and hearing, and made a long sweep of Main Street. Nothing. Far, far too quiet, even for Heidel.

I worked out the parabolic to the Bexter Hotel, and after a small adjustment, heard Bex's voice, then her father's. I was too far away to make out the words, but my quantitatives gave it a positive ID. So Bex was all right, at least for the moment. I made my way back home, and put in a good day's work for making whiskey.

The next morning—it was the quarteryear's double dawn, with both suns rising in the east nearly together—Bex came to me. I brought her inside, and in the moted sunlight of my family's living room, where I now took my rest, when I rested, Bex told me that the glims had taken her father.

"He held back some old Midnight Livet down in the cellar, and didn't deliver it when they called for room service." Bex rubbed her left fist with her right fingers, expertly, almost mechanically, as she'd kneaded a thousand balls of bread dough. "How do they know these things? How do they know, Henry?"

"They can see *around* things," I said. "Some of them can, anyway."

"So they read our thoughts? What do we have left?"

"No, no. They can't see in *there,* at least I'm sure they can't see in your old man's McKinnonite nut lump of a brain. But they probably saw the whiskey down in the cellar, all right. A door isn't a very solid thing for a war-ghost out of its own time and place."

Bex gave her hand a final squeeze, spread it out upon her lap. She stared down at the lines of her palm, then looked up at me. "If you won't fight, then you have to tell *me* how to fight them," she said. "I won't let them kill my father."

"Maybe they won't."

"I can't take that chance."

Her eyes were blazing green, as the suns came full through the window. Her face was bright-lit and shadowed, as if by the steady coals of a fire. You have loved this woman a long time, I thought. You have to tell her something that will be of use. But what could possibly be of use against a creature that had survived—*will* survive—that great and final war—and so must survive *now?* You can't kill the future. That's how the old sergeants would explain battle fate to the recruits. If you are meant to be there, they'd say, then nothing can hurt you. And if you're not, then you'll just fade, so you might as well go out fighting.

"You can only irritate them," I finally said to Bex. "There's a way to do it with the Flash. Talk to that technician, what's his name—"

"Jurven Dvorak."

"Tell Dvorak to strobe the local interrupt, fifty, sixty tetracycles. It'll cut off all traffic, but it will be like a wasp nest to them, and they won't want to get close enough to turn it off. Maybe they'll leave. Dvorak better stay near the node after that too."

"All right," Bex said. "Is that all?"

"Yes," I said. I rubbed my temples, felt the vague pain of a headache, which quickly receded as my internals rushed more blood to my scalp. "Yes, that's it."

Later that day, I heard the crackle of random quantum-tunnel spray, as split, unsieved particles decided their spin, charm, and color without guidance from the world of gravity and cause. It was an angry buzz, like the hum of an insect caught between screen and windowpane, tremendously irritating to listen to for hours on end, if you were unlucky enough to be sensitive to the effect. I put up with it, hoping against hope that it would be enough to drive off the glims.

Bex arrived in the early evening, leading her father, who was ragged and half-crazed from two days without light or water. The glims had locked him in a cleaning closet, in the hotel, where he'd sat cramped and doubled over. After the buzz started, Bex opened the lock and dragged the old man out. It was as if the glims had forgotten the whole affair.

"Maybe," I said. "We can hope."

She wanted me to put the old man up at my house, in case the glims suddenly remembered. Old Furly Bexter didn't like the idea. He rattled on about something in McKinnon's "Letter to the Canadians," but I said yes, he could stay. Bex left me with her father in the shrouds of my living room.

Some time that night, the quantum buzz stopped. And in the early morning, I saw them—five of them—stalking along the road, kicking before them the cowering, stumbling form of Jurven Dvorak. I waited for them on the porch. Furly Bexter was asleep in my parents' bedroom. He was exhausted from his ordeal, and I expected him to stay that way for a while.

When they came into the yard, Dvorak ran to the pump and held to the handle, as if it were a branch suspending him over a bottomless chasm. And for him it was. They'd broken his mind and given him a dream of dying. Soon to be replaced by reality, I suspected, and no pump-handle hope of salvation.

Their leader—or the one who did the talking—was human-looking. I'd have to band out to make a full ID, and I didn't want to give anything away for the moment. He saved me the trouble by telling me himself.

"My name's Marek," he said. "Come from a D-line, not far downtime from here."

I nodded, squinting into the red brightness reflected off my hardpan yard.

"We're just here for a good time," the human continued. "What you want to spoil that for?"

I didn't say anything for a moment. One of Marek's gang spat into the dryness of my dirt.

"Go ahead and have it," I said.

"All right," Marek said. He turned to Dvorak, then pulled out a weapon—not really a weapon though, for it is the tool of behind-the-lines enforcers, prison interrogators, confession extractors. It's called an algorithmic truncheon, a *trunch,* in the parlance. A trunch, used at full load, will strip the myelin sheath from axons and dendrites; it will burn up a man's nerves as if they were fuses. It is a way to kill with horrible pain. Marek walked over and touched the trunch to the leg of Dvorak, as if he were lighting a bonfire.

The Flash technician began to shiver, and then to seethe, like a teapot coming to boil. The motion traveled up his legs, into his chest, out his arms. His neck began to writhe, as if the corded muscles were so many snakes. Then Dvorak's brain burned, as a teapot will when all the water has run out and there is nothing but flame against hot metal. And then Dvorak screamed. He screamed for a long, long time. And then he died, crumpled and spent, on the ground in front of my house.

"I don't know you," Marek said, standing over Dvorak's body and looking up at me. "I know *what* you are, but I can't get a read on *who* you are, and that worries me," he said. He kicked at one of the Flash tech's twisted arms. "But now you know *me.*"

"Get off my land," I said. I looked at him without heat. Maybe I felt nothing inside, either. That uncertainty had been my companion for a long time, my grim companion. Marek studied me for a moment. If I kept his attention, he might not look around me, look inside the house, to find his other fun, Furly Bexter, half-dead from Marek's amusements. Marek turned to the others.

"We're going," he said to them. "We've done what we came for." They turned around and left by the road on which they'd come, the only road there was. After a while, I took Dvorak's body to a low hill and dug him a grave there. I set up a sandstone marker, and since I knew Dvorak came from Catholic people, I scratched into the stone the sign of the cross. Jesus, from the Milky Way. Another glim. Hard to kill.

It took old man Bexter only a week or so to fully recover; I should have known by knowing Bex that he was made of a tougher grit. He began to putter around the house, helping me out where he could, although I ran a tidy one-man operation, and he was more in the way than anything. Bex risked a trip out once that week. Her father again insisted he was going back into town, but Bex told him the glims were looking for him. So far, she'd managed to convince them that she had no idea where he'd gotten to.

I was running low on food and supplies, and had to go into town the following Firstday. I picked up a good backpack load at the mercantile and some chemicals for treating the peat at the druggist, then risked a quick look in on Bex. A sign on the desk told all that they could find her at Thredmartin's, taking her lunch, should they want her. I walked across the street, set my load down just inside Thredmartin's door, in the cloakroom, then passed through the entrance into the afternoon dank of the pub.

I immediately sensed glims all around, and hunched myself in, both mentally and physically. I saw Bex in her usual corner, and walked toward her across the room. As I stepped beside a table in the pub's middle, a glim—it was the halandana—stuck out a long, hairy leg. Almost, I tripped—and in that instant, I almost did the natural thing and cast about for some hold that was not present in the three-dimensional world—but I did not. I caught myself, came to a dead stop, then carefully walked around the glim's outstretched leg.

"Mind if I sit down?" I said as I reached Bex's table. She nodded toward a free chair. She was finishing a beer, and an empty glass stood beside it. Thredmartin usually had the tables clear as soon as the last drop left a mug. Bex was drinking fast. Why? Working up her courage, perhaps.

I lowered myself into the chair, and for a long time, neither of us said anything to the other. Bex finished her beer. Thredmartin appeared, looked curiously at the two empty mugs. Bex signaled for another, and I ordered my own whiskey.

"How's the ranch," she finally asked me. Her face was flush and her lips trembled slightly. She was angry, I decided. At me, at the situation. It was understandable. Completely understandable.

"Fine," I said. "The ranch is fine."

"Good."

Again a long silence. Thredmartin returned with our drinks. Bex sighed, and for a moment, I thought she would speak, but she did not. Instead, she reached under the table and touched my hand. I opened my palm, and she put her hand into mine. I felt the tension in her, the bonework of her hand as she squeezed tightly. I felt her fear and worry. I felt her love.

And then Marek came into the pub looking for her. He stalked across the room and stood in front of our table. He looked hard at me, then at Bex, and then he swept an arm across the table and sent Bex's beer and my whiskey flying toward the wall. The beer mug broke, but I quickly reached out and caught my tumbler of scotch in midair without spilling a drop. Of course, no ordinary human could have done it.

Bex noticed Marek looking at me strangely and spoke with a loud voice that got his attention. "What do you want? You were looking for me at the hotel?"

"Your sign says you're open," Marek said in a reasonable, ugly voice. "I rang for room service. Repeatedly."

"Sorry," Bex said. "Just let me settle up and I'll be right there."

"Be right there *now*,'" Marek said, pushing the table from in front of her. Again, I caught my drink, held it on a knee while I remained sitting. Bex started up from her chair and stood facing Marek. She looked him in the eyes. "I'll *be* there directly," she said.

Without warning, Marek reached out and grabbed her by the chin. He didn't seem to be pressing hard, but I knew he must have her in a painful grip. He pulled Bex toward him. Still, she stared him in the eyes. Slowly, I rose from my chair, setting my tumbler of whiskey down on the warm seat where I had been.

Marek glanced over at me. Our eyes met, and at that close distance, he could plainly see the enhancements under my corneas. I could see his.

"Let go of her," I said.

He did not let go of Bex.

"Who the hell are you?" he asked. "That you tell *me* what to do?"

"I'm just a grunt, same as you," I said. "Let go of her."

The halandana had risen from its chair and was soon standing behind Marek. It-she growled mean and low. A combat schematic of how to handle the situation iconed up into the corner of my vision. The halandana was a green figure, Marek was red, Bex was a faded rose. I blinked once to enlarge it. Studied it in a fractional second. Blinked again to close it down. Marek let go of Bex.

She stumbled back, hurt and mad, rubbing her chin.

"I don't think we've got a grunt here," Marek said, perhaps to the halandana, or to himself, but looking at me. "I think we've got us a genuine sky-falling space marine."

The halandana's growl grew deeper and louder, filling ultra and subsonic frequencies.

"How many systems'd you take out, skyfaller?" Marek asked. "A couple of galaxies worth?" The halandana made to advance on me, but Marek put out his hand to stop it. "Where do you get off? This ain't nothing but small potatoes next to what *you've* done."

In that moment, I spread out, stretched a bit in ways that Bex could not see, but that Marek could—to some extent at least. I encompassed him, all of him, and did a thorough ID on both him and the halandana. I ran the data through some trans-d personnel files tucked into a swirl in n-space I'd never expected to access again. Marek Lambrois. Corporal of a back-line military-police platoon assigned to the local cluster in a couple of possible worlds, deserters all in a couple of others. He was aggression enhanced by trans-weblink anti-alg coding. The squad's fighting profile was notched to the top level at all times. They were bastards who were now *preprogrammed* bastards. Marek was right about them being small potatoes. He and his gang were nothing but mean-ass grunts, small-time goons for some of the nonaligned contingency troops.

"What the hell?" Marek said. He noticed my analytics, although it was too fast for him to get a good glimpse of me. But he did understand something in that moment, something it didn't take enhancement to figure out. And in that moment, everything was changed, had I but seen. Had I but seen.

"You're some bigwig, ain't you, skyfaller? Somebody that *matters* to the outcome," Marek said. "This is your actual, and you don't want to fuck yourself up-time, so you won't fight." He smiled crookedly. A diagonal of teeth, straight and narrow, showed whitely.

"Don't count on it," I said.

"You won't," he said, this time with more confidence. "I don't know what I was worrying about! I can do anything I want here."

"Well," I said. "Well." And then I said nothing.

"Get on over there and round me up some grub." Marek said to Bex. "I'll be waiting for it in room forty-five, little lady."

"I'd rather—"

"Do it," I said. The words were harsh and did not sound like my voice. But they were my words, and after a moment, I remembered the voice. It was mine. From far, far in the future. Bex gasped at their hardness, but took a step forward, moved to obey.

"Bex," I said, more softly. "Just get the man some food." I turned to Marek. "If you hurt her, I don't care about anything. Do you understand? Nothing will matter to me."

Marek's smile widened into a grin. He reached over, slowly, so that I could think about it, and patted my cheek. Then he deliberately slapped me, hard. Hard enough to turn my head. Hard enough to draw a trickle of blood from my lip. It didn't hurt very much, of course. Of course it didn't hurt.

"Don't you worry, skyfaller," he said. "I know exactly where I stand now." He turned and left, and the halandana, its drugs unfinished on the table where it had sat, trailed out after him.

Bex looked at me. I tried to meet her gaze, but did not. I did not look down, but stared off into Thredmartin's darkness. She reached over and wiped the blood from my chin with her little finger.

"I guess I'd better go," she said.

I did not reply. She shook her head sadly, and walked in front of me.

I kept my eyes fixed, far away from this place, this time, and her passing was a swirl of air, a red-brown swish of hair, and Bex was gone. Gone.

> *They sucked down my heart*
> *to a little black hole.*
> *You cannot stab me.*

"Colonel Bone, we've done the prelims on sector eleven sixty-eight, and there are fifty-six class-one civilizations along with two-hundred seventy rationals in stage-one or -two development."

"Fifty-six. Two hundred seventy. Ah. Me."

"Colonel, sir, we can evac over half of them within thirty-six hours local."

"And have to defend them in the transcendent. Chaos neutral. Guaranteed forty percent casualties for us."

"Yes, sir. But what about the civs at least. We can save a few."

> *They wrote down my brain*
> *on a hard knot of space.*
> *You cannot turn me.*

"Unacceptable, soldier."

"Sir?"

"Unacceptable."

"Yes, sir."

All dead. All those millions of dead people. But it was the end of time, and they had to die, so that they—so that we *all*, all in time—could live. But they didn't know, those civilizations. Those people. It was the end of time, but you loved life all the same, and you died the same hard way as always. For nothing. It would be for nothing. Outside, the wind had kicked up. The sky was red with Ferro's dust, and a storm was brewing for the evening. I coated my sclera with a hard and glassy membrane, and, unblinking, I stalked home with my supplies through a fierce and growing wind.

That night, on the curtains of dust and thin rain, on the heave of the storm, Bex came to my house. Her clothes were torn and her face was bruised. She said nothing, as I closed the door behind her, led her into the kitchen, and began to treat her wounds. She said nothing as her worried father sat at my kitchen table and watched, and wrung his hands, and watched because there wasn't anything he could do.

"Did that man . . ." her father said. The old man's voice broke. "Did he?"

"I tried to take the thing, the trunch, from him. He'd left it lying on the table by the door." Bex spoke in a hollow voice. "I thought that nobody was going to do anything, not even Henry, so I had to. I had to." Her facial bruises were superficial. But she held her legs stiffly together, and clasped her hands to her stomach. There was vomit on her dress. "The trunch had some kind of alarm set on it," Bex said. "So he caught me."

"Bex, are you hurting?" I said to her. She looked down, then carefully spread her legs. "He caught me and then he used the trunch on me. Not full strength. Said he didn't want to do permanent damage. Said he wanted to save me for later." Her voice sounded far away. She covered her face with her hands. "He put it in me," she said.

Then she breathed deeply, raggedly, and made herself look at me. "Well," she said. "So."

I put her into my bed, and her father sat in the chair beside it, standing watch for who knew what? He could not defend his daughter, but he must try, as surely as the suns rose, now growing farther apart, over the hard pack of my homeworld desert.

Everything was changed.

"Bex," I said to her, and touched her forehead. Touched her fine, brown skin. "Bex, in the future, we won. I won, my command won it. Really, really big. That's why we're here. That's why we're all here."

Bex's eyes were closed. I could not tell if she'd already fallen asleep. I hoped she had.

"I have to take care of some business, and then I'll do it again," I said in a whisper. "I'll just have to go back up-time and do it again."

Between the first and second rising, I'd reached Heidel, and as Hemingway burned red through the storm's dusty leavings, I stood in the shadows of the entrance foyer of the Bexter Hotel. There I waited.

The halandana was the first up—like me, they never really slept—and it came down from its room looking, no doubt, to go out and get another rubber of its drug. Instead, it found me. I didn't waste time with the creature. With a quick twist in n-space, I pulled it down to the present, down to a local concentration of hate and lust and stupidity that I could kill with a quick thrust into its throat. But I let it live; I showed it myself, all of me spread out and huge, and I let it fear.

"Go and get Marek Lambrois," I told it. "Tell him Colonel Bone wants to see him. Colonel Henry Bone of the Eighth Sky and Light."

"Bone," said the halandana. "I thought—"

I reached out and grabbed the creature's long neck. This was the halandana weak point, and this halandana had a ceramic implant as protection. I clicked up the power in my forearm a level and crushed the collar as I might a tea cup. The halandana's neck carapace shattered to platelets and shards, outlined in fine cracks under its skin.

"Don't think," I said. "Tell Marek Lambrois to come into the street and I will let him live."

This was untrue, of course, but hope never dies, I'd discovered, even in the hardest of soldiers. But perhaps I'd underestimated Marek. Sometimes I still wonder.

He stumbled out, still partly asleep, onto the street. Last night had evidently been a hard and long one. His eyes were a red no detox nano could fully clean up. His skin was the color of paste.

"You have something on me," I said. "I cannot abide that."

"Colonel Bone," he began. "If I'd knowed it was *you*—"

"Too late for that."

"It's never too late, that's what you taught us all when you turned that offensive around out on the Husk and gave the Chaos the what-for. I'll just be going. I'll take the gang with me. It's to no purpose, our staying now."

"You knew enough *yesterday*—enough to leave." I felt the rage, the old rage that was to be, once again. "Why did you do that to her?" I asked. "Why did you—"

And then I looked into his eyes and saw it there. The quiet

desire—beaten down by synthesized emotions, but now triumphant, sadly triumphant. The desire to finally, finally *die*. Marek was not the unthinking brute I'd taken him for after all. Too bad for him.

I took a step toward Marek. His instincts made him reach down, go for the trunch. But it was a useless weapon on me. I don't have myelin sheaths on my nerves. I don't have nerves anymore; I have *wiring*. Marek realized this was so almost instantly. He dropped the trunch, then turned and ran. I caught him. He tried to fight, but there was never any question of him beating me. That would be absurd. I'm Colonel Bone of the Sky-Falling 8th. I kill so that there might be life. *Nobody* beats me. It is my fate, and yours too.

I caught him by the shoulder, and I looped my other arm around his neck and reined him to me—not enough to snap anything. Just enough to calm him down. He was strong, but had no finesse.

Like I said, glims are hard to kill. They're the same as snails in shells in a way, and the trick is to draw them out—way out. Which is what I did with Marek. As I held him physically, I caught hold of him, all of him, *over there*, in the place I can't tell you about, can't describe. The way you do this is by holding a glim still and causing him great suffering, so that they can't withdraw into the deep places. That's what vampire stakes and Roman crosses are all about.

And, like I told Bex, glims are bad ones, all right. Bad, but not the worst. *I* am the worst.

> *Icicle spike*
> *from the eye of a star.*
> *I've come to kill you.*

I sharpened my nails. Then I plunged them into Marek's stomach, through the skin, into the twist of his guts. I reached around there and caught hold of something, a piece of intestine. I pulled it out. This I tied to the porch of the Bexter Hotel.

Marek tried to untie himself and pull away. He was staring at his insides, rolled out, raw and exposed, and thinking—I don't know what. I haven't died. I don't know what it is like to die. He moaned sickly. His hands fumbled uselessly in the grease and phlegm that coated his very own self. There was no undoing the knots I'd tied, no pushing himself back in.

I picked him up, and as he whimpered, I walked down the street with him. His guts trailed out behind us, like a pink ribbon. After I'd gotten about twenty feet, I figured this was all he had in him. I dropped him into the street.

Hemingway was in the northeast and Fitzgerald directly east. They both shone at different angles on Marek's crumple, and cast crazy, mazy shadows down the length of the street.

"Colonel Bone," he said. I was tired of his talking. "Colonel—"

I reached into his mouth, past his gnashing teeth, and pulled out his tongue. He reached for it as I extracted it, so I handed it to him. Blood and drool flowed from his mouth and colored the red ground even redder about him. Then, one by one, I broke his arms and legs, then I broke each of the vertebrae in his backbone, moving up his spinal column with quick pinches. It didn't take long.

This is what I did in the world that people can see. In the twists of other times and spaces, I did similar things, horrible, irrevocable things, to the man. I killed him. I killed him in such a way that he would never come to life again, not in any possible place, not in any possible time. I wiped Marek Lambrois from existence. Thoroughly. And with his death the other glims died, like lights going out, lights ceasing to exist, bulb, filament and all. Or like the quick loss of all sensation after a brain is snuffed out. Irrevocably gone from this timeline, and that was what mattered. Keeping this possible future uncertain, balanced on the fulcrum of chaos and necessity. Keeping it *free,* so that I could go back and do my work.

I left Marek lying there, in the main street of Heidel. Others could do the mopping up; that wasn't my job. As I left town, on the way back to my house and my life there, I saw that I wasn't alone in the dawn-lit town. Some had business out at this hour, and they had watched. Others had heard the commotion and come to windows and porches to see what it was. Now they knew. They knew what I was, what I was to be. I walked alone down the road, and found Bex and her father both sound asleep in my room.

I stroked her fine hair. She groaned, turned in her sleep. I pulled my covers up to her chin. Forty years old, and as beautiful as a child. Safe in my bed. Bex. Bex. I will miss you. Always, always, Bex.

I went to the living room, to the shroud-covered furniture. I sat down in what had been my father's chair. I sipped a cup of my father's best barley-malt whiskey. I sat, and as the suns of Ferro rose in the hard-iron sky, I faded into the distant, dying future.

Six Months, Three Days

INTRODUCTION

He had the ability to see the future and was certain that they would be together for six months and three days, then would part. She had a similar ability, but could see several alternate futures at once, and was anything but certain that they had to part at all. Who would be right? This story won the 2012 Hugo for best short story, was nominated for the Nebula and Theodore Sturgeon Awards, and is under development for NBC television.

* * *

Charlie Jane Anders writes about science fiction for io9.com, and you can find her work in the *McSweeney's Joke Book of Book Jokes, Best Science Fiction of the Year 2009, Sex for America*, and other anthologies. Anders has also contributed to *Mother Jones*, the *Wall Street Journal*, the *San Francisco Chronicle, ZYZZYVA, Pindeldyboz, Strange Horizons*,Tor.com, *The Magazine of Fantasy and Science Fiction, Asimov's Science Fiction Magazine, Lightspeed* and many other publications. She organizes the Writers With Drinks reading series and with Annalee Newitz, she co-edited the anthology *She's Such a Geek* and published an indy magazine called *other* (*a "magazine of pop culture and politics for the new outcasts"*). She wrote a novel called *Choir Boy*, which won a Lambda Literary Award and was a finalist for the Edmund White Award. As a contestant on *To Tell the Truth*, she won $1,000. She has recently sold two novels to Tor, one of them scheduled for early 2016 publication, and has also completed a fantasy novel, and the only question I have is, how did she find the time to write them?

Six Months, Three Days

by Charlie Jane Anders

Judy is nervous but excited, keeps looking at things she's spotted out of the corner of her eye. She's wearing a floral Laura Ashley-style dress with an ankh necklace and her legs are rambunctious, her calves moving under the table. It's distracting because Doug knows that in two and a half weeks, those cucumber-smooth ankles will be hooked on his shoulders, and that curly reddish-brown hair will spill everywhere onto her lemon-floral pillows; this image of their future coitus has been in Doug's head for years, with varying degrees of clarity, and now it's almost here. The knowledge makes Doug almost giggle at the wrong moment, but then it hits him: she's seen this future too—or she may have, anyway.

Doug has his sandy hair cut in a neat fringe that was almost fashionable a couple years ago. You might think he cuts his own hair, but Judy knows he doesn't, because he'll tell her otherwise in a few weeks. He's much, much better looking than she thought he would be, and this comes as a huge relief. He has rude, pouty lips and an upper lip that darkens no matter how often he shaves it, with Elvis Costello glasses. And he's almost a foot taller than her, six foot four. Now that Judy's seen Doug for real, she's re-imagining all the conversations they might be having in the coming weeks and months, all of the drama and all of the sweetness. The fact that Judy can be attracted to him, knowing everything that could lie ahead, consoles her tremendously.

Judy is nattering about some Chinese novelist she's been reading in translation, one of those cruel satirists from the days after the May Fourth Movement, from back when writers were so conflicted they had to rename themselves things like "Contra Diction." Doug is just staring at her, not saying anything, until it creeps her out a little.

"What?" Doug says at last, because Judy has stopped talking and they're both just staring at each other.

"You were staring at me," Judy says.

"I was . . ." Doug hesitates, then just comes out and says it. "I was savoring the moment. You know, you can know something's coming from a long way off, you know for years ahead of time the exact day and the very hour when it'll arrive. And then it arrives, and when it arrives, all you can think about is how soon it'll be gone."

"Well, I didn't know the hour and the day when you and I would meet," Judy puts a hand on his. "I saw many different hours and days. In one timeline, we would have met two years ago. In another, we'd meet a few months from now. There are plenty of timelines where we never meet at all."

Doug laughs, then waves a hand to show that he's not laughing at her, although the gesture doesn't really clarify whom or what he's actually laughing at.

Judy is drinking a cocktail called the Coalminer's Daughter, made out of ten kinds of darkness. It overwhelms her senses with sugary pungency, and leaves her lips black for a moment. Doug is drinking a wheaty Pilsner from a tapered glass, in gulps. After one of them, Doug cuts to the chase. "So this is the part where I ask. I mean, I know what happens next between you and me. But here's where I ask what you think happens next."

"Well," Judy says. "There are a million tracks, you know. It's like raindrops falling into a cistern, they're separate until they hit the surface, and then they become the past: all undifferentiated. But there are an awful lot of futures where you and I date for about six months."

"Six months and three days," Doug says. "Not that I've counted or anything."

"And it ends badly."

"I break my leg."

"You break your leg ruining my bicycle. I like that bike. It's a noble five-speed in a sea of fixies."

"So you agree with me." Doug has been leaning forward, staring at Judy like a psycho again. He leans back so that the amber light spilling out of the Radish Saloon's tiny lampshades turns him the same color as his beer. "You see the same future I do." Like she's passed some kind of test.

"You didn't know what I was going to say in advance?" Judy says.

"It doesn't work like that—not for me, anyway. Remembering the future is just like remembering the past. I don't have perfect recall, I don't hang on to every detail, the transition from short-term memory to long-term memory is not always graceful."

"I guess it's like memory for me too," Judy says.

Doug feels an unfamiliar sensation, and he realizes after a while it's comfort. He's never felt this at home with another human being, especially after such a short time. Doug is accustomed to meeting people and knowing bits and pieces of their futures, from stuff he'll learn later. Or if Doug meets you and doesn't know anything about your future, that means he'll never give a crap about you, at any point down the line. This makes for awkward social interactions, either way.

They get another round of drinks. Doug gets the same beer again, Judy gets a red concoction called a Bloody Mutiny.

"So there's one thing I don't get," Doug says. "You believe you have a choice among futures—and I think you're wrong, you're seeing one true future and a bunch of false ones."

"You're probably going to spend the next six months trying to convince yourself of that," Judy says.

"So why are you dating me at all, if you get to choose? You know how it'll turn out. For that matter, why aren't you rich and famous? Why not pick a future where you win the lottery, or become a star?"

Doug works in tech support, in a poorly ventilated sub-basement of a tech company in Providence, RI, that he knows will go out of business in a couple years. He will work there until the company fails, choking on the fumes from old computers, and then be unemployed a few months.

"Well," Judy says. "It's not really that simple. I mean, the next six months, assuming I don't change my mind, they contain some of the happiest moments of my life, and I see it leading to some good things, later on. And you know, I've seen some tracks where I get rich, I become a public figure, and they never end well. I've got my eye on this one future, this one node way off in the distance, where I die aged 97, surrounded by lovers and grandchildren and cats. Whenever I have a big decision to make, I try to see the straightest path to that moment."

"So I'm a stepping stone," Doug says, not at all bitterly. He's somehow finished his second beer already, even though Judy's barely made a dent in her Bloody Mutiny.

"You're maybe going to take this journey with me for a spell," Judy says. "People aren't stones."

And then Doug has to catch the last train back to Providence, and Judy has to bike home to Somerville. Marva, her roommate, has made popcorn and hot chocolate, and wants to know the whole story.

"It was nice," Judy says. "He was a lot cuter in person than I'd remembered, which is really nice. He's tall."

"That's it?" Marva said. "Oh come on, details. You finally meet the only other freaking clairvoyant on Earth, your future boyfriend, and all you have to say is, 'He's tall.' Uh uh. You are going to spill like a fucking oil tanker, I will ply you with hot chocolate, I may resort to Jim Beam, even."

Marva's "real" name is Martha, but she changed it years ago. She's a grad student studying 18th century lit, and even Judy can't help her decide whether to finish her PhD. She's slightly chubby, with perfect crimson hair and clothing by Sanrio, Torrid and Hot Topic. She is fond of calling herself "mallternative."

"I'm drunk enough already. I nearly fell off my bicycle a couple times," Judy says.

The living room is a pigsty, so they sit in Judy's room, which isn't much better. Judy hoards items she might need in one of the futures she's witnessed, and they cover every surface. There's a plastic replica of a Filipino fast food mascot, Jollibee, which she might give to this one girl Sukey in a couple of years, completing Sukey's collection and making her a friend for life—or Judy and Sukey may never meet at all. A phalanx of stuffed animals crowds Judy and Marva on the big fluffy bed. The room smells like a sachet of whoop-ass (cardamom, cinnamon, lavender) that Judy opened up earlier.

"He's a really sweet guy." Judy cannot stop talking in platitudes, which bothers her. "I mean, he's really lost, but he manages to be brave. I can't imagine what it would be like, to feel like you have no free will at all."

Marva doesn't point out the obvious thing—that Judy only sees choices for herself, not anybody else. Suppose a guy named Rocky asks Marva out on a date, and Judy sees a future in which Marva complains, afterwards, that their date was the worst evening of her life. In that case, there are two futures: One in which Judy tells Marva what she sees, and one in which she doesn't. Marva will go on the miserable date with Rocky, unless Judy tells her what she knows. (On the plus side, in fifteen months, Judy will drag Marva out to a party where she meets the love of her life. So there's that.)

"Doug's right," Marva says. "I mean, if you really have a choice about this, you shouldn't go through with it. You know it's going to be a disaster, in the end. You're the one person on Earth who can avoid the pain, and you still go sticking fingers in the socket."

"Yeah, but . . ." Judy decides this will go a lot easier if there are marshmallows in the cocoa, and runs back to the kitchen alcove. "But going out with this guy leads to good things later on. And there's a realization that I come to as a result of getting my heart broken. I come to understand something."

"And what's that?"

Judy finds the bag of marshmallows. They are stale. She decides cocoa will revitalize them, drags them back to her bedroom, along with a glass of water.

"I have no idea, honestly. That's the way with epiphanies: You can't know in advance what they'll be. Even me. I can see them coming, but I can't understand something until I understand it."

"So you're saying that the future that Doug believes is the only possible future just happens to be the best of all worlds. Is this some Leibniz shit? Does Dougie always automatically see the nicest future or something?"

"I don't think so." Judy gets gummed up by popcorn, marshmallows and sticky cocoa, and coughs her lungs out. She swigs the glass of water she brought for just this moment. "I mean—" She coughs again, and downs the rest of the water. "I mean, in Doug's version, he's only forty-three when he dies, and he's pretty broken by then. His last few years are dreadful. He tells me all about it in a few weeks."

"Wow," Marva says. "Damn. So are you going to try and save him? Is that what's going on here?"

"I honestly do not know. I'll keep you posted."

Doug, meanwhile, is sitting on his militarily neat bed, with its single hospital-cornered blanket and pillow. His apartment is almost pathologically tidy. Doug stares at his one shelf of books and his handful of carefully chosen items that play a role in his future. He chews his thumb. For the first time in years, Doug desperately wishes he had options.

He almost grabs his phone, to call Judy and tell her to get the hell away from him, because he will collapse all of her branching pathways into a dark tunnel, once and for all. But he knows he won't tell her that, and even if he did, she wouldn't listen. He doesn't love her, but he knows he will in a couple weeks, and it already hurts.

"God damnit! Fucking god fucking damn it fuck!" Doug throws his favorite porcelain bust of Wonder Woman on the floor and it shatters. Wonder Woman's head breaks into two jagged pieces, cleaving her magic tiara in half. This image, of the Amazon's raggedly bisected head, has always been in Doug's mind, whenever he's looked at the intact bust.

Doug sits a minute, dry-sobbing. Then he goes and gets his dustpan and brush.

He phones Judy a few days later. "Hey, so do you want to hang out again on Friday?"

"Sure," Judy says. "I can come down to Providence this time. Where do you want to meet up?"

"Surprise me," says Doug.

"You're a funny man."

Judy will be the second long-term relationship of Doug's life. His first was with Pamela, an artist he met in college, who made headless figurines of people who were recognizable from the neck down. (Headless Superman. Headless Captain Kirk. And yes, headless Wonder Woman, which Doug always found bitterly amusing for reasons he couldn't explain.) They were together nearly five years, and Doug never told her his secret. Which meant a lot of pretending to be surprised at stuff. Doug is used to people thinking he's kind of a weirdo.

Doug and Judy meet for dinner at one of those mom-and-pop Portuguese places in East Providence, sharing grilled squid and seared cod, with fragrant rice, with a bottle of heady vinho verde. Then they walk Judy's bike back across the river towards the kinda-sorta gay bar on Wickenden Street. "The thing I like about Providence," says Doug, "is it's one of the American cities that knows its best days are behind it. So it's automatically decadent, and sort of European."

"Well," says Judy, "It's always a choice between urban decay or gentrification, right? I mean, cities aren't capable of homeostasis."

"Do you know what I'm thinking?" Doug is thinking he wants to kiss Judy. She leans up and kisses him first, on the bridge in the middle of the East Bay Bicycle Path. They stand and watch the freeway lights reflected on the water, holding hands. Everything is cold and lovely and the air smells rich.

Doug turns and looks into Judy's face, which the bridge lights have turned yellow. "I've been waiting for this moment all my life." Doug realizes he's inadvertently quoted Phil Collins. First he's mortified, then he starts laughing like a maniac. For the next half hour, Doug and Judy speak only in Phil Collins quotes.

"You can't hurry love," Judy says, which is only technically a Collins line.

Over microbrews on Wickenden, they swap origin stories, even though they already know most of it. Judy's is pretty simple: She was a little kid who overthought choices like which summer camp to go to, until she realized she could see how either decision would turn out. She still flinches when she remembers how she almost gave a valentine in third grade to Dick Petersen, who would have destroyed her. Doug's story is a lot worse: he started seeing the steps ahead, a little at a time, and then he realized his dad would die in about a year. He tried everything he could think of, for a whole year, to save his dad's life. He even buried the car keys two feet deep, on the day of his dad's accident. No fucking use.

"Turns out getting to mourn in advance doesn't make the mourning afterwards any less hard," Doug says through a beer glass snout.

"Oh man," Judy says. She knew this stuff, but hearing it is different. "I'm so sorry."

"It's okay," Doug says. "It was a long time ago."

Soon it's almost time for Judy to bike back to the train station, near that godawful giant mall and the canal where they light the water on fire sometimes.

"I want you to try and do something for me," Judy takes Doug's hands. "Can you try to break out of the script? Not the big stuff that you think is going to happen, but just little things that you couldn't be sure about in advance if you tried. Try to surprise yourself. And maybe all those little deviations will add up to something bigger."

"I don't think it would make any difference," Doug says.

"You never know," Judy says. "There are things that I remember differently every time I think about them. Things from the past, I mean. When I was in college, I went through a phase of hating my parents, and I remembered all this stuff they did, from my childhood, as borderline abusive. And then a few years ago, I found myself recalling those same incidents again, only now they seemed totally different. Barely the same events."

"The brain is weird," Doug says.

"So you never know," Judy says. "Change the details, you may change the big picture." But she already knows nothing will come of this.

A week later, Doug and Judy lay together in her bed, after having sex for the first time. It was even better than the image Doug's carried in his head since puberty. For the first time, Doug understands why people talk about sex as this transcendent thing, chains of selfhood melting away, endless abundance. They looked into each other's eyes the whole time. As for Judy, she's having that oxytocin thing she's always thought was a myth, her forehead resting on Doug's smooth chest—if she moved her head an inch she'd hear his heart beating, but she doesn't need to.

Judy gets up to pee an hour later, and when she comes back and hangs up her robe, Doug is lying there with a look of horror on his face. "What's wrong?" She doesn't want to ask, but she does anyway.

"I'm sorry." He sits up. "I'm just so happy, and . . . I can count the awesome moments in my life on a hand and a half. And I'm burning through them too fast. This is just so perfect right now. And, you know. I'm trying not to think. About."

Judy knows that if she brings up the topic they've been avoiding, they will have an unpleasant conversation. But she has to. "You have to stop this. It's obvious you can do what I do, you can see more than one branch. All you have to do is try. I know you were hurt when you were little, your dad died, and you convinced yourself that you were helpless. I'm sorry about that. But now, I feel like you're actually comfortable being trapped. You don't even try any more."

"I do," Doug is shaking. "I do try. I try every day. How dare you say I don't try."

"You don't really. I don't believe you. I'm sorry, but I don't."

"You know it's true." Doug calms down and looks Judy square in the face. Without his glasses, his eyes look as gray as the sea on a cloudy day. "The thing you told me about Marva—you always know what she's going to do. Yeah? That's how your power works. The only reason you can predict how your own choices will turn out, is because other people's actions are fixed. If you go up to some random guy on the street and slap him, you can know in advance exactly how he'll react. Right?"

"Well sure," Judy says. "I mean, that doesn't mean Marva doesn't have free will. Or this person I've hypothetically slapped." This is too weird a conversation to be having naked. She goes and puts on a Mountain Goats T-shirt and PJ bottoms. "Their choices are just factored in, in advance."

"Right." Doug's point is already made, but he goes ahead and lunges for the kill. "So how do you know that I can't predict your choices, exactly the same way you can predict Marva's?"

Judy sits down on the edge of the bed. She kneads the edge of her T-shirt and doesn't look at Doug. Now she knows why Doug looked so sick when she came back from the bathroom. He saw more of this conversation than she did. "You could be right," she says after a moment. "If you're right, that makes you the one person I should never be in the same room with. I should stay the hell away from you."

"Yeah. You should," Doug says. He knows it will take forty-seven seconds before she cradles his head and kisses his forehead, and it feels like forever. He holds his breath and counts down.

A couple days later, Judy calls in sick at the arts nonprofit where she works, and wanders Davis Square until she winds up in the back of the Diesel Café, in one of the plush leather booths near the pool tables. She eats one of those mint brownies that's like chocolate-covered toothpaste and drinks a lime rickey, until she feels pleasantly ill. She pulls a battered, scotch-taped World Atlas out of her satchel.

She's still leafing through it a couple hours later when Marva comes and sits down opposite her.

"How did you know I was here?" Judy asks.

"Because you're utterly predictable. You said you were ditching work, and this is where you come to brood."

Judy's been single-handedly keeping the Blaze Foundation afloat for years, thanks to an uncanny knack for knowing exactly which grants to apply for and when, and what language to use on the grant proposal. She has a nearly 100 percent success rate in proposal-writing, leavened only by the fact that she occasionally applies for grants she knows she won't get. So maybe she's entitled to a sick day every now and then.

Marva sees that Judy's playing the Travel Game and joins in. She points to a spot near Madrid. "Spain," she says.

Judy's face gets all tight for a moment, like she's trying to remember where she left something. Then she smiles. "Okay, if I get on a plane to Madrid tomorrow, there are a few ways it plays out. That I can see right now. In one, I get drunk and fall off a tower and break both legs. In another, I meet this cute guy named Pedro and we have a torrid three-day affair. Then there's the one where I go to art school and study sculpture. They all end with me running out of money and coming back home."

"Malawi," Marva says. Judy thinks for a moment, then remembers what happens if she goes to Malawi tomorrow.

"This isn't as much fun as usual," Marva says after they've gone to Vancouver and Paris and Sao Paolo. "Your heart isn't in it."

"It's not," Judy says. "I just can't see a happy future where I don't date Doug. I mean, I like Doug, I may even be in love with him already, but . . . we're going to break each other's hearts, and more than that: We're maybe going to break each other's *spirits*. There's got to be a detour, a way to avoid this, but I just can't see it right now."

Marva dumps a glass of water on Judy's head.

"Wha? You—Wha?" She splutters like a cartoon duck.

"Didn't see that coming, did you?"

"No, but that doesn't mean . . . I mean, I'm not freaking omniscient, I sometimes miss bits and pieces, you know that."

"I am going to give you the Samuel Johnson/Bishop Berkeley lecture, for like the tenth time," Marva says. "Because sometimes, a girl just needs a little Johnson."

Bishop George Berkeley, of course, was the "if a tree falls in the forest and nobody hears it, does it make a sound" guy, who argued that objects only exist in our perceptions. One day, Boswell asked Samuel Johnson what he thought of Berkeley's idea. According to Boswell, Johnson's response to this was to kick a big rock "with mighty force," saying, "I refute it thus."

"The point," says Marva, "is that nobody can see everything. Not you, not Doug, not Bishop Berkeley. Stuff exists that your senses can't perceive and your mind can't comprehend. Even if you do have an extra sense the rest of us don't have. Okay? So don't get all doom and gloom on me. Just remember: Would Samuel Johnson have let himself feel trapped in a dead-end relationship?"

"Well, considering he apparently dated a guy named Boswell who went around writing down everything he said . . . I really don't know." Judy runs to the bathroom to put her head under the hot-air dryer.

The next few weeks, Judy and Doug hang out at least every other day and grow accustomed to kissing and holding hands all the time, trading novelty for the delight of positive reinforcement. They're at the point where their cardiovascular systems crank into top gear if one of them sees someone on the street who even looks, for a second, like the other. Doug notices little things about Judy that catch him off guard, like the way she rolls her eyes slightly before she's about to say something solemn. Judy realizes that Doug's joking on some level, most of the time, even when he seems tragic. Maybe especially then.

They fly a big dragon kite on Cambridge Common, with a crimson tail. They go to the Isabella Stewart Gardner, and sip tea in the courtyard. Once or twice, Doug is about to turn left, but Judy stops him, because something way cooler will happen if they go right instead. They discuss which kind of skylight Batman prefers to burst through when he breaks into criminals' lairs, and whether Batman ever uses the chimney like Santa Claus. They break down the taxonomy of novels where Emily Dickinson solves murder mysteries.

Marva gets used to eating Doug's spicy omelettes, which automatically make him Judy's best-ever boyfriend in Marva's book. Marva walks out of her bedroom in the mornings, to see Doug wearing the bathrobe Judy got for him, flipping a perfect yellow slug over and over, and she's like, What *are* you? To Marva, the main advantage of making an omelette is that when it falls apart halfway through, you can always claim you planned to make a scramble all along.

Judy and Doug enjoy a couple months of relative bliss, based on not ever discussing the future. In the back of her mind, Judy never stops looking for the break point, the moment where a timeline splits off from the one Doug believes in. It could be just a split-second.

They reach their three-month anniversary, roughly the midpoint of their relationship. To celebrate, they take a weekend trip to New

York together, and they wander down Broadway and all around the Village and Soho. Doug is all excited, showing off for once—he points out the fancy restaurant where the President will be assassinated in 2027, and the courthouse where Lady Gaga gets arrested for civil disobedience right after she wins the Nobel Peace Prize. Judy has to keep shushing him. Then she gives in, and the two of them loudly debate whether the election of 2024 will be rigged, not caring if people stare.

Once they've broken the taboo on talking about the future in general, Doug suddenly feels free to talk about their future, specifically. They're having a romantic dinner at one of those restaurant/bars, with high-end American food and weird pseudo-Soviet iconography everywhere. Doug is on his second beer when he says, "So, I guess in a couple of weeks, you and I have that ginormous fight about whether I should meet your parents. And about a week after that, I manage to offend Marva. Honestly, without meaning to. But then again, in a month and a half's time, we have that really nice day together on the boat."

"Please don't," Judy says, but she already knows it's too late to stop it.

"And then after that, there's the Conversation. I am not looking forward to the Conversation."

"We both know about this stuff," Judy says. "It'll happen if and when it happens, why worry about it until then?"

"Sorry, it's just part of how I deal with things. It helps me to brace myself."

Judy barely eats her entrée. Doug keeps oversharing about their next few months, like a floodgate has broken. Some of it's stuff Judy either didn't remember, or has blotted out of her mind because it's so dismal. She can tell Doug's been obsessing about every moment of the coming drama, visualizing every incident until it snaps into perfect focus.

By the time Judy gets up and walks away from the table, she sees it all just as clearly as he does. She can't even imagine any future, other than the one he's described. Doug's won.

Judy roams Bleecker and St. Mark's Place, until she claims a small victory: She realizes that if she goes into this one little subterranean bar, she'll run into a cute guy she hasn't seen since high school, and they'll have a conversation in which he confesses that he always had a crush on her back then. Because Doug's not there, he's not able to tell her whether she goes into that bar or not. She does, and she's late getting back to their hotel, even though she and cute high-school guy don't do anything but talk.

Doug makes an effort to be nice the rest of the weekend, even though he knows it won't do him any good, except that Judy holds hands with him on the train back to Providence and Boston.

And then Doug mentions, in passing, that he'll see Judy around, after they break up—including two meetings a decade from now, and one time a full 15 years hence, and he knows some stuff. He starts to say more, but Judy runs to the dining car, covering her ears.

When the train reaches Doug's stop and he's gathering up his stuff, Judy touches his shoulder. "Listen, I don't know if you and I actually do meet up in a decade, it's a blur to me right now. But I don't want to hear whatever you think you know. Okay?" Doug nods.

When the fight over whether Doug should meet Judy's parents arrives, it's sort of a meta-fight. Judy doesn't see why Doug should do the big parental visit, since Judy and Doug are scheduled to break up in ten weeks. Doug just wants to meet them because he wants to meet them—maybe because his own parents are dead. And he's curious about these people who are aware that their daughter can see the future(s). They compromise, as expected: Doug meets Judy's parents over lunch when they visit, and he's on his best behavior.

They take a ferry out to sea, toward Block Island. The air is too cold and they feel seasick and the sun blinds them, and it's one of the greatest days of their lives. They huddle together on deck and when they can see past the glare and the sea spray and they're not almost hurling, they see the glimmer of the ocean, streaks of white and blue and yellow in different places, as the light and wind affect it. The ocean feels utterly forgiving, like you can dump almost anything into the ocean's body and it will still love us, and Judy and Doug cling to each other like children in a storm cellar and watch the waves. Then they go to Newport and eat amazing lobster. For a few days before and a few days after this trip, they are all aglow and neither of them can do any wrong.

A week or so after the boat thing, they hold hands in bed, nestling like they could almost start having sex at any moment. Judy looks in Doug's naked eyes (his glasses are on the nightstand) and says, "Let's just jump off the train now, okay? Let's not do any of the rest of it, let's just be good to each other forever. Why not? We could."

"Why would you want that?" Doug drawls like he's half asleep. "You're the one who's going to get the life she wants. I'm the one who'll be left like wreckage." Judy rolls over and pretends to sleep.

The Conversation achieves mythical status long before it arrives. Certain aspects of The Conversation are hazy in advance, for both Doug and Judy, because of that thing where you can't understand something until you understand it.

The day of the Conversation, Judy wakes from a nightmare, shivering with the covers cast aside, and Doug's already out of bed. "It's today," he says, and then he leaves without saying anything else to Judy, or anything at all to Marva, who's still pissed at him. Judy keeps almost going back to bed, but somehow she winds up dressed, with a toaster pop in her hand, marching towards the door. Marva starts to say something, then shrugs.

Doug and Judy meet up for dinner at Punjabi Dhaba in Inman Square, scooping red-hot eggplant and bright chutney off of metal prison trays while Bollywood movies blare overhead and just outside of their line of vision.

The Conversation starts with them talking past each other. Judy says, "Lately I can't remember anything past the next month." Doug says, "I keep trying to see what happens after I die." Judy says, "Normally I can remember years in advance, even decades. But I'm blocked." She shudders. Doug says, "If I could just have an impression, an afterimage, of what happens when I'm gone. It would help a lot."

Judy finally hears what Doug's been saying. "Oh Jesus, not this. Nobody can see past death. It's impossible."

"So's seeing the future." Doug cracks his samosa in half with a fork, and offers the chunky side to Judy.

"You can't remember anything past when your brain ceases to exist. Because there are no physical memories to access. Your brain is a storage medium."

"But who knows what we're accessing? It could be something outside our own brains."

Judy tries to clear her head and think of something nice twenty years from now, but she can't. She looks at Doug's chunky sideburns, which he didn't have when they'd started dating. Whenever she's imagined those sideburns, she always associated them with the horror of these days. It's sweltering inside the restaurant. "Why are you scared of me?" she says.

"I'm not," Doug says. "I only want you to be happy. When I see you ten years from now, I—"

Judy covers her ears and jumps out of her seat, to turn the Bollywood music all the way up. Standing, she can see the screen, where a triangle of dancing women shake their fingers in unison at an unshaven man. The man smiles.

Eventually, someone comes and turns the music back down. "I think part of you is scared that I really am more powerful than you are," Judy says. "And you've done everything you can to take away my power."

"I don't think you're any more or less powerful than me. Our powers are just different," Doug says. "But I think you're a selfish person. I think you're used to the idea that you can cheat on everything, and it's made your soul a little bit rotten. I think you're going to hate me for the next few weeks until you figure out how to cast me out. I think I love you more than my own arms and legs and I would shorten my already short life by a decade to have you stick around one more year. I think you're brave as hell for keeping your head up on our journey together into the mouth of hell. I think you're the most beautiful human being I've ever met, and you have a good heart despite how much you're going to tear me to shreds."

"I don't want to see you any more," Judy says. Her hair is all in her face, wet and ragged from the restaurant's blast-furnace heat.

A few days later, Judy and Doug are playing foozball at a swanky bar in what used to be the Combat Zone. Judy makes a mean remark about something sexually humiliating that will happen to Doug five years from now, which he told her about in a moment of weakness. A couple days later, she needles him about an incident at work that almost got him fired a while back. She's never been a sadist before now—although it's also masochism, because when she torments him, she already knows how terrible she'll feel in a few minutes.

Another time, Doug and Judy are drunk on the second floor of a Thayer Street frat bar, and Doug keeps getting Judy one more weird cocktail, even though she's had more than enough. The retro pinball machine gossips at them. Judy staggers to the bathroom, leaving her purse with Doug—and when she gets back, the purse is gone. They both knew Doug was going to lose Judy's purse, which only makes her madder. She bitches him out in front of a table of beer-pong champions. And then it's too late to get back to Judy's place, so they have to share Doug's cramped, sagging hospital cot. Judy throws up on Doug's favorite outfit: anise and stomach acid, it'll never come out.

Judy loses track of which unbearable things have already happened, and which lay ahead. Has Doug insulted her parents yet, on their second meeting? Yes, that was yesterday. Has he made Marva cry? No, that's tomorrow. Has she screamed at him that he's a weak mean bastard yet? It's all one moment to her. Judy has finally achieved timelessness.

Doug has already arranged—a year ago—to take two weeks off work, because he knows he won't be able to answer people's dumb tech problems and lose a piece of himself at the same time. He could do his job in his sleep, even if he didn't know what all the callers were going to say before they said it, but his ability to sleepwalk through unpleasantness will shortly be maxed out. He tells his coworker Geoffrey, the closest he has to a friend, that he'll be doing some spring cleaning, even though it's October.

A few days before the breakup, Judy stands in the middle of Central Square, and a homeless guy comes up to her and asks for money. She stares at his face, which is unevenly sunburned in the shape of a wheel. She concentrates on this man, who stands there, his hand out. For a moment, she just forgets to worry about Doug for once—and just like that, she's seeing futures again.

The threads are there: if she buys this homeless man some scones from 1369, they'll talk, and become friends, and maybe she'll run into him once every few weeks and buy him dinner, for the next several years. And in five years, she'll help the man, Franklin, find a place to live, and she'll chip in for the deposit. But a couple years later, it'll all have fallen apart, and he'll be back here. And she flashes on something Franklin tells her eight years from now, if this whole chain of events comes to pass, about a lost opportunity. And then she knows what to do.

"Franklin," she says to wheel-faced guy, who blinks at the sound of his name. "Listen. Angie's pregnant, with your kid. She's at the yellow house with the broken wheelbarrow, in Sturbridge. If you go to her right now, I think she'll take you back. Here's a hundred bucks." She reaches in her new purse, for the entire wad of cash she took out of the bank to hold her until she gets her new ATM card. "Go find Angie." Franklin just looks at her, takes the cash, and disappears.

Judy never knows if Franklin took her advice. But she does know for sure she'll never see him again.

And then she wanders into the bakery where she would have bought Franklin scones, and she sees this guy working there. And she concentrates on him, too, even though it gives her a headache, and she "remembers" a future in which they become friendly and he tells her about the time he wrecked his best friend's car, which hasn't happened yet. She buys a scone and tells the guy, Scott, that he shouldn't borrow Reggie's T-Bird for that regatta thing, or he'll regret it forever. She doesn't even care that Scott is staring as she walks out.

"I'm going to be a vigilante soothsayer," she tells Marva. She's never used her power so recklessly before, but the more she does it, the easier it gets. She goes ahead and mails that Jollibee statue to Sukey.

The day of the big breakup, Marva's like, "Why can't you just dump him via text message? That's what all the kids are doing, it's the new sexting." Judy's best answer is, "Because then my bike would still be in one piece." Which isn't a very good argument. Judy dresses warm, because she knows she'll be frozen later.

Doug takes deep breaths, tries to feel acceptance, but he's all wrung out inside. He wants this to be over, but he dreads it being over. If there was any other way . . . Doug takes the train from Providence a couple hours early, so he can get lost for a while. But he doesn't get lost enough, and he's still early for their meeting. They're supposed to get dinner at the fancy place, but Doug forgot to make the reservation, so they wind up at John Harvard's Brew Pub, in the mall, and they each put away three pints of the microbrews that made John Harvard famous. They make small talk.

Afterwards, they're wandering aimlessly, towards Mass Ave., and getting closer to the place where it happens. Judy blurts out, "It didn't have to be this way. None of it. You made everything fall into place, but it didn't have to."

"I know you don't believe that any more," Doug says. "There's a lot of stuff you have the right to blame me for, but you can't believe I chose any of this. We're both cursed to see stuff that nobody should be allowed to see, but we're still responsible for our own mistakes. I still don't regret anything. Even if I didn't know today was the last day for you and me, I would want it to be."

They are both going to say some vicious things to each other in the next hour or so. They've already heard it all, in their heads.

On Mass Ave., Judy sees the ice cream place opposite the locked side gates of Harvard, and she stops her bike. During their final blow-out fight, she's not eating ice cream, any of the hundred times she's seen it. "Watch my bike," she tells Doug. She goes in and gets a triple scoop for herself and one for Doug, random flavors—Cambridge is one of the few places you can ask for random flavors and people will just nod—and then she and Doug resume their exit interview.

"It's that you have this myth that you're totally innocent and harmless, even though you also believe you control everything in the universe," Doug is saying.

Judy doesn't taste her ice cream, but she is aware of its texture, the voluptuousness of it, and the way it chills the roof of her mouth. There are lumps of something chewy in one of her random flavors. Her cone smells like candy, with a hint of wet dog.

They wind up down by the banks of the river, near the bridge surrounded by a million geese and their innumerable droppings, and Judy is crying and shouting that Doug is a passive aggressive asshole.

Doug's weeping into the remains of his cone, and then he goes nuclear. He starts babbling about when he sees Judy ten years hence, and the future he describes is one of the ones that Judy's always considered somewhat unlikely.

Judy tries to flee, but Doug has her wrist and he's babbling at her, describing a scene where a broken-down Doug meets Judy with her two kids—Raina and Jeremy, one of dozens of combinations of kids Judy might have—and Raina, the toddler, has a black eye and a giant stuffed tiger. The future Judy looks tired, makes an effort to be nice to the future Doug, who's a wreck, gripping her cashmere lapel.

Both the future Judy and the present Judy are trying to get away from Doug as fast as possible. Neither Doug will let go.

"And then 15 years from now, you only have one child," Doug says.

"Let me go!" Judy screams.

But when Judy finally breaks free of Doug's hand, and turns to flee, she's hit with a blinding headrush, like a one-minute migraine. Three scoops of ice cream on top of three beers, or maybe just stress, but it paralyzes her, even as she's trying to run. Doug tries to throw himself in her path, but he overbalances and falls down the river bank, landing almost in the water.

"Gah!" Doug wails. "Help me up. I'm hurt." He lifts one arm, and Judy puts down her bike, helps him climb back up. Doug's a mess, covered with mud, and he's clutching one arm, heaving with pain.

"Are you okay?" Judy can't help asking.

"Breaking my arm hurt a lot more . . ." Doug winces. ". . . than I thought it would."

"Your arm." Judy can't believe what she's seeing. "You broke . . . your arm."

"You can see for yourself. At least this means it's over."

"But you were supposed to break your leg."

Doug almost tosses both hands in the air, until he remembers he can't. "This is exactly why I can't deal with you any more. We both agreed, on our very first date, I break my arm. You're just remembering it wrong, or being difficult on purpose."

Doug wants to go to the hospital by himself, but Judy insists on going with. He curses at the pain, stumbling over every knot and root.

"You broke your arm." Judy's half-sobbing, half-laughing, it's almost too much to take in. "You broke your arm, and maybe that means that all of this . . . that maybe we could try again. Not right away, I'm feeling pretty raw right now, but in a while. I'd be willing to try."

But she already knows what Doug's going to say: "You don't get to hurt me any more."

She doesn't leave Doug until he's safely staring at the hospital linoleum, waiting to go into X-ray. Then she pedals home, feeling the cold air smash into her face. She's forgotten her helmet, but it'll be okay. When she gets home, she's going to grab Marva and they're going straight to Logan, where a bored check-in counter person will give them dirt-cheap tickets on the last flight to Miami. They'll have the wildest three days of their lives, with no lasting ill effects. It'll be epic, she's already living every instant of it in her head. She's crying buckets but it's okay, her bike's headwind wipes the slate clean.

The Day of the
Green Velvet Cloak

INTRODUCTION

She had her immediate future all planned—or planed for her—and tried not to think of troubling doubts . . . until she decided to splurge on a much-too-expensive green velvet cloak, then stepped into a very unusual bookstore that was straight out of the *Twilight Zone* . . .

* * *

Mildred McElroy Clingerman (1918-1997) grew up in Oklahoma and Arizona and attended the University of Arizona, where she later taught. In the 1950s she began writing very excellent science fiction and fantasy stories, many of them published in the prestigious *Magazine of Fantasy and Science Fiction*, whose editor, Anthony Boucher, dedicated the seventh volume of the annual *The Best from Fantasy and Science Fiction* to her, with the praise "most serendipitous of discoveries" appended to the dedication. (And, yes, she had a story in the book—the very effective horror story, "The Wild Wood," which might be even more frightening to a woman than it was to me.) She also sold stories to such "slick" magazines as *Collier's*, *Good Housekeeping*, and *Woman's Home Companion*. To my knowledge, her only book was the short story collection, *A Cupful of Space* (Ballantine, 1961) which has been out of print for much too long. For some time now, SF has been dominated by novels, often of elephantine size, and Clingerman, who wrote no novels, is not as well known as she should be. If you like this story, seek out her other stories, tell your friends, leave graffiti in prominent places. We need a conspiracy!

The Day of the Green Velvet Cloak

by Mildred Clingerman

Exactly one week before she was to be married to Mr. Hubert Lotzenhiser, owner of the Fast and Friendly Loan Company, Mavis O'Hanlon went shopping and, among other things, bought a very expensive mistake. She knew it was a mistake the moment the saleslady counted out the meager change from two fifty-dollar bills— almost the last of Mavis' savings. Still, the green velvet cloak was quite the loveliest mistake Mavis had ever made. For instance, it in no way resembled Hubert, her biggest mistake to date.

Mavis, weaving her way through the crowded department store aisles, glanced briefly in the direction of the exchange desk, then down at the smart box that held the green velvet cloak. No, it was impossible. As usual, the very thought of approaching the exchange desk turned her knees to jelly and set ten thousand butterflies to panic flight in her stomach. Mavis knew very well what Hubert would say of such timid behavior, if he were to find out about it. (She certainly had no intention of telling him.) In the six years of their engagement Hubert had devoted a considerable amount of time and effort to what he called "fibering-up" Mavis' character. She had been subjected to many long, dull lectures on the advantages of self-discipline, which, so far as Mavis could see, consisted chiefly of forcing herself to do all the things she most disliked so that she could turn out to be exactly like Hubert.

Under Hubert's tutelage Mavis had shudderingly tried pot-gardening, dog-patting, and automobile-driving. She was miserable. She balked the night Hubert came to dinner in her apartment and insisted she pursue and kill the two cockroaches the grocer had sacked with the potatoes. She grew so heady with her rebellion that night that she almost broke the engagement. In fact, she was triumphantly convinced she had, till Hubert showed up the next night and overwhelmed her with his bland assumption that all was well. It was all so difficult. She could not clearly recall how she had come to be engaged to Hubert in the first place. Fortunately, Hubert's excessively cautious nature had demanded a long engagement. Unfortunately, the long engagement period was now drawing to a close, and Mavis found it more and more difficult to tell Hubert what a big mistake he was.

After the night of the cockroaches, Mavis had given up her role of the grim quarry slave scourged to her dungeon and gone happily back to being her old chicken-hearted, unfibered self. Now she wished she hadn't. If Hubert's character-building had succeeded, how simple it would be now to tell him (in effect) that she was turning him in at the exchange desk! (But for whom could she exchange him?)

That was a fruitless line of thought. Especially since she couldn't even bring herself to exchange a perfectly useless (but perfectly beautiful) green velvet cloak—which no power on earth could induce her to wear in public, even supposing she should ever have occasion for wearing it. It was impossible to picture herself garbed in the long Victorian garment, sailing into some nightclub on Hubert's arm. Mavis hadn't the courage to bring it off, for one thing. For another, it demanded an escort as unlike Hubert as was humanly possible.

When she left the department store, Mavis headed straight for the Book Nook. After mentally wrestling with two enormous mistakes she felt she deserved a small reward. In Mavis' opinion chicken-hearted people were frequently in need of small rewards—for the things they did and the things they did not do, for success and failure, for joy and despair, and for all in-betweenness.

When she could find it the Book Nook was her favorite second-hand bookstore, and second-hand books were her favorite small rewards. The place was a narrow, dark cave sandwiched between a real-estate office and a surgical-supply shop. She was never quite certain of the address. Sometimes, when it had been months since her last visit, she would return to find that the real-estate office had unaccountably changed into a cubby-hole that sold sneeze powder and exploding cigars; and when she turned into what ought to have been the Book Nook, she ended in a nightmare of trusses, bedpans, and menacing garments with a lot of dangling harness attached.

But on the day of the green cloak the real-estate office displayed its usual ugly photographs of property nobody wanted, while the surgical-supply shop offered a choice of legs or crutches, and she found the Book Nook huddled between them.

There was a new proprietor in charge. But then, there often was. At first glance she found him a vast improvement over his predecessors, though this one was badly in need of a shave. Still, the new man was young and he didn't have a cold. Till then it had been Mavis' experience that all second-hand booksellers suffered from heavy colds and a startling resemblance to stone images squatting on ancient tombs. This one, however, went so far as to raise his head, blink his eyes, and glance pleasantly (if vaguely) in her direction.

Proceeding carefully in the half-gloom, Mavis eased her way into the old-books section, which in places like the Book Nook mostly meant nineteenth-century trash. After a grubby half-hour she emerged with a prize: a chatty description of a European tour made by a wealthy American girl in the year 1877. Mavis had once known a man who collected cigarette lighters that looked like guns or miniature bottles or outdoor privies—he didn't care, just so they in no way resembled cigarette lighters. *Live and let live,* Mavis thought. Cigarette lighters held no charms for her but Victorian travel journals did. Like most collectors she began with sheer greed, trying to cover too much territory, and ended with despair and not enough money. For some time now, she had limited herself to feminine journals that spanned (roughly) the years between 1850 and 1900. As for why she ever began collecting them at all . . . Hubert had asked her that. She had tried answering him with the truth: that people do not live by reason alone—that they only make up reasons to stop other people asking silly questions.

Hubert wasn't pleased with her answer at all, at all. In the end she was forced to retreat behind the conversation-killing remark that history was fascinating. Even Hubert respected history.

When she brought the book to the new proprietor's desk, he blew the dust from it and leafed through it while Mavis waited with money in one hand and tried to steady her small mountain of packages with the other.

"It's marked seventy-five cents," she said. "Right there, on the flyleaf." She laid the money on the desk, but the young man ignored it. He was reading a page in the middle of the book. He closed the book, his finger still marking his place, and looked back to check the author's name.

"Sara . . ." he said. "Only think of Sara's keeping a journal so faithfully. It's exactly what I've been looking for. Thank you . . . thank you." He glanced up at Mavis and smiled very sweetly and went back to his reading. She stared down at the top of his head which resembled a medium grade of sheared beaver. Her feet began to hurt. Impatience always settled in Mavis' feet.

"You want to keep it?" she asked, leaning perilously forward to glare at him over her packages.

"Oh, I don't think that's necessary or even desirable. . . ." He chewed nervously at his lower lip. "But I really ought to *read* it—or anyway, part of. Now, *here's* a nice question of ethics: if one is a time traveler and discovers in the future that one's sister's best friend has been keeping a journal that one is certain to find oneself in, how far is one allowed to read ahead? I mean, of what is to happen, but has not yet happened?" He pondered a moment while Mavis stared at him in bewilderment.

"I rather think," he continued, "that it is perfectly fair for me to read up to the point of my departure, don't you?"

"Oh, by all means," Mavis said, but her sarcasm was lost on the young man.

"Yes, here we are, steaming up the Rhine, a whole party of us." He began to read aloud from the book: *"We broke our journey at Königswinter long enough to climb up to Godesburg Castle. While strolling back T.G. kept us merry with fantastic predictions for the future. J. gaily accused him of having drunk too deeply of the wine at luncheon or of having consulted the raggle-taggle gypsies who waylaid us near the castle. T.G. only laughed and shook his head. J. asked mock-scornfully if he had traveled much into the future. T.G. answered her that he wished he could, more than anything. Mrs. Simmons then exercised her authority as chaperone and begged us to cease our wild talk. Yes,"* he looked up from the book and nodded at Mavis, who was standing before him with her mouth open. "That's exactly the way it was. And then we climbed the Drachenfels and afterwards floated past thirty-three crumbling castles. It must have been two days later when we reached Heidelberg. That's where I excused myself from sightseeing and succumbed to a bookshop." He suddenly stopped talking and fell to reading again the way a hungry man attacks his dinner.

Mavis began unloading all her packages onto the desk. He might well be crazy, but she wanted that book. Short of grappling for it, she saw no way of getting it but to wait for it. She moved around behind the desk, drew up a chair and sat down beside him; she took off her shoes and wiggled her toes. The Book Nook was very quiet, dark, and cool. There were no other customers. She could wait till closing time—still two hours away. Surely it would not take him that long to finish Sara's journal.

The young man paid no attention to her, other than to move his chair a few inches to allow her to squeeze in beside him. He read silently and swiftly for ten minutes, then began groping around on the desk top without lifting his eyes from the page. The hand paused as if it were surprised when it came in contact with Mavis' packages.

"I could stack them here on the floor," she said, "if they're in your way."

"Not at all. The thing is, I believe my cigar case is under them."

Together they lifted the stack. No cigars. The young man ran his hands through the medium grade of sheared beaver and looked desperate.

"Here, have a cigarette." Mavis opened her purse and handed him the package, first taking one for herself. She waited for him to light it, but when she saw that no light was forthcoming she fished out a book of matches. Only then did she glance up at his face. His eyebrows had climbed almost as high as the sheared beaver.

"Oh, I say! You . . . Well, I call it brave of you. There *are* ladies, I know, who . . . who smoke, but to do it in public and carry tobacco about with you . . . I call it brave!"

Nobody else had ever called Mavis brave. She warmed to him. But honesty was strong in her. "Millions of women smoke. Hubert hates it. But, of course you're teasing me. . . . Forgive me, but I do think you're the strangest owner the Book Nook has ever had. If you've finished with it, I'll take the book and go. The money is on the desk."

The young man lighted both cigarettes before he answered. "My dear young lady, I am not the owner of the Book Nook. There was nobody at all here when I arrived in that little alcove back there. It was pitch dark, and I slept on the floor till daylight. That was three days ago. This morning I broke the lock on the front door—the back door is boarded up and nailed solid. I took a short but nerve-racking walk and then crept back into this safe but cheerless hole. It was then I noticed a sign on the street side of the door. It said 'Closed till further notice.' It's still there, I believe. When you came in, I was considering, rather desperately, what I should do next. I do think it was clever of you to find exactly the book I needed! I'd been looking, but there are so many books, and all so higgledy-piggledy . . ." Mavis stared and stared at him, while belief in him grew and grew. For the first time she noticed that his crumpled clothes were very Ivy League. "Are you really out of Sara's journal? I . . . I mean, how did it happen?"

"I really am, Miss—please, what is your name?" Mavis told him. "Mine is Titus Graham, and I ought this minute to be in Heidelberg, and it ought to be the year eighteen-seventy-seven. I don't quite know *how* it happened, except that I went into a bookshop and I found a new book of short stories by a young German whose work I admire. He writes fantastic stories about the future, and I quite lose myself in them, you see. Only this time I lost myself indeed. I had settled myself in a little reading alcove they have there and had begun reading the book. You see, I'd fully intended to buy it and take it back to the hotel with me, till I discovered I'd left all my money in my room. Very embarrassing, but the proprietor insisted I look it over, anyway. I did, and suddenly, here I was."

"But, Mr. Graham, how will you get back?"

"Presumably, by reading in *this* time something that closely relates to the *other* time."

"But will it work?"

"I . . . I hope so." The young man closed his eyes and swayed a little, as if he were suddenly dizzy. He clutched at the edge of the desk, and his teeth began to chatter. His pallor was alarming.

Mavis was on her feet at once, scrambling to put on her shoes. "What is it, Mr. Graham? Are you ill?"

"Not at all. It's just the cold in here. Don't you feel it?"

"Cold nothing!" Mavis was furious with herself. "You're starving, of course. What a witless idiot I am! No money—here three days in this dreadful honking, hooting, cruel city. Frightened, too, I'll bet I But not showing it. Oh, Mr. Graham, you are so *brave!* Here . . ." She dragged the green velvet cloak from its box. "Let me wrap you in this, and then I'll go get some food. I'll be right back."

She was halfway out the door when he called to her. "You are so kind. So very kind. When you come back, don't be alarmed if you don't find me here. I'll try reading the book in the little alcove back there. Perhaps that will help."

"Oh, Mr. Graham, dear, take the book and *try!* Try hard, and I'll hurry."

But again his voice stopped her. "I say . . . I know this is rather presumptuous of me, but I wonder . . . That is, I've never met a woman like you before. You didn't turn a hair when I told you about me—when I was from. I've daydreamed a great deal about the New Woman of the future, so free, so untrammeled and brave. I mean, would you—if you could—go back with me? If we tried reading the book together? I'm saying this badly, but I could take you to my sister . . . And after a while, if you wanted to . . . Miss O'Hanlon, will you marry me in eighteen-seventy-seven?"

Mavis stood in the doorway, her heart pounding. Oh, wouldn't it be wonderful to go back with him—back to a time she'd fit into? Back to the long sunlit days when an hour was a whole hour long, not like these modern ten-minute hours. She knew very well from her persistent reading of Victorian journals that something queer had happened to time even before she was born. And to people. There used to be room enough in the world for all kinds of people—the inefficient, and the chicken-hearted . . . Maybe, with time enough, she could fiber-up her character in her own way. Mightn't she even, in Titus Graham's world, appear to be not only strong-fibered, but perhaps a trifle *fast?* There, she could wear the velvet cloak . . . and no more problems about Hubert. *Hubert.* He fell into her dream the way a boulder might crash into delicate glass castles. She drew herself up as tall as she could, and for the first time in her life felt little tendrils of strength lacing across her spine.

"I thank you, Mr. Graham, dear, from the bottom of my heart. I am honored, but I cannot go. You see, I have not been in this world all that you think I am. I'm a timid rabbit of a girl—not the New Woman you've imagined me to be. A poet once said, 'There grows no herb of help to heal a coward heart,' so there's no sense in my chasing through time to look for it. What I'd better do is stay here and heal myself. Anyway, I mean to try. But right now I must go get you some food."

"In spite of what you say, I should like you to know, Miss O'Hanlon, that my faith in your courage remains unshaken."

They were the last words Mavis ever heard from Titus Graham. Spoken words, that is. When she returned with the sandwiches and coffee, he was gone. In the small alcove in back she found Sara's journal, and after a short but sharp battle with her conscience, she gathered the book up with her packages. After all, she comforted herself, she had left the money for it on the desk. She put the sandwiches and coffee inside the box that had held the green velvet cloak and set them outside on the curb for the trash collector. Resolutely then she left the Book Nook and walked several blocks to find a telephone. Though her voice and hands were shaking, she finally managed to phone the police to them that someone should see to relocking the Book Nook's front door. When they asked for her name, she hung up.

Once safely at home again, Mavis gave in to fatigue and dull discontent. Something strange and wonderful had happened to her, and yet everything was discouragingly the same. She felt there ought to be some glow left, some magic light that would alter her forever. But what was different? There was still Hubert to contend with. There was still the fact that she'd spent almost all her money on the green velvet cloak. What, she wondered, had happened to it? And, oh, if she could only *know* that Mr. Graham was safely home again and no longer hungry. Her eyes fell on Sara's journal . . . *Of course!*

She found the entry almost immediately. Sara had written in Heidelberg in June, 1877: *After a frantic three days' search by our whole party and various Heidelberg officials, T.G. reappeared yesterday and set our fears at rest. He was quite unharmed, but tired and hungry and looking very seedy. None of us endeavored to question him till he had enjoyed some food and rest. Today the physician tells us that he evidently contracted a fever and in his delirium wandered about the city, in a state bordering on loss of memory. It is pitiful to think of poor T. unable to find his way back to his friends and family. The fugue, as the doctor called it, has now passed, and we are assured he will recover fully. T.G. remembers nothing, he says, except that somewhere he met a young woman who was kind to him, giving him her cloak because he was shivering. He had it with him when he returned and will not yet permit it to be removed from his sight. He has got it firmly in his head that she was an extraordinarily beautiful and fearless creature, quite unlike any other young lady of his acquaintance. It is most provoking. He has always admired strong-minded females. Fortunately, I feel myself growing daily more strong-minded . . . The cloak is of green velvet and of a quality that proves its owner (whatever her other attributes) to have been a lady of excellent taste.*

For a moment, Mavis had read enough. Without intending to, Sara had given her enough glow to go on warming. Bravely or not, Mavis could at least live her life with good taste. And it was never good taste to marry a man you didn't love. So much for Hubert. Mavis reached for the telephone and summoned him to their last meeting. While she waited for his arrival she made further plans for the future. She would continue her collection of journals. It would be delightful if now and then she ran across references to Sara and Titus. Of course, they'd marry. Or had married. Mavis hoped so; certainly she didn't mind. In fact, Mavis had no regrets at all, except when she thought of the beautiful green cloak. Never mind, Sara could have it. Mavis would save her money and buy herself another, because it hadn't been a mistake at all. Then why, Mavis wondered, with everything so neatly ordered, did she feel like a leftover pancake in an otherwise empty refrigerator?

She was crying a little and telling herself that she would not cry when her doorbell rang. Mavis was surprised that Hubert had arrived so quickly; he wasn't due for another hour yet. The young man standing before her had hair that resembled a superior grade of sheared beaver, and in his hands he carried a package heavy with red wax seals.

"Miss Mavis O'Hanlon? May I come in? I come on a very strange errand, and it will take time to explain. Forgive me, my name is Titus Graham, the Fourth, if it matters to you." He ran his hands distractedly through the sheared beaver. Mavis remembered to close her mouth—gone suddenly dry—smiled, and invited him in. When he was seated he began again. "You aren't going to believe this, but my great-grandfather—by the way, he was Titus the First. Look, I know I'm not making sense yet, but—that is, when my great-grandfather died in nineteen thirty-five, among his effects was this sealed package with a letter of instructions concerning it. The letter insisted that the package not be opened, but that in a certain year—on this very day—it should be delivered to a Miss Mavis O'Hanlon in this city. Preferably by his unmarried great-grandson, Titus Four. That's me—oh, I told you. Yes . . . well, as a matter of fact, part of my inheritance from him was to be withheld till these conditions were fulfilled. I was pretty young when he died, but I do remember him, and I liked him very much. So, you see, aside from the rest of the inheritance, I'm pleased to do as he asked—am I going too fast for you?"

Mavis cleared her throat and shook her head and brought out a quivery no. Titus IV was looking at her with the quality of sympathy that leads to soothings and murmurings and makes people forget they are strangers. Mavis tried to make her smile repressive but encouraging, cool but warming, hello-but-not-yet. It emerged, she was sure, as a positive leer, which she wiped off at once.

"Well, then," Titus was saying, "it was fairly easy to find you. Luckily, you are the only person of that name in the city. But now comes the hard part. In order to keep the contents of this package you must, before opening it, correctly identify what's inside. Miss O'Hanlon, I know this is silly and impossible, but can you tell me what's inside this package?"

"I can," Mavis said. (Stone-faced and unflinching before a firing squad, an investigating committee, a quizmaster, six detectives, and the income tax bureau . . . brave, cool, alert, snapping her fingers under Hubert's nose . . . waving him into Limbo: Guards! Take him away . . .)

"Miss O'Hanlon?"

"What? Oh! The package, yes. It contains a perfectly beautiful green velvet cloak."

Titus stared at her with deepening interest. "Yes, but how did you know? Not that you wouldn't look lovely in a green velvet cloak. It's the kind of thing that would suit you very well. Oh, I don't mean you need clothes like that, or anything—that is, with or without clothes—that's not what I mean at all!" He grinned wickedly at her. "Put on the cloak, please? And get me out of this hole I've dug for myself."

Mavis broke the seals and opened the package. Somebody had done a miracle of packing, folding the cloak around soft old rolls of the finest lawn to keep the aging velvet from cracking. When she shook out the cloak the room was filled with the scent of roses and lavender, of far-off sunlit days in gardens she'd never know. Mavis smoothed the velvet with trembling fingers, then carefully drew the cloak over her shoulders. "It needs another dress," she said, "and I could lift my hair, like this."

"Do," Titus said. "And we could have dinner at that German place with paintings and red plush."

"It's hardly faded at all," Mavis murmured. "And I've got that cream-colored portrait dress I was going to be—what time is it?"

"Oh, it's early yet. Plenty of time. I want to hear everything. How you knew what was in the package, and how—"

"No," Mavis said. "Not now. There's just time to dress and get away before—I don't believe in Last Meetings, do you?"

"Never," Titus said. "First Meetings, yes. Last Meetings, outlawed. I almost forgot; there's a message that goes with the cloak. Titus the First said to tell Mavis O'Hanlon: *What's past is prologue.* Does that mean anything special to you?"

"I fervently hope so." Mavis grinned back at him while sprinting for her bedroom. "Ten minutes," she called back. . . .

Time paused, as if for a deep breath, before they were caught up in it again and whirled away, so that all the hours of their life together seemed thereafter foreshortened, nostalgic, and as perfectly beautiful as the green velvet cloak.

A Wow Finish

INTRODUCTION

If time travel is possible, time tourists and archaeologists might be walking among us right now. They might be watching historical events, though some historical events, such as visiting Pearl Harbor on December 7, 1941, might be hazardous. Or they might take in a classic movie, such as one which happens to be a very appropriate choice in view of the title of this book . . .

* * *

James Van Pelt's stories have appeared in such publications as *Analog*, *Asimov's Science Fiction Magazine*, *Realms of Fantasy*, *Amazing Stories*, and *Weird Tales*, and his non-fiction work has appeared in *Tangent* magazine. He was a finalist for the 1999 John W. Campbell Award for Best New Writer. His much-praised short story, "The Last of the O-Forms" was a Nebula Award finalist, and many of his stories have appeared in various year's best SF anthologies. In western Colorado, he teaches English at both Fruita Monument High School and Mesa State College. Most importantly to him, his wife Tammy and their three children, Dylan, Samuel, and Joshua, think he tells a pretty good bedtime story.

A Wow Finish

by James Van Pelt

Earle woke up last, on the floor under a sheet. Durance stood at the window, watching the rain, while Hoffman, achingly beautiful, sat on the end of the bed, elbow on knee, chin in hand. They were already dressed.

Of all the field trips to all the times in all the world, she had to choose mine, Earle thought, conscious that he was naked beneath the thin covering. He wondered which of them had put the sheet over him.

"It's a pity we always arrive in a storm," said Durance. He tugged at his dark tie. "And the outfits are uncomfortable." He wore a beige double-breasted suit with matching pants creased so sharply Earle thought he could cut paper with them.

"Allergens," said Hoffman without moving. "The air's cleaner on a rainy day. God knows what you'd react to here. Street dust. Pollutants. Pigeons. It's safer on wet days. Cowardly, perhaps, but safer." She smiled at Earle. "You going to lay there all evening?"

Earle rolled to his side. His clothes were neatly piled beside him. He pulled them under the sheet and dressed there, aware that Hoffman only had to shift her gaze a foot to be looking right at him. It was a struggle to get into the shoes. The stiff leather bit into his ankles, but they had a nice shine to them, and putting them on made him feel more there. More real. Somewhere distant a bell rang. He realized he'd been hearing it for a while. Beyond that a steady rumble quivered just on the edge of his perceptions.

"Look at this phone," said Durance, picking it up. At first Earle thought that it was tied to the table. Durance said, "Wires *and* a dial. How do you work it?"

Hoffman stood from the bed, smoothing the front of her skirt with the edge of her hands. She'd cut her hair short for the trip and given it a curl. "Honestly, it's like you've never been in the field before."

"Nothing before 2020. My master's was on post-rock pop. I got interested in the roots of neuro big band, though. Earle has been in the Twentieth Century, though. I sampled that thing you did on the Hindenberg. Nice work."

Earle struggled with the shirt's buttons. "Beginner's luck. I was a last minute replacement."

Durance shrugged, then put the phone back on the table. "Hard to believe the trouble I'm going through to put in an extra footnote. Tiny Hill and his orchestra are in the Green Room here in the Edison. Harry James is uptown at the Astor, and Benny Goodman opens there tomorrow. Cab Calloway plays the Park Central."

"Pretty good lineup," said Earle.

"I tried talking Hoffman into going with me. A live band has to be better than a dusty old movie. So why go?" Durance laughed and put his hand on Hoffman's shoulder. She leaned into him. Earle turned away, concentrated on tying his shoe.

"Ask Earle. It's *Casablanca*," she said. "Opening week. I don't get it either. The Hindenberg, now that was important, but a film? Well, for a me a theater's as good a place as any."

Durance sniffed. "I read up on the movie. Who can watch this stuff? Ancient black and white that you can't edit while you watch, and bad piano bar music on top of that. Dooley Wilson didn't even play the piano. He was a drummer. Then there's a bunch of Germans singing an off-tune version of "Die Wacht Am Rhein" instead of "Deutschland Uber Alles," which would have made more sense. I wouldn't get anything useful. Hard to believe people would get worked up over it. Twentieth Century sentimentalism."

"I've never seen it," said Hoffman. "Studied the background, though. Vichy, France. The German advances. The resistance movement. Bogart. Bergman. I'm ready."

Earle paused in straightening his jacket. He didn't know that she had never seen the film. There might be hope yet. He dropped the sheet on the bed as he walked to the window. Traffic flowed below, rumbling. "Broadway," he said. "The Great White Way. 1942. Three and a half weeks until Christmas, and an entire world that hasn't seen *Casablanca*." He could feel the cars passing through his fingertips resting on the window sill. "Bogart said, 'When it's December 1941 in Casablanca, what time is it in New York?'"

Durance shrugged. "That's 47th. Broadway is around the corner. It's just an old movie. You could have stayed home and watched it on video."

"And you could listen to big band recordings whenever you want. Why'd *you* make the trip?" said Earle.

Durance glanced at Hoffman. He said, "Experiential research. I'm nanoed to the gills. Download the lot uptime, and I'll have a couple years' work worth of data in my twenty-four hours. No paper's complete anymore without actual field hours," but his glance said it all.

"Me too. Serves me right for asking a direct question," said Earle.

Hoffman slipped her arms into a coat, then flipped the white blouse's collars over the blue wool, as if she's always worn the style. She pulled on a pair of white gloves. Earle could hear Bogart's dialogue in his head: "I remember every detail. The Germans wore grey. You wore blue."

"We'd better get going, Earle. It's a four-block walk, and I want good seats."

Durance said, "I've got a half hour before the band starts here. Last chance at some decent music, Hoffman."

She shook her head at him as she headed for the door.

In the hallway, a sign read, WHEN IN DOUBT, PUT IT OUT.

She ran her fingers along the sign. Earle knew she was calling for info out of habit, but they weren't tied in here. No instant details about whatever they wanted. No augmentation at all. They had to fit in. "Cigarettes?" said Hoffman. She buttoned her coat. "I didn't think the anti-smoking trend came along for another fifty years." She sniffed. "It doesn't smell like it's working either."

Earle adjusted his hat, a dark snap-brim with a black silk band above the brim. "It's a light-dimming measure. They were afraid German submarines might cruise up the Hudson River to shell the Rockefeller Center or something. They never really turned the lights out on Broadway, though."

Hoffman laughed, "That's funny. For a second there I tried to edit out the smell. It's weird to be stuck with one version of the world."

"Nope. Can't change a thing. Just like the natives. No VR ghosts. No info on demand. It's a single-track existence. Besides, you'd stick out wearing your regular headgear."

Earle looked down the long hall, doors opening on each side, a serving tray on the floor next to the nearest room, on the tray a partly eaten sandwich on a plate beside an empty cup. That's exactly it, he thought, that makes this so good. One reality. Of course, even in the editable world, Hoffman had left him.

A bell chimed, and the elevator arrived. Earle started in recognition. That was the bell he'd been hearing. The doors opened to reveal a mirrored back wall. His coat looked good next to hers. Wide lapels. Plain epaulets on the shoulders. Buckled cinch bands at the wrists. He turned his collar up.

"You look like Bogart," Hoffman said.

"In a raincoat and hat, everyone looks like Bogart." He tried not to consider her face in the mirror. "Why'd you choose this trip? There were others to this era."

"I wouldn't have come if I had known that you were here. I'm still research assistant for Dr. Monroe. She's doing that monograph on women's social development in the mid-twentieth. This slot was open. Besides, she wanted me to see how contemporary women react to Ingrid Bergman saying"—she pulled a notecard from her pocket and read—"I don't know what's right any longer. You have to think for both of us."

"You'll love Capitaine Renault then. His hobby is preying on pretty girls who need exit visas but don't have any money."

Hoffman raised her eyebrows. "And this is the classic film you argued was 'the cultural pivot point in American consciousness'?"

If that bothered her, Earle thought, he couldn't wait to see her response to Renault saying, "How extravagant you are, throwing away women like that. Someday they may be scarce."

The elevator opened onto the lobby level.

Hoffman stepped out first. "Heavens. If you love art deco, this is the place."

Gold-rimmed half-dome chandeliers hung from gold chains above the gold and brown carpet. Overstuffed chairs nestled up to tiny tables where a handful of people sipped from china cups.

A pair of sailors in dress whites walked by. "We could catch *The Skin of Our Teeth* if you wanted to see a show," said one.

"I hate Thornton Wilder," said the other. "We've only got two days. I'm going to spend the time snuggling up to that hat check girl or someone just like her."

Hoffman took a step after them, then turned to Earle. "That's the kind of material I need. They're so primitive."

"I don't know. You'd get the same talk in the grad dorms on a Friday night."

"Really?" Hoffman looked offended.

She took a complimentary umbrella from the doorman. Earle waved off the offer. He wanted to feel the rain tapping against his hat, to get more into the moment of time that was *this* time. He needed to submerge in 1942, so that it would be visceral. He couldn't just watch the video because the video wasn't theater. Experiential research meant that there was no substitute for being there. Like Durance, his system practically leaked nanos. They recorded everything he sensed. They made a duplicate of the experience he could return to again and again for study. Better than eyewitness reporting. So, no umbrella. Connect to the moment, walking in the rain with Hoffman, like Paris, where Bogart waited in the rain for Bergman at the train station.

"Where is she? Have you seen her?" Bogart asked. The storm poured down. "No, Mr. Richard," said Sam. "I can't find her." Sam handed Bogart a note. It read in part, "Richard, I cannot go with you or ever see you again." The ink ran in the rain.

They stepped through the doors onto the sidewalk. Earle held his hand out. Droplets pelted his palm. He could imagine the note in it, the ink leaking off the page. A car passed, splashing water onto their shoes.

Hoffman said, "I thought it would be louder. You know, all the gasoline engines."

Rain hissed off the street, drummed steadily against the buildings. Tires whined on the pavement. Lights glistened on the wet surfaces. Two couples, huddled under their umbrellas, hurried into the Edison's doors. This is New York at war, thought Earle. You couldn't tell. Despite gasoline rationing, traffic was heavy. A restaurant sign advertised a variety of steaks. Other than the sailors in the lobby, he hadn't seen military personnel or equipment. Were there anti-aircraft guns on the roofs?

He wanted to ask her about Durance. Hoffman hadn't seen the film. He could say Bogart's line without a hint of irony, "Tell me, who was it you left me for? Was it Durance, or were there others in between?"

Hoffman said, "It's breezy wearing a dress. These nylons aren't insulating at all. What did women do when it snowed?"

"They toughed it out, but they suffered. They took jobs in the factories and raised kids on their own, and waited for terrible telegrams to tell them their husbands weren't coming home." Cars eased by, dripping water from their fenders. Earle strained to see the people within. God, it's 1942, he thought. Soldiers are dying by the thousands. Northern Africa, southern France. Drowning next to the flames of their burning freighters. Broken airplanes tumbling. Many, many more are yet to die.

Hoffman shivered.

They crossed 48th. Low-hanging clouds hid the buildings' tops. The few pedestrians walked briskly under their umbrellas.

"It's amazing how every place in the past feels just like home,"

Hoffman said. "I mean, the air smells different—all those hydrocarbons—and the architecture's dated, but *I'm* the same. I could have been born here just as easily as any other time. Of course, half of my brain feels like it's turned off, but other than that . . ." She stepped around a puddle.

She doesn't see it, thought Earle. There's *nothing* here that's like home. Life here was both straightforward and mysterious. Everything was what it appeared to be, but nothing provided answers. The buildings, the sidewalks, the stores, the people, unaugmented and uneditedable, but all mute, their histories hidden. All of it's different. How could he explain that to her so that she'd know? "If you want to see sights unique to the era, we could cross over a few blocks. St. Patrick's Cathedral and the Waldorf-Astoria are that way." He pointed east, across Broadway.

"The cars are huge!"

A yellow Nash coup cruised by, rain water running off its long hood, the silhouette of a couple, visible for just a moment in the front seat. Packards, Olds, Mercurys, Studebakers, Plymouths, De Sotos, Grahams, Fords, and others he couldn't identify splashed through the shallow pools. A car twice as long as any he'd ever driven in glided on broad whitewalls, a covered spare tire mounted on the running board behind the front wheel. A Cadillac, probably, or a Rio. He whistled in appreciation.

Hoffman walked several steps ahead, hidden beneath her umbrella. What I need, thought Earle, is something she wants. I need a Ugarte to give me letters of transit. A passport to her heart. Ugarte, Peter Lorre in a beautifully done small part, said the letters were "signed by General DeGaull. Cannot be rescinded. Not even questioned." Ugarte killed a pair of German couriers to get them.

Earle shook his head. How did Bogart get Bergman back? He practically called her a whore, but she still loved him. *Casablanca* started as a story of a jilted lover's bitterness. Bogart wanted to punish Bergman for leaving him, but the vengeance went awry. Instead of hurting her, he drew her in. Bergman said, "I can't fight it anymore. I ran away from you once. I can't do it again."

"Tell me about the movie," Hoffman said.

Earle sped up so that he walked beside her.

"*Casablanca* is a pivot point for Americans' attitudes about themselves and the war. They didn't think that at the time. It was just another movie, but when cultural historians look back now, they see it. It's a slice of the times. Go in with an open mind; maybe you'll get more out of it than you believe. If you keep your eyes open, you'll see all sorts of gender attitudes."

Hoffman peeked from under the umbrella. "These gloves aren't very warm either. December in New York is cold," Hoffman said. She jammed her free hand under her armpit. "So what should I be looking for?"

He smiled. "Start with Yvonne. It's implied that she and Bogart have a relationship, but he dumps her in an early scene. She says, 'Where were you last night?' and he says, 'That's so long ago I can't remember.' It's a classic demonstration of Bogart indifference. The really interesting moment is with a Bulgarian girl later in the film. She wants Bogart's advice on love and sacrifice. I don't want to spoil it, but her quandary reflects on what's going on between Bogart, Bergman and Henreid."

"Henreid?"

"Victor Laszlo in the film, Bergman's husband."

"Right. Sorry. I got him mixed up with Greenstreet."

"He owns the Blue Parrot. Another big actor doing a nice turn in a small role."

Hoffman lifted the umbrella so she could look at him. Her eyes caught the oncoming car lights. "Just how many times have you seen this film? You never talked about it a year ago."

"Maybe a hundred."

"Heavens! So you've been a *Casablanca* fan your whole life?"

They crossed 49th. "No, not really. I saw it the first time in January." He blushed. "Well . . . um . . . I was doing a lot of other things too. Have to keep busy, you know."

"It's just hard to believe that a piece of film could be worth the trip." She kept glancing at the traffic to her side, but didn't say anything else as they approached the theater. Her silence was disconcerting. A hundred times, he thought. She'll think I've spent all my days watching romances. How pathetic. But he did watch it a hundred times, reclining in his academic's cubicle, the film playing on the ceiling. Sometimes, while walking on campus, he had edited the world into black and white, and Sam playing "As Time Goes By." University noir, he had thought.

The line into the theater was short. Earle fingered the unfamiliar paper cash in his pocket. Seventy-five cents each for admission. For a moment he panicked when he couldn't remember if dollars were more than cents as he handed the woman at the ticket window a five. She smiled and pushed back a pair of quarters and three dollars.

In the lobby, Hoffman folded the umbrella, after fumbling with the mechanism for a moment, then looked at the change. "Is this any way to run an economy? It's so clumsy, passing around metal and paper. How many people do you think *touched* this? Yuck."

"You sound like Durance," he said.

She laughed. "Sorry. He can be a bit overwhelming. Infectious cynicism. Most of the time I edit him down. I'm going to mingle a bit before the show. See what I can learn."

Earle moved to the edge of the room so he could survey the area. Like the Edison, the lobby was opulent, more like a museum than a theater. He laughed to himself. Experiential research always affected him this way, and it was hard to shake the idea that the world he was walking through was virtual and augmented instead of being actual. This was the *real* world. 1942. A paranoid world at war, although, as someone once told him, it isn't paranoia if they're really out to get you. All kinds of history happened in '42. The Japanese captured Manila, Bataan fell, Roosevelt interned Japanese-Americans, MacArthur left the Phillipines, an oil refinery in California was shelled by a Japanese sub, the civilian draft began. The war hit close to New York too. In June, the FBI arrested four German saboteurs after a U-boat landed them on Long Island.

The people waiting to see *Casablanca* didn't look nervous. They chatted in the low murmur people use when in public. He wondered if the first audiences for *Romeo and Juliet* were the same way. No idea what awaited them inside. It is just another play, they would have been thinking. An idle way to spend a few hours. But the world was different afterwards. Those first audiences were there at the beginning, like people standing in a mountain meadow, unaware that the tiny stream starting at their feet was the progenitor of the Mississippi.

A handful stood near the coatroom. A couple leaned close together under a BUY WAR BONDS poster. Others entered a door into the theater.

"Shall we?" said Hoffman.

They took seats near the front. The room smelled of plush and colognes, and the wet street on people's shoes. Earle eyed the curtain at the front of the room apprehensively. It stretched nearly the length of the stage. "We could be too close. The image might not hold up when you're near the screen."

"They wouldn't have chairs here if it wasn't good." Hoffman sat, then squirmed a bit. "You wouldn't believe what I'm wearing *under* this," she said. "It's all seams and scratchy cloth."

Earle surveyed the theater. *Casablanca* had its opening night three days earlier. Now, fewer than half the seats were filled, almost all folks in their twenties or older. He breathed deeply. His record of the experience would be clearer if he stayed focused and calm. Hormonal imbalances could throw it off. He tried to forget that Hoffman was sitting next to him, her arm against his on the armrest. Slow breaths. Calmness.

The house lights dimmed, and the ceiling to floor curtains drew aside, revealing the screen.

"Very dramatic," said Hoffman. She settled deeper into her seat.

Behind them, a ratchety noise clicked into being, then a beam of light cut through the air to illuminate the screen. Earle turned. Through a small window high on the wall at the back of the theater, the projector glowed as the first film rolled. He nodded. The clicking would be the film pulling through the sprockets and the shutter flicking in front of each frame to give the illusion of movement. *That's* what I'm here for, he thought. All the reading about *Casablanca* had never told him how loud the projection equipment could be. He faced the screen. Movie Tone News, the title said. Reading hadn't told him that the floor would be sticky, or that watching a film in a huge room in the company of strangers felt so . . . well . . . so theatrical. No wonder people went to movies by the millions. This was the era before television, before computers and home theaters and specvids or tactiles or any of the entertainments he was used to. Black and white images of battleships at sea filled the screen.

The narrator's voice boomed through the theater. "Brave sailors on the USS Dakota shot down a record thirty-two enemy planes in a valiant effort in support of the South Pacific campaign." A shadowy plane raced across a grey sky, chased by tracers.

A woman a few seats to his left sat with her hands up to her mouth. Did she know someone in the navy? She might have been twenty, hair curled below her ears, a crucifix dangling from her throat, and she wore a long white skirt covered with a floral pattern, her coat folded on her lap. She appeared to be alone.

In the row in front of them there were three couples, all with the man's arm around the woman's shoulder. More than half the people in the theater were coupled up. It's a *social* occasion, Earle realized. Going to the movies wasn't just about seeing the story, it was, oddly enough, in the darkness of the theater and the noise of the movie, a way to be with someone. Granted, the communication was nonverbal, but the people must have come together to be together.

Hoffman sat beside him. He could put his arm around her. How would she respond? Her hands lightly gripped the armrests. Her legs were uncrossed. Nothing about her body language gave him a clue one way or another about what she was thinking. If he just raised his own arm, he could reach around her. Would she move in close? Her violet perfume filled his nose. From the corner of his eye, in the flickering light of the Movie Tone News, he could see the curve of her cheek, the reflected shine in her eye.

Earle's arm twitched. It would be so easy to make the motion to hold her. He could tell her that it was part of the experience of seeing a movie in 1942. He leaned to the left so he could raise his arm.

Something bumped the back of his chair. Earle turned. It was Durance, his forearms resting on their chair tops. "I figured I could catch Tiny Hill's Orchestra's late show. Thought I'd better see what this

Casablanca fuss was all about. I had a tough time finding you in the dark!"

A sibilant "Shh!" hissed from a row back.

"It's not etiquette to talk in a theater," whispered Hoffman. She didn't appear happy to see him.

"Why not?" Durance said, his voice still too loud. "It's not a live performance."

"Shh," said Earle.

The Warner Bothers' theme trumpets and drums theme filled the auditorium, and the film began.

Earle slid down in the chair until his head rested against the plush. The opening credits played over a map of Africa. He trembled. An arrow traced its way from Paris, across France, through the Mediterranean to end in Casablanca where all refugees without exit visas "wait and wait and wait."

He'd seen the picture a hundred times before. The rhythm of it was familiar—the report of the dead couriers and the stolen letters of transit, the roundup of suspects, the English couple talking to the pickpocket—but he'd never seen the movie like this, in a huge theater, and the atmosphere was different. The people sitting all around him had no idea that they were in the presence of greatness. Earle felt the same way he had at the Hindenberg. 1937. The ship was ridiculously large, only eighty-seven feet shorter than the Titanic. Earle had stood with a crowd to watch the docking. The people oohed and ahhed at her girth. They didn't know. They didn't know, but Earle did. To the unprepared, great moments felt like common ones until they were over.

On the screen, a model airplane flew over a crowded Moroccan street. The people stared hopefully. Hoffman leaned into him. "That's not a very realistic looking airplane."

"Production costs," he whispered back. "Almost everything you see was done in the studio or back lots. No computer help."

She wrinkled her brow. "It's distracting."

"The story is not about the plane."

Scenes flicked by: Germans stepped onto the runway where Renault waited. Bogart played chess by himself at Rick's. Ugarte bragged to Bogart about selling exit Visas cheap. "I don't mind a parasite," said Bogart. "I object to a cut rate one."

Earle craned his neck to see other patrons in the theater. What were they feeling? How did the movie affect them? The woman in the floral print dress leaned forward, but he could see nothing in her or the rest of the audience's attentive faces. For a second, Durance met Earle's gaze, but he looked back to the screen.

Earle turned around. Within minutes, Bergman entered, saw Sam. She had to know right then, Earle thought. Rick was back in her life. The bar was called Rick's and Sam was Rick's best friend. Sam knew too the heartache she brought. Earle could see it in Sam's face. Sam must have been thinking, "run, boss!" Later he would beg Rick to leave. "Please, boss, let's go. There ain't nothing but trouble for you here. We'll take the car and drive all night. We'll get drunk. We'll go fishing and stay away until she's gone."

But Rick waited for a woman. He made Sam play, "As Time Goes By."

Earle's hands rested on his knees. Hoffman had taken the armrest. She stared at the screen, the changing light brightening then shadowing her features.

Bergman walked into Rick's. "Can I tell you a story?" she asked Rick.

"Does it got a wow finish?" he said.

"I don't know the finish yet."

I don't know the finish either, thought Earle. He felt Bogart's pain in his loss of expression. Despite his tough-guy posturing, it was all there beneath. And the film played on, uneditable, inevitable, like history, Earle thought. He wondered what the script of the evening held for him. Was there an inevitable crash coming? Was his Hindenberg moving toward the docking tower, with him on board instead of those poor, doomed people? But, gradually, as the film clicked on, he forgot about Hoffman sitting next to him and Durance behind. He forgot about the other people in the theater. They were all in Casablanca, holding letters of transit close to their hearts, bargaining with bitterness for love. Ignoring the Nazi Major Strasser and his arrogance. Ignoring the pain in the world around them, until the passion became too much. Laszlo led the café's band in "La Marseillaise," overwhelming the Germans' singing of "Die Wacht Am Rhein." Even Yvonne, Bogart's spurned lover who came to the bar with a German officer on her arm, joined in, tears on her cheeks. Bergman looked at her driven husband across the room, who was not thinking of himself or her or of love, but of his occupied France and the German heel in its back. It was an instant where Earle often paused the film to look at Bergman's eyes. The world was in them, filled with respect for Laszlo's courage, with admiration. Anyone would give a lifetime to earn the look that Bergman considered him with, and Laszlo didn't know. He sang the song to its end, the expatriates in the café on their feet, for a moment joined in emotion.

But Earle couldn't pause the film. It rolled on. "Viva la France!" they roared. "Viva La France!"

Like he had a hundred times before, Renault closed the café under Strasser's orders. Bogart said, "How can they close me up? On what grounds?" Renault said, "I'm shocked, shocked to find that gambling is going on here." Just then the croupier handed Renault a handful of cash. "Your winnings, sir." The audience laughed, which woke Earle to his mission. He broke his gaze from the screen. The woman in the floral dress didn't laugh. Her posture was tense. Earle could see she was mesmerized. What's going to happen next? she must be thinking. Her life was involved now, like the audience to any worthwhile story. What's going to happen?

In a few minutes, Bergman would wait for Bogart in his apartment. She'd plead for the letters. Finally, she'd pull a gun on him. "Go ahead and shoot," he'd say. "You'll be doing me a favor." She will put the gun down. "Richard, I tried to stay away. I thought I would never see you again, that you were out of my life." She'll weep. "The day you left Paris, if you knew what I went through. If you knew how much I loved you, how much I still love you." They'd kiss.

Why didn't Bogart see what she was doing? Earle thought. The Bulgarian girl not ten minutes earlier in the film had said, "If someone loved you very much so that your happiness was the only thing she wanted in the world, and she did a bad thing to make certain of it, could you forgive her?"

But that was the beauty. Bogart didn't. He couldn't replay the Bulgarian girl's words. He couldn't edit what Bergman said to him, nor could he tinker with his own heart. Maybe by the end of the film he figured it out, but right then, Bogart went with his own emotions. He forgot his anger and held her, Bergman, with her luminous eyes and high cheekbones and smile like a sunrise.

Hoffman whispered. "You didn't tell me the film had a sense of humor."

Earle felt her breath in his ear, her hand on his arm. "It has irony," he whispered back, keenly aware that Durance sat behind them. Did Bogart send Bergman off with Henreid at the end of the film because he knew she didn't love him? Was he that keen-sighted? And how did he know?

What was Hoffman thinking? Did she care for him in the least?

Earle forced himself to look away from the screen again. He was here to experience *Casablanca* in a world where it hadn't existed before. He had a job to do.

The woman in the floral dress held a handkerchief to her cheek, not moving. Her face was wet with tears. Henreid asked Bergman about the time she thought he was dead. "Were you lonely in Paris?" he asked. "I know how it is to be lonely," he said. Was Henreid forgiving Bergman for the affair with Bogart without even knowing about it? The woman in the floral dress sobbed silently. What was her story? Was her husband at war? Did she believe him to be dead? Even now, was there a lover?

Earle watched, awed. How seldom had he been able to feel the world through someone else. The bend of her wrist. The handkerchief's dangling end. The quiet, wracking sobs that shook her sides. How privileged he felt to be a part of her moment. What a moment of trespass on his part. Everything he hoped for in coming to see *Casablanca* was encompassed by this scene. This would be bigger than his Hindenberg experience.

He looked away, blinking against a momentary sting. It didn't take much to see that his problems didn't amount to—he sought for a comparison, then smiled—a hill of beans. It was Bogart's line. Whatever the woman in the floral dress was going through, his own anxieties couldn't measure up. Earle couldn't know Hoffman's mind any more than Bogart knew Bergman's, and in this time he couldn't edit in messages from her or create pictures of the two of them at romantic vacation stops, or even replay their times together. He was a time traveler stuck in the ever-present and always receding now with the people around him an enigma, like the woman in the floral dress.

On the screen, Bergman slipped away from her motel room to meet Bogart, to tell him of her life after she married Laszlo, how she thought Laszlo was dead when she'd met Bogart in Paris. Earle slid his arm out from under Hoffman's hand, then walked to the rear of the theater. From the back, he could see all the still heads. Earlier in the film he'd heard conversation, but now there was nothing but Bogart and Bergman's voices. Bergman buried her head in Bogart's shoulder. She said the line: "I ran away from you once, I can't do it again."

Earle nodded. He'd seen this moment over and over. It seemed to him that Bergman was exactly torn. She loved her husband, but she also loved Bogart. It was a perfect scene, balancing the two men she loved against the sureness that she would have to leave one behind. Maybe she believed that Laszlo really lived for his work and could go on without her, or maybe she knew that no matter what happened, if she demonstrated her love for Laszlo by deserting him for another man that she had done the right thing. There was no way to tell. Regardless, she chose Bogart and set him in motion for the end of the film.

Who was the audience rooting for? Laszlo seemed a bit of a cold fish, but he was absolutely blameless in his love for his wife and devotion to his anti-Nazism. Bogart was flawed and scarred, but his passion for Bergman redeemed him. And now, in the time the audience watched, France was still occupied. The Vichy government still danced to Germany's pipes. Soldiers were dying over what song the people would sing, "Die Wacht Am Rhine" or "La Marseillaise."

Earle moved to where he could see more of the audience. He imagined how the sequence would replay when he downloaded the nanotech recordings. The noisy projector clicking away in the background. The feel of plush beneath his hands. The hint of rain held in wet coats dripping onto the floor.

Now came the plan, the thinking that Bogart did for Bergman. Bergman believed she was leaving Casablanca with Bogart. They went to the airport. Bogart told Renault to fill out the letters of transit with Laszlo and Bergman's name. Bergman was confused. Bogart explained, the time travelers lament, that if she didn't leave she would regret it, "Maybe not today, maybe not tomorrow, but soon and for the rest of your life." The plane took off. Major Strasser was shot. Bogart and Renault walk into the fog together.

Earle closed his eyes and leaned against the wall. The soundtrack boomed out "La Marseillaise." People clapped. He opened his eyes. Some of the audience was standing, applauding the screen as the curtains closed and the lights came up. They kept clapping. Even though there were no live performers to appreciate their reaction, they applauded. Finally, they turned, gathered their umbrellas and coats to head toward the exits.

"I loved that," said a woman to her companion as they passed Earle on the way out. "Who would have believed Bogart could play a romantic lead?" said another.

Hoffman walked up the aisle, the house lights catching the shimmer in her hair. "You were right to come here. I had no idea," she said, her hand brushing his as she passed. "I'll see you in the lobby." She nodded back into the nearly empty theater.

Only Durance and the woman in the floral dress remained. Durance stood next to her, leaning down over where she was seated, speaking earnestly.

Earle glanced to the exit. Hoffman was already gone. He walked down the aisle toward Durance and the woman. It wasn't until Earle was close enough to touch them that Durance looked up.

"She seemed upset," said Durance.

"I'm better now, really," said the woman. She'd dried her face, but her mascara had smudged. "I don't know what came over me."

"I understand," said Durance. "Look," he said to Earle. "You were right." He fumbled for words, "I didn't think a film . . . it wasn't sentimental." He inhaled deeply, and in the exhalation was a hint of an emotional quiver. "They're doing the show again, aren't they, in a half hour?"

Earle nodded.

"And it will be exactly the same, won't it? They can't change it?" said Durance.

The woman looked at him quizzically.

Earle understood. The film would always play out the same way. Like the Hindenberg. Like all of history, unrolling in its immutable way. That was its charm. "Yes," he said. "Of course."

Durance took a seat next to the woman. "We thought we'd see it again." He gestured toward the exits. "Could you pay for our tickets?" Durance and the woman faced the screen, waiting for the lights to go down and the curtain to open.

In the lobby, Hoffman stood by the door. They stepped onto the sidewalk without speaking, where the rain had slowed to a gentle patter, hinting of snow. A block later, while they waited to cross the street, Hoffman said, "It was a good story."

She was looking into the distance. Not at him.

"Yes," he said.

"It had a good finish."

"Yes."

As they crossed, Hoffman took his arm. He realized she hadn't brought her umbrella. Water ran off the edges of her hat. She said, "What should we do now?"

When they reached the sidewalk, she still held his arm.

Earle thought of Bogart walking into the fog with Renault. It *was* a good ending, a wow finish. Earle said, "I hear that Cab Calloway is playing at the Park Central."

Hoffman smiled in a lingering way that seemed very much like Ingrid Bergman. "Do you know how to dance?"

A passing car splashed water on their legs. Earle didn't care. They had another twenty hours or so in New York, in the city that never sleeps. Meanwhile, in *Casablanca*, Sam sang at his piano, the old song, Bogart's and Bergman's song. Everybody's song.

It's true, Earle thought as the rain came down, as the water gurgled in the gutters, as the undersides of clouds glowing in New York's evening lights twisted slowly above. Sam was right: it's still the same old story, and it would always be, as time goes by.

Backtracked

INTRODUCTION

He had come back from the future, noticeably older, to the consternation of his wife. He knew that something bad was going to happen, something that he had to change or prevent, but he didn't know *what* it was . . .

* * *

Burt Filer is one of science fiction's mysteries. Beginning in the late 1960s, he attracted attention in the field with a string of excellent stories which marked him as a major new talent—and then he sank from sight, no forwarding address. The scant information is that grew up in upstate New York, attending Cornell, earning a degree in Mechanical Engineering in 1961, invented several devices, and was last heard from in Philadelphia. His first published story was "The Hole" in the May, 1967 issue of *If: Worlds of Science Fiction*, and his twelfth and last published work, in 1972, was "Eye of the Beholder" in Harlan Ellison's* *Again, Dangerous Visions*, adding up to a very bright, but (alas) very short career. In his introduction to Filer's story in *Again Dangerous Visions* (which is the source for what little bio info I've just cited), Harlan Ellison* wrote, "His short story 'Backtracked' is one of the finest short stories I have ever read, and it should have won the Nebula in 1968." High praise, indeed.

Backtracked

by Burt Filer

The first thing he saw was Sally staring at him. She was sitting up in the big bed and had four fingers of her left hand wedged in her mouth. For some reason she'd drawn the sheet up around her and held it there with the other arm, as if caught suddenly by a stranger. Fletcher sat up.

"What's the matter? What time is it?" He felt odd and a little woozy. His voice sounded rough and both legs hurt, the good one and the other one.

"You've backtracked," Sally said. She gritted her teeth and gave that quick double shake of hers. The long brown hair fell down, and a curler came out.

Fletcher looked down at the arm he'd hooked around his good knee. It was sunburned and freckled the way August usually made it, but the August of what future year had done this? The fingers were blunter, the nails badly bitten, and the arm itself was thicker by half than the one he'd gone to bed with.

Sally lay back down, blinking, on the verge of tears. "You're older," she said, "a lot older. Why'd you do it?"

Fletcher tossed off the sheet and swung his legs to the floor. "I don't know, but then I wouldn't. It wipes you out completely, they say." Hurrying across the old green rug they'd retired to the bedroom after long service downstairs, he stared at himself in the dressing mirror. At first he didn't believe it.

Gone was the somewhat paunchy but still attractive businessman of thirty-six. The man in the mirror looked more like a Sicilian fisherman, all weather-beaten and knotty. Fletcher looked for several long seconds at the blue veins which wrapped his forearms and calves like fishnets. Both calves. The left, though still as warped as ever, was thick now. It looked strong, but it ached.

Fletcher's face was older by ten years. Etched in the seams about his eyes was the grimness that age brings out through a lifetime of forced smiles. And though the hair on his chest was sunbleached, he could easily see that a good deal of it was actually white. Fletcher shut his eyes, turned away.

Walking around to Sally's side of the bed, he sat down and dropped a hand to her shoulder. "I must have had a good reason. We'll find out soon enough."

It was only six o'clock, but sleep was out of the question, naturally. They dressed. Sally went down the stairs ahead of him, still slim and lithe at thirty-four, and still desirable. The envy of many.

She turned left into the kitchen and he followed, but continued past into the garage. His excuse for privacy was the bicycles, just as hers was breakfast. Leave me alone and I'll get used to it, Fletcher thought. Leave her alone and she can handle it too.

He edged around the bumper of their car to the clutter of his workbench and switched on the light. The bicycles gave him a momentary sense of rightness, gleaming there. They were so slender and functional and spare. Flipping his own over on its back, he checked tension on the derailleur. Perfect.

He righted the thing and dropped the rear wheel into the free rollers. Mounting it, he pedaled against light resistance, the way he'd always dreamed the roads would be.

Maybe they would be now, with these legs. Why had he spent ten years torturing spring into the muscles of a cripple? Sheer vanity, perhaps. But at the cost of wasting those ten years forever, it seemed unreasonable.

Fletcher was sweating, and the speedometer on the rollers said thirty. He was only halfway through the gears, though, so he shifted twice. Fifty.

Maybe he should call Time Central? No, they were duty-bound to give him no help at all. They'd just say that at some point ten years in the future he had gone to them with a request to be backtracked to the present—and that before making the hop his mind had been run through that CLEAR/RESET wringer of theirs.

Sorry, Mr. Fletcher, but it's the only way to minimize temporal contamination and paradox. Bothersome thing, paradox. Your mind belongs to Fletcher of the present; you have no knowledge of the future. You understand, of course.

What he understood was that the body of Fletcher-forty-odd had backtracked to be used by the mind of Fletcher-thirty-six, almost as a beast of burden.

And Fletcher-thirty-six could only wonder why.

A lot of people did it to escape some unhappiness in their later years. It seldom worked. They inevitably became anachronistic misfits among their once-contemporaries. But ten years at Fletcher's age wasn't really that much, and he guessed they'd all get used to him. But would Sally?

Sixty, said the dummy speedometer. Fletcher noted with some surprise that he'd been at it for fifteen minutes. Better slow down, and save some for the trip. What strength! Maybe he'd learn to play tennis. He could see himself trouncing Dave Schenk, Sally looking on from the sidelines—Fletcher was smiling now. Sally would come around. She had a powerful older man in place of a soft young one, a cripple at that. Polio. He'd been one of the last. Other men had held doors open for him ever since, and he'd learned to smile. . . .

Up to fifty again, slow down. And where was breakfast? This body of his hungered. And what had it done, this body? Knowing from bitter experience how slowly it responded to exercise, Fletcher decided that the lost ten years must have been devoted almost exclusively to physical development.

But for what? Some kind of crisis that he might meet with superior strength on the second go-around? And why had he decided to backtrack to this particular morning?

"Fletch, breakfast," Sally called. The voice was lighter and steady. Dismounting, Fletcher stood with his hands in his pockets and watched the silver wheel whir slowly to a stop.

She wouldn't want to discuss it. Not for a while, anyhow. It'd been the same with his leg, back before they were married. He switched the light off and went in.

"It'll be nice after that burns off," he said, nodding out the window.

The bench in the breakfast nook felt hard as he sat on it. Less flesh there now. Sally handed down two plates and joined him. Not across the table but at his side. A show of confidence. They ate slowly, silently.

Fletcher looked over at her profile. With her hair tied back like that she was very patrician. Straight nose, serious mouth. Like Anastasia, Dave Schenk had said, a displaced princess. She caught him looking at her, began to smile, changed her mind, put down her fork.

She faced him squarely. "I think I'll make it, Fletch." She lowered her forehead a fraction, waiting for a reassuring peck, and he gave it to her.

He turned out to have been right about the weather. Within an hour they were pedaling in bright sunlight and had stopped to remove their sweaters. Sally seemed cheerful. For perhaps the third time, Fletcher caught her gazing with frank wonder at his body, especially his leg. He glowed inwardly. Aloud he said, "Forward, troops," and swooped off ahead.

They wound their way up Storm King Mountain. Occasionally a car would grind past them on the steep grades, but soon the two bicycles left the road. They had the clay path which led up to the reservoir all to themselves. May-pale sumacs on the left, and a hundred feet of naked air on the right.

"Hey," said Sally, "slow down." Dismounting, they sat under a big maple. She leaned her head on his shoulder and slid one hand cozily between his upper arm and his ribs. "Oh," she said, and raised her eyebrows.

They sat there for some time. Over them the branches reached across the path and out beyond the cliffs. Below, the Hudson wound in a huge ess, a round green island at one end. It was a wide old river, moving slowly. A tug dragged clumped barges upstream in an efficient line that cut off most of the curves. In the distance a few motorboats buzzed like flies, little white wakes behind them. Crawling along the far shore was a passenger train headed for New York.

It smelled like spring. Rising, Sally went over by the bicycles and bent to pick a white umbrella of Queen Anne's lace. She came back twirling the stalk between her fingers. "Ready." she said.

He set her an easy pace, but did it the hard way himself, not using the lower gears. One of Dave Schenk's subtler tricks. Fletcher wished he were with them today.

At about eleven o'clock they reached the top. Between the power company's storage reservoir and the bluffs was a little park that no one else ever seemed to use. Sally spread most of their food on a weathered wooden picnic table. Then she went over and sat on a broad granite shelf. Fletcher set about starting a fire.

It was taking him quite a while, as he'd forgotten the starter and had to whittle some twigs for tinder. He nicked his thumb, frowned, sucked it, looked up.

Sally was on her feet again, picking more flowers. She paused from time to time to gaze out over the river. The view was even more spectacular here, Fletcher knew, even though too far back to see it himself. They were three or four hundred feet straight above the water.

Running a few feet beyond the main line of the bluff was a grassy promontory. Several bunches of Queen Anne's lace waved above the wild hay and creepers. He wished she'd get away from there and took a breath to tell her to.

Sally screamed as her legs slid out of sight. Twisting midair, she clutched two frantic handfuls of turf.

She was only sixty feet away, but the fireplace and the big old table lay directly between them. Fletcher planted both hands on the smoking stone chimney and vaulted it. The thing was four feet high, but could have been five and he'd still have made it. A dozen running steps, each faster and longer than the last, carried him to the table. He yanked his head down and his right leg up to hurdle it, snapping the leg down on the other side and swinging the weaker one behind. Pain shot through it, and Fletcher nearly sprawled. It took him four steps to straighten out, and in four more he was there.

He hurled himself at the two slender wrists that were falling away, and got one.

Sally screamed again, this time in pain. Fletcher hauled her up to his chin, both sinewy hands around her small white one. Edging backward on his knees, he drew her fully up. Fletcher stood shakily and attempted to help her to her feet. His left leg gave way.

Falling beside her, he lay on the warm granite and tried to catch his breath. It was difficult for some reason.

Her face swam before him, and as he lost consciousness he heard himself repeating, "So that's why, that's why—"

Fletcher's eyelids were burning, so he opened them, to look directly into the sun. He must have been lying there an hour. Sally—his mind leapfrogged back and the breath stopped in his throat. But no, it was over, she lay here beside him now. Fletcher rose to an elbow. His leg throbbed between numbness and intolerable pain, and it looked as if someone had taken an ax to it.

But Sally's wrist looked just as bad. The drying scum near her lips attested to that. As he moved her head gently away from the puddle, she moaned.

It took him ten minutes to crawl over to the table and return with a bottle of wine. They'd brought no water. He sprinkled some on her forehead, then held it to her lips. She came around, fainted, came around again.

Sally had made it about halfway down to the road when she ran into some picnickers. The jeep came at three, and at four they were both in the orthopedic ward at Rockland State.

Fletcher was still dopey with anesthetic and delayed shock. As he told the reporter what had happened, the little man nearly drooled. Their episode had occurred on Saturday. When they were released from the hospital and sent home on Wednesday, their story was still up on page four. On the front porch was a yellow plastic wastebasket full of unopened telegrams and letters.

They hadn't had much privacy at the hospital. So after Sally had made the coffee she sat down opposite Fletcher at the kitchen table and asked, "How've you been?"

"Okay. Still a little disoriented, maybe."

"Yes." She stared into her cup. "Fletch, I guess the first time we went through that, I fell?"

Fletcher nodded. "I'd never have made it to you, the old way." He stared down at the cast on his leg. "Ten years of mine, for all of yours. I'd do it again."

"It wasn't cheap," she said.

"No, it wasn't cheap."

They made love that night. Fletcher had been worried about that, and found his fears justified to some extent. Ten years made a difference. But Sally held him long afterward and cried a little, which was the best with her. He fell asleep feeling reassured for then, but knowing what was to come.

Fletcher dyed his hair and had some minor facial surgery done to smooth out his eyes and throat. He gained ten pounds. He looked pretty much like the Fletcher of thirty-six. A certain amount of romance was attached to his reputation now, and when he changed jobs his salary almost doubled.

His broken left leg never healed solidly, though, and for all intents and purposes he was back to where he'd started. He and Sally remained childless right up until their divorce two years later. She was later married to David Schenk, but Fletcher remained alone.

So Little and So Light

INTRODUCTION

Here's a story of another time patrol and one of their agents, on the trail of a rebel who's back then, recklessly changing the course of history. But when she found him, he seemed to know more about her than she herself knew.

* * *

Sarah A. Hoyt won the Prometheus Award for her novel *Darkship Thieves*, published by Baen, and has authored *Darkship Renegades* (nominated for the following year's Prometheus Award) and *A Few Good Men*, two more novels set in the same universe, with more in the works. She has written numerous short stories and novels in a number of genres, including science fiction, fantasy, mystery, historical novels and historical mysteries, many under a number of pseudonyms, and has been published—among other places—in *Analog*, *Asimov's* and *Amazing*. For Baen, she has also written three books in her popular shape-shifter fantasy series, *Draw One in the Dark*, *Gentleman Takes a Chance*, and *Noah's Boy*. Her *According to Hoyt* is one of the most interesting blogs on the internet. Originally from Portugal, she lives in Colorado with her husband, two sons and the surfeit of cats necessary to a die-hard Heinlein fan.

So Little and So Much

INTRODUCTION

So Little and So Light

by Sarah A. Hoyt

I landed with a stumble at the foot of Calbeck Hill in England in 1066, during the Battle of Hastings when the English routed the Normans for good and all out of England.

The landing was rough, as it sometimes is. I half fell and my feet squelched as I instinctively spread them apart seeking for purchase in the marshy ground. No one saw me appear. The human mind is very good at censoring out the impossible.

I was dressed as a man. Not difficult for a woman of the twenty-third century transported back to the eleventh. More likely to pass as a man than as a woman. Wearing the uniform of a housecarl—a professional soldier—in woolen tunic, and trousers, with a straw padded surcoat under the chain mail hauberk, my breasts, never all that noticeable, were wholly invisible. The conical hat with face shield hid my features and my lack of beard. And the kite-shaped shield, the battle ax in my hand made sure no one got very close to me.

The man next to me made a sound at my stumble, something like, "Hey there, watch it," but then turned forward.

Forward, as all the history books had taught, the forces of William the Bastard fled our side, their mounted cavalry decamping in ground that had never been suited for cavalry. As a trainee time-Hunter, in history of war, I'd heard all about the mistakes William had made. Still, wasn't prepared to see them enacted before my eyes.

Few Breachers make it for battles and confrontations. The romantic mind that thinks the past a better place always goes for parades, for grand events, for triumph and celebration. But this was not a common Breacher. He'd been, before his transgression, a Satrap, a member of a good family, of an hierarchy unbroken for ten generations. And a director of the Time Corps.

Ahead of me, Harold's forces were moving and presently we too started running, chasing the Normans as they fled. Before I'd arrived, already half the forces had abandoned the safety of Caldebeck Hill for the plain where the Normans were fleeing. I joined in the pursuit, excited to finally be in an event we'd studied so often.

For a while it was all a blur as I met the enemy, and had to counter their sword thrusts with my ax blows.

It used to be, back in the beginning, that people were afraid of time travel. They thought any misstep, any foot laid wrong, any butterfly trampled, made us all Breachers and changed history forever.

We've found of course that history is more elastic than that. It takes willful intent and major changes to make history take a different course.

So I lay about with my ax and a clear conscience. It's hard to explain without believing in predestination, but I couldn't kill anyone who hadn't died. Not in a chaotic event like battle.

And to me they weren't quite real, these men I fought.

What was real was the tracker and the time-tagger. The arrows and flashes, in lights, atop my shield, could pass by mere play of light, but I knew what they told me.

The Breacher was here. Very close.

And then the man facing me spoke, in Panlanguage, in a soft throaty voice that barely rose above a whisper, "Ah, Hunter. You've found me." A chuckle. "But too late."

I looked up and for a moment caught a glimpse of the Norman whose heavy sword knocked my ax blow aside. An impression of red hair, of soft red beard, of laughing blue eyes shining from either side of his helmet's nose-piece.

I was so stunned at Panlanguage and at the smile on his eyes that I lowered my ax. He could have killed me then, but he didn't. He only laughed, and then vanished, the bone scales of his armor making a sound as a soft rain while the time-current grabbed him and pulled.

I came to myself as another Norman rushed towards me, and I pushed at the pendant at my neck, the aten that disguised my retrieval mechanism, and which would have become inactive in the absence of the nanites in my living blood, so if I died or lost it, no one could use it.

There was the time current grabbing me like invisible claws, and pulling me, with force that made my teeth rattle.

And then I was in the mission room.

"You failed," Alvin Windham said, even as I dropped my helm and weapon, and started tearing out of the sweat-soaked, uncomfortable clothes.

I undressed completely, and went into the delousing room, saying to the room in general, knowing the pickups would relay the words to Time Command Center, "It was a bloody battle. And he faced me directly, instead of running. And he spoke to me in Panlanguage."

I got out of the delousing room, my body stinging from the short shower of the disinfecting/cleansing solution. The Hunters called it delousing, but I knew it was something else, including inoculating against any virus, any bacteria, anything of the time that might hitch a ride back to the real, present world.

It used to be believed that nothing could attach in the short times a Hunter spent in the past, and then someone who had spent a day in ancient Egypt had brought back the first epidemic flu and killed half of the Hunters. Now we deloused.

The room I entered as I left the delousing was a dressing room, circular, with pegs on the wall. On one of the pegs hung my everyday clothes: short tunic and leggings in a fabric that neither scratched nor clung to your body with sweat. I wanted them so badly. I wanted nothing better than to put them on, to walk out the door into the world where I didn't have to find a dangerous maniac bent on destroying history.

But then I read the words emblazoned around the room, "Time Hunter Corps. Saving the past for the future," and I stayed naked, ready to put on whatever clothes I needed for wherever the Breacher had gone now.

Alvin stood in front of me, in his dark brown uniform, the clipboard in his hands. "We're not faulting you, understand! This is not a common Breacher and this is why we chose you to catch him. We knew it wouldn't be easy." He frowned slightly. "The problem is that he could be anywhere. This is not a home-made time jumper. He stole our best."

I grunted understanding and pulled back at my shoulder-length dark hair and glowered at Alvin. "How did I fail?" I'm nothing special to look at, and he'd seen me—and every other Hunter—naked too often for it to occasion any surprise or any appreciation. Not that there was much to appreciate, as I was no fashion plate. Few Hunters are. Too memorable can kill you when you're back in the past, and we can only take so many legends of the beautiful fairy up the hill.

But he noticed my frown.

He shook his head a little. "We are not quite sure how, but we think he got the ear of William the Bastard. He must have been in the time and place for years, without us seeing it. He must have confounded our tracers. And he . . . he advised William on the use of archers, on the use of ambush. The retreat was a deception. Your momentary comrades were ambushed and massacred."

"The Normans won England?" I said. "But that—"

"For now," Alvin said. "For now. Inside the command we don't change, of course, so we know the truth, and once history settles we will change it again. Ten years. Twenty. But first we need to catch him. We think he's trying to create so many break points, so much instability that we can't repair it; that even within Time Command Center the memories change."

"Can that happen?" I asked.

He shrugged. "We'd think not. But Seth is a Cowden. Not only was he an expert in time and time-disruptions, but his family have been time-experts forever. He might know something we don't." Alvin consulted something on his clipboard. "Ah, there. We found him again."

* * *

We were sliding down the Nile on a boat filled with dancers and servers. I was in the boat of Queen Nefertiti, principal wife of the great innovating pharaoh Akhenaten. Above us the stars shone on a velvet sky. I wore a linen dress with precise pleats, and a wig, having taken the part of a serving lady in the throng of the followers of the queen. Not a real server, but one of the daughters of provincial nobles sent to the court with the pretext of attending the queen and the real aim of perhaps finding an advantageous alliance.

All night my jewelry—the heavy lapis-lazuli looking necklace around my neck—had been communicating through slight shakes that the Breacher was near. But how near?

We were headed for the Heb-Sed of Akhenaten. He had many, having started in the third year of his reign with the Heb-Sed normally reserved by other pharaohs to celebrate thirty years in power.

It was generally acknowledged among historians that it had been such a bold move in celebrating the Heb-Sed, the festival of the tail, that had helped Akhenaten establish a monotheistic religion. And it had been that monotheistic religion that helped consolidate the Egyptian Empire under his son, Tutankhaten, and his sons' sons.

Such a strong empire had Egypt founded that neither Greece nor Rome could dislodge it and little by little their confusing polytheism had been subsumed into the worship of Aten, which in turn had propelled the world into the new era.

Twice during the night, someone had touched me where my back was bare and I'd felt the necklace vibrate. But every time I turned around, I saw only Egyptians. Not the Breacher. And I doubted the tall, redheaded man I'd seen at Hastings could have disappeared in this dark crowd, even if he'd worn a wig.

Presently the boat docked where the preparations had been made for the Pharaoh to run the ritual course and do the dance that would prove both his ability to still rule the country and to have the approval of the gods to do so.

His boat had already docked and his retinue had disappeared past a series of refreshment tents set up to receive him. I had to wait until the Queen and her close attendants left the boat. From where I stood I could see her exquisite profile as she stood.

Near me a voice said, "You, girl," and thrust a linen cushion fringed in gold at me. "Carry this."

I took it. I hadn't had time to establish an identity. Even my command of Egyptian was limited. My goal was not to intrigue, nor to carry on a careful subversion, but to find the Breacher, to neutralize him, to take him back with him or kill him, if I could not take him back for judgment.

Judgment of Breachers was always preferable, but in this case it might not be possible. The Breacher was far too clever and at any rate, if he died before being dragged to the twenty-third century, it would spare his powerful family embarrassment.

On my turn I processed off the boat, holding the cushion to my chest, as though it were precious, which it was, since I'd be severely punished, I was sure, if I lost one of the Queen's possessions. Worse than displeasing one of the Satraps.

We processed past the refreshment tables, and to stand under an awning while the priests pinned a tail to the king, since Heb-Sed or the festival of the tail related to an obscure wolf god. Akhenaten had said the wolf god didn't exist, that all power belonged to Aten. But he still wore the tail.

Just before the run, he stumbled, as though he'd lost balance, and I thought that the sun must be exceptionally hot. After all, Akhenaten was supposed to reign another fifteen years.

A finger caressed my dress at the top. A voice said, speaking throatily in Panlanguage, so that anyone hearing him would think he was making mere, random noises, "He will be dead within the year."

I jumped and tried to turn around, but couldn't. Somehow the cushion—and I couldn't imagine how—was holding me in position, holding me turned forward.

"That is right," he said. "That cushion is a neutralizing device for your necklace and it has . . . other effects. You will neither be able to let go of it nor to turn, till I let you."

I cleared my throat. I wanted to shout, but instead, I spoke in a whisper too, the whisper that prevented us from disturbing those around us. It was no part of the mission of a Time Hunter to create time disturbances. And I would not. "You are mad, Seth Cowden."

He took a deep breath. His finger continued to trace the width of my shoulders, the dip between my shoulder blades. "Perhaps I am, Lady . . . what is your name? Your real name, not the assumed Egyptian one?"

"Iset," I said. "Iset Creuly. But I am not a lady. Not from a Satrap family."

"Ah," he said. "No. You wouldn't be. They don't risk their daughters in these runs."

"I was sent because I've dealt with difficult Breachers before. If you return and turn yourself in," I said, "we'll make accommodations."

This time it was a soft laugh that answered me, "Don't lie to me, Lady Creuly. There are no accommodations for a Breacher who has succeeded. Oh . . ." He paused and seemed to think. "I suppose my family will make sure my death is painless."

I should have told him that he could escape death, that he would be considered mentally disturbed and not fully in control. Surely he was mentally disturbed. Had to be. Why else would someone of a Satrap family run into the past to change it?

But I knew he had been in command, and probably knew the truth better than I did. He was right. Crimes such as his couldn't be forgiven, not even in the Satrap families. And at any rate Akhenaten had stumbled again and I made an involuntary exclamation, lost in the sounds of those around me.

"I wonder," he said, in the tone of a man who dreamed, "What your name was originally. And also why they made such a beautiful woman a Hunter. I thought they chose for lack of memorability?"

I opened my mouth to protest that I was unmemorable, but he only said, "Goodbye, Iset. I wonder what that will be when I next see you. Iset is such a perfect name upon the tongue. Little Isis, a perfect miniature goddess." He laughed softly. "No matter. Akhenaten is done. I have been in his court for years, slowly poisoning all his family in a way undetectable. Even Tutankhaten, soon to become Tutankhamun, will die young and without descendants. If my calculations are right,

Greece and Rome will supplant them and some other religion will give the world names that we can only imagine. And perhaps—"

I couldn't breathe. I wished to believe he was bluffing, but something told me he wasn't. I wished to believe his finger on my skin was an imposition and a boorish trespass, but I felt it was both the taunt of a man who knows in the end he's doomed and the indulgence of a man who found me beautiful. Which was strange and miraculous both.

"Perhaps?" I said, curtly, trying to make him stop tracing arabesques on my skin with his fingertip.

"Perhaps we'll meet again, Iset Creuly. In a freer world."

I stood in the hall of Greenwich Palace, outside the queen's bedroom. This time I had been there for three months, and managed to establish myself as Mary Wingfield, a relation to the Wingfields of Kimbolton Castle.

Alvin, after dressing me down, asking me, "What could you have been thinking, Mary Creuly? You should never have taken that cushion. Did it not occur to you it might contain a nefarious device?" had talked to me about how the Breacher had been traced to the time of Henry VIII, to be precise, to 1535, when the king shared the crown with the beautiful and impetuous Anne Boleyn, his second and final wife, the ancestress of the Tudor dynasty which would retain the English throne until the twenty second century.

She'd given him a daughter, but no son, and in October 1535 she'd miscarried a son. Mid-1636 she'd have her second son, Henry, who would reign as Henry IX. Before he ascended the throne, England would reconcile with the Catholic church. Swayed by the health and vigor of the English heir, and by more material concerns, if the historians were to be believed, Pope Paul III would come to believe Henry VIII's crisis of conscience over his too near relation to Queen Catherine was correct and had been based in divine inspiration.

Everything forgiven, by the time Henry IX climbed the throne on his father's death, he'd be a most Catholic subject. Carefully juggling alliances with Spain and France, the ninth Henry had created the basis of a stable empire.

Queen Anne had given the king two more sons and another daughter, all of whom had been used as marriage fodder around the world. She was sometimes called the mother of kings, and it was true that everyone of royal blood, even all the Satraps in our time, had her blood.

For months I'd watched over her health. I'd managed to get assigned as a lady's maid, and endured endless games of cards to make sure nothing was eaten by the queen, nothing came near her that wasn't carefully monitored by my various disguised apparatus.

If the queen were poisoned, if she died, that would destabilize the future enough that the pieces would be hard enough to put together again. But not on my watch.

As for the Breacher, all my various tracers told me, time and again, that he was nearby, but never close enough to the queen to make a difference. Never close enough to hurt her.

The only times I left her alone at all were while she was sleeping, usually watched over by her women, or when she ordered me away. And even then I kept my tracers on her to make sure the Breacher didn't come near.

It was during one of those times, while I walked in the courtyard at Greenwich palace, my tracer telling me the Breacher was nowhere near the queen, and was in fact quite near me, that I realized he was walking towards me.

As at the Battle of Hastings, he was tall and redheaded, with grey-blue eyes and the shadow of a smile on his lips.

That he recognized me was obvious. I reached under my kirtle for the burner that I kept handy if I came across him. I'd shot men before. No. I'd shot simulations of men before, in exercises. I'd brought in all my captured Breachers alive. I didn't want to shoot him. I wanted to capture him. But he was a difficult one.

"Seth Cowden," I said. "You are under arrest for stealing a time device, for violating the ban on unauthorized time travel, for trying to change the past in order to—"

He grinned at me. He made no effort at all to go for his burner. "Am I, Iset? Is that your name?"

"I am Mary," I said. "Mary Deven."

He smiled a little. "Ah, Mary," he said, testing out my name as though it were an exotic confection upon his tongue. "I must have forgotten."

His smile, his lack of concern with my trying to arrest him disturbed me. "Seth Cowden," I repeated. "You are under arrest. You can let me hold your wrist for transport, or else I will terminate—"

"Yes, yes," he said. He made a gesture with his hand as though dismissing the burner I was pointing at him from under the folds of my kirtle. He had to know it was there, and also that I could shoot through fabric and burn him through the heart. But his eyes were unconcerned. And though I was tall for an Elizabethan woman, he was a giant, as he was tall even for the twenty-third century. He was in fact every bit a Satrap, tall and broad-shouldered, with perfect teeth and a look of complete self-possession. "But first let's walk in this garden. Let me tell you why I did it."

I hesitated. "Tell me—" I said, and then, decidedly. "I don't need to know!"

He shrugged. "Oh, perhaps not. But don't you want to know? You know who I am. The Cowdens have been in charge of the government of Earth and the twenty worlds for centuries. Why would I throw it all away?

"You are disturbed. Your mind—"

"Do I look like a madman to you? Give me your arm, Mary, and I shall walk with you in the garden."

"It is raining!"

"So, you are not a real Elizabethan, whose clothes will be ruined by a little rain, and who can be killed by a cold. Walk with me, Mary. I will tell you why I did what I did, and if you still think I deserve arrest, you can take me back. Or shoot me for all I care. If I still exist when we're done talking."

"If you still exist?"

"Ah, in the multi-universe each individual's life is such a small thing, isn't it? So little and so light. It counts for very little even under the empire, does it not? And the slightest shift can make it vanish."

It was madness of course. What can I tell you, but that Hunters are human too? Aye, and in my case a woman. A woman who had never been rich or connected or, for that matter, beautiful.

I'd been born to a clerk in the Imperial administration, and my rank in life was restricted. That a Satrap wished to speak to me was a little intoxicating. That he'd called me beautiful had to be a ruse, or a trap. But there are traps so seductive we would fall into them willingly. I followed him to the garden, under the fine rain, and he put my arm in his. I could have held his wrist. I could have activated the transport. To this day I don't know why I didn't.

The garden was sad under the rain, but you could tell where things had been planted that when green would make the place delightful. We walked down paths I didn't very well mark, and he talked. "Have you never thought, Mary, that the Empire perhaps cares a little too little about people? About each person?"

"The empire preserves people," I said. "Lines, families, groups of people. Surely individuals are preserved too as part of it."

"But only as part," he said. "And only in their proper ranks."

"The empire is stable," I said. "Over the generations, the families have perfected their peculiar specialties. Each of them is good at what it was born to do, clerks and Satraps, commanders and planners."

He gave me a look, sly, out of the corner of the soft grey eyes. "So, Mary, how many Hunters in your family?"

I shrugged and blushed. "Does it matter then?" I said. "The Hunters are not a clan nor a family specialty. They come from every family and every class, provided they have a taste for adventure, an interest in history, a quick mind."

He grinned. "Aye, then, Mary, from every class. And have you thought, perhaps, that in every class, in every specialized family, there are individuals born whose talents differ from that of their family, that if they were allowed to use their talents, to create their own path, the world might be unimaginably richer?"

"No," I said. "That is madness. Anarchy."

"When I was younger," he said. "I was a Hunter. And on a field mission after a Breacher, I pursued a man who created so much instability that for a few . . . moments? Days? Years? However you measure inexistent time, a society was allowed to exist where the empire had never come about. In it, men were free. Individuals. It was a beautiful— Oh, it was scary," he said, probably having seen my expression, "and maddening and fast and chaotic, but that world, as it was, was also beautiful. No ordered ranks, no classes, no exams for advancement." He sighed. "Their interactions were mad things, with no rhyme or reason. Then the repairers and tracers from headquarters got to cleaning up the time line, and reestablishing it, and I was brought back, and I became one of the planners, and I never saw—" He paused suddenly, both in speech and as though his feet had brought him to an unexpected place. "We," he said. Then stopped again, as though that beginning had no end. He sighed. "When I saw you, the first time you came into the center, a Hunter, newly minted, I realized—" He paused again. "But no, I could never explain it to you, could I?"

And I realized we were standing in the middle of the kitchen garden, where vegetables, stunted by the cold of winter, still remained enough to see what they had been. "I didn't know there was a kitchen garden here," I said.

Which was when the screams echoed, loud, from the main part of the palace, and suddenly, as suddenly as my startled wheeling around to look at him, Seth wasn't there, and there was just me, standing, under the fine rain, my French hood plastered to my hair, my gown sodden, my heart thudding, thudding, thudding.

He'd done something. He'd evaded my careful surveillance. He'd—

I ran. I ran in the direction of the screams, to stand outside the Queen's bedroom. From inside came the screams, the sound of a woman sobbing.

Suddenly the crowd parted, and the king, King Henry VIII in all his majesty, came thundering down the corridors of Greenwich, and into the door of the Queen's room before we had so much as time to curtsey. From inside the crying of a woman stopped, and now came the voice of a man—the king—raised in scolding.

Minutes only, and he came out, saying at the door, "You'll get no more boys from me."

The crying resumed then, quieter. And then minutes later a woman came, carrying something in a folded towel. She looked at us, and she looked at the floor, and she said, "Queen Anne has had a miscarriage of her savior."

I blinked, realizing in shock this was Henry IX, the Great Harry of English history, the ancestor of most of our Satraps. And he'd died. He'd died unborn.

History was tilting on its axis, and I knew the Breacher had done it, but I didn't know how, and I reached for my bracelet and pressed to return to control center.

I was in a room. A broad room, wide round, that looked a little like Time Command Center, and yet wasn't. I looked up, and there was no inscription around the door.

And then Seth Cowden appeared, from an internal door, and smiled at me, "Back so soon, my darling," he said. He extended both hands to me, and took me in his arms. "How was the expedition? Did you find what you wished?"

I was mute for a moment because my first thought was to tell him I knew how he'd done it. Henry IX had died in utero due to something added to his mother's food. I'd monitored the food itself, from the kitchens on, but not what had grown in the kitchen garden. Some fruit, some herb, some winter vegetable had grown with the nanites already upon them that would stop that life, before it was born, that would send history into a different path.

The other part of my brain told me it was all no sense. There was no Time Command Center. There was no Henry IX. England had remained the excommunicated child of Europe, separate. Because of its less rigid adherence to religion, it had spawned a much different culture, one that tolerated different kinds of thought.

The empire that united all the lands of Europe had never coalesced. There was some thought too that a certain rigidity of Egyptian religion, encased in millennia of tradition had never occurred, and the thought that the England itself was very different from the land of Saxons. It all flitted through my mind, like a whirlwind, like scraps of a dream half-remembered. And then it crashed into the thought that I'd been sent to retrieve Seth, that Seth—

But there was no Time Command Center. Time travel was

regulated, in a way, in the sense that it was overseen by several scientific bodies, and that people had to be trained before going back. But the time stream was free to archeologists and sociologists, to investigators and historians.

I was an historian. I'd just gone back to study the Tudor period and to copy some documents relating to Anne Boleyn's trial for witchcraft.

Looking up at Seth, my world solidified. He was my husband of three years, and a chair of history in the University of New America, a planet in Alpha Centauri. It was a new colony, funded after the old Earth country, a free colony that took all those wishing to join it from the heart, and willing to contribute to its mad whirlwind of invention and innovation.

"I found the documents," I said. "And copied them." I removed the French hood and the dress. This was our very own antechamber. Seth was quite wealthy, being older than I and famous in his field, and he had built a time-travel chamber onto our house.

Naked, I allowed Seth to envelope me into his arms, feeling his red beard tickle my face. "I'm so glad we live in a world where I can't have arbitrary charges brought against me, and everyone will go along with a despotic king. I'm so glad that the rights of the individual count for more." I frowned, as a feeling of uneasiness persisted. "It could so easily have been different," I said.

"Very easily," he said, and gently kissed my forehead.

"And in a different world, I might never have met you, even," I said. "Our families being from so different a level of wealth."

"Oh, what does wealth matter, or class," he said, and kissed me again, this time intently, as though kissing me were the only thing of importance in the universe.

Then he took me within, by the hand, into our chamber.

Hours later, we were lying together on our bed, dozing. "I had a dream," I told him. "I think it was a dream. But it is so strange. And the world was quite different. I was hunting you down because you were bent on . . ."

"On?"

"Disrupting the time stream."

He laughed. "Foolishness. Disruptions tend to heal."

"Yes, but not for a while, and I remember it was odd that you . . . I have an idea you killed your own ancestor, in that dream."

"That is madness," he said. Amusement made him narrow his eyes, an expression I knew well. "And quite impossible. Given that women are women, which man can be sure who his ancestor was?"

Just then the communicator played a sharp note, calling our attention. Seth groaned. "Alvin," he said.

Alvin was his assistant, the man who kept all the paperwork in order, the man who made sure that all the events of the day happened on time. Not brilliant, not innovative, but faithful and exact. I had a feeling he bored Seth a little.

Seth pressed a button and a hologram of Alvin appeared in the middle of the room. He was dressed very oddly, in a golden tunic, and strange molding pants, not at all like the loose, informal clothes favored in New America.

He glared at Seth, too, for what I'm sure must be the first time. "You thought you'd been so clever," he said.

Seth sat up straighter, and said, in a tone of deep loathing, "Oh, it is you!" and I got a feeling he wasn't talking about Alvin, or not the Alvin I knew at all. "Very clever sending her after me. You knew I would not hurt her."

"And very poor planning, very unworthy of a Satrap," Alvin said. "To change the whole world for a woman. And a common, low born woman at that."

I opened my mouth to protest, and I might have said something about Alvin needing counseling. But neither of the men paid attention to me.

Alvin said, "Fortunately I found your real ancestor, the Lute player. Did you think I didn't know? Your ancestor looked just like him." He spoke in a low, vicious tone, and I remembered a lute player accused of consorting with Queen Anne, but Queen Anne had been executed and—

Seth grabbed at my wrist. "Whatever happens," he said. "Remember that I love you." He put something in my hand. It felt solid and small. And he closed my fist over it.

Alvin didn't notice the small gesture; he was ranting, "Fortunately I retain my memory. It will take centuries for us to clean up the time stream, but until we do, you will be punished for your actions. Even now, the assassins are destroying your true ancestor, before he can—"

There had been as though a sick twist in my guts, a momentary dizziness. I lay in bed in my small apartment, which overlooked Kansas, the capital city of New America. Outside my window the bustle of the largest city in the system went on. A reflection of light from a passing flyer sent lights chasing into my room.

And I opened my hand and found I was clutching a ring. It was so wide, it would only fit my thumb. I slid it on, hesitantly.

Suddenly I remembered. Hastings and Egypt and Tudor England. But with it came a feeling of Seth, too. And I realized he'd worn this ring that created a bubble of stability in the time stream, a mental barrier against the changes to the past, and allowed you to remember all the adjustments.

An expensive bauble, but then, in the original world we both came from, Seth had been a Satrap. Wealthy beyond the dreams of common people.

And he'd had this bubble, and he'd become a Breacher . . . for love of me.

The memory came with the ring, of the world accidentally created in which we were lovers, and of his despair, until he'd seen me again, in the real? Original world.

I got up from bed and went to the window, and looked out at the tumultuous world outside that would never have happened but for Seth's meddling.

In that first world, it had been ordered, with palaces and slums in very different areas, with castes, with rituals, with rigid control of every individual action.

Individuals. So little and so light in the stream of time, in the pageant of history, in the swirl of the worlds.

But he had roiled time and history for me.

And I remembered too, this world, and our three years together, and the way he laughed, and his teasing look, and the sudden, unexpectedly vulnerable glances he gave me, that spoke of love.

So little and so light.

I clutched my hand in a fist around the ring on my thumb. Alvin had missed something when he'd not destroyed me, when he'd not seen this ring being given to me.

I remembered.

How hard could it be to go back in time and save a man from death? Oh, sure, I knew that scanners and fixers, planners and reweavers of time would all be at work even as I spoke.

But there was a good chance Alvin himself was gone, and any number of his helpers. Satraps had all been descended from Henry IX and who knew how many times Henry IX's wife, Queen Catherine, had been unfaithful.

And yet, even if they all still existed and arrayed themselves against me, they couldn't stop me. Sure, there were many of them, but that just meant I must fight them all.

I remembered our love and our marriage that had only existed in that world created by Breaching the past. Our love for which he had sacrificed all.

I must plunge into the time stream and from it rescue and bring back the one life that mattered to me.

So little and so light. It outweighed all the possible worlds.

The Price of Oranges

INTRODUCTION

What's a fellow to do when his granddaughter, who isn't getting any younger, seems unable to find her Mr. Right? Since he happened to have a secret way of stepping back into the 1930s, when, he thought, there was a Mr. Right on every street corner, the solution was obvious. But there were a few factors he hadn't taken into consideration . . .

* * *

Nancy Kress began writing in the 1970s because, she says, she was not good at embroidery or quilting, her first two choices, selling her first story, "The Earth Dwellers," to Galaxy in 1976. Though her first novels were fantasy, she later concentrated on SF, racking up an impressive array of awards: five Nebulas (for "Out of All Them Bright Stars," "Beggars in Spain," "The Flowers of Aulit Prison," "Fountain of Age," and "After the Fall, Before the Fall, During the Fall"), two Hugos (for "Beggars in Spain" and "The Erdmann Nexus"), a Sturgeon (for "The Flowers of Aulit Prison"), and a John W. Campbell Memorial Award (for Probability Space). Her work has been translated into Swedish, French, Italian, German, Spanish, Polish, Croatian, Lithuanian, Romanian, Japanese, and Russian, and Klingon, none of which she can read. She teaches regularly at summer conferences such as Clarion West and Taos Toolbox. For sixteen years, she was the "Fiction" columnist for Writer's Digest magazine, and has written three books about writing. She lives in Seattle with her husband, writer Jack Skillingstead, and Cosette, the world's most spoiled toy poodle.

The Price of Oranges

by Nancy Kress

"I'm worried about my granddaughter," Harry Kramer said, passing half of his sandwich to Manny Feldman. Manny took it eagerly. The sandwich was huge, thick slices of beef and horseradish between fresh slabs of crusty bread. Pigeons watched the park bench hopefully.

"Jackie. The granddaughter who writes books," Manny said. Harry watched to see that Manny ate. You couldn't trust Manny to eat enough; he stayed too skinny. At least in Harry's opinion. Manny, Jackie—the world, Harry sometimes thought, had all grown too skinny when he somehow hadn't been looking. Skimpy. Stretched feeling. Harry nodded to see horseradish spurt in a satisfying stream down Manny's scraggly beard.

"Jackie. Yes," Harry said.

"So what's wrong with her? She's sick?" Manny eyed Harry's strudel, cherry with real yeast bread. Harry passed it to him. "Harry, the whole thing? I couldn't."

"Take it, take it, I don't want it. You should eat. No, she's not sick. She's miserable." When Manny, his mouth full of strudel, didn't answer, Harry put a hand on Manny's arm. *"Miserable."*

Manny swallowed hastily. "How do you know? You saw her this week?"

"No. Next Tuesday. She's bringing me a book by a friend of hers.

213

I know from this." He drew a magazine from an inner pocket of his coat. The coat was thick tweed, almost new, with wooden buttons. On the cover of the glossy magazine a woman smiled contemptuously. A woman with hollow, starved-looking cheeks who obviously didn't get enough to eat either.

"That's not a book," Manny pointed out.

"So she writes stories, too. Listen to this, just listen. 'I stood in my backyard, surrounded by the false bright toxin-fed green, and realized that the earth was dead. What else could it be, since we humans swarmed upon it like maggots on carrion, growing our hectic gleaming molds, leaving our slime trails across the senseless surface?' Does that sound like a happy woman?"

"Hoo boy," Manny said.

"It's all like that. 'Don't read my things, Popsy,' she says. 'You're not in the audience for my things.' Then she smiles without ever once showing her teeth." Harry flung both arms wide. "Who else should be in the audience but her own grandfather?"

Manny swallowed the last of the strudel. Pigeons fluttered angrily. "She never shows her teeth when she smiles? Never?"

"Never."

"Hoo boy," Manny said. "Did you want all of that orange?"

"No, I brought it for you, to take home. But did you finish that whole half a sandwich already?"

"I thought I'd take it home," Manny said humbly. He showed Harry the tip of the sandwich, wrapped in the thick brown butcher paper, protruding from the pocket of his old coat.

Harry nodded approvingly. "Good, good. Take the orange, too. I brought it for you."

Manny took the orange. Three teenagers carrying huge shrieking radios sauntered past. Manny started to put his hands over his ears, received a look of dangerous contempt from the teenager with green hair, and put his hands on his lap. The kid tossed an empty beer bottle onto the pavement before their feet. It shattered. Harry scowled fiercely but Manny stared straight ahead. When the cacophony had passed, Manny said, "Thank you for the orange. Fruit, it costs so much this time of year."

Harry still scowled. "Not in 1937."

"Don't start that again, Harry."

Harry said sadly, "Why won't you ever believe me? Could I afford to bring all this food if I got it at 1989 prices? Could I afford this coat? Have you seen buttons like this in 1989, on a new coat? Have you seen sandwiches wrapped in that kind of paper since we were young? Have you? Why won't you believe me?"

Manny slowly peeled his orange. The rind was pale, and the orange had seeds. "Harry. Don't start."

"But why won't you just come to my room and *see?*"

Manny sectioned the orange. "Your room. A cheap furnished room in a Social Security hotel. Why should I go? I know what will be there. What will be there is the same thing in my room. A bed, a chair, a table, a hot plate, some cans of food. Better I should meet you here in the park, get at least a little fresh air." He looked at Harry meekly, the orange clutched in one hand. "Don't misunderstand. It's not from a lack of friendship I say this. You're good to me, you're the best friend I have. You bring me things from a great deli, you talk to me, you share with me the family I don't have. It's enough, Harry. It's more than enough. I don't need to see where you live like I live."

Harry gave it up. There were moods, times, when it was just impossible to budge Manny. He dug in, and in he stayed. "Eat your orange."

"It's a good orange. So tell me more about Jackie."

"Jackie." Harry shook his head. Two kids on bikes tore along the path. One of them swerved towards Manny and snatched the orange from his hand. "Aw riggghhhtttt!"

Harry scowled after the child. It had been a girl. Manny just wiped the orange juice off his fingers onto the knee of his pants. "Is everything she writes so depressing?"

"Everything," Harry said. "Listen to this one." He drew out another magazine, smaller, bound in rough paper with a stylized line drawing of a woman's private parts on the cover. On the cover! Harry held the magazine with one palm spread wide over the drawing, which made it difficult to keep the pages open while he read. "She looked at her mother in the only way possible: with contempt, contempt for all the betrayals and compromises that had been her mother's life, for the sad soft lines of defeat around her mother's mouth, for the bright artificial dress too young for her wasted years, for even the leather handbag, Gucci of course, filled with blood money for having sold her life to a man who had long ceased to want it."

"Hoo boy," Manny said. "About a *mother* she wrote that?"

"About everybody. All the time."

"And where *is* Barbara?"

"Reno again. Another divorce." How many had that been? After two, did anybody count? Harry didn't count. He imagined Barbara's life as a large roulette wheel like the ones on TV, little silver men bouncing in and out of red and black pockets. Why didn't she get dizzy?

Manny said slowly, "I always thought there was a lot of love in her."

"A lot of that she's got," Harry said dryly. "Not Barbara—Jackie. A lot of . . . I don't know. Sweetness. Under the way she is."

"The way she is," Harry said gloomily. "Prickly. A cactus. But you're right, Manny, I know what you mean. She just needs someone to soften her up. Love her back, maybe. Although I love her."

The two old men looked at each other. Manny said, "Harry . . ."

"I know, I know. I'm only a grandfather, my love doesn't count, I'm just there. Like air. 'You're wonderful, Popsy,' she says, and still no teeth when she smiles. But you know, Manny—you are right!" Harry jumped up from the bench. "You are! What she needs is a young man to love her!"

Manny looked alarmed. "I didn't say—"

"I don't know why I didn't think of it before!"

"Harry—"

"And her stories, too! Full of ugly murders, ugly places, unhappy endings. What she needs is something to show her that writing could be about sweetness, too."

Manny was staring at him hard. Harry felt a rush of affection. That Manny should have the answer! Skinny wonderful Manny!

Manny said slowly, "Jackie said to me, 'I write about reality.' That's what she said, Harry."

"So there's no sweetness in reality? Put sweetness in her life, her writing will go sweet. She *needs* this, Manny. A really nice fellow!"

Two men in jogging suits ran past. One of their Reeboks came down on a shard of beer bottle. "Every fucking time!" he screamed, bending over to inspect his shoe. "Fucking park!"

"Well, what do you expect?" the other drawled, looking at Manny and Harry. "Although you'd think that if we could clean up Lake Erie . . ."

"Fucking derelicts!" the other snarled. They jogged away.

"Of course," Harry said, "it might not be easy to find the sort of guy to convince Jackie."

"Harry, I think you should maybe think—"

"Not here," Harry said suddenly. "Not here. *There*. In 1937."

"*Harry . . .*"

"Yeah," Harry said, nodding several times. Excitement filled him like light, like electricity. What an idea! "It was different then."

Manny said nothing. When he stood up, the sleeve of his coat exposed the number tattooed on his wrist. He said quietly, "It was no paradise in 1937 either, Harry."

Harry seized Manny's hand. "I'm going to do it, Manny. Find someone for her there. Bring him here."

Manny sighed. "Tomorrow at the chess club, Harry? At one o'clock? It's Tuesday."

"I'll tell you then how I'm coming with this."

"Fine, Harry. Fine. All my wishes go with you. You know that."

Harry stood up too, still holding Manny's hand. A middle-aged man staggered to the bench and slumped onto it. The smell of whiskey rose from him in waves. He eyed Manny and Harry with scorn. "Fucking fags."

"Good night, Harry."

"Manny—if you'd only come . . . money goes so much farther there . . ."

"Tomorrow at one. At the chess club."

Harry watched his friend walk away. Manny's foot dragged a little; the knee must be bothering him again. Harry wished Manny would see a doctor. Maybe a doctor would know why Manny stayed so skinny.

* * *

Harry walked back to his hotel. In the lobby, old men slumped in upholstery thin from wear, burned from cigarettes, shiny in the seat from long sitting. Sitting and sitting, Harry thought—life measured by the seat of the pants. And now it was getting dark. No one would go out from here until the next daylight. Harry shook his head.

The elevator wasn't working again. He climbed the stairs to the third floor. Halfway there, he stopped, felt in his pocket, counted five quarters, six dimes, two nickels, and eight pennies. He returned to the lobby. "Could I have two dollar bills for this change, please? Maybe old bills?"

The clerk looked at him suspiciously. "Your rent paid up?"

"Certainly," Harry said. The woman grudgingly gave him the money.

"Thank you. You look very lovely today, Mrs. Raduski." Mrs. Raduski snorted.

In his room, Harry looked for his hat. He finally found it under his bed—how had it gotten under his bed? He dusted it off and put it on. It had cost him $3.25. He opened the closet door, parted the clothes hanging from their metal pole—like Moses parting the sea, he always thought, a Moses come again—and stepped to the back of the closet, remembering with his body rather than his mind the sharp little twist to the right just past the far gray sleeve of his good wool suit.

He stepped out into the bare corner of a warehouse. Cobwebs brushed his hat; he had stepped a little too far right. Harry crossed the empty concrete space to where the lumber stacks started, and threaded his way through them. The lumber, too, was covered with cobwebs; not much building going on. On his way out the warehouse door, Harry passed the night watchman coming on duty.

"Quiet all day, Harry?"

"As a church, Rudy," Harry said. Rudy laughed. He laughed a lot. He was also indisposed to question very much. The first time he had seen Harry coming out of the warehouse in a bemused daze, he must have assumed that Harry had been hired to work there. Peering at Rudy's round, vacant face, Harry realized that he must hold this job because he was someone's uncle, someone's cousin, someone's something. Harry had felt a small glow of approval; families should take care of their own. He had told Rudy that he had lost his key and asked him for another.

Outside it was late afternoon. Harry began walking. Eventually there were people walking past him, beside him, across the street from him. Everybody wore hats. The women wore bits of velvet or wool with dotted veils across their noses and long, graceful dresses in small prints. The men wore fedoras with suits as baggy as Harry's. When he reached the park there were children, girls in long black tights and hard shoes, boys in buttoned shirts. Everyone looked like it was Sunday morning.

Pushcarts and shops lined the sidewalks. Harry bought a pair of socks, thick gray wool, for 89 cents. When the man took his dollar, Harry held his breath: each first time made a little pip in his stomach. But no one ever looked at the dates of old bills. He bought two oranges for five cents each, and then, thinking of Manny, bought a third. At a candystore he bought *G-8 and His Battle Aces* for fifteen cents. At The Collector's Cozy in the other time they would gladly give him thirty dollars for it. Finally, he bought a cherry Coke for a nickel and headed toward the park.

"Oh, excuse me," said a young man who bumped into Harry on the sidewalk. "I'm so sorry!" Harry looked at him hard: but, no. Too young. Jackie was twenty-eight.

Some children ran past, making for the movie theater. Spencer Tracy in *Captains Courageous*. Harry sat down on a green-painted wooden bench under a pair of magnificent Dutch elms. On the bench lay a newsmagazine. Harry glanced at it to see when in September this was: the 28th. The cover pictured a young blond Nazi soldier standing at stiff salute. Harry thought again of Manny, frowned, and turned the magazine cover down.

For the next hour, people walked past. Harry studied them carefully. When it got too dark to see, he walked back to the warehouse, on the way buying an apple kuchen at a bakery with a curtain behind the counter looped back to reveal a man in his shirt sleeves eating a plate of stew at a table bathed in soft yellow lamplight. The kuchen cost thirty-two cents.

At the warehouse, Harry let himself in with his key, slipped past Rudy nodding over *Paris Nights*, and walked to his cobwebby corner. He emerged from his third-floor closet into his room. Beyond the window, sirens wailed and wailed and would not stop.

"So how's it going?" Manny asked. He dripped kuchen crumbs on the chessboard; Harry brushed them away. Manny had him down a knight.

"It's going to take some time to find somebody that's right," Harry said. "I'd like to have someone by next Tuesday when I meet Jackie for dinner, but I don't know. It's not easy. There are requirements. He has to be young enough to be attractive, but old enough to understand Jackie. He has to be sweet-natured enough to do her some good, but strong enough not to panic at jumping over fifty-two years. Somebody educated. An educated man—he might be more curious than upset by my closet. Don't you think?"

"Better watch your queen," Manny said, moving his rook. "So how are you going to find him?"

"It takes time," Harry said. "I'm working on it."

Manny shook his head. "You have to get somebody here, you have to convince him he is here, you have to keep him from turning right around and running back in time through your shirts . . . I don't know, Harry. I don't know. I've been thinking. This thing is not simple. What if you did something wrong? Took somebody important out of 1937?"

"I won't pick anybody important."

"What if you made a mistake and brought your own grandfather? And something happened to him here?"

"My grandfather was already dead in 1937."

"What if you brought me? I'm already here."

"You didn't live here in 1937."

"What if you brought you?"

"I didn't live here either."

"What if you . . ."

"Manny," Harry said, 'I'm not bringing somebody important. I'm not bringing somebody we know. I'm not bringing somebody for permanent. I'm just bringing a nice guy for Jackie to meet, go dancing, see a different kind of nature. A different view of what's possible. An innocence. I'm sure there are fellows here that would do it, but I don't know any, and I don't know how to bring any to her. From there I know. Is this so complicated? Is this so unpredictable?"

"Yes," Manny said. He had on his stubborn look again. How could somebody so skimpy look so stubborn? Harry sighed and moved his lone knight.

"I brought you some whole socks."

"Thank you. That knight, it's not going to help you much."

"Lectures. That's what there was there that there isn't here. Everybody went to lectures. No TV, movies cost money, they went to free lectures."

"I remember," Manny said. "I was a young man myself. Harry, this thing is not simple."

"Yes, it is," Harry said stubbornly.

"1937 was not simple."

"It will work, Manny."

"Check," Manny said.

That evening, Harry went back. This time it was the afternoon of September 16. On newsstands *The New York Times* announced that President Roosevelt and John L. Lewis had talked pleasantly at the White House. Cigarettes cost thirteen cents a pack. Women wore cotton stockings and clunky, high-heeled shoes. Schrafft's best chocolates were sixty cents a pound. Small boys addressed Harry as "sir."

He attended six lectures in two days. A Madame Trefania lectured on theosophy to a hall full of badly dressed women with thin, pursed lips. A union organizer roused an audience to a pitch that made Harry leave after the first thirty minutes. A skinny, nervous missionary showed slides of religious outposts in China. An archaeologist back from a Mexican dig gave a dry, impatient talk about temples to an audience of three people. A New Deal Democrat spoke passionately about aiding the poor, but afterwards addressed all the women present as "Sister." Finally, just when Harry was starting to feel discouraged, he found it.

A museum offered a series of lectures on "Science of Today—and Tomorrow." Harry heard a slim young man with a reddish beard speak with idealistic passion about travel to the Moon, the planets, the stars. It seemed to Harry that compared to stars, 1989 might seem reasonably close. The young man had warm hazel eyes and a sense of humor. When he spoke about life in a spaceship, he mentioned in passing that women would be freed from much domestic drudgery they now endured. Throughout the lecture, he smoked, lighting cigarettes with a masculine squinting of eyes and cupping of hands. He said that imagination was the human quality that would most help people adjust to the future. His shoes were polished.

But most of all, Harry thought, he had a glow. A fine golden Boy Scout glow that made Harry think of old covers for the *Saturday Evening Post.* Which here cost five cents.

After the lecture, Harry stayed in his chair in the front row, outwaiting even the girl with bright red lipstick who lingered around the lecturer, this Robert Gernshon. From time to time, Gernshon glanced over at Harry with quizzical interest. Finally the girl, red lips pouting, sashayed out of the hall.

"Hello," Harry said. "I'm Harry Kramer. I enjoyed your talk. I have something to show you that you would be very interested in."

The hazel eyes turned wary. "Oh, no, no," Harry said. "Something *scientific.* Here, look at this." He handed Gernshon a filtered Vantage Light.

"How long it is," Gernshon said. "What's this made of?"

"The filter? It's made of . . . a new filter material. Tastes milder and cuts down on the nicotine. Much better for you. Look at this." He gave Gernshon a styrofoam cup from MacDonald's. "It's made of a new material, too. Very cheap. Disposable."

Gernshon fingered the cup. "Who are you?" he said quietly.

"A scientist. I'm interested in the science of tomorrow, too. Like you. I'd like to invite you to see my laboratory, which is in my home."

"In your home?"

"Yes. In a small way. just dabbling, you know." Harry could feel himself getting rattled; the young hazel eyes stared at him so steadily. *Jackie,* he thought. Dead earths. Maggots and carrion. Contempt for mothers. What would Gernshon say? When would Gernshon say *anything?*

"Thank you," Gernshon finally said. "When would be convenient?"

"Now?" Harry said. He tried to remember what time of day it was now. All he could picture was lecture halls.

Gernshon came. It was nine-thirty in the evening of Friday, September 17. Harry walked Gernshon through the streets, trying to talk animatedly, trying to distract. He said that he himself was very interested in travel to the stars. He said it had always been his dream to stand on another planet and take in great gulps of completely unpolluted air. He said his great heroes were those biologists who made that twisty model of DNA. He said science had been his life. Gernshon walked more and more silently.

"Of course," Harry said hastily, "like most scientists, I'm mostly familiar with my own field. You know how it is."

"What is your field, Dr. Kramer?" Gernshon asked quietly.

"Electricity," Harry said, and hit him on the back of the head with a solid brass candlestick from the pocket of his coat. The candlestick had cost him three dollars at a pawn shop.

They had walked past the stores and pushcarts to a point where the locked business offices and warehouses began. There were no passersby, no muggers, no street dealers, no Guardian Angels, no punk gangs. Only him, hitting an unarmed man with a candlestick. He was no better than the punks. But what else could he do? What else could he do? Nothing but hit him softly, so softly that Gernshon was struggling again almost before Harry got his hands and feet tied, well before he got on the blindfold and gag. "I'm sorry, I'm sorry," he kept saying to Gernshon. Gernshon did not look as if the apology made any difference. Harry dragged him into the warehouse.

Rudy was asleep over *Spicy Stories*. Breathing very hard, Harry pulled the young man—not more than 150 pounds, it was good Harry had looked for slim—to the far corner, through the gate, and into his closet.

"Listen," he said urgently to Gernshon after removing the gag. "Listen. I can call the Medicare Emergency Hotline. If your head feels broken. Are you feeling faint? Do you think you maybe might go into shock?"

Gernshon lay on Harry's rug, glaring at him, saying nothing.

"Listen, I know this is maybe a little startling to you. But I'm not a pervert, not a cop, not anything but a grandfather with a problem. My granddaughter. I need your help to solve it, but I won't take much of your time. You're now somewhere besides where you gave your lecture. A pretty long ways away. But you don't have to stay here long, I promise. Just two weeks, tops, and I'll send you back. I promise, on my mother's grave. And I'll make it worth your while. I promise."

"Untie me."

"Yes. Of course. Right away. Only you have to not attack me, because I'm the only one who can get you back from here." He had a sudden inspiration. "I'm like a foreign consul. You've maybe traveled abroad?"

Gernshon looked around the dingy room. "Untie me."

"I will. In two minutes. Five, tops. I just want to explain a little first."

"Where am I?"

"1989."

Gernshon said nothing. Harry explained brokenly, talking as fast as he could, saying he could move from 1989 to September, 1937 when he wanted to, but he could take Gernshon back too, no problem. He said he made the trip often, it was perfectly safe. He pointed out how much farther a small Social Security check, no pension, could go at 1937 prices. He mentioned Manny's strudel. Only lightly did he touch on the problem of Jackie, figuring there would be a better time to share domestic difficulties, and his closet he didn't mention at all. it was hard to keep his eyes averted from the closet door. He did mention how bitter people could be in 1989, how lost, how weary from expecting so much that nothing was a delight, nothing a sweet surprise. He was just working up to a tirade on innocence when Gernshon said again, in a different tone, "Untie me."

"Of course," Harry said quickly, "I don't expect you to believe me. Why should you think you're in 1989? Go, see for yourself. Look at that light, it's still early morning. just be careful out there, is all." He untied Gernshon and stood with his eyes squeezed shut, waiting.

When nothing hit him, Harry opened his eyes. Gernshon was at the door. "Wait!" Harry cried. "You'll need more money!" He dug into his pocket and pulled out a twenty-dollar bill, carefully saved for this, and all the change he had.

Gernshon examined the coins carefully, then looked up at Harry. He said nothing. He opened the door and Harry, still trembling, sat down in his chair to wait.

Gernshon came back three hours later, pale and sweating. "My God!"

"I know just what you mean," Harry said. "A zoo out there. Have a drink."

Gernshon took the mixture Harry had ready in his toothbrush glass and gulped it down. He caught sight of the bottle, which Harry had left on the dresser: Seagram's V.O., with the cluttered, tiny-print label. He threw the glass across the room and covered his face with his hands.

"I'm sorry," Harry said apologetically. "But then it cost only $3.37 the fifth."

Gernshon didn't move.

"I'm really sorry," Harry said. He raised both hands, palms up, and dropped them helplessly. "Would you . . . would you maybe like an orange?"

Gernshon recovered faster than Harry had dared hope. Within an hour he was sitting in Harry's worn chair, asking questions about the space shuttle; within two hours taking notes; within three become again the intelligent and captivating young man of the lecture hall. Harry, answering as much as he could as patiently as he could, was impressed by the boy's resilience. It couldn't have been easy. What if he, Harry, suddenly had to skip fifty-two more years? What if he found himself in 2041? Harry shuddered.

"Do you know that a movie now costs six dollars?"

Gernshon blinked. "We were talking about the moon landing."

"Not any more, we're not. I want to ask *you* some questions, Robert. Do you think the earth is dead, with people sliming all over it like on carrion? Is this a thought that crosses your mind?"

"I . . . no." Harry nodded.

"Good, good. Do you look at your mother with contempt?"

"Of course not. Harry—"

"No, it's my turn. Do you think a woman who marries a man, and maybe the marriage doesn't work out perfect, whose does, but they raise at least one healthy child—say a daughter—that that woman's life has been a defeat and a failure?"

"No. I—"

"What would you think if you saw a drawing of a woman's private parts on the cover of a magazine?"

Gernshon blushed. He looked as if the blush annoyed him, but also as if he couldn't help it.

"Better and better," Harry said. "Now, think careful on this next one—take your time—no hurry. Does reality seem to you to have sweetness in it as well as ugliness? Take your time."

Gernshon peered at him. Harry realized they had talked right through lunch. "But not all the time in the world, Robert."

"Yes," Gernshon said. "I think reality has more sweetness than ugliness. And more strangeness than anything else. Very much more." He looked suddenly dazed. "I'm sorry, I just—all this has happened so—"

"Put your head between your knees," Harry suggested. "There— better now? Good. There's someone I want you to meet."

Manny sat in the park, on their late-afternoon bench. When he saw them coming, his face settled into long sorrowful ridges. "Harry. Where have you been for two days? I was worried, I went to your hotel—"

"Manny," Harry said, "this is Robert."

"So I see," Manny said. He didn't hold out his hand.

"*Him*," Harry said.

"Harry. Oh, Harry."

"How do you do, sir," Gernshon said. He held out his hand. "I'm afraid I didn't get your full name. I'm Robert Gernshon."

Manny looked at him—at the outstretched hand, the baggy suit with wide tie, the deferential smile, the golden Balden-Powell glow. Manny's lips mouthed a silent word: *sir?*

"I have a lot to tell you," Harry said. "You can tell all of us, then," Manny said. "Here comes Jackie now."

Harry looked up. Across the park a woman in jeans strode purposefully toward them. "Manny! It's only Monday!"

"I called her to come," Manny said. "You've been gone from your room two days, Harry, nobody at your hotel could say where—"

"But *Manny*," Harry said, while Gernshon looked, frowning, from one to the other and Jackie spotted them and waved.

She had lost more weight, Harry saw. Only two weeks, yet her cheeks had hollowed out and new, tiny lines touched her eyes. Skinny lines. They filled him with sadness. Jackie wore a blue T-shirt that said LIFE IS A BITCH—THEN YOU DIE. She carried a magazine and a small can of mace disguised as hair spray.

"Popsy! You're here! Manny said—"

"Manny was wrong," Harry said. "Jackie, sweetheart, you look— it's good to see you. Jackie, I'd like you to meet somebody, darling. This is Robert. My friend. My friend Robert. Jackie Snyder."

"Hi," Jackie said. She gave Harry a hug, and then Manny one. Harry saw Gernshon gazing at her very tight jeans.

"Robert's a . . . a scientist," Harry said. It was the wrong thing to say; Harry knew the moment he said it that it was the wrong thing. Science—all science—was, for some reason not completely clear to him, a touchy subject with Jackie. She tossed her long hair back from her eyes. "Oh, yeah? Not *chemical*, I hope?"

"I'm not actually a scientist," Gernshon said winningly. "Just a dabbler. I popularize new scientific concepts, write about them to make them intelligible."

"Like what?" Jackie said.

Gernshon opened his mouth, closed it again. A boy suddenly flashed past on a skateboard, holding a boom box. Metallica blasted the air. Overhead, a jet droned. Gernshon smiled weakly. "It's hard to explain."

"I'm capable of understanding," Jackie said coldly. "Women *can* understand science, you know."

"Jackie, sweetheart," Harry said, "what have you got there? Is that your new book?"

"No," Jackie said, "this is the one I said I'd bring you, by my friend. It's brilliant. It's about a man whose business partner betrays him by selling out to organized crime and framing the man. In jail he meets a guy who has founded his own religion, the House of Divine Despair, and when they both get out they start a new business, Suicide Incorporated, that helps people kill themselves for a fee. The whole thing is just a brilliant denunciation of contemporary America."

Gernshon made a small sound.

"It's a comedy," Jackie added.

"It sounds . . . it sounds a little depressing," Gernshon said.

Jackie looked at him. Very distinctly, she said, "It's reality."

Harry saw Gernshon glance around the park. A man nodded on a bench, his hands slack on his knees. Newspapers and McDonald's wrappers stirred fitfully in the dirt. A trash container had been knocked over. From beside a scrawny tree, enclosed shoulder-height by black wrought iron, a child watched them with old eyes.

"I brought you something else, too, Popsy," Jackie said. Harry hoped that Gernshon noticed how much gentler her voice was when she spoke to her grandfather. "A scarf. See, it's llama wool. Very warm."

Gernshon said, "My mother has a scarf like that. No, I guess hers is some kind of fur."

Jackie's face changed. "What kind?"

"I—I'm not sure."

"Not an endangered species, I hope."

"No. Not that. I'm sure not . . . that."

Jackie stared at him a moment longer. The child who had been watching strolled toward them. Harry saw Gernshon look at the boy with relief. About eleven years old, he wore a perfectly tailored suit and Italian shoes. Manny shifted to put himself between the boy and Gernshon. "Jackie, darling, it's so good to see you . . ."

The boy brushed by Gernshon on the other side. He never looked up, and his voice stayed boyish and low, almost a whisper. "Crack . . ."

"Step on one and you break your mother's back," Gernshon said brightly. He smiled at Harry, a special conspiratorial smile to suggest that children, at least, didn't change in fifty years. The boy's head jerked up to look at Gernshon.

"You talking about my mama?"

Jackie groaned. "No," she said to the kid. "He doesn't mean anything. Beat it."

"I don't forget," the boy said. He backed away slowly.

Gernshon said, frowning, "I'm sorry. I'm not sure exactly what all that was, but I'm sorry."

"Are you for real?" Jackie said angrily. "What the fucking hell *was* all that? Don't you realize this park is the only place Manny and my grandfather can get some fresh air?"

"I didn't—"

"That punk runner meant it when he said he won't forget!"

"I don't like your tone," Gernshon said. "Or your language."

"My language!" The corners of Jackie's mouth tightened. Manny looked at Harry and put his hands over his face. The boy, twenty feet away, suddenly let out a noise like a strangled animal, so piercing all four of them spun around. Two burly teenagers were running toward him. The child's face crumpled; he looked suddenly much younger. He sprang away, stumbled, made the noise again, and hurled himself, all animal terror, toward the street behind the park bench.

"No!" Gernshon shouted. Harry turned towards the shout but Gernshon already wasn't there. Harry saw the twelve-wheeler bearing down, heard Jackie's scream, saw Gernshon's wiry body barrel into the boy's. The truck shrieked past, its air brakes deafening.

Gernshon and the boy rose in the street on the other side.

Car horns blared. The boy bawled, "Leggo my suit! You tore my suit!" A red light flashed and a squad car pulled up. The two burly teenagers melted away, and then the boy somehow vanished as well.

"Never find him," the disgruntled cop told them over the clipboard on which he had written nothing. "Probably just as well." He went away.

"Are you hurt?" Manny said. It was the first time he had spoken. His face was ashen. Harry put a hand across his shoulders.

"No," Gernshon said. He gave Manny his sweet smile. "Just a little dirty."

"That took *guts*," Jackie said. She was staring at Gernshon with a frown between her eyebrows. "Why did you do it?"

"Pardon?"

"Why? I mean, given what that kid is, given—oh, all of it—" she gestured around the park, a helpless little wave of her strong young hands that tore at Harry's heart. "Why bother?"

Gernshon said gently, "What that kid is, is a kid."

Manny looked skeptical. Harry moved to stand in front of Manny's expression before anyone wanted to discuss it. "Listen, I've got a wonderful idea, you two seem to have so much to talk about, about . . . bothering, and . . . everything. Why don't you have dinner together, on me? My treat."

He pulled another twenty dollar bill from his pocket. Behind him he could feel Manny start.

"Oh, I couldn't," Gernshon said, at the same moment that Jackie said warningly, "Popsy. . . ."

Harry put his palms on both sides of her face. "Please. Do this for me, Jackie. Without the questions, without the female protests. Just this once. For me."

Jackie was silent a long moment before she grimaced, nodded, and turned with half-humorous appeal to Gernshon.

Gernshon cleared his throat. "Well, actually, it would probably be better if all four of us came. I'm embarrassed to say that prices are higher in this city than in . . . that is, I'm not able to . . . but if we went somewhere less expensive, the Automat maybe, I'm sure all four of us could eat together."

"No, no," Harry said. "We already ate." Manny looked at him.

Jackie began, offended, "I certainly don't want . . . just what do you think is going on here, buddy? This is just to please my grandfather. Are you afraid I might try to jump your bones?"

Harry saw Gernshon's quick, involuntary glance at Jackie's tight jeans. He saw, too, that Gernshon fiercely regretted the glance the instant he had made it. He saw that Manny saw, and that Jackie saw, and that Gernshon saw that they saw.

Manny made a small noise. Jackie's face began to turn so black that Harry was astounded when Gernshon cut her off with a dignity no one had expected.

"No, of course not," he said quietly. "But *I* would prefer all of us to have dinner together for quite another reason. My wife is very dear to me, Miss Snyder, and I wouldn't do anything that might make her feel uncomfortable. That's probably irrational, but that's the way it is."

Harry stood arrested, his mouth open. Manny started to shake with what Harry thought savagely had better not be laughter. And Jackie, after staring at Gernshon a long while, broke into the most spontaneous smile Harry had seen from her in months.

"Hey," she said softly. "That's nice. That's really, genuinely, fucking nice."

The weather turned abruptly colder. Snow threatened but didn't fall. Each afternoon Harry and Manny took a quick walk in the park and then went inside, to the chess club or a coffee shop or the bus station or the library, where there was a table deep in the stacks on which they could eat lunch without detection. Harry brought Manny a poor boy with mayo, sixty-three cents, and a pair of imported wool gloves, one dollar on pre-season sale.

"So where are they today?" Manny asked on Saturday, removing the gloves to peek at the inside of the poor boy. He sniffed appreciatively. "Horseradish. You remembered, Harry."

"The museum, I think," Harry said miserably.

"What museum?"

"How should I know? He says, 'The museum today, Harry,' and he's gone by eight o'clock in the morning, no more details than that."

Manny stopped chewing. "What museum opens at eight o'clock in the morning?"

Harry put down his sandwich, pastrami on rye, thirty-nine cents. He had lost weight the past week.

"Probably," Manny said hastily, "they just talk. You know, like young people do, just talk. . . ."

Harry eyed him balefully. "You mean like you and Leah did when you were young and left completely alone."

"You better talk to him soon, Harry. No, to her." He seemed to reconsider Jackie. "No, to *him*."

"Talk isn't going to do it," Harry said. He looked pale and determined. "Gernshon has to be sent back."

"Be sent?"

"He's *married*, Manny! I wanted to help Jackie, show her life can hold some sweetness, not be all struggle. What kind of sweetness is she going to find if she falls in love with a married man? You know how that goes! Jackie—" Harry groaned. How had all this happened? He had intended only the best for Jackie. Why didn't that count more? "He has to go back, Manny."

"How?" Manny said practically. "You can't hit him again, Harry. You were just lucky last time that you didn't hurt him. You don't want that on your conscience. And if you show him your, uh . . . your—"

"My closet. Manny, if you'd only come see, for a dollar you could get—"

"—then he could just come back any time he wants. So how?"

A sudden noise startled them both. Someone was coming through the stacks. "Librarians!" Manny hissed. Both of them frantically swept the sandwiches, beer (fifteen cents), and strudel into shopping bags. Manny, panicking, threw in the wool gloves. Harry swept the table free of crumbs. When the intruder rounded the nearest bookshelf, Harry was bent over *Making Paper Flowers* and Manny over *Porcelain of the Yung Cheng Dynasty*. It was Robert Gernshon.

The young man dropped into a chair. His face was ashen. in one hand he clutched a sheaf of paper, the handwriting on the last one trailing off into shaky squiggles.

After a moment of silence, Manny said diplomatically, "So where are you coming from, Robert?"

"Where's Jackie?" Harry demanded.

"Jackie?" Gernshon said. His voice was thick; Harry realized with a sudden shock that he had been crying. "I haven't seen her for a few days."

"A few *days?*" Harry said.

"No. I've been . . . I've been . . ."

Manny sat up straighter. He looked intently at Gernshon over *Porcelain of the Yung Cheng Dynasty* and then put the book down. He moved to the chair next to Gernshon's and gently took the papers from his hand. Gernshon leaned over the table and buried his head in his arms.

"I'm so awfully sorry, I'm being such a baby . . ." His shoulders trembled. Manny separated the papers and spread them out on the library table. Among the hand-copied notes were two slim books, one bound between black covers and the other a pamphlet. *A Memoir of Auschwitz. Countdown to Hiroshima.*

For a long moment nobody spoke. Then Harry said, to no one in particular, "I thought he was going to science museums."

Manny laid his arm, almost casually, across Gernshon's shoulders. "So now you'll know not to be at either place. More people should have only known." Harry didn't recognize the expression on his friend's face, nor the voice with which Manny said to Harry, "You're right. He has to go back."

"But Jackie . . ."

"Can do without this sweetness," Manny said harshly. "So what's so terrible in her life anyway that she needs so much help? Is she dying? Is she poor? Is she ugly? Is anyone knocking on her door in the middle of the night? Let Jackie find her own sweetness. She'll survive."

Harry made a helpless gesture. Manny's stubborn face, carved wood under the harsh fluorescent light, did not change. "Even *him*. . . Manny, the things he knows now—"

"You should have thought of that earlier."

Gernshon looked up. "Don't, I—I'm sorry. It's just coming across it, I never thought human beings—"

"No," Manny said. "But they can. You been here, every day, at the library, reading it all?"

"Yes. That and museums. I saw you two come in earlier. I've been reading, I wanted to know—"

"So now you know," Manny said in that same surprisingly casual, tough voice. "You'll survive, too."

Harry said, "Does Jackie know what's going on? Why you've been doing all this . . . learning?"

"No."

"And you—what will you do with what you now know?"

Harry held his breath. What if Gernshon just refused to go back? Gernshon said slowly, "At first, I wanted to not return. At all. How can I watch it, World War II and the camps—I have relatives in

Poland. And then later the bomb and Korea and the gulags and Vietnam and Cambodia and the terrorists and AIDS—"

"Didn't miss anything," Harry muttered.

"And not be able to do anything, not be able to even hope, knowing that everything to come is already set into history—how could I watch all that without any hope that it isn't really as bad as it seems to be at the moment?"

"It all depends what you look at," Manny said, but Gernshon didn't seem to hear him.

"But neither can I stay, there's Susan and we're hoping for a baby . . . I need to think."

"No, you don't," Harry said. "You need to go *back*. This is all my mistake. I'm sorry. You need to go back, Gernshon."

"Lebanon," Gernshon said. "D.D.T. The Cultural Revolution. Nicaragua. Deforestation. Iran—"

"Penicillin," Manny said suddenly. His beard quivered. "Civil rights. Mahatma Gandhi. Polio vaccines. Washing machines." Harry stared at him, shocked. Could Manny once have worked in a hand laundry?

"Or," Manny said, more quietly, "Hitler. Auschwitz. Hoovervilles. The Dust Bowl. What you look at, Robert."

"I don't know," Gernshon said. "I need to think. There's so much . . . and then there's that girl."

Harry stiffened. "Jackie?"

"No, no. Someone she and I met a few days ago, at a coffee shop. She just walked in. I couldn't believe it. I looked at her and just went into shock—and maybe she did too, for all I know. The girl looked exactly like me. And she felt like—I don't know. It's hard to explain. She felt like *me*. I said hello but I didn't tell her my name; I didn't dare." His voice fell to a whisper. "I think she's my granddaughter."

"Hoo boy," Manny said.

Gernshon stood. He made a move to gather up his papers and booklets, stopped, left them there. Harry stood, too, so abruptly that Gernshon shot him a sudden, hard look across the library table. "Going to hit me again, Harry? Going to kill me?"

"Us?" Manny said. "Us, Robert?" His tone was gentle.

"In a way, you already have. I'm not who I was, certainly."

Manny shrugged. "So be somebody better."

"Damn it, I don't think you understand—"

"I don't think you do, Reuven, boychik. This is the way it is. That's all. Whatever you had back there, you have still. Tell me, in all that reading, did you find anything about yourself, anything personal? Are you in the history books, in the library papers?"

"The Office of Public Documents takes two weeks to do a search for birth and death certificates," Gernshon said, a little sulkily.

"So you lost nothing, because you really know nothing," Manny said. "Only history. History is cheap. Everybody gets some. You can have all the history you want. It's what you make of it that costs."

Gernshon didn't nod agreement. He looked a long time at Manny, and something moved behind the unhappy hazel eyes, something that made Harry finally let out a breath he didn't know he'd been holding. It suddenly seemed that Gernshon was the one that was old. And he was—with the fifty-two years he'd gained since last week, he was older than Harry had been in the 1937 of *Captains Courageous* and the wide-brimmed fedoras and clean city parks. But that was the good time, the one that Gernshon was going back to, the one Harry himself could choose, if it weren't for Jackie and Manny . . . still, he couldn't watch as Gernshon walked out of the book stacks, parting the musty air as heavily as if it were water.

Gernshon paused. Over his shoulder he said, "I'll go back. Tonight. I will."

After he had left, Harry said, "This is my fault."

"Yes," Manny agreed.

"Will you come to my room when he goes? To . . . to help?"

"Yes, Harry."

Somehow, that only made it worse.

Gernshon agreed to a blindfold. Harry led him through the closet, the warehouse, the street. Neither of them seemed very good at this; they stumbled into each other, hesitated, tripped over nothing. In the warehouse Gernshon nearly walked into a pile of lumber, and in the sharp jerk Harry gave Gernshon's arm to deflect him, something twisted and gave way in Harry's back. He waited, bent over, behind a corner of a building while Gernshon removed his blindfold, blinked in the morning light, and walked slowly away.

Despite his back, Harry found that he couldn't return right away. Why not? He just couldn't. He waited until Gernshon had a large head start and then hobbled towards the park. A carousel turned, playing bright organ music: September 24. Two children he had never noticed before stood just beyond the carousel, watching it with hungry, hopeless eyes. Flowers grew in immaculate flower beds. A black man walked by, his eyes fixed on the sidewalk, his head bent. Two small girls jumping rope were watched by a smiling woman in a blue-and-white uniform. On the sidewalk, just beyond the carousel, someone had chalked a swastika. The black man shuffled over it. A Lincoln Zephyr V-12 drove by, $1090. There was no way it would fit through a closet.

When Harry returned, Manny was curled up on the white chenille bedspread that Harry had bought for $3.28, fast asleep.

"What did I accomplish, Manny? What?" Harry said bitterly. The day had dawned glorious and warm, unexpected Indian summer. Trees in the park showed bare branches against a bright blue sky. Manny wore an old red sweater, Harry a flannel workshirt. Harry shifted gingerly, grimacing, on his bench. Sunday strollers dropped ice cream wrappers, cigarettes, newspapers, Diet Pepsi cans, used tissues, popcorn. Pigeons quarreled and children shrieked.

"Jackie's going to be just as hard as ever and why not?" Harry continued. "She finally meets a nice fellow, he never calls her again. Me, I leave a young man miserable on a sidewalk. Before I leave him, I ruin his life. While I leave him, I ruin my back. *After* I leave him, I sit here guilty. There's no answer, Manny."

Manny didn't answer. He squinted down the curving path.

"I don't know, Manny. I just don't know."

Manny said suddenly, "Here comes Jackie."

Harry looked up. He squinted, blinked, tried to jump up. His back made sharp protest. He stayed where he was, and his eyes grew wide.

"Popsy!" Jackie cried. "I've been looking for you!"

She looked radiant. All the lines were gone from around her eyes, all the sharpness from her face. Her very collar bones, Harry thought dazedly, looked softer. Happiness haloed her like light. She held the hand of a slim, red-haired woman with strong features and direct hazel eyes.

"This is Ann," Jackie said. "I've been looking for you, Popsy, because . . . well, because I need to tell you something." She slid onto the bench next to Harry, on the other side from Manny, and put one arm around Harry's shoulders. The other hand kept a close grip on Ann, who smiled encouragement. Manny stared at Ann as at a ghost.

"You see, Popsy, for a while now I've been struggling with something, something really important. I know I've been snappy and difficult, but it hasn't been—everybody needs somebody to love, you've often told me that, and I know how happy you and Grammy were all those years. And I thought there would never be anything like that for me, and certain people were making everything all so hard. But now . . . well, now there's Ann. And I wanted you to know that."

"Happy to meet you," Ann said. She had a low, rough voice and a sweet smile. Harry felt hurricanes, drought, sunshine.

Jackie said, "I know this is probably a little unexpected—"

Unexpected. "Well—" Harry said, and could say no more.

"It's just that it was time for me to come out of the closet."

Harry made a small noise. Manny managed to say, "So you live here, Ann?"

"Oh, yes. All my life. And my family, too, since forever."

"Has Jackie . . . has Jackie met any of them yet?"

"Not yet," Jackie said. "It might be a little . . . tricky, in the case of her parents." She smiled at Ann. "But we'll manage."

"I wish," Ann said to her, "that you could have met *my* grandfather. He would have been just as great as your Popsy here. He always was."

"Was?" Harry said faintly.

"He died a year ago. But he was just a wonderful man. Compassionate and intelligent."

"What . . . what did he do?"

"He taught history at the university. He was also active in lots of organizations—Amnesty International, the ACLU, things like that. During World War II he worked for the Jewish rescue leagues, getting people out of Germany."

Manny nodded. Harry watched Jackie's teeth.

"We'd like you both to come to dinner soon," Ann said. She smiled. "I'm a good cook."

Manny's eyes gleamed.

Jackie said, "I know this must be hard for you—" but Harry saw that she didn't really mean it. She didn't think it was hard. For her it was so real that it was natural weather, unexpected maybe, but not strange, not out of place, not out of time. In front of the bench, sunlight striped the pavement like bars.

Suddenly Jackie said, "Oh, Popsy, did I tell you that it was your friend Robert who introduced us? Did I tell you that already?"

"Yes, sweetheart," Harry said. "You did."

"He's kind of a nerd, but actually all right." After Jackie and Ann left, the two old men sat silent a long time. Finally Manny said diplomatically, "You want to get a snack, Harry?"

"She's happy, Manny."

"Yes. You want to get a snack, Harry?"

"She didn't even recognize him."

"No. You want to get a snack?"

"Here, have this. I got it for you this morning." Harry held out an orange, a deep-colored navel with flawless rind: seedless, huge, guaranteed juicy, nurtured for flavor, perfect.

"Enjoy," Harry said. "It cost me ninety-two cents."

The Secret Place

INTRODUCTION

The government had assigned the young geologist to a boring and, he thought, useless job, looking for something that he knew wasn't there. What *was* there was a mystery involving a strangely withdrawn young woman whose brother had died under inexplicable circumstances, and who now seemed to live in some sort of dream world. Or was it a dream world? Without giving away the story, I think I can save the reader the bother of looking up the word, and mention that the Miocene lasted from about 23 million to 5 million years ago. (But feel free to look it up for further details.) This story won the Nebula Award of the Science Fiction Writers of America and was nominated for the Hugo Award.

* * *

Richard M. McKenna (1913-1964), born in Idaho, joined the U.S. Navy in 1931, serving for 22 years, including active sea duty in both World War II and the Korean War as a Chief Machinist's Mate. Afterward, he attended the University of North Carolina in Chapel Hill on the G.I. Bill, studying creative writing. His first published story, "Casey Agonistes," appeared in *The Magazine of Fantasy and Science Fiction* in 1957, and, as writer and editor Ben Bova wrote, "immediately established him as a writer to be watched." In 1962, he published the novel *The Sand Pebbles*, which was serialized in *The Saturday Evening Post*, won the $10,000 1963 Harper Prize Novel competition, and became a 1966 movie, starring Steve McQueen. Unfortunately, in 1964 a heart attack cut short a career that promised to be brilliant. His other books, all posthumously published, are *Casey Agonistes and Other Science Fiction and Fantasy Stories*, *The Sons of Martha*, and *Left-Handed Monkey Wrench*.

The Secret Place

by Richard McKenna

This morning my son asked me what I did in the war. He's fifteen and I don't know why he never asked me before. I don't know why I never anticipated the question.

He was just leaving for camp, and I was able to put him off by saying I did government work. He'll be two weeks at camp. As long as the counselors keep pressure on him, he'll do well enough at group activities. The moment they relax it, he'll be off studying an ant colony or reading one of his books. He's on astronomy now. The moment he comes home, he'll ask me again just what I did in the war, and I'll have to tell him.

But I don't understand just what I did in the war. Sometimes I think my group fought a death fight with a local myth and only Colonel Lewis realized it. I don't know who won. All I know is that war demands of some men risks more obscure and ignoble than death in battle. I know it did of me.

It began in 1931, when a local boy was found dead in the desert near Barker, Oregon. He had with him a sack of gold ore and one thumb-sized crystal of uranium oxide. The crystal ended as a curiosity in a Salt Lake City assay office until, in 1942, it became of strangely great importance. Army agents traced its probable origin to a hundred-square-mile area near Barker. Dr. Lewis was called to duty as a reserve colonel and ordered to find the vein. But the whole area was overlain by thousands of feet of Miocene lava flows and of course it was geological insanity to look there for a pegmatite vein. The area had no drainage pattern and had never been glaciated. Dr. Lewis protested that the crystal could have gotten there only by prior human agency.

It did him no good. He was told he's not to reason why. People very high up would not be placated until much money and scientific effort had been spent in a search. The army sent him young geology graduates, including me, and demanded progress reports. For the sake of morale, in a kind of frustrated desperation, Dr. Lewis decided to make the project a model textbook exercise in mapping the number and thickness of the basalt beds over the search area all the way down to the prevolcanic Miocene surface. That would at least be a useful addition to Columbia Plateau lithology. It would also be proof positive that no uranium ore existed there, so it was not really cheating.

That Oregon countryside was a dreary place. The search area was flat, featureless country with black lava outcropping everywhere through scanty gray soil in which sagebrush grew hardly knee high. It was hot and dry in summer and dismal with thin snow in winter. Winds howled across it at all seasons. Barker was about a hundred wooden houses on dusty streets, and some hay farms along a canal. All the young people were away at war or war jobs, and the old people seemed to resent us. There were twenty of us, apart from the contract drill crews who lived in their own trailer camps, and we were gown against town, in a way We slept and ate at Colthorpe House, a block down the street from our headquarters. We had our own "gown" table there, and we might as well have been men from Mars.

I enjoyed it, just the same. Dr. Lewis treated us like students, with lectures and quizzes and assigned reading. He was a fine teacher and a brilliant scientist, and we loved him. He gave us all a turn at each phase of the work. I started on surface mapping and then worked with the drill crews, who were taking cores through the basalt and into the granite thousands of feet beneath. Then I worked on taking gravimetric and seismic readings. We had fine team spirit and we all knew we were getting priceless training in field geophysics. I decided privately that after the war I would take my doctorate in geophysics. Under Dr. Lewis, of course.

In early summer of 1944 the field phase ended. The contract drillers left. We packed tons of well logs and many boxes of gravimetric data sheets and seismic tapes for a move to Dr. Lewis's Midwestern university. There we would get more months of valuable training while we worked our data into a set of structure contour maps. We were all excited and talked a lot about being with girls again and going to parties. Then the army said part of the staff had to continue the field search. For technical compliance, Dr. Lewis decided to leave one man, and he chose me.

It hit me hard. It was like being flunked out unfairly. I thought he was heartlessly brusque about it.

"Take a Jeep run through the area with a Geiger once a day," he said. "Then sit in the office and answer the phone."

"What if the army calls when I'm away?" I asked sullenly.

"Hire a secretary," he said. "You've an allowance for that."

So off they went and left me, with the title of field chief and only myself to boss. I felt betrayed to the hostile town. I decided I hated Colonel Lewis and wished I could get revenge. A few days later old Dave Gentry told me how.

He was a lean, leathery old man with a white mustache and I sat next to him in my new place at the "town" table. Those were grim meals. I heard remarks about healthy young men skulking out of uniform and wasting tax money. One night I slammed my fork into my half-emptied plate and stood up.

"The army sent me here and the army keeps me here," I told the dozen old men and women at the table. "I'd like to go overseas and cut Japanese throats for you kind hearts and gentle people, I really would! Why don't you all write your Congressman?"

I stamped outside and stood at one end of the veranda, boiling. Old Dave followed me out.

"Hold your horses, son," he said. "They hate the government, not you. But government's like the weather, and you're a man they can get ahold of."

"With their teeth," I said bitterly.

"They got reasons," Dave said. "Lost mines ain't supposed to be found the way you people are going at it. Besides that, the Crazy Kid mine belongs to us here in Barker."

He was past seventy and he looked after horses in the local feedyard. He wore a shabby, open vest over faded suspenders and gray flannel shirts and nobody would ever have looked for wisdom in that old man. But it was there.

"This is big, new, lonesome country and it's hard on people," he said. "Every town's got a story about a lost mine or a lost gold cache. Only kids go looking for it. It's enough for most folks just to know it's there. It helps 'em to stand the country."

"I see," I said. Something stirred in the back of my mind.

"Barker never got its lost mine until thirteen years ago," Dave said. "Folks just naturally can't stand to see you people find it this way, by main force and so soon after."

"We know there isn't any mine," I said. "We're just proving it isn't there."

"If you could prove that, it'd be worse yet," he said. "Only you can't. We all saw and handled that ore. It was quartz, just rotten with gold in wires and flakes. The boy went on foot from his house to get it. The lode's got to be right close by out there."

He waved toward our search area. The air above it was luminous with twilight and I felt a curious surge of interest. Co'onel Lewis had always discouraged us from speculating on that story. If one of us brought it up, I was usually the one who led the hooting and we all suggested he go over the search area with a dowsing rod. It was an article of faith with us that the vein did not exist. But now I was all alone and my own field boss.

We each put up one foot on the veranda rail and rested our arms on our knees. Dave bit off a chew of tobacco and told me about Owen Price.

"He was always a crazy kid and I guess he read every book in town," Dave said. "He had a curious heart, that boy."

I'm no folklorist, but even I could see how myth elements were already creeping into the story. For one thing, Dave insisted the boy's shirt was torn off and he had lacerations on his back.

"Like a cougar clawed him." Dave said. "Only they ain't never been cougars in that desert. We backtracked that boy till his trail crossed itself so many times it was no use, but we never found one cougar track."

I could discount that stuff, of course, but still the story gripped me. Maybe it was Dave's slow, sure voice; perhaps the queer twilight; possibly my own wounded pride. I thought of how great lava upwellings sometimes tear loose and carry along huge masses of the country rock. Maybe such an erratic mass lay out there, perhaps only a few hundred feet across and so missed by our drill cores, but rotten with uranium. If I could find it, I would make a fool of Colonel Lewis. I would discredit the whole science of geology. I, Duard Campbell, the despised and rejected one, could do that. The front of my mind shouted that it was nonsense, but something far back in my mind began composing a devastating letter to Colonel Lewis and comfort flowed into me.

"There's some say the boy's youngest sister could tell where he found it, if she wanted," Dave said. "She used to go into that desert with him a lot. She took on pretty wild when it happened and then was struck dumb, but I hear she talks again now." He shook his head. "Poor little Helen. She promised to be a pretty girl."

"Where does she live?" I asked.

"With her mother in Salem," Dave said. "She went to business school and I hear she works for a lawyer there."

Mrs. Price was a flinty old woman who seemed to control her daughter absolutely. She agreed Helen would be my secretary as soon as I told her the salary. I got Helen's security clearance with one phone call; she had already been investigated as part of tracing that uranium crystal. Mrs. Price arranged for Helen to stay with a family she knew in Barker, to protect her reputation. It was in no danger. I meant to make love to her, if I had to, to charm her out of her secret, if she had one, but I would not harm her. I knew perfectly well that I was only playing a game called "The Revenge of Duard Campbell." I knew I would not find any uranium.

Helen was a plain little girl and she was made of frightened ice.

She wore low-heeled shoes and cotton stockings and plain dresses with white cuffs and collars. Her one good feature was her flawless fair skin against which her peaked, black Welsh eyebrows and smoky blue eyes gave her an elfin look at times. She liked to sit neatly tucked into herself, feet together, elbows in, eyes cast down, voice hardly audible, as smoothly self-contained as an egg. The desk I gave her faced mine and she sat like that across from me and did the busy work I gave her and I could not get through to her at all.

I tried joking and I tried polite little gifts and attentions, and I tried being sad and needing sympathy. She listened and worked and stayed as far away as the moon. It was only after two weeks and by pure accident that I found the key to her.

I was trying the sympathy gambit. I said it was not so bad, being exiled from friends and family, but what I could not stand was the dreary sameness of that search area. Every spot was like every other spot and there was no single, recognizable place in the whole expanse. It sparked something in her and she roused up at me.

"It's full of just wonderful places," she said.

"Come out with me in the Jeep and show me one," I challenged.

She was reluctant, but I hustled her along regardless. I guided the Jeep between outcrops, jouncing and lurching. I had our map photographed on my mind and I knew where we were every minute, but only by map coordinates. The desert had our marks on it: well sites, seismic blast holes, wooden stakes, cans, bottles and papers blowing in that everlasting wind, and it was all dismally the same anyway.

"Tell me when we pass a 'place' and I'll stop," I said.

"It's all places," she said. "Right here's a place."

I stopped the Jeep and looked at her in surprise. Her voice was strong and throaty. She opened her eyes wide and smiled; I had never seen her look like that.

"What's special, that makes it a place?" I asked.

She did not answer. She got out and walked a few steps. Her whole posture was changed. She almost danced along. I followed and touched her shoulder.

"Tell me what's special," I said.

She faced around and stared right past me. She had a new grace and vitality and she was a very pretty girl.

"It's where all the dogs are," she said.

"Dogs?"

I looked around at the scrubby sagebrush and thin soil and ugly black rock and back at Helen. Something was wrong.

"Big, stupid dogs that go in herds and eat grass," she said. She kept turning and gazing. "Big cats chase the dogs and eat them. The dogs scream and scream. Can't you hear them?"

"That's crazy!" I said. "What's the matter with you?"

I might as well have slugged her. She crumpled instantly back into herself and I could hardly hear her answer.

"I'm sorry. My brother and I used to play out fairy tales here. All this was a kind of fairyland to us." Tears formed in her eyes. "I haven't been here since . . . I forgot myself. I'm sorry."

I had to swear I needed to dictate "field notes" to force Helen into that desert again. She sat stiffly with pad and pencil in the Jeep while I put on my act with the Geiger and rattled off jargon. Her lips were pale and compressed and I could see her fighting against the spell the desert had for her, and I could see her slowly losing.

She finally broke down into that strange mood and I took good care not to break it. It was weird but wonderful, and I got a lot of data. I made her go out for "field notes" every morning and each time it was easier to break her down. Back in the office she always froze again and I marveled at how two such different persons could inhabit the same body. I called her two phases "Office Helen" and "Desert Helen."

I often talked with old Dave on the veranda after dinner. One night he cautioned me.

"Folks here think Helen ain't been right in the head since her brother died," he said. "They're worrying about you and her."

"I feel like a big brother to her," I said. "I'd never hurt her, Dave. If we find the lode, I'll stake the best claim for her."

He shook his head. I wished I could explain to him how it was only a harmless game I was playing and no one would ever find gold out there. Yet, as a game, it fascinated me.

Desert Helen charmed me when, helplessly, she had to uncover her secret life. She was a little girl in a woman's body. Her voice became strong and breathless with excitement and she touched me with the same wonder that turned her own face vivid and elfin. She ran laughing through the black rocks and scrubby sagebrush and momentarily she made them beautiful. She would pull me along by the hand and sometimes we ran as much as a mile away from the Jeep. She treated me as if I were a blind or foolish child.

"No, no, Duard, that's a cliff!" she would say, pulling me back.

She would go first, so I could find the stepping stones across streams. I played up. She pointed out woods and streams and cliffs and castles. There were shaggy horses with claws, golden birds, camels, witches, elephants and many other creatures. I pretended to see them all, and it made her trust me. She talked and acted out the fairy tales she had once played with Owen. Sometimes he was enchanted and sometimes she, and the one had to dare the evil magic of a witch or giant to rescue the other. Sometimes I was Duard and other times I almost thought I was Owen.

Helen and I crept into sleeping castles, and we hid with pounding hearts while the giant grumbled in search of us and we fled, hand in hand, before his wrath.

Well, I had her now. I played Helen's game, but I never lost sight of my own. Every night I sketched in on my map whatever I had learned that day of the fairyland topography.

Its geomorphology was remarkably consistent.

When we played, I often hinted about the giant's treasure. Helen never denied it existed, but she seemed troubled and evasive about it. She would put her finger to her lips and look at me with solemn, round eyes.

"You only take the things nobody cares about," she would say. "If you take the gold or jewels, it brings you terrible bad luck."

"I got a charm against bad luck and I'll let you have it too," I said once. "It's the biggest, strongest charm in the whole world."

"No. It all turns into trash. It turns into goat beans and dead snakes and things," she said crossly. "Owen told me. It's a rule, in fairyland."

Another time we talked about it as we sat in a gloomy ravine near a waterfall. We had to keep our voices low or we would wake up the giant. The waterfall was really the giant snoring and it was also the wind that blew forever across that desert.

"Doesn't Owen ever take anything?" I asked.

I had learned by then that I must always speak of Owen in the present tense.

"Sometimes he has to," she said. "Once right here the witch had me enchanted into an ugly toad. Owen put a flower on my head and that made me be Helen again."

"A really truly flower? That you could take home with you?"

"A red and yellow flower bigger than my two hands," she said. "I tried to take it home, but all the petals came off."

"Does Owen ever take anything home?"

"Rocks, sometimes," she said. "We keep them in a secret nest in the shed. We think they might be magic eggs."

I stood up. "Come and show me."

She shook her head vigorously and drew back. "I don't want to go home," she said. "Not ever."

She squirmed and pouted, but I pulled her to her feet.

"Please, Helen, for me," I said. "Just for one little minute."

I pulled her back to the Jeep and we drove to the old Price place. I had never seen her look at it when we passed it and she did not look now. She was freezing fast back into Office Helen. But she led me around the sagging old house with its broken windows and into a tumbledown shed. She scratched away some straw in one corner, and there were the rocks. I did not realize how excited I was until disappointment hit me like a blow in the stomach. They were worthless waterworn pebbles of quartz and rosy granite. The only thing special about them was that they could never have originated on that basalt desert.

After a few weeks we dropped the pretense of field notes and simply went into the desert to play. I had Helen's fairyland almost completely mapped. It seemed to be a recent fault block mountain with a river parallel to its base and a gently sloping plain across the river. The scarp face was wooded and cut by deep ravines and it had castles perched on its truncated spurs. I kept checking Helen on it and never found her inconsistent. Several times when she was in doubt I was able to tell her where she was, and that let me even more deeply into her secret life. One morning I discovered just how deeply.

She was sitting on a log in the forest and plaiting a little basket out of fern fronds. I stood beside her. She looked up at me and smiled.

"What shall we play today, Owen?" she asked.

I had not expected that, and I was proud of how quickly I rose to it. I capered and bounded away and then back to her and crouched at her feet.

"Little sister, little sister. I'm enchanted," I said. "Only you in all the world can uncharm me."

"I'll uncharm you," she said, in that little girl voice. "What are you, brother?"

"A big, black dog," I said. "A wicked giant named Lewis Rawbones keeps me chained up behind his castle while he takes all the other dogs out hunting."

She smoothed her gray skirt over her knees. Her mouth drooped.

"You're lonesome and you howl all day and you howl all night," she said. "Poor doggie."

I threw back my head and howled.

"He's a terrible, wicked giant and he's got all kinds of terrible magic," I said. "You mustn't be afraid, little sister. As soon as you uncharm me I'll be a handsome prince and I'll cut off his head."

"I'm not afraid." Her eyes sparkled. "I'm not afraid of fire or snakes or pins or needles or anything."

"I'll take you away to my kingdom and we'll live happily ever afterward. You'll be the most beautiful queen in the world and everybody will love you."

I wagged my tail and laid my head on her knees. She stroked my silky head and pulled my long black ears.

"Everybody will love me," she was very serious now. "Will magic water uncharm you, poor old doggie?"

"You have to touch my forehead with a piece of the giant's treasure," I said. "That's the only onliest way to uncharm me."

I felt her shrink away from me. She stood up, her face suddenly crumpled with grief and anger.

"You're not Owen, you're just a man! Owen's enchanted and I'm enchanted too and nobody will ever uncharm us!"

She ran away from me and she was already Office Helen by the time she reached the Jeep.

After that day she refused flatly to go into the desert with me. It looked as if my game was played out. But I gambled that Desert Helen could still hear me, underneath somewhere, and I tried a new strategy. The office was an upstairs room over the old dance hall and, I suppose, in frontier days skirmishing had gone on there between men and women. I doubt anything went on as strange as my new game with Helen.

I always had paced and talked while Helen worked. Now I began mixing common-sense talk with fairyland talk and I kept coming back to the wicked giant, Lewis Rawbones.

Office Helen tried not to pay attention, but now and then I caught Desert Helen peeping at me out of her eyes. I spoke of my blighted career as a geologist and how it would be restored to me if I found the lode. I mused on how I would live and work in exotic places and how I would need a wife to keep house for me and help with my paper work. It disturbed Office Helen. She made typing mistakes and dropped things. I kept it up for days, trying for just the right mixture of fact and fantasy, and it was hard on Office Helen.

One night old Dave warned me again.

"Helen's looking peaked, and there's talk around. Miz Fowler says Helen don't sleep and she cries at night and she won't tell Miz Fowler what's wrong. You don't happen to know what's bothering her, do you?"

"I only talk business stuff to her," I said. "Maybe she's homesick. I'll ask her if she wants a vacation." I did not like the way Dave looked at me. "I haven't hurt her. I don't mean her any harm, Dave," I said.

"People get killed for what they do, not for what they mean," he said. "Son, there's men in this here town would kill you quick as a coyote, if you hurt Helen Price."

I worked on Helen all the next day and in the afternoon I hit just the right note and I broke her defenses. I was not prepared for the way it worked out. I had just said, "All life is a kind of playing. If you think about it right, everything we do is a game." She poised her pencil and looked straight at me, as she had never done in that office, and I felt my heart speed up.

"You taught me how to play, Helen. I was so serious that I didn't know how to play."

"Owen taught me to play. He had magic. My sisters couldn't play anything but dolls and rich husbands and I hated them."

Her eyes opened wide and her lips trembled and she was almost Desert Helen right there in the office.

"There's magic and enchantment in regular life, if you look at it right," I said. "Don't you think so, Helen?"

"I know it!" she said. She turned pale and dropped her pencil. "Owen was enchanted into having a wife and three daughters and he was just a boy. But he was the only man we had and all of them but me hated him because we were so poor." She began to tremble and her voice went flat. "He couldn't stand it. He took the treasure and it killed him." Tears ran down her cheeks. "I tried to think he was only enchanted into play-dead and if I didn't speak or laugh for seven years, I'd uncharm him."

She dropped her head on her hands. I was alarmed. I came over and put my hand on her shoulder.

"I did speak." Her shoulders heaved with sobs. "They made me speak, and now Owen won't ever come back."

I bent and put my arm across her shoulders.

"Don't cry, Helen. He'll come back," I said. "There are other magics to bring him back."

I hardly knew what I was saying. I was afraid of what I had done, and I wanted to comfort her. She jumped up and threw off my arm.

"I can't stand it! I'm going home!"

She ran out into the hall and down the stairs and from the window I saw her run down the street, still crying. All of a sudden my game seemed cruel and stupid to me and right that moment I stopped it. I tore up my map of fairyland and my letters to Colonel Lewis and I wondered how in the world I could ever have done all that.

After dinner that night old Dave motioned me out to one end of the veranda. His face looked carved out of wood.

"I don't know what happened in your office today, and for your sake I better not find out. But you send Helen back to her mother on the morning stage, you hear me?"

"All right, if she wants to go," I said. "I can't just fire her."

"I'm speaking for the boys. You better put her on that morning stage, or we'll be around to talk to you."

"All right, I will, Dave."

I wanted to tell him how the game was stopped now and how I wanted a chance to make things up with Helen, but I thought I had better not. Dave's voice was flat and savage with contempt and, old as he was, he frightened me.

Helen did not come to work in the morning. At nine o'clock I went out myself for the mail. I brought a large mailing tube and some letters back to the office. The first letter I opened was from Dr. Lewis, and almost like magic it solved all my problems.

On the basis of his preliminary structure contour maps Dr. Lewis had gotten permission to close out the field phase. Copies of the maps were in the mailing tube, for my information. I was to hold an inventory and be ready to turn everything over to an army quartermaster team coming in a few days. There was still a great mass of data to be worked up in refining the maps. I was to join the group again and I would have a chance at the lab work after all.

I felt pretty good. I paced and whistled and snapped my fingers. I wished Helen would come, to help on the inventory. Then I opened the tube and looked idly at the maps. There were a lot of them, featureless bed after bed of basalt, like layers of a cake ten miles across. But when I came to the bottom map, of the prevolcanic Miocene landscape, the hair on my neck stood up.

I had made that map myself. It was Helen's fairyland. The topography was point by point the same.

I clenched my fists and stopped breathing. Then it hit me a second time, and the skin crawled up my back.

The game was real. I couldn't end it. All the time the game had been playing me. It was still playing me.

I ran out and down the street and overtook old Dave hurrying toward the feedyard. He had a holstered gun on each hip.

"Dave, I've got to find Helen," I said.

"Somebody seen her hiking into the desert just at daylight," he said. "I'm on my way for a horse." He did not slow his stride. "You better get out there in your stinkwagon. If you don't find her before we do, you better just keep on going, son."

I ran back and got the Jeep and roared it out across the scrubby sagebrush. I hit rocks and I do not know why I did not break something. I knew where to go and feared what I would find there. I knew I loved Helen Price more than my own life and I knew I had driven her to her death.

I saw her far off, running and dodging, I headed the Jeep to intercept her and I shouted, but she neither saw me nor heard me. I stopped and jumped out and ran after her and the world darkened. Helen was all I could see, and I could not catch up with her.

"Wait for me, little sister!" I screamed after her. "I love you, Helen! Wait for me!"

She stopped and crouched and I almost ran over her. I knelt and put my arms around her and then it was on us.

They say in an earthquake, when the direction of up and down tilts and wobbles, people feel a fear that drives them mad if they can not forget it afterward. This was worse. Up and down and here and there and now and then all rushed together. The wind roared through the rock beneath us and the air thickened crushingly above our heads. I know we clung to each other, and we were there for each other while nothing else was and that is all I know, until we were in the Jeep and I was guiding it back toward town as headlong as I had come.

Then the world had shape again under a bright sun. I saw a knot of horsemen on the horizon. They were heading for where Owen had been found. That boy had run a long way, alone and hurt and burdened.

I got Helen up to the office. She sat at her desk with her head down on her hands and she quivered violently. I kept my arm around her.

"It was only a storm inside our two heads, Helen," I said, over and over. "Something black blew away out of us. The game is finished and we're free and I love you."

Over and over I said that, for my sake as well as hers. I meant and believed it. I said she was my wife and we would marry and go a thousand miles away from that desert to raise our children. She quieted to a trembling, but she would not speak. Then I heard hoofbeats and the creak of leather in the street below and then I heard slow footsteps on the stairs.

Old Dave stood in the doorway. His two guns looked as natural on him as hands and feet. He looked at Helen, bowed over the desk, and then at me, standing beside her.

"Come on down, son. The boys want to talk to you," he said.

I followed him into the hall and stopped.

"She isn't hurt," I said. "The lode is really out there, Dave, but nobody is ever going to find it."

"Tell that to the boys."

"We're closing out the project in a few more days," I said. "I'm going to marry Helen and take her away with me."

"Come down or we'll drag you down!" he said harshly. "We'll send Helen back to her mother."

I was afraid. I did not know what to do,

"No, you won't send me back to my mother!"

It was Helen beside me in the hall. She was Desert Helen, but grown up and wonderful. She was pale, pretty, aware and sure of herself.

"I'm going with Duard," she said. "Nobody in the world is ever going to send me around like a package again."

Dave rubbed his jaw and squinted his eyes at her.

"I love her, Dave," I said. "I'll take care of her all my life."

I put my left arm around her and she nestled against me. The tautness went out of old Dave and he smiled. He kept his eyes on Helen.

"Little Helen Price," he said, wonderingly. "Who ever would've thought it?" He reached out and shook us both gently. "Bless you youngsters," he said, and blinked his eyes.

"I'll tell the boys it's all right."

He turned and went slowly down the stairs. Helen and I looked at each other, and I think she saw a new face too.

That was sixteen years ago. I am a professor myself now, graying a bit at the temples. I am as positivistic a scientist as you will find anywhere in the Mississippi drainage basin. When I tell a seminar student "That assertion is operationally meaningless," I can make it sound downright obscene. The students blush and hate me, but it is for their own good. Science is the only safe game, and it's safe only if it is kept pure. I work hard at that, I have yet to meet the student I cannot handle.

My son is another matter. We named him Owen Lewis, and he has Helen's eyes and hair and complexion. He learned to read on the modern sane and sterile children's books. We haven't a fairy tale in the house but I have a science library. And Owen makes fairy tales out of science. He is taking the measure of space and time now, with Jeans and Eddington. He cannot possibly understand a tenth of what he reads, in the way I understand it. But he understands all of it in some other way privately his own.

Not long ago he said to me, "You know, Dad, it isn't only space that's expanding. Time's expanding too, and that's what makes us keep getting farther away from when we used to be."

And I have to tell him just what I did in the war. I know I found manhood and a wife. The how and why of it I think and hope I am incapable of fully understanding. But Owen has, through Helen, that strangely curious heart. I'm afraid. I'm afraid he will understand.

Palely Loitering

INTRODUCTION

Here's a very unusual park, where one can take a walk on a time-bridge and end up one day in the past or future. But youngsters don't always follow the rules, and when the story's narrator jumped *off* the bridge, something definitely not to be done, he began a chain of events that would affect the rest of his life. This story won the British Science Fiction Association 1979 award for best short fiction, and also was a runner-up for the 1980 Hugo and Locus awards in the novelette and novella categories.

* * *

Christopher Priest was born in Cheshire, England. He began writing soon after leaving school and has been a full-time freelance writer since 1968. He has published thirteen novels, four short story collections and a number of other books, including critical works, biographies, novelizations and children's non-fiction. His novel *The Separation* won both the Arthur C. Clarke Award and the British Science Fiction Association Award. In 1996 Priest won the James Tait Black Memorial Prize for his novel *The Prestige*. He has been nominated four times for the Hugo award. He has won several awards abroad, including the Kurd Lasswitz Award (Germany), the Eurocon Award (Yugoslavia), the Ditmar Award (Australia), and Le Grand Prix de L'Imaginaire (France). In 2001 he was awarded the Prix Utopia (France) for lifetime achievement. He has written drama for radio

(BBC Radio 4) and television (Thames TV and HTV). In 2006, *The Prestige* was filmed by director Christopher Nolan, went to number one U.S. box office in its first week, and received two Academy Award nominations. Another novel, *The Glamour,* is soon to be filmed in the UK by director Gerald McMorrow. Chris Priest's most recent novel, *The Adjacent,* was published by Gollancz in 2013, and in the USA by Titan Books in April 2014. He is Vice-President of the H. G. Wells Society. In 2007, an exhibition of installation art based on his novel *The Affirmation* was mounted in London. As a journalist he has written features and reviews for *The Times*, the *Guardian*, the *Independent*, the *New Statesman*, the *Scotsman*, and many different magazines.

Palely Loitering

by Christopher Priest

I

During the summers of my childhood, the best treat of all was our annual picnic in Flux Channel Park, which lay some fifty miles from home. Because my father was set in his ways, and for him no picnic would be worthy of its name without a joint of freshly roasted cold ham, the first clue we children had was always, therefore, when Cook began her preparations. I made a point every day of slipping down unnoticed to the cellar to count the hams that hung from steel hooks in the ceiling, and as soon as I found one was missing I would hurry to my sisters and share the news. The next day, the house would fill with the rich aroma of ham roasting in cloves, and we three children would enter an elaborate charade: inside we would be brimming over with excitement at the thought of the adventure, but at the same time restraining ourselves to act normally, because Father's announcement of his plans at breakfast on the chosen day was an important part of the fun.

We grew up in awe and dread of our father, for he was a distant and strict man. Throughout the winter months, when his work made its greatest demands, we hardly saw him, and all we knew of him were the instructions passed on to us by Mother or the governor. In the summer months he chose to maintain the distance, joining us only for meals, and spending the evenings alone in his study. However, once a year my father would mellow, and for this alone the excursions to the Park would have been cause for joy. He knew the excitement the trip held for us and he played up to it, revealing the instinct of showman and actor.

Sometimes he would start by pretending to scold or punish us for some imaginary misdemeanour, or would ask Mother a misleading question, such as whether it was that day the servants were taking a holiday, or he would affect absentmindedness; through all this we would hug our knees under the table, knowing what was to come. Then at last he would utter the magic words "Flux Channel Park," and, abandoning our charade with glee, we children would squeal with delight and run to Mother, the servants would bustle in and clear away the breakfast, there would be a clatter of dishes and the creak of the wicker hamper from the kitchen . . . and at long last the crunching of hooves and steel-rimmed wheels would sound on the gravel drive outside, as the taxi-carriage arrived to take us to the station.

II

I believe that my parents went to the Park from the year they were married, but my own first clear memory of a picnic is when I was seven years old. We went as a family every year until I was fifteen. For nine summers that I can remember, then, the picnic was the happiest day of the year, fusing in memory into one composite day, each picnic much like all the others, so carefully did Father orchestrate the treat for us. And yet one day stands out from all the others because of a moment of disobedience and mischief, and after that those summery days in Flux Channel Park were never quite the same again.

It happened when I was ten years old. The day had started like any other picnic day, and by the time the taxi arrived the servants had gone on ahead to reserve a train compartment for us. As we clambered into the carriage, Cook ran out of the house to wave us away, and she gave each of us children a freshly peeled carrot to gnaw on. I took mine whole into my mouth, distending my cheeks, and sucking and nibbling at it slowly, mashing it gradually into a juicy pulp. As we rattled down to the station I saw Father glancing at me once or twice, as if to tell me not to make so much noise with my mouth . . . but it was a holiday from everything, and he said nothing.

My mother, sitting opposite us in the carriage, issued her usual instructions to my sisters. "Salleen," (my elder sister), "you're to keep an eye on Mykle. You know how he runs around." (I, sucking my carrot, made a face at Salleen, bulging a cheek with the carrot and squinting my eyes.) "And you, Therese, you must stay by me. None of you is to go too close to the Channel." Her instructions came too soon—the train-ride was of second-order interest, but it came between us and the Park.

I enjoyed the train, smelling the sooty smoke and watching the steam curl past the compartment window like an attendant white wraith, but my sisters, especially Salleen, were unaccustomed to the motion and felt sick. While Mother fussed over the girls and summoned the servants from their compartment further down the train, Father and I sat gravely beside each other. When Salleen had been taken away down the train and Therese had quietened I started to fidget in my seat, craning my neck to peer forward, seeking that first magical glimpse of the silvery ribbon of the Channel.

"Father, which bridge shall we cross this time?" And, "Can we cross *two* bridges today, like last year?"

Always the same answer. "We shall decide when we arrive. Keep still, Mykle."

And so we arrived, tugging at our parents' hands to hurry them, waiting anxiously by the gate as the entrance fees were paid. The first dashing run down the sloping green sward of the Park grounds, dodging the trees and jumping high to see along the Channel, shouting disappointment because there were too many people there already, or not enough. Father beamed at us and lit his pipe, flicking back the flaps of his frock-coat and thrusting his thumbs into his waistcoat, then strolled beside Mother as she held his arm. My sisters and I walked or ran, depending on our constitutional state, heading towards the Channel, but slowing when awed by its closeness, not daring to approach. Looking back, we saw Father and Mother waving to us from the shade of the trees, needlessly warning us of the dangers.

As always, we hurried to the tollbooths for the time bridges that crossed the Channel, for it was these bridges that were the whole reason for the day's trip. A line of people was waiting at each booth, moving forward slowly to pay the entrance fee: families like ourselves with children dancing, young couples holding hands, single men and women glancing speculatively at each other. We counted the people in each queue, eagerly checked the results with each other, then ran back to our parents.

"Father, there are only twenty-six people at the Tomorrow Bridge!"

"There's *no one* at the Yesterday Bridge!" Salleen, exaggerating as usual.

"Can we cross into Tomorrow, Mother?"

"We did that last year." Salleen, still disgruntled from the tram, kicked out feebly at me. "Mykle *always* wants to go to Tomorrow!"

"No I don't. The queue is longer for Yesterday!"

Mother, soothingly, "We'll decide after lunch. The queues will be shorter then."

Father, watching the servants laying our cloth beneath a dark old cedar tree, said, "Let us walk for a while, my dear. The children can come too. We will have luncheon in an hour or so."

Our second exploration of the Park was more orderly, conducted, as it was, under Father's eye. We walked again to the nearest part of the Channel—it seemed less risky now, with parents there—and followed one of the paths that ran parallel to the bank. We stared at the people on the other side.

"Father, are they in Yesterday or Tomorrow?"

"I can't say, Mykle. It could be either."

"They're nearer to the Yesterday Bridge, stupid!" Salleen, pushing me from behind.

"That doesn't mean anything, stupid!" Jabbing back at her with an elbow.

The sun reflecting from the silvery surface of the flux fluid (we sometimes called it water, to my father's despair) made it glitter and sparkle like rippling quicksilver. Mother would not look at it, saying the reflections hurt her eyes, but there was always something dreadful about its presence so that no one could look too long. In the still patches, where the mystifying currents below briefly let the surface settle, we sometimes saw upside-down reflections of the people on the other side.

Later: we edged around the tolls, where the lines of people were longer than before, and walked further along the bank towards the east.

Then later: we returned to the shade and the trees, and sat in a demure group while lunch was served. My father carved ham with the precision of the expert chef: one cut down at an angle towards the bone, another horizontally across to the bone, and the wedge of meat so produced taken away on a plate by one of the servants. Then the slow, meticulous carving beneath the notch. One slice after another, each one slightly wider and rounder than the one before.

As soon as lunch was finished we made our way to the tollbooths and queued with the other people. There were always fewer people waiting at this time of the afternoon, a fact that surprised us but which our parents took for granted. This day we had chosen the Tomorrow Bridge. Whatever the preferences we children expressed Father always had the last word. It did not, however, prevent Salleen from sulking, nor me from letting her see the joys of victory.

This particular day was the first time I had been to the Park with any understanding of the Flux Channel and its real purpose. Earlier in the summer, the governor had instructed us in the rudiments of spatio-temporal physics . . . although that was not the name he gave to it. My sisters had been bored with the subject (it was boys' stuff, they declared), but to learn how and why the Channel had been built was fascinating to me.

I had grown up with a general understanding that we lived in a world where our ancestors had built many marvellous things that we no longer used or had need for. This awareness, gleaned from the few other children I knew, was of astonishing and miraculous achievements, and was, as might be expected, wildly inaccurate. I knew as a fact, for instance, that the Flux Channel had been built in a matter of days, that jet-propelled aircraft could circumnavigate the world in a matter of minutes, and that houses and automobiles and railway trains could be built in a matter of seconds. Of course the truth was quite different, and our education in the scientific age and its history was constantly interesting to me.

In the case of the Flux Channel, I knew by my tenth birthday that it had taken more than two decades to build, that its construction had cost many human lives, and that it had taxed the resources and intelligence of many different countries.

Furthermore, the principle on which it worked was well understood today, even though we had no use for it as it was intended.

We lived in the age of starflight, but by the time I was born mankind had long lost the desire to travel in space.

The governor had shown us a slowed-down film of the launching of the craft that had flown to the stars: the surface of the Flux Channel undulating as the starship was propelled through its deeps like a huge whale trying to navigate a canal. Then the hump of its hull bursting through the surface in a shimmering spray of exploding foam, and the gushing wake sluicing over the banks of the Channel and vanishing instantaneously. Then the actual launch, with the starship soaring into the sky, leaving a trail of brilliant droplets in the air behind it.

All this had taken place in under one-tenth of a second. Anyone within twenty-five miles of the launch would have been killed by the shockwave, and it is said that the thunder of the starship's passage could be heard in every country of the Neuropean Union. Only the automatic high-speed cameras were there to witness the launching. The men and women who crewed the ship—their metabolic functions frozen for most of the flight—would not have felt the strain of such a tremendous acceleration even if they had been conscious. The flux field distorted time and space, changed the nature of matter. The ship was launched at such a high relative velocity that by the time the technicians returned to the Flux Channel it would have been outside the Solar System. By the time I was born, seventy years after this, the starship would have been . . . who knows where?

Behind it, churning and eddying with temporal mystery, the Flux

Channel lay across more than a hundred miles of the land, a scintillating, dazzling ribbon of light, like a slit in the world that looked towards another dimension.

There were no more starships after the first and that one had never returned. When the disturbance of the launching had calmed to a degree where the flux field was no longer a threat to human life, the stations that tapped the electricity had been built along part of its banks. A few years later, when the flux field had stabilized completely, an area of the countryside was landscaped to create the Park and the time bridges were built.

One of these traversed the Channel at an angle of exactly ninety degrees, and to walk across it was no different from crossing any bridge across any ordinary river.

One bridge was built slightly obtuse of the right-angle, and to cross it was to climb the temporal gradient of the flux field; when one emerged on the other side of the Channel, twenty-four hours had elapsed.

The third bridge was built slightly acute of the right-angle, and to cross to the other side was to walk twenty-four hours into the past. Yesterday, Today and Tomorrow existed on the far side of the Flux Channel, and one could walk at will among them.

III

While waiting in line at the tollbooth, we had another argument about Father's decision to cross into Tomorrow. The Park management had posted a board above the paydesk, describing the weather conditions on the other side. There was wind, low cloud, sudden showers. My mother said that she did not wish to get wet. Salleen, watching me, quietly repeated that we had been to Tomorrow last year. I stayed quiet, looking across the Channel to the other side.

(Over there the weather seemed to be as it was here: a high, bright sky, hot sunshine. But what I could see was Today: yesterday's Tomorrow, tomorrow's Yesterday, today's Today.)

Behind us the queue was thinning as other, less hardy, people drifted away to the other bridges. I was content, because the only one that did not interest me was the Today Bridge, but to rub in my accidental victory I whispered to Salleen that the weather was good on the Yesterday side. She, in no mood for subtle perversity, kicked out at my shins and we squabbled stupidly as my father went to the toll.

He was an important man. I heard the attendant say, "But you shouldn't have waited, sir. We are honoured by your visit." He released the ratchet of the turnstile, and we filed through.

We entered the covered way of the bridge, a long dark tunnel of wood and metal, lit at intervals by dim incandescent lamps. I ran on ahead, feeling the familiar electric tingle over my body as I moved through the flux-field.

"Mykle! Stay with us!" My father, calling from behind.

I slowed obediently and turned to wait. I saw the rest of the family coming towards me. The outlines of their bodies were strangely diffused, an effect of the field on all who entered it. As they reached me, and thus came into the zone I was in, their shapes became sharply focused once more.

I let them pass me, and followed behind. Salleen, walking beside me, kicked out at my ankles.

"Why did you do that?"

"Because you're a little pig!"

I ignored her. We could see the end of the covered way ahead. It had become dark soon after we started crossing the bridge—a presage of the evening of the day we were leaving—but now daylight shone again and I saw pale blue morning light, misty shapes of trees. I paused, seeing my parents and sisters silhouetted against the light. Therese, holding Mother's hand, took no notice of me, but Salleen, whom I secretly loved, strutted proudly behind Father, asserting her independence of me. Perhaps it was because of her, or perhaps it was that morning light shining down from the end of the tunnel, but I stayed still as the rest of the family went on.

I waved my hands, watching the fingertips blur as they moved across the flux field, and then I walked on slowly. Because of the blurring my family were now almost invisible. Suddenly I was a little frightened, alone in the flux field, and I hastened after them. I saw their ghostly shapes move into daylight and out of sight (Salleen glanced back towards me), and I walked faster.

By the time I had reached the end of the covered way, the day had matured and the light was that of mid-afternoon. Low clouds were scudding before a stiff wind. As a squall of rain swept by I sheltered in the bridge, and looked across the Park for the family. I saw them a short distance away, hurrying towards one of the pagoda-shaped shelters the Park authorities had built. Glancing at the sky I saw there was a large patch of blue not far away, and I knew the shower would be a short one. It was not cold and I did not mind getting wet, but I hesitated before going out into the open. Why I stood there I do not now recall, but I had always had a childish delight in the sensation of the flux field, and at the place where the covered way ends the bridge is still over a part of the Channel.

I stood by the edge of the bridge and looked down at the flux fluid. Seen from directly above it closely resembled water, because it seemed to be clear (although the bottom could not be seen), and did not have the same metallic sheen or quicksilver property it had when viewed from the side. There were bright highlights on the surface, glinting as the fluid stirred, as if there were a film of oil across it.

My parents had reached the pagoda—whose colourful tiles and paintwork looked odd in this dismal rain—and they were squeezing in with the two girls, as other people made room for them. I could see my father's tall black hat, bobbing behind the crowd.

Salleen was looking back at me, perhaps envying my solitary state, and so I stuck out my tongue at her. I was showing off. I went to the edge of the bridge, where there was no guard rail, and leaned precariously out above the fluid. The flux field prickled around me. I saw Salleen tugging at Mother's arm, and Father took a step forward into the rain. I poised myself and jumped towards the bank, flying above the few inches of the Channel between me and the ground. I heard a roaring in my ears, I was momentarily blinded, and the charge of the flux field enveloped me like an electric cocoon.

I landed feet-first on the muddy bank, and looked around me as if nothing untoward had happened.

IV

Although I did not realize it at first, in leaping from the bridge and moving up through a part of the flux-field, I had travelled in time. It happened that I landed on a day in the future when the weather was as grey and blustery as on the day I had left, and so my first real awareness, when I looked up, was that the pagoda had suddenly emptied. I stared in horror across the parkland, not believing that my family could have vanished in the blink of an eye.

I started to run, stumbling and sliding on the slippery ground, and I felt a panicky terror and a dread of being abandoned. All the cockiness in me had gone. I sobbed as I ran, and when I reached the pagoda I was crying aloud, snivelling and wiping my nose and eyes on the sleeve of my jacket.

I went back to where I had landed, and saw the muddy impressions of my feet on the bank. From there I looked at the bridge, so tantalizingly close, and it was then that I realized what I had done, even though it was a dim understanding.

Something like my former mood returned then and a spirit of exploration came over me. After all, it was the first time I had ever been alone in the Park. I started to walk away from the bridge, following a tree-lined path that went along the Channel.

The day I had arrived in must have been a weekday in winter or early spring because the trees were bare and there were very few people about. From this side of the Channel I could see that the toll-booths were open, but the only other people in the Park were a long way away.

For all this, it was still an adventure and the awful thoughts about where I had arrived, or how I was to return, were put aside.

I walked a long way, enjoying the freedom of being able to explore this side without my family. When they were present it was as if I could only see what they pointed out, and walk where they chose. Now it was like being in the Park for the first time.

This small pleasure soon palled. It was a cold day and my light summer shoes began to feel sodden and heavy, chafing against my toes. The Park was not at all how I liked it to be. Part of the fun on a normal day was the atmosphere of shared daring, and mixing with people you knew had not all come from the same day, the same time. Once, my father, in a mood of exceptional capriciousness, had led us to and fro across the Today and Yesterday Bridges, showing us time-slipped images of himself which he had made on a visit to the Park the day before. Visitors to the Park often did such things. During the holidays, when the big factories were closed, the Park would be full of shouting, laughing voices as carefully prepared practical jokes of this sort were played.

None of this was going on as I tramped along under the leaden sky. The future was for me as commonplace as a field.

I began to worry, wondering how I was to get back. I could imagine the wrath of my father, the tears of my mother, the endless jibes I would get from Salleen and Therese. I turned around and walked quickly back towards the bridges, forming a half-hearted plan to cross the Channel repeatedly, using the Tomorrow and Yesterday Bridges in turn, until I was back where I started.

I was running again, in danger of sobbing, when I saw a young man walking along the bank towards me. I would have paid no attention to him, but for the fact that when we were a short distance apart he sidestepped so that he was in front of me.

I slowed, regarded him incuriously, and went to walk around him. . . but much to my surprise he called after me.

"Mykle! It is Mykle, isn't it?"

"How do you know my name?" I said, pausing and looking at him warily.

"I was looking for you. You've jumped forward in time, and don't know how to get back."

"Yes, but—"

"I'll show you how. It's easy."

We were facing each other now, and I was wondering who he was and how he knew me. There was something much too friendly about him. He was very tall and thin, and had the beginnings of a moustache darkening his lip. He seemed adult to me, but when he spoke it was with a hoarse, boyish falsetto.

I said, "It's all right, thank you, sir. I can find my own way."

"By running across the bridges?"

"How did you know?"

"You'll never manage it, Mykle. when you jumped from the bridge you went a long way into the future. About thirty-two years."

"This is. . . ?" I looked around at the Park, disbelieving what he said. "But it feels like—"

"Just like Tomorrow. But it isn't. You've come a long way. Look over there." He pointed across the Channel, to the other side. "Do you see those houses? You've never seen those before, have you?"

There was an estate of new houses, built beyond the trees on the Park's perimeter. True, I hadn't noticed them before, but it proved nothing. I didn't find this very interesting, and I began to sidle away from him, wanting to get on with the business of working out how to get back.

"Thank you, sir. It was nice to meet you."

"Don't call me 'sir'," he said, laughing. "You've been taught to be polite to strangers, but you must know who *I* am."

"N-no . . ." Suddenly rather nervous of him I walked quickly away, but he ran over and caught me by the arm.

"There's something I must show you,' he said. "This is very important. Then I'll get you back to the bridge."

"Leave me alone!" I said loudly, quite frightened of him.

He took no notice of my protests, but walked me along the path beside the Channel. He was looking over my head, across the Channel, and I could not help noticing that whenever we passed a tree or a bush which cut off the view he would pause and look past it before going on. This continued until we were near the time bridges again, when he came to a halt beside a huge sprawling rhododendron bush.

"Now," he said. "I want you to look. But don't let yourself be seen."

Crouching down with him, I peered around the edge of the bush. At first I could not imagine what it was I was supposed to be looking at, and thought it was more houses for my inspection. The estate did, in fact, continue all along the further edge of the Park, just visible beyond the trees.

"Do you see her?" He pointed, then ducked back. Following the direction, I saw a young woman sitting on a bench on the far side of the Channel.

"Who is she?" I said, although her small figure did not actually arouse much curiosity in me.

"The loveliest girl I have ever seen. She's always there, on that bench. She is waiting for her lover. She sits there every day, her heart filled with anguish and hope."

As he said this the young man's voice broke, as if with emotion, and I glanced up at him. His eyes were moist.

I peered again around the edge of the bush and looked at the girl, wondering what it was about her that produced this reaction. I could hardly see her, because she was huddled against the wind and had a shawl drawn over her hair. She was sitting to one side, facing towards the Tomorrow Bridge. To me, she was approximately as interesting as the houses, which is not to say very much, but she seemed important to the young man.

"Is she a friend of yours?" I said, tuning back to him.

"No, not a friend, Mykle. A symbol. A token of the love that is in us all."

"What is her name?" I said, not following this interpretation.

"Estyll. The most beautiful name in the world."

Estyll: I had never heard the name before, and I repeated it softly.

"How do you know this?" I said. "You say you—"

"Wait, Mykle. She will turn in a moment. You will see her face."

His hand was clasping my shoulder, as if we were old friends, and although I was still shy of him it assured me of his good intent. He was sharing something with me, something so important that I was honoured to be included.

Together we leaned forward again and looked clandestinely at her. By my ear, I heard my friend say her name, so softly that it was almost a whisper. A few moments passed, then, as if the time vortex above the Channel had swept the word slowly across to her, she raised her head, shrugged back the shawl, and stood up. I was craning my neck to see her but she turned away. I watched her walk up the slope of the Park grounds, towards the houses beyond the trees.

"Isn't she a beauty, Mykle?"

I was too young to understand him fully, so I said nothing. At that age, my only awareness of the other sex was that my sisters were temperamentally and physically different from me. I had yet to discover more interesting matters. In any event, I had barely caught a glimpse of Estyll's face.

The young man was evidently enraptured by the girl, and as we watched her move through the distant trees my attention was half on her, half on him.

"I should like to be the man she loves," he said at last.

"Do you . . . love her, sir?"

"Love? What I feel is too noble to be contained in such a word." He looked down at me, and for an instant I was reminded of the haughty disdain that my father sometimes revealed when I did something stupid. "Love is for lovers, Mykle. *I* am a romantic, which is a far grander thing to be."

I was beginning to find my companion rather pompous and overbearing, trying to involve me in his passions. I was an argumentative child, though, and could not resist pointing out a contradiction.

"But you said she was waiting for her lover," I said.

"Just a supposition."

"I think you are her lover, and won't admit it."

I used the word disparagingly, but it made him look at me thoughtfully. The drizzle was coming down again, a dank veil across the countryside. The young man stepped away suddenly. I think he had grown as tired of my company as I had of his.

"I was going to show you how to get back," he said. "Come with me." He set off towards the bridge, and I went after him. "You'll have to go back the way you came. You jumped, didn't you?"

"That's right," I said, puffing a little. It was difficult keeping up with him.

As we reached the end of the bridge, the young man left the path and walked across the grass to the edge of the Channel. I held back, nervous of going too close again.

"Ah!" said the young man, peering down at the damp soil. "Look, Mykle . . . these must be your footprints. This was where you landed."

I went forward warily and stood just behind him.

"Put your feet in these marks and jump towards the bridge."

Although the metal edge of the bridge was only an arm's length away from where we were standing it seemed a formidable jump, especially as the bridge was higher than the bank. I pointed this out.

"I'll be behind you," the young man said. "You won't slip. Now . . . look on the bridge. There's a scratch on the floor. Do you see it? You have to aim at that. Try to land with one foot on either side, and you'll be back where you started."

It all seemed rather unlikely. The part of the bridge he was pointing out was wet with rain and looked slippery. If I landed badly I would fall; worse, I could slip backwards into the flux fluid. Although I sensed that my new friend was right—that I could only get back by the way I had come—it did not *feel* right.

"Mykle, I know what you're thinking. But I made that mark. I've done it myself. Trust me."

I was thinking of my father and his wrath, so at last I stepped forward and put my feet in the squelching impressions I had made as I landed. Rainwater was oozing down the muddy bank towards the flux fluid, but I noticed that as it dripped down to touch the fluid it suddenly leaped back, just like the droplets of whisky on the side of the glass my father drank in the evenings.

The young man took a grip on my belt, holding on so that I should not slip down into the Channel.

"I'll count to three, then you jump. I'll give you a shove. Are you ready?"

"I think so."

"You'll remember Estyll, won't you?"

I looked over my shoulder. His face was very close to mine.

"Yes, I'll remember her," I said, not meaning it.

"Right . . . brace yourself. It's quite a hop from here. One . . ."

I saw the fluid of the Channel below me and to the side. It was glistening eerily in the grey light.

". . . two . . . three . . ."

I jumped forward at the same instant as the young man gave me a hefty shove from behind. Instantly, I felt the electric crackle of the flux field, I heard again the loud roaring in my ears and there was a split-second of impenetrable blackness. My feet touched the edge of the time bridge and I tripped, sprawling forward on the floor. I slithered awkwardly against the legs of a man standing just there, and my face fetched up against a pair of shoes polished to a brilliant shine. I looked up.

There was my father, staring down at me in great surprise. All I can now remember of that frightful moment is his face glaring down at me, topped by his black, curly brimmed, stovepipe hat. He seemed to be as tall as a mountain.

V

My father was not a man who saw the merit of short, sharp punishment, and I lived under the cloud of my misdeed for several weeks.

I felt that I had done what I had done in all innocence, and that the price I had to pay for it was too high. In our house, however, there was only one kind of justice and that was Father's.

Although I had been in the future for only about an hour of my subjective time, five or six hours had passed for my family and it was twilight when I returned. This prolonged absence was the main reason for my father's anger, although if I had jumped thirty-two years, as my companion had informed me, an error of a few hours on the return journey was as nothing.

I was never called upon to explain myself. My father detested excuses.

Salleen and Therese were the only ones who asked what had happened, and I gave them a shortened account: I said that after I jumped into the future, and realized what I had done, I explored the Park on my own and then jumped back. This was enough for them. I said nothing of the youth with the lofty sentiments, nor of the young lady who sat on the bench. (Salleen and Therese were thrilled enough that I had catapulted myself into the distant future, although my safe return did make the end of the story rather dull.) Internally, I had mixed feelings about my adventure. I spent a lot of time on my own—part of my punishment was that I could only go into the playroom one evening a week, and had to study more diligently instead—and tried to work out the meaning of what I had seen.

The girl, Estyll, meant very little to me. She certainly had a place in my memory of that hour in the future, but because she was so fascinating to my companion I remembered her through him, and she became of secondary interest.

I thought about the young man a great deal. He had gone to such pains to make a friend of me, and to include me in his private thoughts, and yet I remembered him as an intrusive and unwelcome presence. I often thought of his husky voice intoning those grand opinions, and even from the disadvantage of my junior years, his callow figure—all gangly limbs, slicked-back hair and downy moustache—was a comical one. For a long time I wondered who he could be. Although the answer seems obvious in retrospect it was some years before I realized it and whenever I was out in the town I would keep my eyes open in case we happened to meet.

My penance came to an end about three months after the picnic. This parole was never formally stated but understood by all concerned. The occasion was a party our parents allowed us to have for some visiting cousins and after that my misbehaviour was never again directly mentioned.

The following summer, when the time came around for another picnic in Flux Channel Park, my father interrupted our excited outpourings to deliver a short speech, reminding us that we must all stay together. This was said to us all, although Father gave me a sharp and meaningful look. It was a small, passing cloud, and it threw no shadow on the day. I was obedient and sensible throughout the picnic . . . but as we walked through the Park in the gentle heat of the day, I did not forget to look out for my helpful friend, nor for his adored Estyll. I looked, and kept looking, but neither of them was there that day.

VI

When I was eleven I was sent to school for the first time. I had spent my formative years in a household where wealth and influence were taken for granted, and where the governor had taken a lenient view of my education. Thrown suddenly into the company of boys from all walks of life, I retreated behind a manner of arrogance and condescension. It took two years to be scorned and beaten out of this, but well before then I had developed a wholehearted loathing for education and all that went with it. I became, in short, a student who did not study, and a pupil whose dislike for his fellows was heartily reciprocated.

I became an accomplished malingerer, and with the occasional connivance of one of the servants I could readily feign a convincing though unaccountable stomach ailment, or develop infectious-looking rashes. Sometimes I would simply stay at home. More frequently I would set off into the countryside on my bicycle and spend the day in pleasant musings.

On days like this I pursued my own form of education by reading, although this was by choice and not by compulsion. I eagerly read whatever novels and poetry I could lay my hands on: my preference in fiction was for adventure, and in poetry I soon discovered the romantics of the early nineteenth century, and the then much despised desolationists of two hundred years later. The stirring combinations of valour and unrequited love, of moral virtue and nostalgic wistfulness, struck deep into my soul and made more pointed my dislike of the routines of school.

It was at this time, when my reading was arousing passions that my humdrum existence could not satisfy, that my thoughts turned to the girl called Estyll.

I needed an object for the stirrings within me. I envied the romantic poets their soulful yearnings, for they, it seemed to me, had at least had the emotional experience with which to focus their desires. The despairing desolationists, lamenting the waste around them, at least had known life. Perhaps I did not rationalize this need quite so neatly at the time, but whenever I was aroused by my reading it was the image of Estyll that came most readily to mind.

Remembering what my companion had told me, and with my own sight of that small, huddled figure, I saw her as a lonely, heartbroken waif, squandering her life in a hopeless vigil. That she was unspeakably beautiful, and utterly faithful, went without saying.

As I grew older, my restlessness advanced. I felt increasingly isolated, not only from the other boys at school, but also from my family. My father's work was making more demands on him than ever before and he was unapproachable. My sisters were going their own separate ways: Therese had developed an interest in ponies, Salleen in young men.

Nobody had time for me, no one tried to understand.

One autumn, some three or four years after I started school, I surrendered at last to the stirrings of soul and flesh, and attempted to allay them.

VII

I selected the day with care, one when there were several lessons at school where my absence would not be too obvious. I left home at the usual time in the morning, but instead of heading for school I rode to the city, bought a return ticket to the Park at the railway station, and settled down on the train.

During the summer there had been the usual family outing to the Park, but it had meant little to me. I had outgrown the immediate future. Tomorrow no longer concerned me.

I was vested with purpose. When I arrived at the Park on that stolen day I went directly to the Tomorrow Bridge, paid the toll, and set off through the covered way towards the other side. There were more people about than I had expected, but it was quiet enough for what I wanted to do. I waited until I was the only one on the bridge, then went to the end of the covered way and stood by the spot from which I had first jumped. I took a flint from my pocket and scratched a thin but deep line in the metal surface of the bridge.

I slipped the flint back in my pocket then looked appraisingly at the bank below. I had no way of knowing how far to jump, only an instinct and a vague memory of how I had done it before. The temptation was to jump as far as possible, but I managed to suppress it.

I placed my feet astride the line, took a deep breath . . . and launched myself towards the bank.

A dizzying surge of electric tingling, momentary darkness, and I sprawled across the bank.

Before I took stock of my surroundings I marked the place where I had landed. First I scraped a deep line in the soil and grass with the flint, pointing back towards the mark on the bridge (which was still visible, though less bright), then I tore away several tufts of grass around my feet to make a second mark. Thirdly, I stared intently at the precise place, fixing it in memory, so there would be no possibility of not finding it again.

When satisfied, I stood up and looked around at this future.

VIII

It was a holiday. The Park was crowded with people, all gay in summer clothes. The sun shone down from a cloudless sky, a breeze rippled the ladies' dresses, and from a distant pagoda a band played stirring marches. It was all so familiar that my first instinct was that my parents and sisters must be somewhere about and my illicit visit would be discovered. I ducked down against the bank of the Channel, but then I laughed at myself and relaxed; in my painstaking anticipation of this exploit I had considered the possibility of meeting people I knew, and had decided that the chance was too slender to be taken seriously. Anyway, when I looked again at the people passing— who were paying me no attention—I realized that there were subtle differences in their clothes and hair-styles, reminding me that for all the superficial similarities I had indeed travelled to the future.

I scrambled up to the tree-lined pathway and mingled with the throng, quickly catching the spirit of the day. I must have looked like any other schoolboy, but I felt very special indeed. After all, I had now leaped into the future twice.

This euphoria aside, I was there with a purpose, and I did not forget it. I looked across to the other bank, searching for a sight of Estyll. She was not by the bench, and I felt a crushing and illogical disappointment, as if she had deliberately betrayed me by not being there. All the frustration of the past months welled up in me, and I could have shouted with the agony of it. But then, miraculously it seemed, I saw her some distance away from the bench, wandering to and fro on the path on her side, glancing occasionally towards the Tomorrow Bridge. I recognized her at once, although I am not sure how; during that other day in the future I had barely seen her, and since then my imagination had run with a free rein, yet the moment I saw her I knew it was she.

Gone was the shawl and the arms that had been wrapped for warmth about her body were now folded casually across her chest. She was wearing a light summer frock, coloured in a number of pastel shades, and to my eager eyes it seemed that no lovelier clothes could have been worn by any woman in the world. Her short hair fell prettily about her face, and the way she held her head, and the way she stood, seemed delicate beyond words.

I watched her for several minutes, transfixed by the sight of her. People continued to mill past me, but for all I was aware of them they might not have been there.

At last I remembered my purpose, even though just seeing her was an experience whose joys I could not have anticipated. I walked back down the path, past the Tomorrow Bridge and beyond to the Today Bridge. I hastened across and let myself through the exit turnstile on the other side. Still in the same day, I went up the path towards where I had seen Estyll.

There were fewer people on this side of the Channel, of course, and the path was less crowded. I looked around as I walked, noticing that custom had not changed and that many people were sitting in the shade of the trees with the remains of picnic meals spread out around them. I did not look too closely at these groups—it was still at the back of my mind that I might see my own family here.

I passed the line of people waiting at the Tomorrow tollbooth and saw the path continuing beyond. A short distance away, walking slowly to and fro, was Estyll.

At the sight of her, now so near to me, I paused.

I walked on, less confidently than before. She glanced in my direction once, but she looked at me in the same uninterested way as she looked at everybody. I was only a few yards from her, and my heart was pounding and I was trembling. I realized that the little speech I had prepared—the one in which I introduced myself, then revealed myself as witty and mature, then proposed that she take a walk with me—had gone from my mind. She looked so grown-up, so sure of herself.

Unaware of my concentrated attention on her, she turned away when I was within touching distance of her. I walked on a few more paces, desperately unsure of myself. I turned and faced her.

For the first time in my life I felt the pangs of uncontrollable love. Until then the word had had no meaning for me but as I stood before her I felt for her a love so shocking that I could only flinch away from it. How I must have appeared to her I cannot say. I must have been shaking, I must have been bright with embarrassment. She looked at me with calm grey eyes and an enquiring expression, as if she detected that I had something of immense importance to say. She was so beautiful! I felt so clumsy!

Then she smiled, unexpectedly, and I had my cue to say something. Instead, I stared at her, not even thinking of what I could say, but simply immobilized by the unexpected struggle with my emotions. I had thought love was so simple.

Moments passed and I could cope with the turbulence no more. I took a step back and then another. Estyll had continued to smile at me during those long seconds of my wordless stare, and as I moved away her smile broadened and she parted her lips as if to say something. It was too much for me. I turned away, burning with embarrassment, and started to run. After a few steps, I halted and looked back at her. She was still looking at me, still smiling.

I shouted, "*I love you!*"

It seemed to me that everyone in the Park had heard me. I did not wait to see Estyll's reaction. I ran away. I hurried along the path, then ran up a grassy bank and into the shelter of some trees. I ran and ran, crossing the concourse of the open-air restaurant, crossing a broad lawn, diving into the cover of more trees beyond.

It was as if the physical effort of running would stop me thinking, because the moment I rested the enormity of what I had done flooded in on me. It seemed that I had done nothing right and everything wrong. I had had a chance to meet her and I had let it slip through my fingers. Worst of all, I had shouted my love at her, revealing it to the world. To my adolescent mind it seemed there could have been no grosser mistake.

I stood under the trees, leaning my forehead against the trunk of an old oak, banging my fist in frustration and fury.

I was terrified that Estyll would find me and I never wanted to see her again. At the same time I wanted her and loved her with a renewed passion . . . and hoped, but hoped secretly, that she would be searching for me in the Park, and would come to me by my tree and put her arms around me.

A long time passed and gradually my turbulent and contradictory emotions subsided.

I still did not want to see Estyll, so when I walked down to the path I looked carefully ahead to be sure I would not meet her. When I stepped down to the path itself—where people still walked in casual enjoyment, unaware of the drama—I looked along it towards the bridges, but saw no sign of her. I could not be sure she had left so I hung around, torn between wincing shyness of her and profound devotion.

At last I decided to risk it and hurried along the path to the tollbooths. I did not look for her and I did not see her. I paid the toll at the Today Bridge and returned to the other side. I located the marks I had made on the bank beside the Tomorrow Bridge, aimed myself at the scratch on the bridge floor, and leaped across towards it.

I emerged in the day I had left. Once again, my rough-and-ready way of travelling through time did not return me to a moment precisely true to elapsed time, but it was close enough. When I checked my watch against the clock in the toll-booth, I discovered I had been gone for less than a quarter of an hour. Meanwhile, I had been in the future for more than three hours.

I caught an earlier train home and idled away the rest of the day on my bicycle in the countryside, reflecting on the passions of man, the glories of young womanhood, and the accursed weaknesses of the will.

IX

I should have learned from experience, and never tried to see Estyll again, but there was no quieting the love I felt for her. Thoughts of her dominated every waking moment. It was the memory of her smile that was central. She had been encouraging me, inviting me to say the very things I had wanted to say, and I missed the chance. So, with the obsession renewed and intensified, I returned to the Park and did so many times.

Whenever I could safely absent myself from school and could lay my hands on the necessary cash I went to the Tomorrow Bridge and leapt across to the future. I was soon able to judge that dangerous leap with a marvellous instinctive skill. Naturally, there were mistakes. Once, terrifyingly, I landed in the night, and after that experience I always took a small pocket flashlight with me. On two or three occasions my return jump was inaccurate, and I had to use the timebridges to find the day I should have been in.

After a few more of my leaps into the future I felt sufficiently at home to approach a stranger in the Park and ask him the date. By telling me the year he confirmed that I was exactly twenty-seven years into the future . . . or, as it had been when I was ten, thirty-two years ahead. The stranger I spoke to was apparently a local man and by his appearance a man of some substance, and I took him sufficiently into my confidence to point out Estyll to him. I asked him if he knew her, which he said he did, but could only confirm her given name. It was enough for me, because by then it suited my purpose not to know too much about her.

I made no more attempts to speak to Estyll. Barred from approaching her by my painful shyness I fell back on fantasies, which were much more in keeping with my timid soul. As I grew older, and became more influenced by my favourite poets, it seemed not only more sad and splendid to glorify her from a distance, but appropriate that my role in her life should be passive.

To compensate for my nervousness about trying to meet her again, I constructed a fiction about her.

She was passionately in love with a disreputable young man, who had tempted her with elaborate promises and wicked lies. At the very moment she had declared her love for him, he had deserted her by crossing the Tomorrow Bridge into a future from which he had never returned. In spite of his shameful behaviour her love held true and every day she waited in vain by the Tomorrow Bridge, knowing that one day he would return. I would watch her covertly from the other side of the Channel, knowing that her patience was that of the lovelorn. Too proud for tears, too faithful for doubt, she was at ease with the knowledge that her long wait would be its own reward.

In the present, in my real life, I sometimes dallied with another fiction: that *I* was her lover, that it was for me she was waiting. This thought excited me, arousing responses of a physical kind that I did not fully understand.

I went to the Park repeatedly, gladly suffering the punishments at school for my frequent, and badly excused, truancies. So often did I leap across to that future that I soon grew accustomed to seeing other versions of myself, and realized that I had sometimes seen other young men before, who looked suspiciously like me, and who skulked near the trees and bushes beside the Channel and gazed across as wistfully as I. There was one day in particular—a lovely, sunny day, at the height of the holiday season—that I often lighted on, and here there were more than a dozen versions of myself, dispersed among the crowd.

One day, not long before my sixteenth birthday, I took one of my now customary leaps into the future and found a cold and windy day, almost deserted. As I walked along the path I saw a child, a small boy, plodding along with his head down against the wind and scuffing at the turf with the toes of his shoes. The sight of him, with his muddy legs and tear-streaked face, reminded me of that very first time I had jumped accidentally to the future. I stared at him as we approached each other. He looked back at me and for an instant a shock of recognition went through me like a bolt of electricity. He turned his eyes aside at once and stumped on by, heading towards the bridges behind me. I stared at him, recalling in vivid detail how I had felt that day, and how I had been fomenting a desperate plan to return to the day I had left, and as I did so I realized—at long last—the identity of the friend I had made that day.

My head whirling with the recognition I called after him, hardly believing what was happening.

"Mykle!" I said, the sound of my own name tasting strange in my mouth. The boy turned to look at me and I said a little uncertainly, "It is Mykle, isn't it?"

"How do you know my name?" His stance was truculent and he seemed unwilling to be spoken to.

"I . . . was looking for you," I said, inventing a reason for why I should have recognized him. "You've jumped forward in time, and don't know how to get back."

"Yes, but—"

"I'll show you how. It's easy."

As we were speaking a distracting thought came to me: so far I had, quite accidentally, duplicated the conversation of that day. But what if I were to change it consciously? Suppose I said something that my "friend" had not; suppose young Mykle were not to respond in the way I had? The consequences seemed enormous and I could imagine this boy's life—my own life—going in a direction entirely different. I saw the dangers of that and I knew I had to make an effort to repeat the dialogue, and my actions, precisely.

But just as it had when I tried to speak to Estyll, my mind went blank.

"It's all right, thank you, sir," the boy was saying. "I can find my own way."

"By running across the bridges?" I wasn't sure if that was what had been said to me before, but I knew that had been my intention.

"How did you know?"

I found I could not depend on that distant memory, and so, trusting to the inevitable sweep of destiny, I stopped trying to remember. I said whatever came to mind.

It was appalling to see myself through my own eyes. I had not imagined that I had been quite such a pathetic-looking child. I had every appearance of being a sullen and difficult boy. There was a stubbornness and a belligerence that I both recognized and disliked. And I knew there was a deeper weakness too. I could remember how I had seen myself, my older self, that is. I recalled my "friend" from this day as callow and immature, and mannered with a loftiness that did not suit his years. That I (as child) had seen myself (as young man) in this light was condemnation of my then lack of percipience. I had learned a lot about myself since going to school and I was more adult in my outlook than the other boys at school. What is more, since falling in love with Estyll I had taken great care over my appearance and clothes and whenever I made one of these trips to the future I looked my best.

However, in spite of the shortcomings I saw in myself-as-boy, I felt sorry for young Mykle and there was certainly a feeling of great spirit between us. I showed him what I had noticed of the changes in the Park and then we walked together towards the Tomorrow Bridge. Estyll was there on the other side of the Channel. I told him what I knew of her. I could not convey what was in my heart, but knowing how important she was to become to him, I wanted him to see her and love her.

After she had left, I showed him the mark I had made in the surface of the bridge. After I had persuaded him to make the leap—with several sympathetic thoughts about his imminent reception—I wandered alone in the blustery evening, wondering if Estyll would return. There was no sign of her.

I waited almost until nightfall, resolving that the years of admiring her from afar had been long enough. Something that young Mykle said had deeply affected me.

Allowing him a glimpse of my fiction, I had told him, "She is waiting for her lover." My younger self had replied, "I think you are her lover, and won't admit it."

I had forgotten saying that. I would not admit it, for it was not strictly true, but I would admit to the wish that it were so.

Staring across the darkening Channel, I wondered if there were a way of making it come true. The Park was an eerie place in that light, and the temporal stresses of the flux field seemed to take on a tangible presence. Who knew what tricks could be played by Time? I had already met myself—once, twice, and seen myself many times over—and who was to say that Estyll's lover could *not* be me?

In my younger self I had seen something about my older self that I could not see on my own. Mykle had said it, and I wanted it to be true. I would make myself Estyll's lover, and I would do it on my next visit to the Park.

X

There were larger forces at work than those of romantic destiny, because soon after I made this resolution my life was shaken out of its pleasant intrigues by the sudden death of my father.

I was shocked by this more profoundly than I could ever have imagined. In the last two or three years I had seen very little of him and thought about him even less. And yet, from the moment the maid ran into the drawing-room, shrilling that my father had collapsed across the desk in his study, I was stricken with the most awful guilt. It was I who had caused the death! I had been obsessed with myself, with Estyll . . . if only I had thought more of him he would not be dead!

In those sad days before the funeral my reaction seemed less than wholly illogical. My father knew as much about the workings of the flux field as any man alive, and after my childhood adventure he must have had some inkling that I had not left matters there. The school must have advised him of my frequent absences and yet he said nothing. It was almost as if he had been deliberately standing by, hoping something might come of it all.

In the days following his death, a period of emotional transition, it seemed to me that Estyll was inextricably bound up with the tragedy. However much it flew in the face of reason, I could not help feeling that if I had spoken to Estyll, if I had acted rather than hidden, then my father would still be alive.

I did not have long to dwell on this. When the first shock and grief had barely passed, it became clear that nothing would ever be quite the same again for me. My father had made a will, in which he bequeathed me the responsibility for his family, his work and his fortune.

I was still legally a child and one of my uncles took over the administration of the affairs until I reached my majority. This uncle, deeply resentful that none of the fortune had passed to him, made the most of his temporary control over our lives. I was removed from school and made to start in my father's work. The family house was sold, the governor and the other servants were discharged, and my mother was moved to a smaller household in the country. Salleen was quickly married off, and Therese was sent to boarding school. It was made plain that I should take a wife as soon as possible.

My love for Estyll—my deepest secret—was thrust away from me by forces I could not resist.

Until the day my father died I did not have much conception of what his work involved, except to know that he was one of the most powerful and influential men in the Neuropean Union. This was because he controlled the power stations which tapped energy from the temporal stresses of the flux field. On the day I inherited his position I assumed this meant he was fabulously wealthy, but I was soon relieved of this misapprehension. The power stations were state controlled and the so-called fortune comprised a large number of debentures in the enterprise. In real terms these could not be cashed, thus explaining many of the extreme decisions taken by my uncle. Death duties were considerable, and in fact I was in debt because of them for many years afterwards.

The work was entirely foreign to me and I was psychologically and academically unready for it, but because the family was now my responsibility, I applied myself as best I could. For a long time, shaken and confused by the abrupt change in our fortunes, I could do nothing but cope.

My adolescent adventures in Flux Channel Park became memories as elusive as dreams. It was as if I had become another person.

(But I had lived with the image of Estyll for so long that nothing could make me forget her. The flame of romanticism that had lighted my youth faded away, but it was never entirely extinguished. In time I lost my obsessive love for Estyll, but I could never forget her wan beauty, her tireless waiting.)

By the time I was twenty-two I was in command of myself. I had mastered my father's job. Although the position was hereditary, as most employment was hereditary, I discharged my duties well and conscientiously. The electricity generated by the flux field provided roughly nine-tenths of all the energy consumed in the Neuropean Union, and much of my time was spent in dealing with the multitude of political demands for it. I travelled widely, to every state in Federal Neurop, and further abroad.

Of the family: my mother was settling into her long years of widowhood and the social esteem that naturally followed. Both my sisters were married. Of course I too married in the end, succumbing to the social pressures that every man of standing has to endure. When I was twenty-one I was introduced to Dorynne, a cousin of Salleen's husband, and within a few months we were wed. Dorynne, an intelligent and attractive young woman, proved to be a good wife, and I loved her. When I was twenty-five, she bore our first child: a girl. I needed an heir, for that was the custom of my country, but we rejoiced at her birth. We named her . . . well, we named her Therese, after my sister, but Dorynne had wanted to call her Estyll, a girl's name then very popular, and I had to argue against her. I never explained why.

Two years later my son Carl was born, and my position in society was secure.

XI

The years passed, and the glow of adolescent longing for Estyll dimmed still further. Because I was happy with my growing family, and fulfilled by the demands of my work, those strange experiences in Flux Channel Park seemed to be a minor aberration from a life that was solid, conventional and unadventurous. I was no longer romantic in outlook. I saw those noble sentiments as the product of immaturity and inexperience. Such was the change in me that Dorynne sometimes complained I was unimaginative.

But if the romance of Estyll faded with time, a certain residual curiosity about her did not. I wanted to know: what had become of her? Who was she? Was she as beautiful as I remembered her?

Setting out these questions has lent them an urgency they did not possess. They were the questions of idle moments, or when something happened to remind me of her. Sometimes, for instance, my work took me along the Flux Channel, and then I would think briefly of her. For a time a young woman worked in my office, and she had the same name. As I grew older, a year or more would sometimes pass without a thought of Estyll.

I should probably have gone for the rest of my life with these questions unanswered if it had not been for an event of major world importance. When the news of it became known it seemed for a time to be the most exciting event of the century, as in some ways it was. The starship that had been launched a hundred years before was returning.

This news affected every aspect of my work. At once I was involved in strategic and political planning at the highest level.

What it meant was this: the starship could only return to Earth by the same means as it had left. The Flux Channel would have to be reconverted, if only temporarily, to its original use. The houses in its vicinity would have to be evacuated, the power stations would have to be disconnected, and the Park and its time bridges would have to be destroyed.

For me, the disconnection of the power stations—with the inevitable result of depriving the Neuropean Union of most of its electricity—created immense problems. Permission had to be sought from other countries to generate electricity from fossil deposits for the months the flux stations were inoperable, and permission of that sort could only be obtained after intricate political negotiation and bargaining. We had less than a year in which to achieve this.

But the coming destruction of the Park struck a deeper note in me, as it did in many people. The Park was a much loved playground, familiar to everyone, and, for many people, ineradicably linked with memories of childhood. For me, it was strongly associated with the idealism of my youth and with a girl I had loved for a time. If the Park and its bridges were closed, I knew that my questions about Estyll would never be answered.

I had leapt into a future where the Park was still a playground, where the houses beyond the trees were still occupied. Through all my life I had thought of that future as an imaginary or ideal world, one unattainable except by a dangerous leap from a bridge. But that future was no longer imaginary. I was now forty-two years old. It was thirty-two years since I, as a ten-year-old boy, had leapt thirty-two years into the future.

Today and Tomorrow co-existed once more in Flux Channel Park.

If I did not act in the next few weeks, before the Park was closed, I should never see Estyll again. The memory of her flared into flame again, and I felt a deep sense of frustration. I was much too busy to go in search of a boyhood dream.

I delegated. I relieved two subordinates from work in which they would have been better employed, and told them what I wanted them to discover on my behalf. They were to locate a young woman or girl who lived, possibly alone, possibly not, in one of the houses that bordered the Park.

The estate consisted of some two hundred houses. In time, my subordinates gave me a list of over a hundred and fifty possible names, and I scanned it anxiously. There were twenty-seven women living on the estate who were called Estyll. It was a popular name.

I returned one employee to his proper work, but retained the other, a woman named Robyn. I took her partially into my confidence. I said that the girl was a distant relative and that I was anxious to locate her, but for family reasons I had to be discreet. I believed she was frequently to be found in the Park. Within a few days, Robyn confirmed that there was one such girl. She and her mother lived together in one of the houses. The mother was confined to the house by the conventions of mourning (her husband had died within the last two years), and the daughter, Estyll, spent almost every day alone in the Park. Robyn said she was unable to discover why she went there.

The date had been fixed when Flux Channel Park would be closed to the public, and it was some eight and a half months ahead. I knew that I would soon be signing the order that would authorize the closure. One day between now and then, if for no other reason, Estyll's patient waiting would have to end.

I took Robyn further into my confidence. I instructed her to go to the Park and, by repeated use of the Tomorrow Bridge, go into the future. All she was to report back to me was the date on which Estyll's vigil ended. Whether Robyn wondered at the glimpses of my obsession she was seeing, I cannot say, but she went without demur and did my work for me. When she returned, she had the date: it was just over six weeks away.

That interview with Robyn was fraught with undertones that neither side understood. I did not want to know too much, because with the return of my interest in Estyll had come something of that sense of romantic mystery. Robyn, for her part, clearly had seen something that intrigued her. I found it all most unsettling.

I rewarded Robyn with a handsome cash bonus and returned her to her duties. I marked the date in my private diary, then gave my full attention to the demands of my proper work.

XII

As the date approached I knew I could not be at the Park. On that day there was to be an energy conference in Geneva and there was no possibility of my missing it. I made a futile attempt to change the date, but who was I against fifty heads of state? Once more I was tempted to let the great preoccupation of my youth stay forever unresolved, but again I succumbed to it. I could not miss this one last chance.

I made my travel arrangements to Geneva with care and instructed my secretarial staff to reserve me a compartment on the one overnight train which would get me there in time.

It meant that I should have to visit the Park on the day before the vigil was to end, but by using the Tomorrow Bridge I could still be there to see it.

At last the day came. I had no one to answer to but myself. Shortly after midday I left my office and had my driver take me to the Park. I left him and the carriage in the yard beyond the gate, and with one glance towards the estate of houses I went into the Park.

I had not been in the Park itself since my last visit just before my father died. Knowing that one's childhood haunts often seem greatly changed when revisited years later I had been expecting to find the place smaller, less grand than I remembered it. But as I walked slowly down the gently sloping sward towards the tollbooths, it seemed that the magnificent trees, and the herbaceous borders, the fountains, the pathways, and all the various kinds of landscaping in the Park gardens were just as I recalled them.

But the smells! In my adolescent longing I had not responded to those. The sweet bark, the sweeping leaves, the clustered flowers. A man with a mowing machine clattered past, throwing up a moist green smell, and the shorn grass humped in the mower's hood like a sleeping furry animal. I watched the man as he reached the edge of the lawn he was cutting, turned the machine, then bent low over it to start it up the incline for his return. I had never pushed a mower, and as if this last day in the Park had restored my childhood I felt an urge to dash across to him and ask him if I might try my hand.

I smiled to myself as I walked on: I was a well-known public figure, and in my drape suit and tall silk hat I should certainly have cut a comic sight.

Then there were the sounds. I heard, as if for the first time (and yet also with a faint and distracting nostalgia), the metallic click of the turnstile ratchets, the sound of the breeze in the pines that surrounded the Park, and the almost continuous soprano of children's voices. Somewhere, a band was playing marches.

I saw a family at picnic beneath one of the weeping willows. The servants stood to one side, and the paterfamilias was carving a huge joint of cold beef. I watched them surreptitiously for a moment. It might have been my own family, a generation before; people's delights did not change.

So taken was I by all this that I had nearly reached the tollbooths before I remembered Estyll. Another private smile: my younger self would not have been able to understand this lapse. I was feeling more relaxed, welcoming the tranquil surroundings of the Park and remembering the past, but I had grown out of the obsessive associations the place had once had for me.

I had come to the Park to see Estyll, though, so I went on past the tollbooths until I was on the path that ran beside the Channel. I walked a short way, looking ahead. Soon I saw her, and she was sitting on the bench, staring towards the Tomorrow Bridge.

It was as if a quarter of a century had been obliterated. All the calm and restful mood went from me as if it had never existed, to be replaced by a ferment of emotions that was the more shocking for being so unexpected.

I came to a halt, turned away, thinking that if I looked at her any more she would surely notice me.

The adolescent, the immature, the romantic child . . . I was still all of these, and the sight of Estyll awakened them as if from a short nap. I felt large and clumsy and ridiculous in my over-formal clothes, as if I were a child wearing a grandparent's wedding outfit. Her composure, her youthful beauty, the vital force of her vigil . . . they were enough to renew all those inadequacies I had felt as a teenager.

But at the same time there was a second image of her, one which lay above the other like an elusive ghost. I was seeing her as an adult sees a child.

She was so much younger than I remembered her! She was smaller. She was pretty, yes . . . but I had seen prettier women. She was dignified, but it was a precocious poise, as if she had been trained in it by a socially conscious parent. And she was young, so very young! My own daughter, Therese, would be the same age now, perhaps slightly older.

Thus torn, thus acutely conscious of my divided way of seeing her, I stood in confusion and distraction on the pathway, while the families and couples walked gaily past.

I backed away from her at last, unable to look at her any more. She was wearing clothes I remembered too well from the past: a narrow white skirt tight around her legs, a shiny black belt, and a dark-blue blouse embroidered with flowers across the bodice.

(I remembered—I remembered so much, too much. I wished she had not been there.)

She frightened me because of the power she had, the power to awaken and arouse my emotions. I did not know what it was. Everyone has adolescent passions, but how many people have the chance to revisit those passions in maturity?

It elated me, but also made me deeply melancholic. Inside I was dancing with love and joy, but she terrified me. She was so innocently, glowingly young, and I was now so old.

XIII

I decided to leave the Park at once . . . but changed my mind an instant later. I went towards her, then turned yet again and walked away.

I was thinking of Dorynne, but trying to put her out of my mind. I was thinking of Estyll, obsessed again.

I walked until I was out of sight of her, then took off my hat and wiped my brow. It was a warm day but I knew that the perspiration was not caused by the weather. I needed to calm myself, wanted somewhere to sit down and think about it . . . but the Park was for pleasure, and when I went towards the open air restaurant to buy a glass of beer, the sight of all the heedless merriment was intrusive and unwelcome.

I stood on the uncut grass, watching the man with the mower, trying to control myself. I had come to the Park to satisfy an old curiosity, not to fall again into the traps of childhood infatuation. It was unthinkable that I should let a young girl of sixteen distract me from my stable life. It had been a mistake, a stupid mistake, to return to the Park.

But inevitably there was a deeper sense of destiny beneath my attempts to be sensible. I knew, without being able to say why, that Estyll was waiting there at her bench for me, and that we were destined at last to meet.

Her vigil was due to end tomorrow and that was just a short distance away. It lay on the far side of the Tomorrow Bridge.

XIV

I tried to pay at the tollbooth but the attendant recognized me at once. He released the ratchet of the turnstile with such a sharp jab of his foot that I thought he might break his ankle. I nodded to him and passed through into the covered way.

I walked across briskly, trying to think no more about what I was doing or why. The flux field prickled about my body.

I emerged into bright sunlight. The day I had left was warm and sunny, but here in the next day it was several degrees hotter. I felt stiff and overdressed in my formal clothes, not at all in keeping with the reawakened, desperate hope that was in my breast. Still trying to deny that hope I retreated into my daytime demeanour, opening the front of my coat and thrusting my thumbs into the slit-pockets of my waistcoat, as I sometimes did when addressing subordinates.

I walked along the path beside the Channel, looking across for a sight of Estyll on the other side.

Someone tugged at my arm from behind and I turned in surprise.

There was a young man standing there. He was nearly as tall as me but his jacket was too tight across his shoulders and his trousers were a fraction too short, revealing that he was still growing up. He had an obsessive look to him but when he spoke it was obvious he was from a good family.

"Sir, may I trouble you with a question?" he said, and at once I realized who he was.

The shock of recognition was profound. Had I not been so preoccupied with Estyll I am sure meeting him would have made me speechless. It was so many years since my time jumping that I had forgotten the jolting sense of recognition and sympathy.

I controlled myself with great difficulty. Trying not to reveal my knowledge of him, I said, "What do you wish to know?"

"Would you tell me the date, sir?" I started to smile, and glanced away from him for a moment, to straighten my face. His earnest eyes, his protuberant ears, his pallid face and quiffed-up hair!

"Do you mean today's date, or do you mean the year?"

"Well . . . both actually, sir."

I gave him the answer at once, although as soon as I had spoken I realized I had given him today's date, whereas I had stepped forward one day beyond that. No matter, though: what he, I, was interested in was the year.

He thanked me politely and made to step away. Then he paused, looked at me with a guileless stare (which I remembered had been an attempt to take the measure of this forbidding-looking stranger in a frock coat), and said, "Sir, do you happen to live in these parts?"

"I do," I said, knowing what was coming. I had raised a hand to cover my mouth, and was stroking my upper lip.

"I wonder if you would happen to know the identity of a certain person, often to be seen in this Park?"

"Who—?"

I could not finish the sentence. His eager, pinkening earnestness was extremely comical. I spluttered an explosive laugh. At once I turned it into a simulated sneeze, and while I made a play with my handkerchief I muttered something about hay fever. Forcing myself to be serious I returned my handkerchief to my pocket and straightened my hat. "Who do you mean?"

"A young lady, of about my own age." Unaware of my amusement he moved past me and went down the bank to where there was a thick cluster of rosebushes. From behind their cover he looked across at the other side. He made sure I was looking too, then pointed.

I could not see Estyll at first, because of the crowds, but then saw that she was standing quite near to the queue for the Tomorrow Bridge. She was wearing her dress of pastel colours—the clothes she had been wearing when I first loved her.

"Do you see her, sir?" His question was like a discordant note in a piece of music.

I had become perfectly serious again. Just seeing her made me want to fall into reflective silence. The way she held her head, the innocent composure.

He was waiting for a reply, so I said, "Yes . . . yes, a local girl."

"Do you know her name, sir?"

"I believe she is called Estyll."

An expression of surprised pleasure came over his face and his flush deepened. "Thank you, sir. Thank you."

He backed away from me, but I said, "Wait!" I had a sudden instinct to help him, to cut short those months of agony. "You must go and talk to her, you know. She wants to meet you. You mustn't be shy of her."

He stared at me in horror, then turned and ran into the crowd. Within a few seconds I could see him no more.

The enormity of what I had done struck me forcibly. Not only had I touched him on his most vulnerable place, forcing him to confront the one matter he had to work out for himself in his own time, but impetuously I had interfered with the smooth progression of events. In *my* memory of the meeting, the stranger in the silk hat had not given unsolicited advice!

A few minutes later, as I walked slowly along the path, pondering on this, I saw my younger self again. He saw me and I nodded to him, as an introduction, perhaps, to telling him to ignore what I had said, but he glanced away uninterestedly as if he had never seen me before.

There was something odd about him: he had changed his clothes, and the new ones fitted better.

I mused over this for a while until I realized what must have happened. He was not the same Mykle I had spoken to—he was still myself, but here, on this day, from another day in the past!

A little later I saw myself again. This time I—he—was wearing the same clothes as before. Was it the youth I had spoken to? Or was it myself from yet another day?

I was quite distracted by all this but never so much that I forgot the object of it all. Estyll was there on the other side of the Channel and while I paced along the pathway I made certain she was never out of my sight. She had waited beside the tollbooth queue for several minutes, but now she had walked back to the main path and was standing on the grassy bank, staring, as I had seen her do so many times before, towards the Tomorrow Bridge. I could see her much better there: her slight figure, her young beauty.

I was feeling calmer at last. I no longer saw a double image of her. Meeting myself as a youth, and seeing other versions of myself, had reminded me that Estyll and I, apparently divided by the flux field, were actually united by it. My presence here was inevitable.

Today was the last day of her vigil, although she might not know it, and I was here because I was supposed to be here. She was waiting, and I was waiting. I could resolve it, I could resolve it now!

She was looking directly across the Channel, and seemed to be staring deliberately at me, as if the inspiration had struck her in the same instant. Without thinking, I waved my arm at her. Excitement ran through me. I turned quickly, and set off down the path towards the bridges. If I crossed the Today Bridge I should be with her in a matter of a few seconds! It was what I had to do!

When I reached the place where the Tomorrow Bridge opened on to this side I looked back across the Channel to make sure of where she was standing.

But she was no longer waiting! She too was hurrying across the grass, rushing towards the bridges. As she ran she was looking across the Channel, looking at me!

She reached the crowd of people waiting by the tollbooth and I saw her pushing past them. I lost sight of her as she went into the booth.

I stood at my end of the bridge, looking down the ill-lit covered way. Daylight was a bright square two hundred feet away.

A small figure in a long dress hurried up the steps at the far end and ran into the wooden tunnel. Estyll came towards me, raising the front of her skirt as she ran. I glimpsed trailing ribbons, white stockings.

With each step, Estyll moved further into the flux field. With each frantic, eager step towards me, her figure became less substantial. She was less than a third of the way across before she had blurred and dissolved into nothing.

I saw her mistake! She was crossing the wrong bridge! When she reached this side—when she stood where I stood now—she would be twenty-four hours too late.

I stared helplessly down the gloomy covered way, watching as two children slowly materialized before me. They pushed and squabbled, each trying to be the first to emerge into the new day.

XV

I acted without further delay. I left the Tomorrow Bridge and ran back up the slope to the path. The Today Bridge was about fifty yards away, and, clapping a hand on the top of my hat, I ran as fast as I could towards it. I thought only of the extreme urgency of catching Estyll before I lost her. If she realized her mistake and began to search for me, we might be forever crossing and recrossing the Channel on one bridge after another—forever in the same place, but forever separated in time.

I scrambled on to the end of the Today Bridge, and hurried across. I had to moderate my pace, as the bridge was narrow and several other people were crossing. This bridge, of the three, was the only one with windows to the outside. As I passed each one I paused to look anxiously towards each end of the Tomorrow Bridge, hoping for a glimpse of her.

At the end of the bridge I pushed quickly through the exit turnstile, leaving it rattling and clattering on its ratchet.

I set off at once towards the Tomorrow Bridge, reaching for the money to pay the toll. In my haste I bumped into someone. It was a woman and I murmured an apology as I passed, affording her only a momentary glance. We recognized each other in the same instant. It was Robyn, the woman I had sent to the Park. But why was she here now?

As I reached the tollbooth I looked back at her again. She was staring at me with an expression of intense curiosity but as soon as she saw me looking she turned away. Was this the conclusion of the vigil she had reported to me on? Is this what she had seen?

I could not delay. I pushed rudely past the people at the head of the queue and threw some coins on to the worn brass plate where the tickets were ejected mechanically towards the buyer. The attendant looked up at me, recognized me as I recognized him.

"Compliments of the Park again, sir," he said, and slid the coins back to me.

I had seen him only a few minutes before—yesterday in his life. I scooped up the coins and returned them to my pocket. The turnstile clicked as I pushed through. I went up the steps and entered the covered way.

Far ahead: the glare of daylight of the day I was in. The bare interior of the covered way, with lights at intervals. No people.

I started to walk and when I had gone a few paces across the flux field, the daylight squared in the far end of the tunnel became night. It felt much colder.

Ahead of me: two small figures, solidifying, or so it seemed, out of the electrical haze of the field. They were standing together under one of the lights, partly blocking the way.

I went nearer and saw that one of them was Estyll. The figure with her had his head turned away from me. I paused.

I had halted where no light fell on me, and although I was only a few feet away from them I would have seemed as they seemed to me—a ghostly, half-visible apparition. But they were occupied with each other and did not look towards me.

I heard him say, "Do you live around here?"

"In one of the houses by the Park. What about you?"

"No. . . I have to come here by train." The hands held nervously by his side, the fingers curling and uncurling.

"I've often seen you here," she said. "You stare a lot."

"I wondered who you were."

There was a silence then, while the youth looked shyly at the floor, apparently thinking of more to say. Estyll glanced beyond him to where I was standing, and for a moment we looked directly into each other's eyes.

She said to the young man, "It's cold here. Shall we go back?"

"We could go for a walk. Or I could buy you a glass of orange."

"I'd rather go for a walk."

They turned and walked towards me. She glanced at me again, with a frank stare of hostility. I had been listening in and she well knew it. The young man was barely aware of my presence. As they passed me he was looking first at her, then nervously at his hands. I saw his too-tight clothes, his quiff of hair combed up, his pink ears and neck, his downy moustache. He walked clumsily as if he were about to trip over his own feet, and he did not know where to put his hands.

I loved him, I had loved her.

I followed them a little way, until light shone in again at the tollbooth end. I saw him stand aside to let her through the turnstile first. Out in the sunshine she danced across the grass, letting the colours of her dress shine out, and then she reached over and took his hand. They walked away together, across the newly cut lawns towards the trees.

XVI

I waited until Estyll and I had gone and then I too went out into the day. I crossed to the other side of the Channel on the Yesterday Bridge, and returned on the Today Bridge.

It was the day I had arrived in the Park, the day before I was due in Geneva, the day before Estyll and I were finally to meet. Outside in the yard, my driver would be waiting with the carriage.

Before I left I went for one more walk along the path on this side of the Channel and headed for the bench where I knew Estyll would be waiting.

I saw her through the crowd: she was sitting quietly and watching the people, dressed neatly in her white skirt and dark blue blouse.

I looked across the Channel. The sunshine was bright and hazy and there was a light breeze. I saw the promenading holidaymakers on the other side: the bright clothes, the festive hats, the balloons and the children. But not everyone blended with the crowd.

There was a rhododendron bush beside the Channel. Behind it I could just see the figure of a youth. He was staring across at Estyll. Behind him, walking along deep in thought, was another Mykle. Further along the bank, well away from the bridges, another Mykle sat in long grass overlooking the Channel. I waited, and before long another Mykle appeared.

A few minutes later yet another Mykle appeared, and took up position behind one of the trees over there. I did not doubt that there were many more, each unaware of all the others, each preoccupied with the girl who sat on the bench a few feet from me.

I wondered which one it was I had spoken to. None of them, perhaps, or all of them?

I turned towards Estyll at last and approached her. I went to stand directly in front of her and removed my hat.

"Good afternoon, miss," I said. "Pardon me for speaking to you like this."

She looked up at me in sharp surprise. I had interrupted her reverie. She shook her head, but turned on a polite smile for me.

"Do you happen to know who I am?" I said.

"Of course, sir. You're very famous." She bit her lower lip, as if wishing she had not answered so promptly. "What I meant was—"

"Yes," I said. "Do you trust my word?" She frowned then, and it was a consciously pretty gesture—a child borrowing a mannerism from an adult. "It will happen tomorrow," I said.

"Sir?"

"Tomorrow," I said again, trying to find some subtler way of putting it. "What you're waiting for . . . it will happen then."

"How do you—?"

"Never mind that," I said. I stood erect, running my fingers across the brim of my hat. In spite of everything she had the uncanny facility of making me nervous and awkward. "I'll be across there tomorrow," I said, pointing to the other side of the Channel. "Look out for me. I'll be wearing these clothes, this hat. You'll see me wave to you. That's when it will be."

She said nothing to this, but looked steadily at me. I was standing against the light, and she could not have been able to see me properly. But I could see her with the sun on her face, and with light dancing in her hair and her eyes.

She was so young, so pretty. It was like pain to be near her.

"Wear your prettiest dress," I said. "Do you understand?"

She still did not answer, but I saw her eyes flicker towards the far side of the Channel. There was a pinkness in her cheeks and I knew I had said too much. I wished I had not spoken to her at all.

I made a courtly little bow and replaced my hat.

"Good-day to you, miss," I said.

"Good-day, sir."

I nodded to her again, then walked past her and turned on to the lawn behind the bench. I went a short way up the slope, and moved over to the side until I was hidden from Estyll by the trunk of a huge tree.

I could see that on the far side of the Channel one of the Mykles I spotted earlier had moved out from his hiding place. He stood on the bank in clear view. He had apparently been watching me as I spoke to Estyll, for now I could see him looking across at me, shading his eyes with his hand.

I was certain that it was him I had spoken to.

I could help him no more. If he now crossed the Channel twice, moving forward two days, he could be on the Tomorrow Bridge to meet Estyll as she answered my signal.

He stared across at me and I stared back. Then I heard a whoop of joy. He started running.

He hurried along the bank and went straight to the Today Bridge. I could almost hear the hollow clumping of his shoes as he ran through the narrow way, and moments later he emerged on this side. He walked, more sedately now, to the queue for the Tomorrow Bridge.

As he stood in line, he was looking at Estyll. She, staring thoughtfully at the ground, did not notice.

Mykle reached the tollbooth. As he went to the pay desk, he looked back at me and waved. I took off my hat and waved it. He grinned happily.

In a few seconds he had disappeared into the covered way, and I knew I would not see him again. I had seen happen what was to happen next.

I replaced my hat and walked away from the Channel, up through the stately trees of the Park, past where the gardener was still pushing his heavy mower against the grass, past where many families were sitting beneath the trees at their picnic luncheons.

I saw a place beneath a wide old cedar where I and my parents and sisters had often eaten our meals. A cloth was spread out across the grass, with several dishes set in readiness for the meal. An elderly couple was sitting here, well under the shade of the branches. The lady was sitting stiffly in a folding canvas chair, watching patiently as her husband prepared the meat. He was carving a ham joint, taking slices from beneath the notch with meticulous strokes. Two servants stood in the background, with white linen cloths draped over their forearms.

Like me, the gentleman was in formal wear. His frock coat was stiff and perfectly ironed, and his shoes shone as if they had been polished for weeks. On the ground beside him, his silken stove-pipe hat had been laid on a scarf.

He noticed my uninvited regard and looked up at me. For a moment our gaze met and we nodded to each other like the gentlemen we were. I touched the brim of my hat, wished him and the lady good-afternoon. Then I hurried towards the yard outside. I wanted to see Dorynne before I caught the train to Geneva.